BIRMINGHAM CITY
UNIVERSITY
DISCARDED

Sensibility in Transformation

Creative Resistance to Sentiment from the Augustans to the Romantics

Essays in Honor of Jean H. Hagstrum

EDITED BY

Syndy McMillen Conger

Rutherford • Madison • Teaneck
Fairleigh Dickinson University Press
London and Toronto: Associated University Presses

UNIVERSITY OF CENTRAL ENG[LAND]
INFORMATION SERVICES

© 1990 by Associated University Presses, Inc.

All rights reserved. Authorization to photocopy items for internal or personal use, or the internal or personal use of specific clients, is granted by the copyright owner, provided that a base fee of $10.00, plus eight cents per page, per copy is paid directly to the Copyright Clearance Center, 27 Congress Street, Salem, Massachusetts 01970. [0-8386-3352-8/90 $10.00+8¢ pp, pc.]

Associated University Presses
440 Forsgate Drive
Cranbury, NJ 08512

Associated University Presses
25 Sicilian Avenue
London WC1A 2QH, England

Associated University Presses
P.O. Box 488, Port Credit
Mississauga, Ontario
Canada L5G 4M2

The paper used in this publication meets the requirements of the American National Standard for Permanence of Paper for Printed Library Materials Z39.48-1984.

Library of Congress Cataloging-in-Publication Data

Sensibility in transformation : creative resistance to sentiment from the Augustans to the Romantics : essays in honor of Jean H. Hagstrum / Syndy McMillen Conger, editor.
p. cm.
Bibliography: p.
"Bibliography of works by Jean H. Hagstrum": p.
Includes index.
Contents: The conscious speakers / Leland E. Warren — "They caught fire at each other" / Mark S. Madoff — Sensibility as argument / Stephen Cox — Madness and lust in the age of sensibility / John A. Dussinger — What kind of heroine is Mary Wollstonecraft? / Catherine N. Parke — Sensibility and the walk of reason / Mitzi Myers — Sense and sensibility / James Thompson — The role of feeling in the formation of romantic ideology / Lore Metzger — Persecutions of the infinite / Robert Platzner.
ISBN 0-8386-3352-8 (alk. paper)
1. English literature—18th century—History and criticism. 2. Sentimentalism in literature. 3. English literature—19th century—History and criticism. 4. Romanticism—England. 5. Hagstrum, Jean H. I. Hagstrum, Jean H. II. Conger, Syndy M.
PR449.S4S4 1990
820.9'353—dc20 88-46055
CIP

UNIVERSITY OF CENTRAL ENGLAND
Book no 07640463
Subject no 820.9353/Con
INFORMATION SERVICES

PRINTED IN THE UNITED STATES OF AMERICA

To Jean H. Hagstrum

Sensibility in Transformation

Jean H. Hagstrum is John C. Shaffer Professor Emeritus of English and the Humanities at Northwestern University.

Contents

Contributors

SYNDY MCMILLEN CONGER, Professor of English at Western Illinois University, has published a monograph, *Matthew G. Lewis, Charles Robert Maturin, and the Germans* (1977), and various articles on Anglo-German literary relations of the eighteenth and nineteenth centuries, Gothic fiction, and women writers of sensibility including Charlotte Smith, Ann Radcliffe, Mary Wollstonecraft, Jane Austen, and Mary Shelley.

PETER V. CONROY, JR., is Chair of the French Department at the University of Illinois, Chicago. His main area of interest is the French eighteenth-century novel. In addition to his book on Laclos, *Intimate, Intrusive, and Triumphant: Readers in the "Liaisons Dangereuses"* (1987) and a monograph, *Crebillon Fils: Techniques of the Novel* (1972), he has published essays on various eighteenth-century topics like garden design, Voltaire and smallpox, Marivaux, l'abbé Prévost, and Rousseau.

STEPHEN COX is Associate Professor of Literature at the University of California. He is the author of "*The Stranger within Thee*": *Concepts of the Self in Late-Eighteenth-Century Literature*, and of essays on William Blake and other literary figures.

JOHN A. DUSSINGER has been a member of the English Department at the University of Illinois since 1965 and has also taught in Scandinavia and in England. Besides numerous articles and reviews in the major scholarly journals, he is the author of *The Discourse of the Mind in Eighteenth-Century Fiction* (1974); his *In the Pride of the Moment: Encounters in Jane Austen's World* has just been published by Ohio State University Press (1989).

MARK S. MADOFF is Associate Professor and Acting Head in the Department of Literature and Philosophy at Royal Roads Military College, Victoria, B.C. His publications on eighteenth-century topics include studies of Sterne, Swift, Gothic fiction, reactions to the French Revolution, and the motif of conspiracy. His main research entails a book-length examination of conspiracy fears, conspiracy fictions, and conspiratorial secret societies.

LORE METZGER is Professor of English at Emory University. She is a contributing editor to *Marginalia*, vol. 12 (in five parts) of The Collected Works of S. T. Coleridge (1980-) and author of *One Foot in Eden: Modes of Pastoral Romantic Poetry* (1986). She has also published articles on Romantic, Victorian, and modern subjects in *JHI*, *Comparative Literature*, *MLQ*, *Victorian Poetry*, *Contemporary Literature*, and *Genre*. She is currently at work on a study of Goethe's *Faust, Part Two*, as a social text.

MITZI MYERS has published numerous essays on Mary Wollstonecraft and other women writers. Her book-in-progress on early women writers for the young is funded by grants from the Children's Literature Association, the American Philosophical Society, and the National Endowment for the Humanities. She is currently a Research Associate of the UCLA center for the Study of Women.

CATHERINE N. PARKE, Associate Professor of English at the University of Missouri, has edited two books and produced essays on a wide range of subjects, including Samuel Johnson, Sir Joshua Reynolds, an eighteenth-century novel of education, Jane Austen, and Gaston Bachelard. She is also a published poet, translator, and film critic.

ROBERT PLATZNER is Professor of Humanities and Religious Studies at California State University, Sacramento, where he has taught since 1970. His publications include articles and reviews on contemporary science fiction, the Gothic romance, Jewish mysticism, and the autobiographical writings of Thomas De Quincey. His doctoral dissertation, *The Metaphysical Novel in England*, was published by Arno Press, and more recently he has co-authored two instructional volumes for Behrman House on *The Mishnah* and *The Midrash*. He is contributing editor to *Studia Mystica* and is presently engaged in developing a new model for post-war covenant theology.

JAMES THOMPSON is Associate Professor of English at the University of North Carolina at Chapel Hill. He is the author of *Language in Wycherley's Plays* (1984), along with articles on various Restoration and eighteenth-century subjects. His most recent book *Between Self and World: The Novels of Jane Austen*, was published by the Pennsylvania State University Press in 1987.

LELAND E. WARREN, an Associate Professor of English at Kansas State University, is an editor in English and American literature for *The Eighteenth Century: A Current Bibliography* and corresponding editor of *Eighteenth-Century Life*. Among his publications are essays on Wordsworth, De Quincey, Charlotte Lennox, Sterne, Fielding, and eighteenth-century guides to conversation. This last essay will be the first chapter of a study he is now writing on the relationships between conversation and narrative theory in eighteenth-century England.

Introduction

SYNDY McMILLEN CONGER

Ever since Laurence Sterne described sensibility paradoxically as the "source inexhausted of all that's precious in our joys, or costly in our sorrows," its ambiguity has bedeviled artists and critics who sought its close acquaintance. How could sensibility contribute both to the irascibility of a Matthew Bramble and the tranquillity of an Uncle Toby? To the strength of a Parson Adams and the weakness of a Harley? To the virtue of a Clarissa and the vice of an Ambrosio? Even its early apologists often wavered in its defense. Sterne's works admit close proximity between sensibility and comedy, Mackenzie's Harley between sensibility and pathetic ineffectuality, and Goethe's Werther between sensibility and personal tragedy. Goethe and Mackenzie both eventually recant their faith in sensibility: Goethe in a dramatic parody called "The Triumph of Sensibility," and Mackenzie in the "Account of the German Theatre," where he laments the late-century divorce of sentiment and morality.

Mackenzie's essay isolates the single most important cause of the eventual reaction against the literature of sensibility: its increasing moral complacency. In the German sentimental plays Mackenzie is reviewing, spontaneous emotion has become the single proof of virtue and wisdom and the one irrevocable value. Moreover, its cultivation is no longer a means to any other end (benevolence, for example) but an end in itself, a shift in attitude that alarmed many of Mackenzie's contemporaries. Fearful for the future of the English church, state, and family, Edmund Burke attacks sensibility as a dangerously immoral and subversive continental heterodoxy.[1] Equally alarmed about the future of womankind, Mary Wollstonecraft expresses the suspicion that sensibility is a seductive and manipulative doctrine designed to keep women silly and subjugated.[2] The fact that Wollstonecraft is on other issues Burke's ideological opponent underlines the persistent ambiguity of the idea that they both come to distrust. By the 1790s it was equally possible to believe either that the sentimental ethic could precipitate the decline of established institutions or that it could reinforce the status quo.

The problem was not so much with the concept itself as with its prolonged popularity. By the end of the century it had become an overdetermined linguistic sign, laden not only with occasionally incompatible values but with the sometimes contradictory hopes and fears that cluster around those values. It was and remains, as Raymond Williams admits in *Keywords*, a "very difficult word,"[3] which, depending upon context, denoted a wide range of sensitivities—to feelings both violent and gentle, and either physiological or emotional, to nature, to art, even to life in general: "a use much like that of modern *awareness* (not only *consciousness* but *conscience*)." On the connotative level, the term becomes even more complex, implying, on the one hand, positive assumptions about the virtue of human emotion and the natural goodness of humankind, yet offering, on the other hand, to raise doubts about itself: is sensibility psychologically healthy? moral? manly? true? wise?

Persisting uncertainties about the nature of sensibility have led critics of this century to inquire repeatedly into its origins in philosophy, religion, a rising bourgeoisie, and an emerging medical science. By far the most widely accepted explanation has been R. S. Crane's in his "Suggestions toward a Genealogy of the 'Man of Feeling' " (1934).[4] Crane traces to the sermons of seventeenth-century latitudinarian divines what he believes to be the four key tenets of the sentimental ethic: (1) "The identification of virtue with acts of benevolence"; (2) "the assumption that such 'good Affections' are natural"; (3) "the anti-stoical praise of sensibility"; (4) "the complacent emphasis on . . . 'Self-approving Joy.' " Crane's theory, which largely supplanted an earlier one that the origins of sensibility are found in the secular philosophy of the third Earl of Shaftesbury, stimulated several fruitful revisionary studies of the literature of the later eighteenth century: most notably, Northrop Frye, "Towards Defining an Age of Sensibility" (1959); Martin C. Battestin, *The Moral Basis of Fielding's Art* (1959); Stuart M. Tave, *The Amiable Humorist* (1960); Louis I. Bredvold, *The Natural History of Sensibility* (1962); R. F. Brissenden, *Virtue in Distress: Studies in the Novel of Sentiment from Richardson to Sade* (1974); Stephen D. Cox, *"The Stranger Within Thee": Concepts of the Self in Late-Eighteenth-Century Literature* (1980); Jean Hagstrum, *Sex and Sensibility* (1980); and Mary Poovey, *The Proper Lady and the Woman Writer* (1984). Recent Marxist critics identify sensibility as a middle-class phenomenon although they differ about its sociological function. Terry Eagleton believes that the literature of sensibility represents "the English bourgeoisie's attempt to wrest a degree of ideological hegemony from the aristocracy";[5] continental Marxists tend instead to view that literature as bourgeois flight into interiority in the face of political impotence.[6] Finally, Karl M. Figlio in England, Sergio Moravia in Italy, and G. S. Rousseau in this country are uncovering roots for sensibility in the late seventeenth-century physiological investigations by scientists and medical men.

These multiple theories of origin strengthen the sense of the pervasiveness of sensibility in the eighteenth century in both literature and culture, scientific and philosophic discourse, but unfortunately they also intensify the problem of the term's ambiguity. In the last ten years, some of the earliest doubts about sensibility have resurfaced, receiving their clearest articulation from Donald Greene and feminist critic Mary Poovey. Greene maintains in his "Latitudinarianism and Sensibility: The Genealogy of the 'Man of Feeling' Reconsidered,"[7] in explicit opposition to Crane, that the sentimental ethic was never a mainstream force in the eighteenth century. "The latitudinarians were never more than a small minority in the church," Greene insists; the ethic of the majority was Augustinian and stressed the depravity of the human race. Moreover, Greene continues, the assertion that the tenets Crane isolates were new and revolutionary at the time is for the most part an illusion: the first "three elements of the 'complex' were far from novel in the eighteenth century, and if the fourth existed then, Anglicanism cannot be held responsible for it." A number of recent scholars, including Cox, Frans De Bruyn, Elizabeth Dutchie, Jean H. Hagstrum, and John D. Sheriff, have answered Greene's charges persuasively, but they have yet to dismiss them altogether. At the heart of Greene's essay is, after all, the arguable conviction that the eighteenth-century English held an essentially medieval view of human nature as fallible, of the human heart as untrustworthy. Mary Poovey, who represents a growing number of feminist critics, shares this conviction. She sees sensibility as part of a reactionary ideology of propriety working to stifle women and keep them subordinate. It encouraged them to cultivate their emotions at the expense of their physical, moral, spiritual, and intellectual growth; and it trapped them in a paralyzing paradox: they were acknowledged freely to be men's superiors in the exercise of feeling, but at the same time they were reminded that excess exhibition of feeling demonstrated weakness of character and inferiority to men.

Both Greene's and Poovey's challenges reinforce a long-standing suspicion about the literature of sensibility: that it is just tearful literature and, therefore, not worth thinking about very much. If some students of the phenomenon have erred by claiming too much for the influence of sensibility on subsequent developments in art and life from the Romantic novel to the French Revolution, others have erred by viewing the phenomenon reductively and pejoratively, mistaking "outward expression" for "inward reality."[8] This is not to suggest that the literature of sensibility cannot degenerate into cheap sentimentalism; it not only can, it has. As students of a sentimental century, however, we have some obligation to rein in our suspicion of tears long enough to listen to the authors and subsequent critics of sensibility, especially Brissenden and Eagleton, who see its literary expressions as liberating rather than manipulative, as sublime rather than bathetic, as evidence of sincerity rather than duplicity, as revolutionary rather than repressive.

More than any other recent scholar, Jean Hagstrum has supplied a persuasive and plausible apology for sensibility. His *Sex and Sensibility: Ideal and Erotic Love From Milton to Mozart*, which traces changes in representations of women, relationships, and love through eighteenth-century literature, art, and music, investigates, extends, and verifies most persuasively the claim first made by Friedrich Schiller at the end of the eighteenth century that the literature of sensibility was part of a major shift in European mentality: that if it was in its beginnings an idea only entertained seriously by a few unorthodox individuals, by mid-century it had become the New Orthodoxy. More important, that New Orthodoxy, for Schiller as for Hagstrum, involved much more than an endorsement of feeling, although it certainly did include that. Eighteenth-century sensibility also ushered in the era of a new consciousness, a modern consciousness that was emotionally and intellectually sensitive to both internal and external stimuli, and self-conscious and reflective about those stimuli: newly uncertain about the nature and boundaries of the self; newly skeptical about a reality that no longer seemed to be immutable or self-evidently right; and newly suspicious of representations of that reality that did not take the subject—and the subjective—into account.

The essays in this volume seek to extend Hagstrum's work, revealing connections between sensibility and other key preoccupations of the age—conversation (Leland E. Warren), the self (Mark S. Madoff), the rhetoric of rights (Stephen Cox), the irrational (John Dussinger), the feminine ideal (Catherine N. Parke and Mitzi Myers), marriage and romance (James Thompson), the poetic imagination (Lore Metzger), and the sublime (Robert Platzner)—and attempting to measure the transformations arising from the resulting cross-fertilization. The sections are arranged in an order that best represents the degree of receptiveness to the New Orthodoxy. The literature of instruction discussed in Part I was the most resistant, tending to present the literature of sensibility with reservations in order to reinforce existing norms; nevertheless, the ideology of feeling did gradually manage to make an imprint on its long-established forms. The eighteenth-century artists discussed in Part II were moderately resistant, bending or modifying form, technique, or content only to accommodate but never to surrender completely to the tenets of the new faith. Only the nineteenth-century authors treated in Part III can be said to have embraced that new faith and to have achieved, as a result, radical breaks with their past profound enough to contribute to that major transformation in literary form and content that we have come to label "Romanticism."

The approaches to sensibility in these essays are wide ranging, touching on manners and morals, on gender and various genres, and on science, religion, politics, economics, and aesthetics. The diversity dramatizes the pervasive nature of what Cox calls a "protean intellectual force" in the century, and underlines at the same time the many remaining opportunities for further research. There is, however, also much unity in this variety in the double focus on sensibility and metamorphosis. Each essay, like the items selected for the appended bibliography, contributes to a better general understanding of the phenomenon of sensibility as well as to some specific facet of the topic; and each essay also discovers transformation in or by means of the concept of sensibility, transformations in artists, in their works of art, or in their—or others'—general attitudes. Essentially, the transformations documented here emerge from reception stories. All the artists in this volume grappled repeatedly with the cluster of occasionally incompatible ideas that were associated with sensibility, and all struck their own compromises with that intractable tradition. In the struggle, they often asked new questions, created new character types or new narrative strategies or persuasive techniques, or constructed new aesthetic theories or feminist doctrines.

Such a brief introduction cannot do justice to the number and range of new insights into sensibility and its transformations in these essays. A suggestive—but by no means exhaustive—list, however, would have to include the following. Cox and Madoff face the problem of inauthenticity that has nagged students of sensibility from its beginnings in ways that make that problem seem much less troublesome. Cox, Metzger, and Thompson offer new ways of viewing the political implications of sensibility and, as they do, they make much clearer the political ambiguity of the term by the late eighteenth century. Dussinger, Parke, and Platzner clarify the nature of the same kind of ambiguity in the aesthetic sphere, offering among them examples of sensibility both as a crippler and as an enabler of the thinkers and artists who were bold enough to entertain its tenets. Finally, Cox, Dussinger, Myers, Parke, and Warren all shed valuable light on the recent question about the nature of the relationship between sensibility and enlightenment feminism by directing attention to that late-century feminist and anatomist of sensibility, Mary Wollstonecraft.

Two essays focus directly on Wollstonecraft's ambivalent and creative resistance to sensibility—Parke's and Myers's. Three others divide on their understanding of Wollstonecraft's relationship to the New Orthodoxy. Warren, on the one hand, posits Wollstonecraft as Austen's foil, a disciple of sensibility to contrast with Austen's belief in conversation. On the other hand, Cox to a greater and Dussinger to a lesser extent, emphasize Wollstonecraft's charges against sensibility: that it was artificial, unprincipled, and conservative—a tool of the patriarchy for the continued repression of woman. It is true that, for a brief period in the 1790s when sensibility was under siege from both the anti-Jacobin champions of church, state, and family, and the Jacobin prophets of reason, Wollstonecraft's faith in sensibility wavered. In a larger sense, however, Wollstonecraft's life and writings were, as Parke's essay indicates, a continuing tribute to, as well as a stringent test of, sensibility. By the last decade of her life, she had, more than any of her contemporaries, measured and weighed its strengths alongside its vulnerabilities. Perhaps because she never entirely resolved the ambiguity of her response to sensibility, these essayists find hers the keenest and most valuably candid analysis of this "very difficult word" in the late eighteenth century, the analysis that, more than many others, provides a rich context for understanding the moral and aesthetic concerns of her contemporaries. She most eloquently "calls us back into the struggle," as Warren's essay puts it, "on which Austen's art is built."

All together, then, the contributors to this collection refocus attention on the wide-ranging effects of sensibility between roughly 1690 and 1830. They depict an "age of sensibility" that was "in transformation" in two interwoven senses: the sentimental ethic was transforming the attitudes and forms of British culture and literature, but it was also concomitantly undergoing considerable transformation itself, sloughing off its eccentric surface traits to gain recognition as a normative part of the human and the artist's psyche and to contribute to larger shifts in attitude toward both public and private virtue. The contributors to this volume are unanimous in their wish to dedicate it to Jean H. Hagstrum, whose work on their subject continues to inspire them to see sensibility as an enriching and dynamic force at work in the shaping of early modern culture.

Notes

1. On Burke's stand, see Peter Stanlis's essay "Burke and the Sensibility of Rousseau," in *Thought* (1961): 246–76.
2. This is Wollstonecraft's stance in *Vindication of the Rights of Woman* (1792).
3. Raymond Williams, *Keywords: A Vocabulary of Culture and Society* (New York: Oxford, 1976), pp. 235–38.
4. Crane's essay appeared in *ELH* 1, no. 3 (1934): 205–30.
5. Terry Eagleton, *The Rape of Clarissa* (Minneapolis: University of Minnesota Press, 1982), p. 4.
6. For a recent explication of this point of view, see Gerhart Sauder, *Empfindsamkeit* (Stuttgart: Metzler, 1974), pp. 50–55.
7. Greene's article was published in *Modern Philology* 75.2 (1977): 159–83. The two specific quotations are from pp. 181 and 160. All of Greene's critics are listed in the bibliography. For a summary presentation of Poovey's argument, see her first chapter, "The Proper Lady."
8. John Sheriff, *The Good Natured Man: The Evolution of a Moral Ideal, 1660–1800.* (University: University of Alabama Press, 1982), p. 76.

Sensibility in Transformation

PART I
Marking Boundaries: Sensibility and the Literature of Instruction

The Conscious Speakers

Sensibility and the Art of Conversation Considered

LELAND E. WARREN

> "Sensibility is the most exquisite feeling of which the human soul is susceptible: when it pervades us, we feel happy; and could it last unmixed, we might form some conjecture of the bliss of those paradisiacal days, when the obedient passions were under the domination of reason, and the impulses of the heart did not need correction."

> "Sensibility is indeed the foundation for all our happiness. . . . But it is only to be felt; it escapes discussion."

So writes the tortured heroine of Mary Wollstonecraft's novel *Mary, A Fiction* (1788).[1] These passages appear in "a rhapsody on sensibility" the young woman composes in an effort to understand why, in the midst of despair at the failure of reason to provide any grounds for action, "the affections which bound her to her fellow creatures began again to play, and reanimated nature." Having completed her analysis, she returns home, where she meets "a man, past the meridian of life, of polished manners, and a dazzling wit."

> He endeavoured to draw Mary out, and succeeded; she entered into conversation, and some of her artless flights of genius struck him with surprise; he found she had a capacious mind, and that her reason was as profound as her imagination was lively. She glanced from earth to heaven, and caught the light of truth. Her expressive countenance showed what passed in her mind, and her tongue was ever the faithful interpreter of her heart; duplicity never threw a shade over her words or actions. (53–54)

While Mary's rhapsody conveys the stock features of a "sensibility" both admired and ridiculed in the last decades of the eighteenth century—a sensibility about which Wollstonecraft herself showed considerable ambivalence—my interest is in the juxtaposition here of a scene depicting the intensely private, almost solipsistic aspect of this sensibility ("when it pervades us, we feel happy") with an episode that is very opposite, one in which Mary displays herself through talk to a man whose characteristics define him as a representative of the public world. I wish to use this collocation as a starting point for considering the relationships between two phenomena to which the eighteenth century gave much attention but which may appear initially to have little to do with one another: sensibility and conversation. While scholarly attention to sensibility is a very old matter and the good talk long credited to the eighteenth century has recently begun to be subjected to closer analysis, there has been little effort to identify connections between the two.[2] Such an examination can, I think, open new lines of inquiry in the discussions of these often nebulous terms.

Although Wollstonecraft's depiction of an unresolved conflict between conversation and sensibility is novelistically clumsy, it does bring into relief the complex of relationships between her era's attitudes toward the two. Later in this essay I suggest that tension between conversation and sensibility, between the differing assumptions concerning the proper relation between society and the individual implied by these highly charged words, marks the novels of Jane Austen, a near contemporary of and far better novelist than Wollstonecraft. At that point, I hope to show how an understanding of the opposed tendencies of these two writers—Wollstonecraft toward sensibility, Austen toward conversation—may make us better readers of each of them. But first it is necessary to consider some common grounds shared by writings on sensibility with those on conversation. Together, accounts of these phenomena may offer a modest addition to our understanding of the ways by which eighteenth-century men and women tried to define themselves in relation to a public discourse in the process of change.

1

Although eighteenth-century theorists of sensibility and conversation provide a bewildering range of definitions, all suggest an obvious difference between the two. Conversation can—and in the eighteenth century usually did—refer to a whole range of social relations. Sensibility, in contrast, refers to the system or systems through which the individual responds to experience. Whether thought of as an ethical or as a psychological concept, the emphasis is on the individual. We might conclude, then, that conversation and sensibility represented opposites in discussions about the relationship between self and society. Conversation was often prescribed as a guard against or prescription for the dangers of isolation, one of which came to be identified as an excess of sensibility. For example, in *The Theory of Moral Sentiments* (1759), Adam Smith wrote: "Society and conversation are the most powerful remedies for restoring the mind to its tranquility. . . . Men of retirement and speculation, who are apt to sit brooding at home over either grief or resentment, though they may often have more humanity, more generosity, and a nicer sense of honour, yet seldom possess that equality of temper which is so common among men of the world."[3] Because Smith's statement follows logically from a detailed account of the operations of sympathy that precedes it, he is not simply repeating what became a virtual truism. But most of the guides to conversation could variously make the point without offering much evidence or argument, confident they were repeating advice their readers would assume to be sound. Although such advice was directed at anyone who might be attracted to solitude, society as embodied in conversation seemed particularly necessary for one group disbarred from living in "the world"—young women. Therefore, tract after tract insists that young ladies seek solid conversation in order to escape the personal fantasies to which their situations make them prey.

In her novel *The Female Quixote* (1752), Charlotte Lennox portrays her heroine, Arabella, as a sad product of female isolation working in conjunction with a powerful imagination. Arabella is so convinced of the reality of the world she shapes from the romances that are her only companions that her actions suggest insanity. Only by finally yielding to the authority of public reason in the person of a clergyman is she redeemed for the unromantic but useful life of a good wife. However, Lennox elsewhere wrote that "of all the pains of educating [daughters] none is comparable to that of bringing up a child who is deficient in sensibility." For although "lively and sensible tempers are subject to terrible deviations," though "passion and presumption hurry them away, nevertheless have they great resources, and frequently are seen to come back, after having ran great lengths . . . whereas we have no hold upon indolent tempers, their thoughts are but the wandering of the mind."[4]

Adam Smith makes a related point in speaking of the admiration we feel for the "delicate precision of [the] moral judgments" of one "whose censure and applause are upon all occasions suited with the greatest accuracy to the value or unworthiness of the object." The actions of such a person, Smith admits, may be very different from his moral determinations:

> Virtue requires habit and resolution of mind as well as delicacy of sentiment; and, unfortunately, the former qualities are sometimes wanting where the latter is in the greatest perfection. This disposition of mind,

> however, though it may sometimes be attended with imperfections, is incompatible with any thing that is grossly criminal, and is the happiest foundation upon which the superstructure of perfect virtue can be built. There are many men who mean very well, and seriously purpose to do what they think their duty, who, notwithstanding, are disagreeable on account of the coarseness of their moral sentiments.[5]

In such statements the social world in which conversations take place is where virtue is finally judged, because it is there that purpose or potentiality must reveal itself in action. But it is clear that all must begin with the sensibility of the individual; if this is coarse or weak, then little can be expected.

Sensibility, then, is an attribute that exalts the self. Although dangerous, it is also necessary, for it is both a means of refined discrimination and a source of energy. Conversation embodies the other, the social context that restrains the individual, making his or her energy and discrimination available to all and protecting the individual from himself.

It would appear then that we are also dealing, on the one hand, with a quality that is more or less innate and, on the other, with a skill or art that can to some extent be learned or improved. Certainly, the number of books printed during this period bearing such titles as *The Art of Conversation* or *The Whole Art of Converse* suggests that conversation is a practical skill that can be taught. Such books offer a wide variety of materials for using in different conversations as well as both general and specific advice about what to say and how to say it in these different social contexts. Many also offer sample conversations or even present their entire texts in dialogues intended both to state guidelines and to provide examples of the advice put into action. Conversation seen in this light is something outside the self, a material that can be grasped and used as a tool to function in the social world. And, of course, as with any matter that the self can use to its advantage, conversation is also available for others to use against it. This exteriority of conversation also appears in the economic imagery that marks so many of these manuals, imagery that depicts speaking as spending or investing and conversations as markets in which one may gain or lose.

I know of no text claiming to teach the whole art of sensibility; indeed, I assume such a title would be oxymoronic. Certainly, there is false sensibility, and any quality that is valued and for which visible characteristics are recognized can be feigned. Eighteenth-century texts offer us an ample gallery of the false and the feigners, but teaching the thing itself seems impossible, for, as Wollstonecraft's

Mary wrote, "It escapes discussion." Hannah More's poem *Sensibility* (1782) makes the same point:

Sweet Sensibility! Thou secret pow'r
Who shed'st thy gifts upon the natal hour,
Like fairy favours; art can never seize,
Nor affectation catch thy pow'r to please:
Thy subtile essence still eludes the chains
Of definition, and defeats her pains.

More's poem shows a keen awareness of the potential for hypocrisy in the cultivation of tears, attacking the woman who "weeps o'er Werter while her children starve" and suggesting the danger of reading "perverted Sterne," for true sensibility will always reveal itself in action. Nevertheless, the poem dwells most on the intensely private pleasures available only to those who possess sweet sensibility:

The fine wrought spirit feels acuter pains;
Where glow exalted sense and taste refin'd,
There keener anguish rankles in the mind;
There, feeling is diffus'd thro' ev'ry part,
Thrills in each nerve, and lives in all the heart.[6]

2

Most of the conversation guides published earlier in our period were reprints of or in the tradition of renaissance courtesy books, and this influence remained strong. In such works the justification for mastering the art of conversation is clear and very practical. We may take as an interesting example Obadiah Walker's *Of the Education, Especially of Young Gentlemen* (1673). "It is necessary [Walker writes] for everyone, that would bring his purpose to effect . . . to *master the wills* and powers of those he makes use of; to make them . . . to work cheerfully and readily for him; which is by *Civility* to *let* or *insinuate* himself into their good liking, and *voluntary assistance*." As if uneasy about encouraging duplicity, Walker goes on to argue that "Every *civil person*" only does what "a good Courtier" does "for his interest" and "*as a good Christian*, for the glory of God [does when he] *mortifies* all his own passions and humours, and *puts on* those, which are for his purpose."[7]

That Walker is a somewhat transitional figure is indicated by the fact that while addressing "every civil person," he still alludes to the good courtier's conduct as a model for emulation. Further, if the advice quoted above makes him sound remarkably cynical, he writes elsewhere that one should have a "readiness to do courtesies to all," should "*assist* and pleasure all, even the unknown," and should "*strive* to render good alwaies even for evil."[8] On the basis of such advice Walker, according to W. Lee Ustick, exemplifies a new type of courtesy book writer that appeared in the second half of the seventeenth century, one who emphasized a regard for others rather than mere cultivation of the self. "The spirit of the times, which made men distrustful of themselves, seems to have caused men to look searchingly into their own souls, inquiring whether they could justify themselves—not only before their fellows, but before God."[9] Such attempts at justification required a close evaluation of one's actions toward others.

Ustick's argument is that in such seventeenth-century texts we see the emergence of sensibility: not only an emphasis on the need to cultivate a sense of responsibility toward others and a desire to do good for them, but a powerful expression of the pleasure that comes from the satisfaction of knowing that one has committed such goodness. Clearly Ustick is correct in finding elements of sensibility in such works. But we can find a similar tone in conversation books published much earlier. For example, in a work first translated into English in 1581, M. Stephen Guazzo defines "civil conversation" as "an honest virtuous, and sociable kind of living in the world." But such converse is not a mere ornament of life, for "he who keeps no Company, has no experience; without Experience there can be no Judgment; and without Judgment, what is a Man better than a Brute." We use the experiences we have with others in conversation as a means of correcting faults we might not otherwise be aware of, and through such correction we move closer to the moral perfection that should be our goal. Such intercourse is pleasant in itself and in its consequences: "true pleasure . . . is that which is naturally reciprocal and is enjoyed in common with other Persons."[10]

In short, although conversation may embody the other that stands outside the self and that is necessary for the existence of the inner sensibility, it is an outside that writers on conversation insist must be brought inside. And if this complicates any effort to separate neatly the realm of sensibility from that of conversation, so do the many accounts of conversation that attribute to it pleasures that later writers will often find specific to sensibility. The art of conversation is in many formulations equivalent to the art of civility, which "consists only in containing ones self."[11] In others it is the "art of pleasing." In all these the essence of conversation is controlling oneself in company so as to please others, and a primary way of doing this is to make them feel that they are pleasing you. As suggested by Walker's statement above, this can be the strategy of a courtier, a strategy to gain control over others. But this is misused conversation just as feigned or false sensibility is a kind of desecration of human potential, for, as Fielding wrote in his "Essay on Conversation," the "profit" we are to gain in conversation should come from "the consciousness of pleasing" that we feel.[12]

Few will be surprised to find evidence of sensibility in a work by Fielding, but I stress that his "Essay on Conversation" is firmly within the tradition of conversation books going back to the Renaissance. The speaker who luxuriates in the conversational skills he has mastered, who can stand apart from himself as he talks with others and see the pleasure he gives, and who can take satisfaction in the awareness that he intends only good toward those he pleases clearly has much in common with the man or woman of sensibility contemplating with pleasure the worthiness of his or her feelings.

3

But there is something we have left out of the account, because our self-satisfied conversationist lacks one ingredient essential to the true person of sensibility, lacks what R. F. Brissenden has referred to as the "notion of a necessarily reasonable feeling."[13] Consider the declaration from Frances Brooke's novel *Emily Montague* (1769) that the religion and virtue of women are due not to "principles found on reason and argument" but derive from "elegance of mind, delicacy of moral taste, and a certain quick perception of the beautiful and becoming in everything." Mary Wollstonecraft is even more emphatic: sensibility, she wrote, is "the result of acute senses, finely fashioned nerves, which vibrate at the slightest touch, and convey such clear intelligence to the brain, that it does not require to be arranged by the judgment."[14]

As this last passage shows, the concept of necessary reasonableness was often grounded in certain beliefs about physiology. In a recent essay, John Mullan writes of this "peculiar myth" according to which "only men of a particular merit or refinement [were thought] to suffer from" ailments specifically associated with sensibility. Hypochondria in men and hysteria in women, although "afflictions," were also signs of "privilege." After quoting Richard Blackmore's *Treatise of the Spleen and Vapours* (1725)—"Hypchondriacal Persons [are] endowed with a great Share of Understanding and Judgment, with a strong and clear Reason, a quick Apprehension and Vivacity of Fancy and Imagination, even above other Men"—Mullan goes on to point out that in mid-eighteenth century novels "the apotheosis of 'sensibility' typically involves the production of certain kinds of retreat or specialization. Sensibility and the pleasures of sentiment with which it is associated are not represented prescriptively, not represented as strictly available models of behavior."[15] If sensibility depends largely on innate qualities, qualities related to physiology, then it is hardly surprising that even the boldest writer hesitates about claiming to teach it.

But if no one can teach sensibility, those who would tell their readers how to use the sensibility of others are legion, and, not surprisingly, often conversation offers the means of access to a level of understanding and judgment beyond the capabilities of most. Conversation therefore becomes not only the other that restrains the self, but also the consumer of the consequences of those flights. And this grants a possible value to female talk that could otherwise be considered merely frivolous. According to one manual, "one very agreeable circumstance [of conversing with ladies] is the *politesse* of their language. . . . Though they do not invent new words, yet the terms they express themselves in wear the semblance of novelty, and seem purposely framed for their thoughts. Custom, in some sort, receives its sanction from them: For, according to the determination of their ruelles, new words and expressions are either made current or proscribed."[16] Conversation can provide access to discriminations that many of us are incapable of making, distinctions that have little to do with reason and that can therefore never be taught. The result of this contact is a refined public discourse, a conversation embodying a degree of sensibility possessed by few individuals.

Or should I say possessed by few men? The passage quoted is typical in implying that all women have by virtue of their sex a degree of sensibility very rare in men. I will not argue here what I assume most of us will grant: that this tendency to endow women with superior sensibility was also a means of declaring them fragile, unsuited to positions of power. I do, however, wish to make two points about the supposed correlation between one's sex and one's sensibility. First, although this served to justify limited roles for women in society, it did attribute to them dominance in certain areas that were becoming increasingly important in the eighteenth century, and so could help them have greater respect for themselves as individuals and as a sex. Mary Poovey has shown how Wollstonecraft was able for a time to apply to herself the image of "the stereotypical sentimental heroine" as a means of "gaining some distance—hence control—over her own emotionalism" and thereby "to conceive of

[a] present emotional turmoil as part of a larger, recognizable characterization." Of more general applicability is a passage quoted by Poovey in which Mrs. Thrale writes, perhaps with some irony, of the potential advantages for women in a literary fashion that emphasized individual feeling and in which "all Meaning is needless, and Thought superfluous."[17]

Mrs. Thrale's tone should warn us that thought was not always assumed to be an exclusively male domain, and this leads to my second point: sensibility was not, of course, solely a female trait. After all, how could a quality often equated with "humanity" be left solely to the dominated sex? If emphasis on either a physiological or a sociological basis for sensibility made an abundance of women of feeling likely—women on the whole being more delicate physically and living in relative isolation that encourages development of the feelings—it did not rule out male counterparts, for privileged males might be subject to similar conditions. But men of sensibility do stand out and arouse awe, because they are less common and their endowments are remarkable in persons who must live more in the world where sensibility supposedly makes one continuously vulnerable. All the more reason, then, to regard the man who joins power and sensibility as the ideal toward which all should aspire.

Sensibility and conversation, as code words for individual feeling and reason subject to verification by others, respectively, are powers constitutive of both the ideal individual, without regard to sex, and of society as a whole. But clearly particular individuals will differ greatly in the degree of thought or feeling they possess, and defining—not to mention attaining—a proper balance within society between the two qualities is not easy. Just as Wollstonecraft could argue that sensibility might be good for men but bad for women—women generally being given too little encouragement to control their feelings, men too often refusing to recognize their feelings[18]—so the degree to which society needs to exalt one or the other will depend on particular, time-bound conditions. Thus the "notion of a necessarily reasonable feeling" may seem more plausible if we consider it in the context of a transformed notion of conversation, one in which feeling was not to be excluded from good talk or seen merely as ornament to it but was to serve as one of its major sources of truth. When Adam Smith writes of the sensible individual whose "censure and applause" are always correct and when Wollstonecraft's Mary conveys "the light of truth" to her auditor, the authors give evidence of societal faith in a source of truth whose operations are not available to rational explanation. But these passages also suggest how the potential threat posed by such mysterious sources is deflected by a conviction that their assertions can be checked against truth as already determined by the consensus embodied in conversation. "Normal" persons can be impressed by such paragons only because they already know the truths these figures speak, and they are impressed because men or women of sensibility do not require the laborious processes of reason or the long round of experience others need to attain their knowledge.

4

Established as a kind of oracle by the consensus of society embodied in conversation, the man or woman of feeling, in turn, verifies the values of that consensus. Raymond Williams has written that in the eighteenth century sensibility was "essentially, a social generalization of certain personal qualities, or, to put it another way, a personal appropriation of certain social qualities. It thus belongs in an important formation which includes **TASTE** . . . cultivation and *discrimination*."[19] To understand the logic of this "social generalization" or "personal appropriation," we need to look at some further connotations of our key terms. The association of sensibility with withdrawal from the active world can make it an image of weakness and vulnerability, but the connection can also convey objectivity and purity. Free of, above, the desires that dominate the masculine world of social action, the man or woman of sensibility sees clearly and speaks with utter sincerity. In contrast, conversation, as the nexus through which the individual urges his desires upon social authority, is always in danger of degenerating into nothing more than a market place in which, in Archbishop Tillotson's phrase, each is engaged in "driving a trade of dissimulation."[20] But if conversation admits and is partially guided by sensibility, then the acts and values underwritten by conversation can appear to reflect more than the current and temporary state of a never-ending struggle for individual power. Sensibility, then, may be seen as a quality that transforms social interchange, elevating the potentially crass verbal contests that make up the secular world to an arena for genuine communion.

We may put this another way, by saying that sensibility makes it possible for a certain conception of conversation to assume the force of an ideology. Conversation was extolled as the way an entire society could participate in defining a workable reality, a social context in which all could have a voice and upon which all could draw, but no writer could explain how such a discourse could emerge or function. The ideal conversation always depends upon openness and equality among its participants, but that openness requires admitting very few into the exchange. Consequently, the values of this discourse will actually reflect the needs of the small, self-conscious group that accepts this particular notion of conversation. Making sensibility a part of this idealized talk masks the exclusiveness that conversation both requires and nourishes, because if sensibility makes available the enduring truth of mankind, that which rises above the contingencies of time and place, then can it matter that all classes and conditions of people are not participants in the talk?

Here, then, is a problem that lies at the heart of most if not all of the positive evaluations of both sensibility and conversation in the eighteenth century, a common problem that finally offers the best justification for considering the two together. If sensibility was made vulnerable by the idea of a necessarily rational feeling, investing in conversation as a source of value was rendered suspect by the belief in a necessarily rational and representative community of speakers. And if sensibility was treated cautiously by conversation, respected only after being taken over by conversation, it could, in turn, perceive the emptiness of conversation.

In the Wollstonecraft episode with which I began, Mary does more than perform for the male listener; she also observes and (presumably) listens to him, penetrating the surface of his talk: "He was human, despised meanness; but was vain of his abilities, and by no means a useful member of society. He talked often of the beauty of virtue; but not having any solid foundation to build the practice on, he was only a shining, or rather a sparkling character: and though his fortune enabled him to hunt down pleasure, he was discontented" (55). Here Mary's sensibility allows her to perceive that far from guaranteeing a stabilizing contact with truth, conversation may reward the self-regarding cultivation of oral skills and encourage the egotism it is supposed to control. In another of Wollstonecraft's novels, *The Wrongs of Woman* (1798), her heroine writes that "True sensibility, the sensibility which is the auxiliary of virtue and the soul of genius, is in society so occupied with the feelings of others, as scarcely to regard its own sensations" (176). The qualifier "in society" leaves in force the warnings of sensibility's dangers, but it is more notable that here true sensibility sounds like "true politeness" as defined in countless manuals: the first requirement of "the art of pleasing others in conversation." Attached to "politeness" or "sensibility," "true" declares that the attribute finds its legitimate objects outside the self, but the continual need for the adjective signals the fear—if not the certainty—that we rarely encounter the true version, and that neither conversation nor sensibility offers hope for a reconciliation between self and society.

5

In Wollstonecraft the apparent hopelessness of reconciliation is at the heart of abortive fictions in which women feel strongly but to no satisfying end and in which they are rarely given a hearing in the conversation of the world. Inchoate and clumsily written, both *Mary* and *The Wrongs of Woman* nevertheless have a raw power that certainly derives from Wollstonecraft's determination to speak her personal truth through thinly disguised characters. Whatever regard Wollstonecraft's fictions gain, however, comes at a high price: her shrill voice, embodied in the extremes of character and plot as well as in the direct polemics of the novels, is too easily dismissed. In Jane Austen we find a near contemporary of Wollstonecraft who speaks with a more finely tuned voice, who is a much better conversationist, but whose words nevertheless endorse much of what Wollstonecraft would tell us. Although Austen's novels could hardly differ from Wollstonecraft's more in all the ways that usually matter in fiction, their "happy" endings do not imply a rejection of Wollstonecraft's bleak message; rather they argue the need to live with a recognition that the fallen nature of human communication makes outward signs of both sensibility and politeness suspect. One way of defining Austen's superiority as a novelist is to show how she made supreme comedy from this fallen condition, but my somewhat humble concern here will be to suggest briefly how her works bring to a kind of culmination the interchanges between sensibility and conversation I have been describing.

In a recent study, James Boyd White considers Austen's novel *Emma* among a series of texts he uses to illuminate the "processes . . . [by which] we define ourselves and others in what we say, how we create community and reconstitute our culture in language."[21] In the company of the *Iliad*, Thucydides, Plato's *Gorgias*, Swift's *A Tale of a Tub*, Johnson's *Rambler*, Burke's *Reflections on the Revolution in France*, and the United States Constitution, *Emma* may at first appear out of place. But White's analysis justifies the inclusion and thus helps us to see how Austen pays homage to an ideology of conversation while raising serious questions about it. Through her "conversation, rational and playful" with Knightley, Emma comes to reject her view of "manners as artificial modes of behavior to be adopted as techniques of social success" and to see them instead as "the application of the whole intelligence to the meaning of what one says and does, to the nature of the relationships—the friendships—one establishes with others, and to the character one makes for oneself in the process." And, as Emma perfects herself through her talk with Knightley, so the readers grow through their engagement with Austen's voice: "It is this movement of mind into harmony with mind that is responsible for the sense, shared by so many readers of Jane Austen, that one has a secretly privileged and personal relationship with her, a special kind of friendship" (174–86).

As White describes it, *Emma* has near affinities with conversation books that offer examples of ideal conversations to observe and that try to engage readers in a conversation with the author intended to bring such talk into their lives. The appeal of this idealization of conversation is perhaps best seen in White's response to this aspect of the novel.

> Emma has the force of mind and will, the insistence on meaning, that enable her to maintain the artifices by which life is given significance, the fictions that constitute the culture that she and Mr. Knightley have made out of the materials of their world. This means that she, with him, can create on the only scale on which it is possible, in conversation with another, the stable society and stable values that are absent from the world around her. She has the imaginative power to be a source of meaning and language, a true partner in conversation, equal to anyone. (189)

Here White conveys not only the emotional appeal of the novel, but how that appeal is bound up with a notion of social order based on personal contact. But White is primarily concerned with tracing the political implications of the relationships he describes, for if the reader manages to become the perfected self that Emma's growth directs him toward, the key problem remains: "How can we move from an ideally created world of two, in the text or in the world, to a larger world of social and political life and action" (191). And, although this is not an implication of the problem that White addresses, how can the reader, secure in a world of two, or at least few, be confident that the image of perfection upon which this possibility of movement outward is based be anything other than the product of an exclusive conversational relationship that makes such movement impossible?

White's account of *Emma* serves as a part of his argument bearing not just upon different sorts of relationships between self and society as they are implied by different texts but also upon a progression over time in these relationships. Although the chapter on *Emma* precedes those on Burke's *Reflections* and the U.S. Constitution, works chronologically before *Emma*, the three together shape an analysis of the modern age: *Emma* serves to define the desire for a society based on "kindness" and "conversation," Burke discusses the difficulty of creating such a society without denying a voice to many of those who make it up, and the Constitution stands as the best means created thus far of reconciling the desire promulgated in Austen with the reality defined by Burke. The Constitution is a vehicle for conversation, because it invites discussion in response to which it can change. It gives a place to all in the conversation of the society for which it is a basis and makes mutual regard a prime value among society's members.

I have given so much space to White's book because it demonstrates eloquently the continuing appeal of a model of social interaction that claims to balance the needs of the individual with those of society. But we may use Austen's finely etched depictions of the interplay between conversation and sensibility to draw a more sobering lesson.

Emma is an excellent conversationist, not just because she speaks well but because she understands the inner dynamics of verbal intercourse and takes pains to master their intricacies. But Emma has to learn the proper use of this power. In Austen's last heroine, Anne Elliot, skill and wisdom are united from the beginning of the novel. Anne knows "the power of conversation" to establish a union with Wentworth that will redeem their seven-year separation,[22] but she also knows "that every little social commonwealth should dictate its own matters of discourse" and that "the art of knowing our own nothingness beyond our own circle" is an essential part of any true self-knowledge (69). She fully understands too the "art of pleasing" as practiced by Mrs Clay in her efforts to gain the attentions of Sir Walter (46), and as practiced on a far more sophisticated level by Walter Elliot:

> Various as were the tempers in her father's house, he pleased them all. He endured too well, he stood too well with everybody. He had spoken to [Anne] with some degree of openness of Mrs Clay; had appeared completely to see what Mrs Clay was about, and to hold her in contempt; and yet Mrs Clay found him as agreeable as anybody. (173)

Although Mrs Clay may be duplicitous and Mr Elliot certainly is, the more significant problem is with a publicly available art that invites duplicity by substituting outward gestures for inner convictions. It is hardly surprising that Mr Elliot can please Sir Walter or Mrs Clay, but he is equally satisfying to Lady Russell, and his ability to please her is consonant with her certainty that Wentworth cannot be a suitable husband for Anne. Lady Russell's "prejudices on the side of ancestry" are part of her regard for forms intended to define a stable community in which there is absolute congruence between how one appears and the values one accepts, forms by which the spontaneity of a Wentworth and his cheerful acceptance of the need to make one's own way in the world are immediately suspect. In Lady Russell, who "was, generally speaking, rational and consistent" (425), the force of this prejudice suggests a deeply seated fear of the individual self and a strong desire to immerse oneself in the conversation of the world as protection against unreliable personal feelings.

Marilyn Butler has argued that *Persuasion* is a "muddle" because its "manner, style, and language" give weight to the inner life of Anne while its form—"the element which in the last resort must express a novel's meaning"—conveys Austen's usual "scepticism about the qualities that make up [the inner life]—intuition, imagination, original insight." For Butler this flaw in the novel shows most clearly in its "failure to define the tempter-figure," the figure who in the other novels "embodied self-sufficiency, a whole intellectual system of individualism or self-interest that the more social and outward-turning ethic of the novel was designed to counter." In *Persuasion*, "where Anne's inner world is implicitly vindicated, there is little that is significant for William Walter Elliot to represent."[23]

Butler's observations are acute, but I think her determination everywhere to refute those who find hints of radicalism in Austen's fiction leads her to an ill-founded conclusion. Walter Elliot represents something very significant, indeed, for he is an embodiment of self-interest who has adopted successfully the signs of the "social and outward-turning ethic" and so constitutes a real threat, not to Anne, but to that ethic as a force in society and so to the possibility of a society based on "kindness" and "conversation." Butler is correct to point out that the novel's criticisms of the aristocrats Sir Walter and Lady Russell "belong to a familiar kind of conservative social comment," but she is also aware that here the criticism derives from the inner life, the sensibility, of an individual whose "word had no weight" with those around her rather than from the public conversation that should enunciate values. What Butler sees as muddle I read as the logical development of attitudes implicit throughout Austen's fiction. A high regard for "true" conversation and "true" sensibility restrained by a realistic assessment of how both ideals are debased in practice may lead to a confused novel, if the test is whether the work conveys a straightforward political message. If, however, the test is the degree to which the novel conveys the tensions between opposed ideals that makes all simple messages dubious, the confusion here may not be in the novel but in the society it depicts.

6

Yet I do not deny the cogency of Butler's criticism, because if we praise Austen for a comic vision so dependent on mastery of form, we may consider violations of that form to be flaws. Put differently, if I fault Wollstonecraft for failing to resolve in her art the problems it identifies, can I fairly praise an Austen novel that uses form to elide rather than confront the same problems? I suggest that in the novels of both Wollstonecraft and Austen we witness a conflict between conversation, embodied in a form intended to give the writer a voice in the world's talk, and sensibility, expressed through the highly individual voice of the author. Both authors recognized the power of these ideals in their society, and both were themselves attracted to their promise, even as they saw the lies that lay at their heart.

At the risk of disturbing the troubled ghost of Mary Wollstonecraft, I would argue that in her fiction she speaks as a woman of sensibility, one for whom the individual perceptions of truth can admit no compromise with the conversation of the world. In contrast, Austen masters that conversation and so pleases her readers even as she introduces doubts about the nature of social relationships. It is hardly surprising that Wollstonecraft has rarely been allowed a hearing: even today, hers is not an easy presence. It is much easier to listen to Austen, who herself understood so well the art of pleasing by making her readers feel a part of true conversation, conversation that satisfies even as it demands that all give their best toward its success. Austen's loyalty to a form that enacts the power of conversation suggests finally not her insistence that the self be repressed but a conviction that, properly understood, conversation offers a practical means by which the self can grow toward its fullest potential.

But just as Austen is suspicious about the voice that too easily pleases all, her readers should be uncomfortable with a formulation that neatly resolves the conflict between self and other. Austen, I believe, always wished to point beyond the book to the social world, in which actual conversations bear little relationship to those described in texts. If as readers we feel comfortable with Austen, feel, in James Boyd White's words, that we "have a secretly privileged and personal relationship with her," we may need to listen more readily to Wollstonecraft, to a voice that utterly denies such accommodation. Both Austen and Wollstonecraft knew the seductions of conversation and sensibility; only Austen spoke so well of their delusive appeal that we may think we have escaped it. Wollstonecraft calls us back into the struggle on which Austen's art is built.

Notes

1. Mary Wollstonecraft, *"Mary" and "The Wrongs of Woman"*, ed. Gary Kelly (New York: Oxford University Press, 1980), pp. 53–54. Subsequent references will appear parenthetically in the text.

2. Because scholarship on sensibility and the closely related concepts of sentiment and sentimental is vast, and because this work can be readily located through standard bibliographies, I offer no selected list here. On conversation I cite William Matthews, "Polite Speech in the Eighteenth Century," *English* 1 (1937): 493–511 and Herbert Davis, "The Conversation of the Augustans," in *The Seventeenth Century: Studies in the History of English Thought and Literature from Bacon to Pope, by Richard Foster Jones and Others Writing in his Honor* (Stanford, 1951), pp. 181–97, as typical of the few brief early treatments of the topic. Indications of recent interest in the relations between conversation and literature in the 18th century are Ann Cline Kelley's "Swift's *Polite Conversation*: An Eschatological Vision," *Studies in Philology*, 73 (1976): 204–24; Clive T. Probyn's "Realism and Raillery: Augustan Conversation and the Poetry of Swift," *Durham University Journal* n.s. 39 (1977): 1–14; Glenn J. Brodhead's "Samuel Johnson and the Rhetoric of Conversation," *SEL* 20 (1980): 461–74; my own essays "The Constant Speaker: Aspects of Conversation in *Tristram Shandy*," *University of Toronto Quarterly* 46 (1976): 51–67; "Of the Conversation of Women: *The Female Quixote* and the Dream of Perfection," *Studies in Eighteenth-Century Culture* 11 (1982): 367–80; and two very recent books: Roy Roussel's *The Conversation of the Sexes: Seduction and Equality in Selected 17th and 18th Century Texts* (New York: Oxford, 1986), and Carey McIntosh's *Common and Courtly Language: The Stylistics of Social Class in Eighteenth-Century British Literature* (Philadelphia: University of Pennsylvania Press, 1986). For evidence of the interest in conversation in the 18th century see Glenn J. Brodhead's "A Bibliography of the Rhetoric of Conversation in England, 1660–1800," *Rhetoric Society Quarterly* 10 (1980): 43–48; and my own " 'Turning Reality Round Together': Guides to Conversation in 18th Century England," *Eighteenth-Century Life* 8, n.s. 3 (1983): 65–87.

3. Adam Smith, *The Theory of Moral Sentiments* (1759; reprint ed., New York: Augustus M. Kelley, 1966), p. 25.

4. Charlotte Lennox, *The Ladies Museum*, 2nd ed. (London: for J. Newberry and J. Coote, n.d.), p. 687. This is a collected edition of a periodical that was published from March 1760 through February 1761. According to Duncan Isles, although the periodical is "nominally" by Lennox, it "contains many contributions by her friends" ("A Chronology of Charlotte Lennox," *The Female Quixote*, ed. Margaret Dalziel [London, Oxford University Press, 1970], p. xxii). Whether this passage was written by Lennox or not, it clearly expresses an opinion she held.

5. Smith, pp. 475–76.

6. Hannah More, *The Complete Works of Hannah More* (London: for T. Cadell and W. Davies, 1818), 18:171.

7. Obadiah Walker, *Of the Education, Especially of Young Gentlemen* (Oxford, 1673), pp. 211–13.

8. Ibid., pp. 229, 233–34.

9. W. Lee Ustick, "Changing Ideals of Aristocratic Character and Conduct in Seventeenth-Century England," *Modern Philology* 30 (1932): 162.

10. M. Stephen Guazzo, *The Art of Conversation* (London, 1738), pp. 38, 31, 8.

11. Antoine DeCourtin, *The Rules of Civility; or, the Maxims of Genteel Behavior* (London: 1703), p. 204.

12. Henry Fielding, *Miscellanies. Vol. One.*, ed. Henry Knight Miller (Middletown, Conn.: Wesleyan University Press, 1972), p. 145.

13. R. F. Brissenden, *Virtue in Distress: Studies in the Novel of Sentiment from Richardson to Sade* (New York: Barnes & Noble, 1974), p. 55.

14. Both Brooke and Wollstonecraft are quoted in J. M. S. Tompkins, *The Popular Novel in England 1770–1800* (1932; reprint ed., Lincoln: University of Nebraska Press, 1961), pp. 94–95.

15. John Mullan, "Hypochondria and Hysteria: Sensibility and the Physicians," *The Eighteenth Century: Theory and Interpretation* 25 (1984): 145–49.

16. Morvan de Bellegarde, *Models of Conversation for Persons of Polite Education* (London, 1703), p. 303.

17. Mary Poovey, *The Proper Lady and the Woman Writer* (Chicago: The University of Chicago Press, 1989), pp. 53, 37.

18. Poovey makes this point, 102.

19. Raymond Williams, *Keywords* (New York: Oxford University Press, 1976), p. 236.

20. Although I quote this passage from *Spectator No. 103*, it comes from Tillotson's sermon "Of Sincerity Toward God and Man." For a useful account of the widespread influence of this sermon in the eighteenth century, see Jonathan Lamb, "The Comic Sublime and Sterne's Fiction," *ELH* 48 (1981): 112.

21. James Boyd White, *When Words Lose Their Meaning: Constitution and Reconstitution of Language, Character, and Community* (Chicago: University of Chicago Press, 1984), p. x. Subsequent page references will appear parenthetically in the text.

22. Jane Austen, *Persuasion*, ed. D. W. Harding (Harmondsworth, England: Penguin, 1974), p. 243. Subsequent references will appear parenthetically in the text.

23. Marilyn Butler, *Jane Austen and the War of Ideas* (Oxford: The Clarendon Press, 1975), pp. 290, 280–81.

"They caught fire at each other"
Laurence Sterne's Journal of the Pulse of Sensibility

MARK S. MADOFF

The most vexing problems of interpretation in the literature of sensibility will probably appear in writings about self: diaries, journals, memoirs, meditations, and, of course, full-fledged autobiographies.[1] In few other modes of writing is sensibility more naked yet complicated—and that is saying a great deal, because, as Jean H. Hagstrum has noted, sensibility is a complicated idea at the best of times.[2] In brief, the problem is that autobiographies often insist upon the authenticity and authority of the feelings that they contain, yet the mode's openness to self-fabrication, irony, self-deception, and ignorance contradicts that insistence. In an autobiography of a subject of acute sensibility, we may expect an interpretive palimpsest without layers of stable pigment. The shaky epistemological standing of autobiography aggravates the problems of reading a work of sensibility; conversely, the indulgence of sensibility, with its endorsement for *artifices* of feeling, also aggravates the problems of reading autobiography.

Therefore, sharpening our understanding of either mode of writing also should sharpen our understanding of the other. This essay seeks to apply recent refinements in the criticism of autobiography, by James Olney, Georges Gusdorf, Barrett J. Mandel, Elizabeth Bruss, and Patricia Meyer Spacks, to a very problematic autobiographical work of sensibility: Laurence Sterne's *Journal to Eliza*. The benefits of this approach will appear as the essay moves through three stages. First, it describes some of the general interpretive problems in autobiography and the solutions offered by recent criticism of autobiography. In general, there are three solutions: the polyvalence of autobiography, the consequent transference of autobiographical truth from extrinsic to intrinsic references, and the fictiveness of autobiography. The essay then focusses on the particular problems of the *Journal* that are open to the solutions offered in criticism of autobiography. Finally, the essay narrows further to interpret the most difficult constructions of feeling and identity in the

Journal: the Pygmalion myth and the metaphor of illness. It interprets these with help both generally from criticism of autobiography and, because the *Journal* is filled with the peculiar sensibility of the diseased, particularly from Susan Sontag's semiotics of illness.[3]

* * *

Recent critical work on autobiography has concentrated on the problem of reliability—the epistemological standing of autobiographical utterances or "acts," as one critic calls them. Indeed, the most valuable result of that work has been a series of generally congruent schemes for explaining the nature of truth in autobiography in the face of apparent contradictions by extrinsic findings, such as biographies or histories,[4] or by internal dissonance, such as that generated by posturing sensibility.

The first step in critical refinement is to admit disorder or uncertainty where it has been denied. The newer criticism of autobiography assumes an essential irrationality of its subject—an imperfection in the autobiographers' attempts at rationalizing the material. Just as Stephen Spender's essay on "Confessions and Autobiography" admits the paradox that scrupulous self-examination entails *in*sensibility,[5] so the most recent criticism of autobiography accepts the semiotic equivalent of Heisenberg's Uncertainty Principle.[6]

Central in the pioneering critical work of Georges Gusdorf[7] is the idea that unreliability in autobiography is a function of the pull betwen rationalizing intention and ultimately irrational material. This pull shows, for example, in Gusdorf's typology: he distinguishes "journal" from "autobiography" according to the superior rational objectivity of the latter.[8] If Gusdorf thus claims for autobiography such qualities as continuity, distance, and objectivity, all consistent with rational self-consciousness, his *qualifiers* on this list are characteristic of the general direction of new criticism of autobiography and highly relevant to a better understanding of the reliability that belongs to the *Journal to Eliza*. Gusdorf admits that "the original sin of autobiography is first one of logical coherence and rationalization. The narrative is conscious, and since the narrator's consciousness directs the narrative, it seems to him incontestable that it has also directed his life. In other words, the act of reflecting that is essential to conscious awareness is transferred, by a kind of unavoidable optical illusion, back to the stage of the event itself."[9]

Gusdorf and his followers construct similar polyvalent systems of autobiographical meaning and reliability. They insist that any fair interpretation of autobiography must account for what we find even in the most blatant, apparently simple autobiography: the ulterior, the creation of "a sort of posthumous propaganda for posterity," because there is "a considerable gap between the avowed plan of autobiography, which is simply to retrace the history of a life, and its deepest intentions, which are directed toward a kind of apologetics or theodicy of the individual being. This gap explains the puzzlement and the ambivalence of the literary genre."[10] And, because "any autobiography is a moment of the life it recounts,"[11] it cannot be the simple referential structure that Gusdorf's initial list of qualities implies. At the second level of his argument, Gusdorf asserts that "the significance of autobiography should . . . be sought beyond truth and falsity, as those are conceived by simple common sense."[12] Historical verification reveals only one valence of an autobiography: it is also a work of art *and* a structure of deep personal signification. Even an autobiography that misstates the history of its author bears the value of its images.[13]

Gusdorf claims a deeper operation of autobiographical polyvalence, hence a different sense of reliability than what comes from correspondence to historical fact or from intrinsic consistency. Ultimately, he says, the significance of an autobiography is anthropological. Therefore, it yields to interpretations neither historical nor aesthetic: "there is need of a second critique that instead of verifying the literal accuracy of the narrative or demonstrating its artistic value would attempt to draw out its innermost, private significance by viewing it as the symbol . . . or the parable of a consciousness in quest of its own truth."[14] This "second critique" implies an awareness of what Barret J. Mandel calls the quality of "ratification" in autobiography: the confirmation of formal integrity in the author's life after it has been created as an object in language.[15]

Autobiography is reliable inasmuch as it may tell a truth greater than the sum of its factual, intentional claims. Claims in autobiography receive authority from the act of utterance, and at worst they are true to the liar who utters them.

Elizabeth Bruss has developed two largely congruent schemes to account for reliability or authority in autobiography. She asserts that "to count as autobiography a text must have a certain implicit situation, a particular relationship to other texts and to the scene of its enactment." In the latter of Bruss's schemes, her values or measurements of reliability are the "parameters" that "define this situation."[16] In an earlier scheme, Bruss regards autobiographical reliability in terms of an author-reader contract.[17] Bruss reminds us that "an autobiographer can be convicted of 'insincerity' or worse if he is caught in a premeditated distortion."[18] Bruss's notion of an author-reader contract includes not only the threat of verification or exposure that the reader brings to that contract but also the threat of elusiveness and inadvertance that the author brings.

Patricia Meyer Spacks argues that "to tell a story of the self is to create a fiction."[19] By comparing eighteenth-century "realistic" fiction with eighteenth-century autobiography, Spacks explores the boundaries of "premeditated distortion." She compares the ontological conditions of autobiography and fiction: "Characters in fiction exist as objects of someone else's imagination. The heroes and heroines of autobiography achieve identity as objects of their own imagination. . . . Autobiographies and novels alike must achieve form, by discovery and invention. . . . Novelist and autobiographer must find the causality that produces plot."[20] In the composition of either kind of discourse, memory easily gets confused with imagination, knowledge with fancy.[21] The most compelling autobiographies of the eighteenth century, such as those by Boswell, Gibbon, Hume, and Cowper, express fear of indeterminacy—the desperation to stave off nullity by rationalizing an identity.[22] Spacks adds to Gusdorf's anthropological and Mandel's psychological motives for autobiography the effects of a skeptical climate of ideas that admits uncertainty as an important factor in man's works.

Spacks's discussion of James Boswell the autobiographer is especially pertinent to the case of Sterne's *Journal* and illustrates the value of her synthesis of fiction and autobiography. She notes three issues: Boswell's acknowledgment of the uncertainties, yet necessity, of self-creation; his sense of responsibility for the product of self-creation; and the illusion of formlessness in his autobiographies. Of the sense of uncertainty, she remarks that

> James Boswell, who invents himself, in various versions, before the reader's eyes ('I have discovered,' he writes, 'that we may be in some degree whatever character we choose') epitomizes the uncertainty—not unmixed with exhilaration at the range of possibilities—that afflicts some of the century's autobiographers. . . . His writing exists less to make an impression on the world than to explain himself to himself. The journals embody an endless struggle to make sense out of his life, a struggle of interpretation in which one form of self-understanding gives way to another in a conflict-ridden sequence that creates drama from the act of writing.

Radically converting the notion of stable identity to which novelists such as Fielding or Richardson aspire, "Boswell insists" that "identity," as far as the self is concerned, "is made."[23]

If personal identity is malleable, then the shaper is responsible for the resulting shapes or shapelessness. Spacks concludes that "Boswell probably makes the problem of responsibility more vivid than any other writer of his century, conveying both his confidence that a man can be, by effort, whoever he chooses and his repeated discovery that he cannot simply select a role and inhabit it for more than a few hours or days at a time."[24] Although, in an ordinary sense, Boswell's shifts of self-image must have seemed irresponsible, Spacks's intensive analysis of his journals reveals that Boswell took responsibility, as a dramatist does, for his play, with the unusual twist that for him the dramatic action consists mainly of his efforts to turn himself into words.[25]

Spacks interprets the apparent formlessness of Boswell's autobiography in ways especially useful in solving the problems of Sterne's *Journal*. Boswell is a journalist, "an autobiographer of the moment, concerned with the pattern of a day or a week rather than a life."[26] His insistence upon trying out various versions of himself results in multiple, apparently fragmentary, ephemeral dramatic texts. Yet Spacks argues "for the unity not simply of 'large sections' but of volumes, and even of the whole sequence of volumes" of Boswell's autobiographical works. "And this kind of unity," she insists, "testifies the presence in Boswell's journals of a coherent 'plot'. . . ."[27] It is this suggestion that we understand the structure of journal-writing in terms of plot, with its features of development and vicissitude, rather than in terms of historical consistency, that is the major refinement of critical method achieved by Spacks's theory of autobiographical fictiveness.

★ ★ ★

The three critical gains obtained from newer work on autobiography—a sense of textual polyvalence, a transference of authority from extrinsic reference to intrinsic consistency, and a sense of fictiveness—have particular applications to the problems of Laurence Sterne's *Journal to Eliza*.

Those problems are special cases of the generally problematic situation of autobiography. First, there is the problem of reliability or authority. The "I" of the *Journal* is hard to identify, not only because of this voice's shifting aliases, Yorick and Bramin, but also because the reader may want to compare it with the "I" of Laurence Sterne's other letters and with the externally-observed historical personage called Laurence Sterne. The "I" of the *Journal* admits that he is a mask. To what extent does the mask *become* a surrogate self? If the making and wearing of such a mask is an act of dishonesty, is admitting to wearing one a compensatory act of honesty? The "I" of the *Journal* has a different character from either of Sterne's more famous personae, Tristram Shandy or Parson Yorick, yet he often shares Yorick's name, and he appeals intertextually to a career that lies partly inside, partly outside of all of Sterne's literary texts—including the text that he is making as "he" writes. For example, there are frequent references in the *Journal* to the composing of *A Sentimental Journey*. Several kinds of extrinsic evidence cast doubt upon the claims of sensibility within the *Journal*; intrinsic evidence is also problematic. Does strong insistence upon a certain emotional response—the grief of separation, for example—make or unmake that response? Can an "I" who often stresses his own mercurial nature be believed when he also stresses his sincerity?

Second, there are problems of structure or coherence. The *Journal* lacks the qualities in autobiography that at least make the illusion of wholeness, qualities that Gusdorf and Spacks discuss. A contrast illustrates this shortcoming. The "Memoirs" that Lydia Sterne de Medalle, Sterne's daughter, included in her edition of the *Letters* (1775)[28] span an entire life: they contain both implicit and explicit commitments to explain, in a voice that seems to be the subject's, Sterne's origins, private life, and (briefly) public career—although there are significant gaps or misstatements in all three areas.[29] The *Journal*, however, covers six and a half months (from 12 April to 1 November 1767), and it confines its remarks to a single area of the journalist's experience: his alienation from the lover who he believes will sustain his life. Moreover, the textual history and editorial presentation of the *Journal* underline its incoherence: there is reasonable doubt that Sterne undertook and kept the *Journal* as a continuous register of experience, and Lewis Perry Curtis has it interspersed with the *Letters* in his edition, arguing that it should be read that way.[30]

Despite the superficial formlessness or incoherence of Sterne's *Journal*, it has a coherent plot in the anthropological sense that Gusdorf endorses and the fictive sense that Spacks endorses. The dramatic principle of the plot is the Pygmalion-and-Galatea myth: Yorick/Bramin's efforts to imagine the perfect companion for his soul by transforming an initiate, the Bramine, also known as Mrs. Daniel Draper (Elizabeth Sclater); his efforts to *secure* the ideal image. The *Journal*, with its effects (and affectations) of sharing intimacies, also serves to teach an undefined audience of other initiates into sensibility about the savoring of intimacies and the personal uses of fine sensibility. These plot lines complement the more sociable purpose that Sterne declared in writing *A Sentimental Journey*, the text whose composition forms one of the sub-plots of the *Journal*: "I told you my design in it was to teach us to love the world and our fellow creatures better than we do—so it runs most upon those gentler passions and affections, which aid so much to it."[31]

Alan Howes gives a succinct account of the facts upon which Sterne's self-dramatizing imagination was at work:

> Sterne met Mrs. Daniel Draper (née Elizabeth Sclater) (1744–1778) during January of 1767 while she was on a visit to England from India. Sterne's wife had elected to remain in the south of France after Sterne's second Continental tour. Sterne began a sentimental flirtation with Mrs. Draper similar to those he had carried on before with other women; but, worn out in body and spirit, he was pulled more deeply into this friendship with his Eliza (sometimes called his Bramine) than he had ever been before. . . . Yet he thought of the relationship at least partly as contributing to his literary projects. . . . After Mrs. Draper's return to India in April at her husband's summons, Sterne began a *Journal to Eliza*. . . . the relationship was obviously innocent, though more important to Sterne than a mere flirtation.[32]

Pat Rogers has observed the signs that self-dramatization is the purpose of the *Journal*, while comparing Sterne's method as a journal-writer with Swift's (a comparison further authorized by Sterne's likening of Eliza to Swift's Stella[33]): "Swift uses his journal to achieve a mock intimacy, in an attempt to negotiate a difficult relationship; he attains a spurious ease of communication which was not possible in his ordinary dealings with Stella. . . . Sterne employs a similar device so as to concentrate all his emotional and psychic energy, which separation might otherwise have dispersed. . . . he elevates the journal itself to an independent magnitude far beyond its real dimension."[34]

A few other "facts," less verifiable, are the subjects of Sterne's magnifications in the *Journal*. In the spring of 1767 he suffered a recurrence of his pulmonary tuberculosis; his physicians also diagnosed (at first he said they had misdiagnosed) his symptoms as syphilis.[35] Mrs. Draper, an Anglo-Indian married to a responsible officer of the East India Company, stayed in England, where their two children were in school, for two years after Daniel Draper's return to station in Bombay, because his stingy, serious character and exclusive attention to duty were making him odious to her.[36] Sterne was bargaining, emotionally and legally, with his wife Elizabeth (Lumley) for a permanent marital separation, and Elizabeth was behaving badly, importuning and threatening him with her return from France.[37]

The odd turn to the re-enactment of the Pygmalion-Galatea myth in the *Journal* is that Bramin/Pygmalion/Sterne is engaged not only in making the image of Bramine/Galatea/Draper live as his ideal but also in reforming his own inner life. Shortly after meeting Mrs. Draper, Sterne sent her a packet of his books, with a covering note in which he declared a strange imperative of his heart: "I know not how it comes in—but I'm half in love with you.—I ought to be wholy so—for I never valued, (or saw more good Qualities to value,)—or thought more of one of Y^{r} Sex than of You.—"[38]

The *Journal*, then, is a would-be textual fulfillment of the imperative "I ought to be wholy so," although its primary function is to make the other, Galatea/Eliza, wholly what Sterne would have her be. The modal "ought" hints at a potential for insincerity in the text of the ensuing journal-by-correspondence. As the *Journal*'s elements became known through *Letters from Yorick to Eliza* (1773), some debate followed about Pygmalion's sincerity and about what heat it actually generated in the *Journal* entries. In 1790, in an essay "On the Inconsistency of affected Sensibility," Vicesimus Knox regarded the correspondence as an evil turn of popular taste, and, incidentally, indicated how strong was the popular taste for such correspondences:

> Bad passions, and bad actions the consequence of them, have always been common, and will continue to be so in the present condition of human nature; but to boast of them as doing honour to the heart, under the name of *lovely and delicate sensibility*, is peculiar to the fashionable of the present age. Mr. Sterne and Mrs. Draper have too many imitators. A goat is a personage of as great sensibility and sentiment as most of them.[39]

In the July 1781 number of the *Monthly Review*, Samuel Badcock complained of "the large quantities of that insipid trash, called *Sentimental Letters, Sentimental Effusions, &c. &c.* which had been poured upon us, under the sanction of Yorick's name . . . without one grain of wit or acuteness. . . . Every coxcomb who was versed in the small talk of love, and who had acquired the knack of writing without thinking, fancied himself to be another YORICK! and as it was exceedingly easy to assume the virtue of sentiment, and as easy to adopt its cant, the ELIZAS too, were very numerous!"[40] Of the *Letters from Yorick to Eliza* (1775) (containing ten of the *Journal* letters) and of Lydia de Medalle's edition of Sterne's *Letters*, Henry Mackenzie, who appreciated keenly Sterne's true sensibility, wrote: "in these Letters I discover little of that intimacy with the Heart, that delicate Feeling which apply'd itself to the Pulse of Nature & trac'd her thro' her finest Recesses."[41]

Several features of the *Journal* or of its situation raise doubt about Sterne's *sincerity.* It is not only through the multiplication of names, especially for himself (Yorick, Bramin, even Sterne[42]) that the voice of the *Journal* confounds the issue of his identity and origin. These disguises might be dismissed as mere pet names, such as lovers often adopt, but the preamble to the *Journal*, dated 10–22 April 1767, complicates such a dismissal by heaping fiction upon truth upon fiction:

> This Journal wrote under the fictitious Names of Yorick & Draper—and sometimes of the Bramin & Bramine—but tis a Diary of the miserable feelings of a person separated from a Lady for whose Society he languish'd—
>
> The real Names—are foreigne—& the Acc^{t} a Copy from a french Mans^{t}—in M^{r} Ss hands—but wrote as it is, to cast a Viel over them—[43]

Sterne adds that there is "a counterpart," from Eliza's point of view, but that Yorick's words "seem to have little Merit beyond their honesty & truth—"[44] And how much "honesty & truth" is that? Perhaps it is honest confusion: Yorick, for instance, is a fictitious name, indeed a name from two fictions *by Sterne*, but "Draper" *removes* the "Viel" from the "Lady" in question. The *Sermons of Mr. Yorick* had appeared in a fifth edition by 1763,[45] rendering the pen name "Yorick" a banner, rather than a shelter, for Laurence Sterne. Moreover, in the *Journal* and attendant letters, Yorick recounts his flourishing of Eliza's painted miniature image, as well as his verbal flourishing of her image, before anyone who would admire it. So a veil of code names would have been superfluous by the time Sterne was making it.[46] And, to further compound the confusion about the place of this text, only the preamble directs the *Journal* toward a public readership, from whom protection might be necessary.

Self-plagiarism also taints the sincerity of the *Journal*. Curtis runs beside the first of Sterne's letters in his edition (a courtship letter to Elizabeth Lumley) eight passages from the *Journal*, composed, it would seem, twenty-seven years later, during Sterne's intense longing for the second Elizabeth, Mrs. Draper. The passages are recycled from the earlier letter almost verbatim. Of course, neither Elizabeth Draper nor readers of the *Journal* in letter form in the 1770s knew of this self-plagiarism, but Sterne must have known, unless one believes that the repetitions were accidental. The effect is all the more startling in light of Yorick's continual complaints to Eliza about his wife's injustices and importunings. The new Elizabeth might have expected not to get the old Elizabeth's cast-off wooing.[47]

So placing the *Journal*'s characters within the context of other texts where they appear differently, even as recipients of each other's mail, lowers the truth-value of the text (in Bruss's terms) and imperils its identity-value, because it is doubtful whether "the logically distinct roles of author, narrator, and protagonist are conjoined, with the same individual occupying a position both in the context, the associated 'scene of writing,' and within the text itself."[48] Even Yorick expresses a distinction of identities—among author, narrator, and protagonist—for he narrates a sequence of events that matches Sterne's course of activities over the period of the *Journal*. Against this sequential pattern is set the primary self-revelatory non-narrative of the *Journal*, a sequence of reports, like a physician's graph, on three closely joined kinds of health: physical, psychic, and relational. Bringing together Pat Rogers's remark about the magnification of events in the *Journal* with Gusdorf's encouragement of fictional, rather than historical, truth-testing, the meaning of the *Journal*'s primary structure—Pygmalion's and Galatea's health-reports—may be discovered.

Thirty-four of the *Journal*'s entries are devoted partly or mainly to illness. These tend to be grouped in the first half of the text. The graph rises when Yorick is able to translate himself to his Coxwold cottage and plunges into a different, more figurative illness before the English sojourn of Elizabeth Sterne and Lydia. On Easter Sunday (20 April 1767), for example, Yorick writes the following: "was not disappointed [in being visited by "the greatest delusions of love" in his dreams]—yet awoke in the most acute pain—Something Eliza is wrong with me—you should be ill out of Sympathy—& yet you are too ill already—my dear friend—all day at home—in extream dejection."[49] By June 20th, however, outside the *Journal* he is blithely assuring the unidentified A. L—e: "I am in still better health, my dear L...e, than when I wrote last to you—owing I believe to my riding out every day with my friend H[all] whose castle lies near the sea—."[50] And on July 2nd, he plagiarizes his own letter (of June 7th) to A. L—e, in describing to Eliza Draper his idyll at Coxwold: "—tis a Land of Plenty—I sit down alone to Venison, fish or Wild foul—or a couple of fouls—with Curds, and strawberrys & Cream, and all the simple clean plenty w[ch] a rich Vally can produce—."[51] The *Journal* contains the strange business of the venereal diagnosis reported to Eliza on April 24th, which Yorick both denies and fretfully acknowledges, while retaining his written fantasies of eventually taking Eliza as his wife, without connecting the suspected taint to the attractiveness of his marriage suit. The *Journal* also contains a romantic self-diagnosis, Yorick declaring in the third entry (as he had already declared in nearly the same words to Elizabeth Lumley three decades before); "worn out with fevers of all kinds but most, by that fever of the heart with wch I'm eternally wasting, & shall waste till I see Eliza again."[52] He confirms this association between loss and illness in two other entries in April: "poor Sick-headed, sick hearted Yorick! Eliza has made a Shadow of thee—I am absolutely good for nothing, as every mortal is who can think & talk but upon one thing!"; and "the Loss of Eliza, and attention to that one Idea, brought on a fever—."[53]

Thus Sterne creates a metaphor of physical illness, love, and obsession. Were it not for his or Yorick's accompanying detailed accounts of physical debilitation,[54] this linkage might be mere cliché. But evidence of real blood, probably from a tubercular hemorrhage, mingles with the tears of romantic cliché. Sterne creates a very complex figure (in a letter preceding the *Journal*) in which Yorick, having soaked all his India handkerchiefs with his blood, awakens to find the breast of his shirt "steeped in tears," tears which Eliza, with "filial affection," like a second Lydia Sterne, is enjoined to collect in a bottle, and she is imagined kneeling as a comforter before him, receiving the blessing of Esau, the wanderer, from "Isaac" Sterne.[55] The implicit metaphor of tears as blood describes the dramatic tendency of the *Journal* proper: it treats the keen experience of sensations, even those of suffering, as a means of perserving vitality, of transforming the inanimate—like Galatea's graven image—into the animate; the far-off, abstract wife of an East India Company officer, whose painted likeness can be carried to dinner parties, into a warm presence, a daughter-lover.

To understand the peculiar sensibility at play in the *Journal*, it is necessary to reckon with the metaphorical potency of the disease that wracked from Laurence Sterne's lungs the blood that became tears that became a daughter-lover's keepsake of her father-lover. It is necessary to reckon with tuberculosis as an instrument of sensibility that shapes the text in several ways.

After surveying many representations of "consumptives" in Western literature, Susan Sontag derives the same metaphor as Sterne: illness, love, and obsession—particularly self-obsession. "TB is celebrated as the disease of born victims," she writes, "of sensitive, passive people who are not quite life-loving enough to survive. . . . And while the standard representation of a death from TB places the emphasis on the perfected sublimation of feeling, the recurrent figure of the tubercular courtesan indicates that TB was also thought to make the sufferer sexy."[56] In its literary uses, tuberculosis has contradictory meanings of repression and passion. It is also a way of resolving the contradiction between repression and passion, because the dis-ease of the disease answers equally well to either quality of character: "it was also a way of describing sexual feelings—while lifting the responsibility for libertinism, which is blamed on a state of objective, physiological decadence or deliquescence. . . . it was a way of affirming the value of being more conscious, more complex psychologically. Health becomes banal, even vulgar."[57]

In a text such as the *Journal*, the polarity of passion and repression is translated into the pace of life as the journalist experiences it, reflectively. If the *Journal* were clocked for *speed,* in this sense, it would be a puzzling object, for the entries swing between bouts of manic activity and delightful *longeurs*—between life at a gallop and a life of cultivated, therapeutic sloth. The alternation is illustrated in its most compressed format in an entry from mid-July. On July 15th Sterne visits John Hall-Stevenson at Crazy Castle; the next day, Hall visits him at Shandy Hall; the 18th Sterne/Yorick spends with Archbishop Drummond of York; by the 19th he is at the spas in Harrogate, taking the waters and complaining of his impatience with females. This does not seem the career of an invalid. By the 29th, he is in York for the races, where he laments the frantic round: "am tired to death with the hurrying pleasures of these races—I want still & silent ones—so return home to morrow, in search of them—I shall find them as I sit contemplating over thy passive picture. . . ."[58] "Hurrying pleasures" and the "passive picture," speed and lethargy—these are the two poles of tuberculosis as a disease (or indulgence) of sensibility. They correspond, respectively, to the assertion of selfhood, through action for its own sake, and the acceptance of oblivion. But even the acceptance of death is self-assertion, in that it entails a minute recording of the sensations of wasting away. As Sontag observes, "it is with TB that the idea of individual illness was articulated, along with the idea that people are made more conscious as they confront their deaths. . . . Sickness was a way of making people 'interesting'. . . ."[59]

Finally, tuberculosis is a liberation, a declaration of irresponsibility. Not only is the sufferer somehow seductive and feverish, but he is free. Citing the many tuberculosis victims who wandered the world in search of health, Sontag concludes that "TB became a new reason for exile, for a life that was mainly traveling," as was certainly true for the Sternean sentimental tourist. The chronic invalidism of the tubercular patient "was a way of retiring from the world without having to take responsibility for the decision. . . ."[60] Sontag refers to the general effect of "the TB myth," the effect of "validating so many possibly subversive longings and turning them into cultural pieties."[61] Prominent among these cultural pieties is the sanctity of strong feelings, of high sensibility. Sontag parallels the increasing emphasis on sensibility as a cultural virtue with changes from premodern to modern attitudes toward fatal diseases. By the time of Rousseau (or Sterne), "as excess feelings become positive, they are no longer analogized—in order to denigrate them—to a terrible disease. Instead, disease is seen as the vehicle of excess feeling. TB is the disease that makes manifest intense desire; that discloses, in spite of the reluctance of the individual, what the individual does not want to reveal."[62]

The "I" of the *Journal to Eliza* therefore becomes easier to identify, as well as the "you" implicit in the address of a *journal*, normally a private, self-reflexive form, to some reader—to Eliza. The "I" is a hobby-horsical version of Laurence Sterne (that student, in fiction, of hobby-horses), and he rides two chargers that, as Sontag shows, share one harness: his disease of body and his disease of emotion. In the face of the first affliction, Christian patience might have been expected of the Rev. Mr. Yorick. But Sterne, except for not actually publishing the letters that comprise the *Journal* (the drama of his fever for Mrs. Draper was apparently public enough otherwise), suffered from little of the reticence that Sontag associates with the mythical etiology of tuberculosis as a disease of sexual passion. If "TB is the disease that makes manifest intense desire," the *Journal* is an instructional sampler of the manifestations both of the organic disease and especially of the psychic pains and pleasures accompanying the analogous, perhaps pre-conditional, disease of the heart. The *Journal* makes manifest, without apparent reservation, all that tuberculosis and disease disclose of the individual.

In the *Journal*, Yorick insists that the acts of disclosure (what Bruss calls "autobiographical acts") and the act of reading the disclosure-text are parts of an instructional and constructional process. The pre-*Journal* letters contain some aphoristic instruction to Eliza, such as the punning self-advertising variant of the Socratic "Know thyself": "REVERENCE THYSELF" ("reverend thyself"?).[63] But the drama inside and outside the *Journal* would teach Yorick and Eliza to reverence their feelings, particularly their participation in each other's sorrows. In a passage replete with prophetic and homiletic allusions, Sterne likens their companionship in suffering to a safe anchorage:

> what a sad Story thou hast told me of thy Sufferings & Despondences, from St Iago, till thy meeting wth the Dutch Ship—twas a sympathy above Tears—I trembled every Nerve as I went from line to line—& every moment the Acc^{t} comes across me—I suffer all I felt, over & over again—will providence suffer all this anguish without end—& without pity? . . . I am tried my dear Bramine in the furnace of Affliction as much as thou—by the time we meet, We shall be fit only for each other—& should cast away upon any other Harbour.[64]

On 14 June 1767, anticipating the arrival of Elizabeth Sterne and Lydia, Sterne again dramatizes Yorick as a victim who may suffer as much from the pains of his own imagination as from the pains of actual events: "I want you to comfort me my dear Bramine—& reconcile my mind to 3 Months misery— . . . for sitting as I do, expecting sorrow—is suffering it—"[65] But he adds, in the guise of a parson addressing Heaven, that Eliza is "an Object," "thrown . . . in my Way," towards which his suffering may be directed. The disingenuity of the ecclesiastical voice is very important, because if Eliza is "an Object," she is the product of the journalist's sensible imagination more than of heavenly providence. The dis-ease of anguish is self-made, Yorick admits, through the process of anticipation and imagination. First, Eliza is the cure for Yorick's disease. Second, she is a student of his way of bearing the disease; Yorick hopes that she may bear, and even finely appreciate, her own sufferings, which he remakes to his own image as he imagines them over distance. Third, Eliza is a benign disease herself—a fever that both consumes[66] and redeems him. "You" in the *Journal* thus refers to the reconstructed Eliza, to the inferred reader-student, and to the journal-keeper as self-instructor.

The climax of the self-reflexive drama enacted in the *Journal to Eliza* is the consummation of a marriage of sensibilities: the joining of Pygmalion and Galatea. The union appears within the *Journal*: it is an intertextual revision of their lives, a revision that leads from the fever of sensation toward the extinction of all sensation, the null-point of selfhood. It is a revision that, not coincidentally, eliminates objects of less aesthetically, sentimentally valid feelings—hatred, jealously, envy—such as Elizabeth Sterne or Daniel Draper. And, appropriately for the Sternean sense of design, the consummation or end-point comes in the middle of the text, in the entry for 17 June 1767, on which Yorick reports: "I have brought y^r^ name *Eliza*! and Picture into my work—where they will remain—when You & I are at rest for ever. Some Annotator or explainer of my works in this place will take occasion, to speak of the Friendship wch Subsisted so long & faithfully betwixt Yorick & the Lady he speaks of—." There follows a fair account of Eliza Sclater Draper and of Laurence Sterne's (at this point he calls himself "our Author") encounter with her. He writes that "Mrs Draper had a great thirst for Knowledge," presumably including knowledge of high sensibility. Once Yorick "became her Admirer—they caught fire, at each other at the same time—& they w^d^ often say, without reserve to the world, & without any Idea of saying wrong in it, That their Affections for each other were *unbounded*." Then, the consummation: "Mr Draper dying in the Year xxxx—This Lady return'd to England, & Yorick the year after becoming a Widower—They were married—& retiring to one of his Livings in Yorkshire, where was a most romantic Situation—they lived & died happily—and are spoke of with honour in the parish to this day—"[67] Like Boswell, however, Sterne is remarkably aware of the intertextual relationships (where even lives are texts) of artifice and sensibility, for the next day's entry asks Eliza: "How do you like the History of this couple, Eliza?—is it to your mind?—or shall it be written better in some sentimental Evening after your return—tis a rough Sketch—but I could make it a pretty picture, as the outlines are just—"[68]

To annotators or explainers, the outlines of the relationship between Sterne's exercise of sensibility in the *Journal to Eliza* and the theoretical models of autobiography-criticism are also just. The *Journal* is full of signs of internal consistency or ratification. In particular, the personal or mutual myth within the text is consistent, and it is singularly appropriate to the dramatization of a marriage of sensibilities, because it concerns the transformation of an abstract image into a sympathetic, living creature. Yet the ontological and historical situation of the *Journal* is difficult to fix, for reasons which this paper has explored in part. Further application of such tools as the autobiography-critics have developed is worthwhile, if only because Sterne the journalist of sensibility produces a text as much trampled by hobby-horses as laid out carefully by a rational, even-tempered autobiographer.

Notes

1. John Pilling notes the definitional problems of the term "autobiography" in the opening of his *Autobiography and Imagination: Studies in Self-Scrutiny* (London:Routledge & Kegan Paul, 1981) pp. 1–2. Like Pilling, I will use the term here as a shorthand for *all* self-reflexive discourse.

2. In carrying out an etymological trace of "sense," "sensible," and "sensibility," Jean H. Hagstrum remarks that, by the middle of the eighteenth-century, just before Sterne flourished as an exponent of sensibility, "it became a central term of complex and multiple signification covering such meanings as perceptibility by the senses, the readiness of an organ to respond to sensory stimuli, mental perception, the power of the emotions, heightened emotional consciousness, and quickness of feeling. . . . The word is . . . related to fine excess or deplorable excess and in either meaning is a much stronger word than we now think of it as being. . . . yet the most important fact about the eighteenth-century use of the word was not that its meaning of sexual passion was fully maintained but that it was concurrently civilized and 'tenderized' . . . until it became almost indistinguishable from the latest eighteenth-century meaning of 'sentimental.' " (Hagstrum, *Sex and Sensibility: Ideal and Erotic Love from*

Milton to Mozart [Chicago and London: University of Chicago Press, 1980], p. 9.) The applications of Hagstrum's observation about "tenderized" sexual passion to Sterne's *Journal* will become obvious in the final, interpretive section of this essay. Hagstrum himself evidently sees Sterne as the culmination of this most important development of the idea during the eighteenth century (Hagstrum, pp. 11–12).

3. There is no particular affinity between Sontag's semiotic study, *Illness as Metaphor* (New York: Farrar, Straus and Giroux, 1978) and the work of Gusdorf, Mandel, Bruss, or Spacks. However, after taking advantage of the autobiography-critics' methods in order to clarify how Sterne's *Journal* is something other than a tissue of lies, I saw that Sontag's account of literary pathology was the next explanatory step toward an understanding of this peculiar autobiographical fixation, this myth-making with experiences of consumption as the prime raw material.

4. A specimen both of the contradictions and of an older way of handling them comes from the annals of literary, Sternean pilgrimage. In 1826, when William Hazlitt embarked on his own less sentimental journey through France and Italy, he found that Sterne's Maria, that famous pathetic object of sensibility, was unknown in the *real* town of Moulins, where Yorick "met" her. Rhetorically, Hazlitt asked: "Is it an injury done us by an author to have invented for us what we should not have met with in reality?" In other words, if a sensible autobiographer stakes strong feeling and apparently passionate self-revelation upon an unreal encounter with an unreal person, what else may he have betrayed into unreliability? What, the question implied, is Yorick's status? Perhaps Hazlitt's answer was well-suited to an age of suspended disbelief: "Let us leave the realities to shift for themselves, and think only of those bright tracts that have been reclaimed for us by the fancy. . . ." Disallowing any pun on shifting realities, Hazlitt assumes that the tracts best "reclaimed for us by the fancy" (in this case, by sensibility parodying itself) are the "bright" ones, as if only pleasing, self-flattering illusions could have this special exemption from correspondence to other facts. Hazlitt also ignores the peculiarly disturbing effect of accounts of "what we should not have met with in reality" when they punctuate an insistently self-reflexive mode of discourse. Hazlitt, *Notes of a Journey Through France and Italy* (1826), quoted in *Sterne: The Critical Heritage*, ed. Alan B. Howes (London: Routledge & Kegan Paul, 1974), p. 363.

5. Stephen Spender, "Confessions and Autobiography" (*The Making of a Poem*, 1962), in *Autobiography: Essays Theoretical and Critical*, ed. James Olney (Princeton: Princeton University Press, 1980), p. 118.

6. James Olney sets this innovation nicely into historical context. He recalls the origin of the term "autobiography," and notes that there has been a recent tendency to emphasize the *autos* (hence the frequency of "self" and "I" in the titles of critical works on the subject), at the expense of the *bios*—the shaping consciousness at the expense of the life's events. Yet when the reverse slant prevailed, it was too easy for critics of autobiography to treat the *bios* as fairly simple, stable material, nearly unfalsifiable by the autobiographer. Hazlitt's move when confronted with the fictitious Maria (see note 4) is a corollary of such a simplified idea of *bios*: when the *bios* seems unstable, one pretends that the instability does not really matter. Olney, however, reminds us of the particularity of any *bios* as material for self-reflection: life is disease as well as "bright tracts" (Olney, "Autobiography and the Cultural Moment," *Autobiography*, pp. 19–22; see also Olney, "Some Versions of Memory/Some Versions of *Bios*: The Ontology of Autobiography," *Autobiography*, pp. 236–48).

7. Olney's history of autobiography-criticism traces serious critical attention to the genre back to 1956, when Georges Gusdorf's "*Conditions et limites de l'autobiographie*" was published (Olney, "Autobiography and the Cultural Moment," *Autobiography*, p. 9).

8. "The author of a private journal, noting his impressions and mental states from day to day, fixes the portrait of his daily reality without any concern for continuity. Autobiography, on the other hand, requires a man to take a distance with regard to himself in order to reconstitute himself in the focus of his special unity and identity across time" (Gusdorf, "Conditions and Limits of Autobiography," trans. James Olney, *Autobiography*, p. 35). Gusdorf argues that the invention of metal-backed mirrors was a breakthrough in establishing ripe conditions for autobiography (pp. 32–33); in the *Journal,* Sterne presents Yorick as fixated on Eliza's painted miniature image; because his interest in Eliza is largely narcissistic, a mirror would have been equally appropriate for his contemplation. In the *Journal*, Eliza as "other" at best has an uncertain status.

9. Gusdorf, p. 41. Barret J. Mandel advances a parallel argument about the difference between "consciousness" (or "ego") and "being" as agents or censors of autobiographical creation; "being" is more comprehensive and authentic. As these terms might suggest, Mandel, like Gusdorf, bases his new theoretical structure for autobiography on the systems of depth psychology (Mandel, "Full of Life Now," *Autobiography*, pp. 49–50).

10. Ibid., pp. 36, 39. As if he had Sterne specifically in mind, Gusdorf says that "the man who recounts himself is himself searching his self through his history; he is not engaging in an objective and disinterested pursuit but in a work of personal justification. Autobiography appeases the more or less anguished uneasiness of an aging man who wonders if his life has not been lived in vain, frittered away haphazardly, ending now in simple failure" (Gusdorf, p. 39).

11. Ibid., p. 43.

12. Ibid.

13. For example, of Chateaubriand's lying autobiographies Gusdorf says what might be said as well of the *Journal to Eliza*: "there is a truth affirmed beyond the fraudulent itinerary and chronology, a truth of the man, images of himself and of the world, reveries of a man of genius, who, for his own enchantment and that of his readers, realizes himself in the unreal" (Gusdorf, p. 43).

14. Ibid., p. 44.

15. In terms of depth psychology, Mandel explains that "the ongoing activity of writing discloses the being's ratification of the ego's illusion of the past, thereby solidifying it. The acceptance of the illusion, occurring in the present where meaning is possible, is what makes an autobiography capable of telling the truth." Mandel, unlike Gusdorf, at least tries to treat the epistemological crux of the problem of reliability using his idea of ratification. In explaining ratification, he describes a model that will be valuable later in this essay for its application to the *Journal to Eliza*:

> In many autobiographies the ratification is negative—the light of now shines on the illusion the ego puts forth and reveals it as false. In this case, the autobiographer has not chosen one of many truths. He or she has lied; ego has attempted to manipulate and distort, to *prevent* disclosure. The being does not choose or ratify what the ego is alleging it has done. One's being knows—*is*—the truth even when one's mind goes unconscious. In these autobiographies the reader experiences disease with the autobiography. It seems as if the author is lying . . . although readers cannot always easily put their finger on the lie. . . . even in these autobiographies the duality exists between mind and being, between the assertion and the ratification. . . . Very often the autobiographical disclosure of the author's experience . . . is that what he or she is saying veers from what is "truly" remembered. Since the ego is in conflict with the truth, the reader very often gets the message. (Mandel, pp. 64–66)

16. "Truth-value. An autobiography purports to be consistent with other evidence; we are conventionally invited to compare it with other documents that describe the same events (to determine its veracity) and with anything that author may have said or written on other occasions (to determine its sincerity).

Act-value. Autobiography is a personal performance, an action that exemplifies the character of the agent responsible for that action and how it is performed.

Identity-value. In autobiography, the logically distinct roles of author, narrator, and protagonist are conjoined, with the same individual occupying a position both in the context, the associated 'scene of writing,' and within the text itself" (Elizabeth W. Bruss, "Autobiography in Film," in *Autobiography*, pp. 299–300).

17. " . . . a claim is made for the truth-value of what the autobiography reports—no matter how difficult that truth-value might be to ascertain, whether the report treats of private experiences or publicly observable occasions." And "the audience is expected to accept these reports as true, and is free to 'check up' on them or attempt to discredit them" (Bruss, *Autobiographical Acts: The Changing Situation of a Literary Genre* [Baltimore and London: Johns Hopkins University Press, 1976], p. 11).

18. Ibid., p. 11.

19. Patricia Meyer Spacks, *Imagining a Self: Autobiography and Novel in Eighteenth-Century England* (Cambridge and London: Harvard University Press, 1976) p. 311. Among the eighteenth-century novels in this comparative study is *Tristram Shandy*.

20. Ibid., p. 20.

21. Ibid., pp. 4, 12.

22. Ibid., pp. 13–16.

23. Ibid., p. 16.

24. Ibid., p. 306.

25. Ibid , pp. 228–29, 231–32.

26. Ibid., p. 16.

27. Ibid., p. 228.

28. Reprinted, with extensive notes, in *Letters of Laurence Sterne*, ed. Lewis Perry Curtis (Oxford: At the Clarendon Press, 1935), pp. 1–9.

29. Mark S. Madoff, "Laurence Sterne's Name on the Ceiling," *Transactions of the Samuel Johnson Society of the Northwest*, 11 (Calgary, 1980): 31–44.

30. *Letters*, ix: Curtis says that he includes the *Journal* and the *Memoirs* because "it has been my intention to incorporate as much biographical material as possible. . . . These in their proper places are of use in presenting the chronology of his life." The *Journal* was not issued as a linear text until Wilbur L. Cross named it by analogy to Swift's *Journal to Stella* and included it in his 1904 edition of Sterne's *Works*. See Cross, *The Life and Times of Laurence Sterne* (New Haven: Yale University, 1929), pp. 429–40, for a brief bibliographic history of the *Journal*.

31. Sterne to Mrs. William James, 12 November 1767, *Letters*, p. 401.

32. Howes (ed.), *Sterne: The Critical Heritage*, p. 187, n. 1.

33. Sterne to Mrs. Daniel Draper, March 1767: "Not Swift so loved his Stella, Scarron his Maintenon, or Waller his Sacharissa, as I will love, and sing thee, my wife elect! All those names, eminent as they were, shall give place to thine, Eliza" (*Letters*, p. 319).

34. Pat Rogers, "Sterne and Journalism." In *The Winged Skull: Papers from the*

Laurence Sterne Bicentenary Conference, ed. Arthur H. Cash and John M. Stedmond (London: Methuen for Kent State University Press, 1971), p. 143. Like Gusdorf, Rogers recognizes the operation of ulterior motives; in the *Journal*, Rogers asserts, "there is an ulterior motive which takes the sequence right out of the conventional diary form" (p. 143).

35. See Cross, pp. 441–44; Cross does not treat seriously the venereal diagnosis, but implies that this outbreak really was yet another tubercular relapse. Percy Fitzgerald passes right over the crucial passage in the *Journal* (*The Life of Laurence Sterne* [London: Chatto & Windus, 1906], pp. 354–55), although he does, probably unintentionally, join the medical fraternity's view with his phrase "mercurial Yorick" (p. 355). In the *Journal* of 31 May 1767, Yorick says that he is resuming mercury treatments, which he suspended because of harsh side effects, "merely for quietness sake" (*Letters*, p. 347). In *Laurence Sterne: The Early & Middle Years* (London: Methuen, 1975), Arthur Cash gives Sterne's own account, to Hall-Stevenson, of his first tubercular attack, when he was a student at Cambridge (p. 61). Cash traces the conviction of Sterne's syphilitic condition to George Saintsbury's introductory essay to his edition of *A Sentimental Journey* and the *Journal* (1926) and to Lodwick Hartley's *This is Lorence* (1943) (Cash, p. 135, n. 2).

36. Cross (p. 430) at first depicts the Drapers' marriage as normal, and attributes the separation of 1765 to kindness: Eliza needed to recover from childbirth and from the heat of India. But Cross later (p. 433) admits that Mrs. Draper was out of love with her husband by the time she received his letter recalling her to India in 1767, and that the odiousness of the prospect of a reunion probably contributed to her illness, with which Sterne so lavishly commiserated.

37. In the *Journal* entry for 2 June 1767, Sterne describes "this unexpected visit" by Elizabeth and Lydia as "neither a visit of friendship or form—but tis a visit, such as I know you will never make me,—of pure Interest—to pillage What they can from me" (*Letters*, p. 347). Sterne goes on to describe in detail the possible terms of a separation settlement (pp. 347–48). Cross (pp. 454–58) gives a very full version of this complicated transaction: early in the spring of 1767 (Curtis tentatively dates the letter 9 March) Sterne had written Lydia begging her to convince Elizabeth to return to Yorkshire for good (Cross, p. 455 and *Letters*, p. 307).

38. Dated by Curtis late January 1767 (*Letters*, p. 298).

39. Knox, *Winter Evenings* 2:159, quoted in *Sterne: The Critical Heritage*, p. 255. Among the sentimental imitations resembling the *Journal* were the anonmyous *Letters from Eliza to Yorick* (1775), *Unfortunate Sensibility; or, the Life of Mrs. L ***** written by Herself in a series of Sentimental Letters* (1784: "dedicated to Mr. Yorick in the Elysian Fields"), "Peter Pennyless"'s *Sentimental Lucubrations* (1770), and William Combe's *Original Letters of Sterne* (1788).

40. Unsigned review in *Monthly Review*, 65 (July 1781): 65–66, quoted in *Sterne: The Critical Heritage*, p. 248.

41. Letter from Henry Mackenzie to Elizabeth Rose, quoted in *Sterne: The Critical Heritage*, p. 233.

42. Eva C. van Leewen, *Sterne's 'Journal to Eliza': A Semiological and Linguistic Approach to the Text* (Tübingen: Gunter Narr, 1981), p. 126. Van Leewen's study is a very careful sifting of the text, much more extensive and methodologically various than this paper. Although it contains two sections on "fictivity," it does not draw particularly upon autobiography-criticism.

43. *Letters*, p. 322.

44. *Letters*, p. 322; part of the general controversy surrounding Sterne's correspondence with Mrs. Draper, in which letters of doubtful origin abound, is the question of the authenticity of anything like this "counterpart." Certainly much of

the imitators' ingenuity went into imagining Eliza's responses to the published letters of Yorick—many of the latter also being forgeries.

45. Cross, p. 601.

46. Curtis, *Letters*, p. 306, n. 2: "Sterne made no secret of his infatuation." Curtis cites the letter by Richard Griffith (published in *A Series of Genuine Letters, between Henry and Frances*, 1786), who met Sterne in September 1767 and heard him speak at length of a relationship with Eliza that Griffith deduced to be platonic. See also *Sterne: The Critical Heritage*, pp. 185–87.

47. The self-plagiarism issue is entangled in the controversy, mainly between Lewis Perry Curtis and Margaret Shaw, over the authenticity of the letter from Laurence Sterne to Elizabeth Lumley. If the letter is a forgery by Lydia Sterne de Medalle, as Curtis contends, then self-plagiarism and the attendant interpretive problems are out of the question. Shaw's position is that the letter is authentic and the self-plagiarism real. Having summarized their positions, Duke Maskell examines in great detail a set of significant differences between the letter and the corresponding passages of the *Journal* (*Notes and Queries*, August 1970, pp. 303–7). His conclusion (p. 307), based upon some ingenious reconstruction of motives for Sterne or his daughter to alter the text, is that Shaw's theory of self-plagiarism is more consistent with the evidence. I would add that self-plagiarism is also consistent with Sterne's tendency to treat all his writings as one playfully mingled intertext.

48. Bruss, "Autobiography in Film," p. 300.

49. *Letters*, p. 325.

50. Ibid., pp. 368–69.

51. Ibid., p. 371.

52. Ibid., p. 323.

53. Ibid., pp. 324–25.

54. Ibid., pp. 320, 343.

55. Tentatively dated 20 March 1767, Ibid., p. 320.

56. Sontag, p. 25.

57. Ibid., pp. 25–26.

58. *Letters*, pp. 380–81, 384.

59. Sontag, p. 30.

60. Ibid., p. 34.

61. Ibid., p. 34.

62. Ibid., p. 45.

63. *Letters*, p. 321.

64. 1 August 1767, Ibid., p. 384.

65. Ibid., p. 357.

66. Sontag (pp. 9–10) unpacks some of the etymological and metaphorical sense of the term "consumption" as a synonym for pulmonary tuberculosis (it was used as early as 1398), and her larger discussion of tuberculosis as a trope implies the association between the disease and overactive passions.

67. *Letters*, pp. 358–59.

68. Ibid., p. 359.

Sensibility as Argument

STEPHEN COX

In *A Vindication of the Rights of Woman*, Mary Wollstonecraft attacks sentimental literature for depicting women as fragile angels of sensibility who are too innocent and delicate to assume an active equality with men and who must therefore remain in their sheltered and benighted place. In such literature, she says, "there is a display of cold artificial feelings, and that parade of sensibility which boys and girls should be taught to despise as the sure mark of a little vain mind. Florid appeals are made to heaven, and to the *beauteous innocents*, the fairest images of heaven here below, whilst sober sense is left far behind.—This is not the language of the heart, nor will it ever reach it, though the ear may be tickled."[1] Sensibility appears, in short, as an insidious form of political argument, an artificial rhetoric designed to manipulate its audience into conforming to traditional social structures.

It is easy to sympathize with Wollstonecraft. As Jean Hagstrum's work has demonstrated, sensibility was an enormously capacious and highly flexible concept. Like other such large, vague, value-laden ideas, it could easily adapt itself to a variety of argumentative purposes. In certain texts, it adapts itself so well that one is justified in wondering if there is much to it except an artificial rhetoric—very little "heart," but a great deal of manipulative "language."

This essay will examine some of the salient characteristics of sensibility employed as argument, especially moral and (broadly speaking) political argument. Much of what I have to say supports Wollstonecraft's general thesis about the function of sensibility as a tool of intellectual mastery and manipulation. But there is evidence to support a contrary thesis, too: if sensibility was adaptable to many kinds of argument, it was also deviously resistant to argument; not only do writers who try to argue against sensibility find the charms of their adversary impossible to withstand, but writers who wish to exploit sensibility find themselves struggling to master the oddly recalcitrant concept they are trying to employ. Eighteenth-century political argument could manipulate and transform the concept of sensibility, but sensibility could transform, distort, and even destroy political argument. One reason for the gradual decline of confidence in the vocabulary and rhetoric of sensibility—for the process by which particular expressions of sensibility came increasingly to be dismissed as sentimentality, in the worst sense of that word—may actually be the resistant strength of sensibility as a concept, a concept capable of revealing the inadequacies of the rhetorical formulations that were based on it. The fortunes of sensibility employed as argument lend further support to Hagstrum's idea that sensibility was not merely an artistic mode but a protean intellectual force and moral problem.[2]

The argument of sensibility might be very loosely defined as persuasive discourse that tends to equate intellectual authority with the power to display or elicit emotional susceptibility. Some typical rhetorical devices employed by the argument of sensibility were listed by Hannah More in a poem on the subject; she mentions "exclamations, tender tones, fond tears, / And all the graceful drapery" of "Pity" or "Feeling."[3] These devices are equally useful in novels, poems, and polemics—as are larger devices of persuasion, such as the delineation of characters and situations capable of awakening the audience's spontaneous sensibility. The appeal to emotional spontaneity is of great importance, because the argument of sensibility is often an obvious substitute for argument that attempts to produce conviction by careful analysis of facts and skeptical testing of hypotheses. In More's words, spontaneous sensibility is an "untaught goodness," a "hasty moral! sudden sense of right!" Edmund Burke is thinking along similar lines when he discusses the type of artistic effect that appeals to "natural impulses" and therefore enables its audience to judge matters by "the first intuitive glance, without any elaborate process of reasoning."[4] It would be incorrect to say that the argument of sensibility distinguishes itself from other types of argument by eliminating inference from facts, but the facts involved in this type of argument are the facts of subjective states.

There is, perhaps, no context in which the argument of sensibility could not be used. Jane Austen satirizes its adaptability in the delicious scene in *Sense and Sensibility* that describes how Edward Ferrars' relatives try to persuade him not to marry the woman he intends to marry. They remind him of his duty to feel "affection" for them; they threaten to withdraw their own affection (as well as their financial support); and when he remains resolute, his brother-in-law damns him as "unfeeling," professing astonishment "at the obstinacy which could resist such arguments as these. . . . We must all feel for him. . . . Poor Edward! I feel for him sincerely."[5] The assumption is that strong feeling is equivalent to argumentative authority; the fact is that Edward's relatives possess a strong feeling that he does not; the correct conclusion, they believe, ought spontaneously to follow.

One need look no further than the Burke-Paine controversy concerning the merits of the French Revolution to discover how useful sensibility might be to a great variety of arguments. But here, of course, sensibility is much more than witless emotional aggression. In his *Reflections on the Revolution in France*, Burke is supremely conscious of his mode of argument; he is conscious, in fact, that his argument begins and ends in heightened consciousness, and he emphasizes the self-consciousness toward which his rhetoric is addressed. "One is interested," he says, describing the distresses of the Queen of France, "that beings made for suffering should suffer well": the sufferer who is conscious of her proper role ought to evoke the self-conscious *interest* of her audience. The audience reveals its moral quality by the nature of its self-conscious interest, and Burke is just as concerned with prescribing the proper consciousness of the audience as he is with examining the performance of his tragic actress: "Oh! What a revolution! and what an heart must I have, to contemplate without emotion that elevation and that fall!"[6] It was obvious enough to some people in Burke's audience that what he calls "my sensibility on that most melancholy occasion" constituted an argument that substituted facts of consciousness for facts of history. His friend Philip Francis informed him that "all that you say of the Queen is pure foppery," and contrasted arguments based on careful consideration of historical fact with arguments based on Burke's consciousness of the Queen's beauty and suffering. Burke held out for the argument of sensibility, asking querulously if he were "obliged to prove juridically the Virtues of all those I shall see suffering . . . before I endeavour to interest others in their sufferings?"[7]

Burke's liberal critics were certain to attack him for relying too heavily on the argument of sensibility, for creating even in himself a consciousness in opposition to the facts: "As to the tragic paintings by which Mr. Burke has outraged his own imagination, and seeks to work upon that of his readers, they are very well calculated for theatrical representation, where facts are manufactured for the sake of show, and accommodated to produce, through the weakness of sympathy, a weeping effect."[8] Thus Thomas Paine. But consciousness is an argumentative weapon that anyone can use. Paine quickly seizes it. What is the Queen's consciousness of her sufferings compared with the people's consciousness of their own? "When men are sore with the sense of oppressions, and menaced with the prospect of new ones, is the calmness of philosophy, or the palsy of insensibility, to be looked for?" Paine's famous epigram on Burke—"He pities the plumage, but forgets the dying bird"—is not so much a critique of sensibility as an attempt to conserve and direct it. Paine himself operates on the premise that feeling is good argument; the problem is that Burke's feelings are not spontaneous, and therefore not authentic: "he degenerates into a composition of art, and the genuine soul of nature forsakes him." Like Burke, Paine judges the authority both of himself and of his opponents against a standard of consciousness, testifying that it is truly "painful" for him "to behold" Burke's failure to be "affected by the reality of distress touching his heart." Burke had said that "the true lawgiver ought to have an heart full of sensibility"; Paine would disagree only on the current location of such hearts, in London or in Paris.[9]

James T. Boulton has observed that "the very strength of [Burke's] feelings is a salient feature of the case he is arguing: the traditional order takes full account of natural feelings; the revolutionists deny them."[10] But if sensibility is often roughly synonymous with self-conscious feeling,[11] the kind of feeling that can distinguish one individual from another, then one might expect the argument of sensibility to be more easily exploited by liberal proponents of the integrity of individuals and their rights than by conservative proponents of social adhesion and social authority. R. F. Brissenden has analyzed the connections between late-eighteenth-century revolutionary ideology and the ideology of the sensibility movement, and he has explored some of the ways in which such conservative polemicists as the writers of the *Anti-Jacobin* exposed, and derided, the same connections.[12] Yet the *Anti-Jacobin* finds its own uses for sensibility, lamenting the lack of any healthy form of that quality in "cold-hearted" Jacobinism and its English friends.[13] A recent analyst of Robespierre's sentiment-imbued rhetoric declares that "In oratory, at least, right and left spoke the same language."[14]

All of this adds strength to Wollstonecraft's reasons for distrusting sensibility as an artificial and unprincipled mode of discourse, although not to her portrayal of sensibility as a distinctly conservative mode. It is interesting that she herself is unable to avoid this mode; she herself is willing to employ as argument supposedly "artless" but actually very theatrical pictures of heartfelt sentiments and sensibilities.[15] But her most important and inclusive objection to the argument of sensibility is to its lack of authenticity: she views it as a socially conservative force *because* it replaces truly spontaneous and individual consciousness with externally imposed imitations of feeling.

Yet the question of authenticity cannot simply be reduced to the question of whether sensibility involved a literally spontaneous overflow of powerful feelings, either in author or in audience. There is also the question of whether the discourse of sensibility could authenticate itself in action by producing the spontaneity of consciousness from which it was supposedly derived and to which it supposedly appealed. In regard to this question something like a general reply to Wollstonecraft can be abstracted from the theories presented in the late Michel Foucault's *History of Sexuality*. Although nothing seems more natural and spontaneous than "sexuality," Foucault argues that its modern forms were in large part created by Enlightenment discourse. This discourse included a moral, scientific, and religious investigation of sex; it attempted to incorporate sex into a conscious "system of knowledge" and to provide new means of examining it to determine its degree of healthiness and naturalness. In so doing, discourse "problematized," "valorized," and "optimized" its subject; as it struggled to fit sexual activity into the categories of the understood, the valued, and the morally desirable, it transformed selected types of naturally occurring behavior into conscious ideals of healthiness and naturalness that deserved cultivation.[16]

Sexuality and sensibility are so closely allied that the eighteenth century often considered the former as a subset of the latter, and Foucault's argument, with all its ungainly terms and diffuse speculations, is useful in suggesting what may happen to any such human experience when it is identified as both a problem and an ideal. In the eighteenth century, sensibility also was "problematized," "valorized," and "optimized" by being incorporated into systems of normative discourse that identified certain motions of consciousness as the subject of analysis, education, and discipline, as a moral ideal to be cultivated with a high degree of *self*-consciousness. This intellectual process is fundamental to Adam Smith's *Theory of Moral Sentiments*. According to Smith, "delicate sensibility" is now expected and, indeed, "required in civilized nations." Real virtue, however, "requires, surely, a sensibility, much beyond what is possessed by the rude vulgar of mankind."[17] A truly virtuous sensibility does not manifest itself solely in one's conformity to social mores, however decent and humane these may be; it is represented by the consciousness—individual and uncoerced, yet carefully educated and scrutinized—that one is acting and feeling meritoriously when judged against an ideal standard.[18] Smith's work is a treatise on the educational process that enables people of sensibility to internalize social expectations and incorporate them into consciousness, idealizing yet personalizing them. It is also, like many other eighteenth-century works of sensibility, an examination book by which readers can measure the degree to which they have acquired the spontaneity of individual consciousness that is expected of them. Such works might function in this way even for their authors. Burke was proud that he could pass the test of his own description of the suffering queen of France: "Tears came again into my Eyes almost as often as I lookd at the description. They may again."[19]

The eighteenth century's extensive and varied program in the education of consciousness, exploring and exemplifying, as it did, the complex and delicate processes of internalization, was capable of producing a remarkable range of conscious states. Marianne, in *Sense and Sensibility*, has profited so much from her education in the refinement of consciousness that she is rightly suspected, not of merely "giving way" to feelings, as people have always done, but of "feeding and encouraging" them "as a duty." She has even learned the fashionable individualism manifested in uniquely sensitive responses to nature—an individualism that leads her, ironically, to reject fashionably sentimental "jargon" in order to cultivate only her fully personal "feelings."[20] Sensibility is too strong for its own rhetoric. Austen, of course, is satirizing Marianne's habit of turning sensibility into a duty and a code, but she is not satirizing Fanny Price, the heroine of *Mansfield Park*, when Fanny reproaches herself for "shameful insensibility" because she does not feel grief in a social situation in which she feels that she *ought* to feel it. "She really grieved because she could not grieve": an educated, self-conscious sensibility may still be an authentic sensibility, authentic in its feeling for all the complications of individual and social, spontaneous and dutiful response.[21] Raymond Williams's definition of sensibility is even more mystifying than the concept it defines, but it reflects the dualities of the concept: "It was, essentially, a social generalization of certain personal qualities, or, to put it another way, a personal appropriation of certain social qualities."[22] By "problematizing" consciousness, by "valorizing," testing, and examining it, and by positing an ideal self-consciousness that could perform these functions of testing and examination, the discourse of sensibility might go far toward establishing precisely the complicated forms of self-consciousness that its artificial rhetoric idealized.

The eighteenth-century novel of sensibility is generally a structure of "delicate complications." Political discourse, including political discourse that finds its way into the novel, often appears less delicate and less complex. But sensibility is problematized in this discourse also. The sensibility of Austen's Marianne is double: it is both a reflex of social attitudes and an individual complication and idealization of those attitudes. Sensibility manifests a similar doubleness in political rhetoric. The argument of sensibility is problematized as discourse that must function both to provide education in the type of consciousness that is, or should be, socially "required" and to encourage the development of an ideally individual self-consciousness.

Here it may be helpful to look at the argument of sensibility contained in that encyclopedia of liberal sentiments, Thomas Day's novel for children (and others), *Sandford and Merton*. Day provides a plentiful supply of "exclamations, tender tones, fond tears." His novel's hero, little Harry Sandford, a man of sensibility at the age of six, is "so very good-natured . . . to every thing" that he loves not only people but birds and horses and pigs and "even toads and frogs, and spiders, and such kind of disagreeable animals, which most people destroy where-ever they find them."[23] Little Harry's sensibility takes the form it does because he is an exponent of Day's program of social and political reformation. Harry and his tutor, Mr. Barlow, enjoy discoursing about people's (and animals') individual rights. They are Christians, but their religion is strictly the social gospel. Harry believes that Christ came to reform a world in which "the great folks" were all busy overeating and oversleeping "and amusing themselves," without taking any "care of the poor."[24] The world still stands in need of reformation, and Harry energetically preaches to it in word and deed. He is a self-conscious individual in an irritatingly self-righteous way. One would expect him to annoy, not just the great folks, but everyone else who would rather eat a lamb than talk about its rights. One is therefore surprised to discover that his constant display of humane "sentiments" makes him "a great favourite with every body."[25]

Clearly, Harry is not so much a character as a political argument. He and the strangely responsive community in which he lives are the blueprints for a new order of sentimental liberalism, and the argumentative assurance that such an order will naturally appeal to everyone's consciousness. Day's rhetoric exemplifies the doubleness of the argument of sensibility; it appeals simultaneously to the statistical norm of "every body's" natural or socially required reactions and to the ideal norm established by people of rare and refined sensibility. Day implies that virtually everyone in his audience will naturally respond to the sentiments that his arguments exploit and valorize, but he also invites his audience to recognize and value the distinctiveness of these sentiments, their superiority to vulgar, statistically "natural" emotions. By appealing to natural, universal, or "required" sympathies, Day's rhetoric, like that of Paine and Burke, embraces the widest possible audience, the lowest common denominator of consciousness; by positing an ideal, it flatters a selected audience and discriminates among the types of consciousness capable of being indulged.

Exploitation of the language of sensibility to discriminate among different types of consciousness, and thereby among different types of political roles and attitudes, appears in the English novel as early as Richardson's *Clarissa* (1747–51). This novel is anything but a blueprint for utopia, but it has an important political dimension. It has often been read, in fact, as a manifesto of the middle class. But *Clarissa*'s argument of sensibility renders its politics much more complicated than those of a middle-class declaration of a right to hegemony. Clarissa Harlowe and her creator are, indeed, members of the middle class (though from very different subspecies of that class), and Richardson uses Clarissa's sensibility to cast a disparaging light upon the aristocracy's supposed barbarity of feeling. But her sensibility distinguishes her chiefly from other members of her own class, a class from which, in the course of the novel, she becomes exiled and self-exiled. It is true that Clarissa's sensibility makes her responsive not just to her own moral principles but also to the feelings of other people in society.[26] But to regard her special sensibility as an unfortunate function of her economic class[27] is to take the individuality from individualism and to obscure the structure of Richardson's argument.

The novel makes a distinction between middle-class consciousness and self-consciousness, and it uses the quality of Clarissa's rhetoric to enforce the distinction. No one else can talk or write like Clarissa. To Alexander Pope, true wit was "Nature to advantage dressed,/ What oft was thought, but ne'er so well expressed,"[28] but Clarissa's rhetoric is "natural" in another way; it has the seductive doubleness of the argument of sensibility: "She had a talent of saying uncommon things in such an easy manner that everybody thought they could have said the same; and which yet required both genius and observation to say them."[29] Her rhetorical ability is a powerful threat to her authoritarian, bourgeois family as well as to her aristocratic would-be seducer. Even after she is dead, her distinctively nuanced style comes back to haunt them. Her family finds, for instance, that she has bequeathed her library to her cousin Dolly, hoping that Dolly's "friendly grief" may be "mellowed by time into a remembrance more sweet than painful." The reading of Clarissa's will provokes her brusquely bourgeois sister into revealing an inferior state of consciousness: Bella "grudge[s] the library," arguing that "as she and her sister never bought the same books, she would take that to herself, and would *make it up* to her Cousin Dolly *one way or other*."[30] Never bought the same books! Failure to share Clarissa's literary taste is damning in itself. And consider the crudeness of Bella's style, as compared with the well-meditated sensitivity of Clarissa's. The novel's discourse gives a psychological rather than an economic turn to its politics: it discriminates the class of Clarissas from the class of Bellas and invites all the novel's readers to congratulate themselves on their ability to appreciate a triumphantly individual style; thus is the self-consciousness of sensitive readers educated and encouraged.

Listening to Clarissa's will, the members of her family discover what they "called *flights, and such whimsies as distinguish people of imagination from those of judgment.*"[31] The quality of their language proves them right, at least about the insuperable difference in character between people who speak in the jargon of a crude materialism and people who are at ease with the language of sensibility. Although Clarissa's relatives consider some expressions of her feelings unnatural and "monstrous," their crudeness of feeling argues that they themselves are the monsters, the aliens from minimally decent society.[32] A realist might argue that the relatives' language and conduct are no stranger, no more unusual, than Clarissa's, but the double argument of sensibility asserts that she, like little Harry, deserves the love of everybody by acting as nobody else ever acted.

Yet this brings up the problem that, more than any other, seems to have worried writers who employed the argument of sensibility. If sensibility can be used to associate the ideal with the normal and to make the most unusual forms of conduct appear natural and necessary; further, if sensibility is a wild card that can be played in virtually any hand, lending itself to virtually any argumentative purpose, then the various meanings of "sensibility" need to be investigated with special care, so that one can tell just what sort of sensibility ought properly to be appealed to and what sort ought properly to be rejected. This is to problematize the definition of sensibility and to bring up the question of discrimination again, but this time the question of discrimination among different types of sensibility. The concept was so valuable, and yet so many-sided, that the argument *of* sensibility was constantly turning into an argument *about* sensibility.

The eighteenth-century novel makes that argument into a structural principle. In works of comparatively simple structure, such as *Sandford and Merton*, conflicts among and within characters generally involve the distinction between having and not having sensibility. In more complex works, the conflict is itself a double one, and characters have the option of having or not having sensibility *and* of having the right or the wrong variety of it. Clarissa is distinguished not just from her insensate kin but also from her sexual assailant Lovelace, who has more than enough of the kind of sensibility that runs naturally into sensual extremes. Laclos' *Liaisons Dangereuses* has a different moral pattern, but it also distinguishes three types of characters: dully normal persons, brilliantly evil persons of sensibility, and naively good-natured persons of sensibility. Goethe's *The Sufferings of Young Werther* offers another variation on the structural principle. Werther, the ultimate man of feeling, classes Albert, whom he regards as a man of real though constricted sensibility, among the dull, unspiritual people whose lives he does not wish to replicate; and Lotte, who is strongly attracted to Werther's intensely self-conscious sensibility, must decide between the two men. The conflicts in the novel climax in her choice, which she makes in a despairing flight from the complexities of self-consciousness that Werther demands of her. Such novels are not just arguments about sensibility; they are arguments in which sensibility of one kind or another does plenty of arguing. And sensibility is so problematized, so suspicious and equivocal a thing, that arguments representing the wrong kind often succeed, while arguments for the preferred kind often fail. The strength of Clarissa's moral feelings cannot convince Lovelace to mend his ways; Werther, expressing his sensibility with gestures and tears and readings from Ossian, cannot prevail upon Lotte to embrace his variety of mystically sensuous sensibility; but the evil arguments of Laclos' Merteuil and Valmont succeed in ruining the lives of the people who choose to listen to them.

The examples I have chosen draw special attention to what the eighteenth century regarded as the most equivocal aspect of sensibility, its close alliance with sexuality. I cannot hope to add anything to Jean Hagstrum's analysis, in *Sex and Sensibility,* of the century's difficulties in clarifying the proper relations of those concepts. In the most general terms, however, the difficulty with using sensibility for argumentative purposes lay in the necessity of setting some limits to a concept that was able to embrace every form of self-consciousness and self-indulgence. It was not just a problem of sexual morality; it was a problem with political implications too, arising from the difficulty of discriminating, among all possible varieties of consciousness, the type that might offer the surest basis for one's social values.

In her poem "Sensibility" (1782), Hannah More, later a leading warrior in the anti-Jacobin cause, makes one of the century's most vigorous efforts to argue about the concept in such a way as to distinguish and conserve an authentic, socially valuable sensibility. Along the way, she brings up most of the established eighteenth-century distinctions between sensibility's true and false varieties.

False sensibility, she says, is affected, "counterfeit," merely a matter of fashion; or it runs to the other extreme, becoming authentic in the worst way: then it is selfish, immoral, the enemy of "principle." True sensibility is sober, reasonable, kindly, charitable; it is instinctive and spontaneous, yet for all its apparent naturalness it represents the responses of people whose "parts" are "superior."[33] Several difficulties are implicit in these attempts at discrimination, but on the whole they work to conserve the problematized notion of true sensibility by making it sound like little more than a routine notion of upright living. What, one wonders, was all the excitement about?

More realizes, however, that her descriptions of sensibility somehow fail to distinguish its fundamental quality: "Thy subtile essence still eludes the chains / Of Definition, and defeats her pains." Sensibility is more than a matter of specific moral actions; it would be incorrect to say "that by deeds alone this love's exprest." And sensibility is more than a matter of words, more than a matter of jargon that was beginning to sound feeble and conformist, even to such devotees as Hannah More and Austen's Marianne. More reviews the common verbal formulas for evoking sensibility, making the point that these "external marks" of sensibility's argument need to be distinguished from the emotional "things themselves" of which they are merely the "outward sign."[34] Sensibility is such a subtly individual state of consciousness that it exposes its own vocabulary as crude and insufficient. It cannot describe itself: "To those who know thee not, no words can paint, / And those who know thee, know all words are faint!" Sensibility can use discourse but cannot be enclosed by it; one could say, as a corollary to this, that sensibility has no certain boundaries or limitations. It adds a new dynamic to whatever forces, bad or good, happen to inspire each individual. The consequence is that sensibility apparently cannot be depended upon as a stable moral concept:

> 'Tis not peculiar to the wise and good;
> 'Tis passion's flame, the virtue of the blood. . . .
> If, ill-directed, it pursues the wrong,
> It adds new strength to what before was strong;
> Breaks out in wild irregular desires,
> Disorder'd passions, and illicit fires.[35]

More wants to enlist the concept of natural yet ideal feeling in her argument for traditional moral and social relations. She does so, however, at the cost of devaluing sensibility's verbal formulas as inauthentic or superficial and of depicting its emotional content as dangerously real. Despite her perceptiveness, her effort to fit sensibility to her social ideology raises several questions for every one it answers.

The same might be said of liberal attempts to come to terms with the concept. The writers of the *Anti-Jacobin* were not the first to notice difficulties in the liberals' appeals to sensibility. Even such a simple-minded liberal as Thomas Day shows himself aware of them. Although Day praises the "energy of soul" of "untutored" people who respond to "nature" and are "unincumbered by [social] forms and ceremonies," he knows that sensibility needs to be carefully limited if it is not to destroy his own political platform. One of the first ideological crises in *Sandford and Merton* occurs when a pupil of Mr. Barlow, suffering from an excess of sensibility for a needy family, gives them a loaf of bread that he has appropriated from Mr. Barlow, thus infringing his rights. The pupil's reward is a lecture on the evil of theft.[36] Later, when Day discusses the horrors that ensue when sensibility becomes "vile sensuality," he emphasizes the political aspect of the problem: people who cultivate nothing but their sensibility render themselves effeminate, incapable of "vindicating their natural rights by arms."[37] Mr. Barlow is so distrustful of the emotionally responsive human nature on which his philosophy is presumably based that he accuses most people—"the generality"—of a constant tendency to give "an unbounded loose" to their passions, and he argues in a not very libertarian manner that the moral "legislator" should try to diminish "inequality" by refusing to make "the slightest concessions in favour either of human pride or sensuality."[38]

If Day had had the opportunity to read William Blake's *Visions of the Daughters of Albion* (1793), he might have discovered the full extent to which the liberal argument of sensibility could become politically self-subverting. The poem is ostensibly a vindication of individual freedom and, in some respects, of natural rights. Oothoon, its protagonist, has been raped by the slave-holding tyrant Bromion; in a series of arguments she defends her native dignity and her right to pursue love that is "free as the mountain wind!"[39] Although the word "sensibility" never appears in this work, the premise of Oothoon's arguments is that every creature has a fundamental, passionate sensibility (even "infancy" is happily "lustful"), and that this sensibility needs and deserves to be expressed in a fully individual form: "Are not different joys / Holy, eternal, infinite! and each joy is a Love" (6.4, 5.5–6; E 49, 48).

Like many other arguments of sensibility, *Visions* has a structure of double discrimination: Oothoon argues not merely against the materialist Bromion but also against her lover Theotormon, a man of vaporish sentiment who would rather contemplate his narrow and passive self-consciousness than do anything to help Oothoon. Against Bromion, Oothoon ably maintains the idea that real feeling is more than mere "sense"; this is an argument for the spirituality of individual feeling that had been common since the time of *Clarissa*. Against Theotormon, however, she argues that individual sensibility should not be limited in any way, that to limit it means to corrupt or destroy it. When Oothoon declares that she will catch for Theotormon "girls of mild silver, or of furious gold," and delightedly "view their wanton play/ In lovely copulation bliss on bliss . . . lustful as the first born beam" (7.24–27, E 50), she is carrying the ideal of individual enjoyment of sensibility to the same terrible extreme to which Day (not to mention the conservatives of the 1790s) feared it might be taken.

In Blake's hands, the argument of sensibility has transcended and devalued all its normal rhetoric and sober political purposes. One may well be skeptical about whether the argument should still be called "political." An ideal of all-embracing, fully spontaneous gratification admits no political ideas of rights, natural or otherwise, simply because the notion of rights implies the notion of limits and duties: my individual right implies your individual duty to respect that right.[40] But this concept of limitation or duty is inconsistent with Oothoon's argument, and it is not surprising that Blake shows little interest in discussing "rights" anywhere else in his works. Around 1810, Blake remarked that Paine and his fellow liberals were mistaken in their political aims because "you cannot have Liberty in this World without what you call Moral Virtue & you cannot have Moral Virtue without the Slavery of that half of the Human Race who hate what you call Moral Virtue."[41] The remark has often been attributed to Blake's disillusionment with the specific results of the French Revolution. But it is also explicable as a coming to terms with the inherently anti-political nature of an argument for unlimited spiritual freedom, for "All the Passions Emanat[ing] Uncurbed in their Eternal Glory."[42]

Goethe had noted the politically corrosive effects of sensibility in the scene in which Werther argues for the life of a servant who has slain his rival in love. Werther believes that to limit sensibility is not to be worthy of having it, and he sees the case from the passionate murderer's perspective. The authorities of course argue that "all law would be annulled, all the security of the state destroyed," if Werther's view were admitted. The psychologically interesting effect of this exchange is that Werther recognizes that his opponents "might be in the right, yet it [is] as if he must renounce his own inmost

existence in order to confess it."[43] In this contest between individualism and lawful conformity, it is difficult to decide that one argument has been defeated and another vindicated. The argument of sensibility has been carried to its extreme, and it is an uncomfortable extreme, even for Werther. Yet there is something about the argument that the succeeding two centuries have not been able to dismiss, any more than they have been able to dismiss Oothoon's ideal of complete freedom and gratification. The something to which I refer is not the seductive appeal to conformism that Wollstonecraft discovered in the discourse of sensibility, nor is it the formulas of the discourse that More helped to discredit simply by examining them candidly. It is the sense that individual consciousness has more value than any specific arguments it may generate. Whatever we may feel (even indifference) about the arguments of Werther or his antagonists, we remain interested in the complexities of the arguers' consciousness. Perhaps in this respect Werther has managed to win the argument, because his position is that the worth of the individual somehow transcends the specifics of the individual's words or actions.

If one is searching for the enduring values fostered by the argument of sensibility, it is instructive to consult Elizabeth Hamilton's anti-Jacobin novel *Memoirs of Modern Philosophers* (1800). Hamilton's book, which was very popular in its day, is that exceedingly rare political satire that is still funny two centuries later. Much of the fun is at the expense of sensibility. When Miss Botherim, the "heroine," decides to bother an eligible young man into falling in love with her, she can think of no better method than to concoct a philosophical treatise about why he ought to love her. The index of her treatise reveals her basic argumentative equipment:

> *Moral sensibility, thinking sensibility, importunate sensibility; mental sensation, pernicious state of protracted and uncertain feeling; congenial sympathy, congenial sentiment, congenial ardour; delicious emotions, melancholy emotions, frenzied emotions; tender feeling, energetic feeling, sublimised feeling; the germ, the bud, and the full-grown fruits of general utility, &c. &c.* "Yes," cried she, in extacy, when she had finished the contents, "this will do! Here is argument irresistible; here is a series of calculations, enough to pour conviction on the most incredulous mind."

Botherim plans to publish her correspondence under the title of *The Sweet Sensations of Sensibility, or the Force of Argument.*[44]

Cant, jargon, self-important verbiage: plainly, the rhetoric of sensibility has been around long enough to weary any normal audience; Hamilton can depend upon a mere list of its formulas to make

Botherim's supposedly radical argument look horribly stale. As Jean Hagstrum has remarked, "we get a strong sense of ending" for sensibility, as a literary movement, when we find that it has become a convenient object of satire.[45] Hamilton does not seek merely to illustrate silliness and lack of authenticity in a set of verbal formulas; she is also worried about the political conclusions to which a devotion to sensibility may lead. Botherim and her philosophic friends have little difficulty in using the argument of sensibility to posit an ideal of completely unrestricted, and therefore anti-social, individual freedom. When the trustee of Botherim's fortune introduces the subject of her "lawful issue," she declares, in words that Hamilton obviously intends to be deeply disturbing, "I shall have no lawful issue. . . . I hate lawful issue, and every thing that is lawful" (3:91). As with Oothoon's declarations, the question is not merely sexual; Botherim's statement has a much wider, political significance: "*every thing* that is lawful."

But the irony is that the argument of unlimited sensibility, as Hamilton sees it, works as efficiently toward the destruction of individual freedom as toward its advancement. In Botherim's circle, individual emotions are respected much more than individual rights. A leading ideologist among her friends develops the argument that because he is a person of "great passions," and therefore of great "virtue," he should be entitled to sacrifice other people's interests to his own, even if this means killing those people. "What a charming contrivance is this guillotine!" he muses. "How effectually does it stop the mouths of troublesome people. . . . Does not the philosophy, I now profess, teach that there is no such thing as right?"—by which he means individual rights to life and property (1:73–75).[46] Again, the political logic of sensibility is involved in a process of self-destruction: the more stringently the premise of individual sensibility's prerogatives is applied, the farther from liberal individualism it seems to impel the argument.

Like Wollstonecraft, however, Hamilton finds a place for sensibility in her own argument; like More, she devalues the rhetorical formulas of sensibility but cannot do without the emotional thing itself. Sensibility, to Hamilton, is too important to be allowed to disfigure itself in debased expressions. She creates a cast of positive characters whose true sensibility distinguishes them both from the fanatics in Botherim's party and from commonplace people who have no special degree of feeling. While conventional members of society ignore the sufferings of the poor and occupy themselves with status-seeking, and while Botherim propagandizes for abstract, utopian causes, Hamilton's real heroine Mrs. Fielding spends her time in charitable activities, including the operation of an asylum for destitute women. She is more than a sentimentalist: "Mrs. Fielding's sensibility was not of that nature which can content itself with dropping a graceful tear to the misery which an active exertion of benevolence has power to relieve" (3:75). In Mrs. Fielding, Hamilton creates an image of social sensibility that she can use to reprove other people's sensibility for not being social enough.

But this summary statement runs the risk of picturing Hamilton's ideal as merely a higher form of that socialized and conventionalized sensibility to which both Wollstonecraft and More objected. In fact, Hamilton's respect for sensibility results in her placing the emphasis of her novel as much on regard for the individual as on regard for social order. It is true that Hamilton sees, as clearly as Wollstonecraft, that institutional expressions of sensibility function as a means of socialization; Mrs. Fielding's humanitarian institution reforms fallen women, not by using punishment, which would create resistance, but by using a program of "kindness and humanity" and of work that helps them regain "the invigorating stimulus of self-approbation" (3:317, 83). Yet sensibility is not just a collection of internalized rewards and restraints. It is a state of consciousness, a state that characteristically manifests itself not just in the ability to follow social rules but in the ability to make sensitive distinctions, and to make them for oneself. If the argument of sensibility generally includes an argument of discriminations, the state of mind to which it appeals, and which it attempts to create, also thrives on the habit of discrimination. As part of her effort to distinguish true from false sensibility, Hamilton tries to refute the notion that there is a necessity in "importunate sensibility" that naturally deprives people of their power to judge and discriminate. She uses her characters to suggest that this conception of sensibility is merely the product of "abstract reasoning"; moral sensibility is "spontaneous" but not "necessarian" (a difficult but real distinction); an inspection of one's own "feelings" and "consciousness" demonstrates that one is quite capable of using one's sensibility to make accurate moral judgments (2:46–60, 79–80). And the distinctions that sensibility makes are not simply products of social distinctions. Hamilton complains about people who cannot distinguish "sensibility" to class-bound rules and forms from a real awareness of the "infinite variety" of "tempers and dispositions" of people in all social classes (1:268; 3:73–81, 218–19); she denounces "all the system-makers" who have "laid down the law" for women, treating them not as thinking beings but as "mere machines" (1:198); and she emphasizes her heroine's ability to take action for herself without waiting for support from government or society (3:81).[47]

Richardson's novel was obsessively concerned with the choices that Clarissa's sensibility makes. Even in discussing the details of her daily schedule, she exclaims, "I have my choice: *who* can wish for more? . . . You see what *freewill* enables one to do."[48] Hamilton's argument also emphasizes individual choice. The victims of false sensibility may like to portray themselves as driven by emotional necessities, but they are not, after all, mere machines; their consciousness tells them that they can choose their systems of values. Not every novel of sensibility emphasizes individual choice, and in those that do, as I have observed, the choices often get made badly. Yet the focus on sensibility as an ideal of individual consciousness and yet as a problem for individual consciousness, as an argument and also as something worth arguing about, imparts a positive value to the intricacies of consciousness that establishes standards for the ways in which we still read literature. Again, we may regard Werther as a mistaken idealist in his conflict with the authorities, or we may side with him; but his possession of an individual and intricate consciousness still represents a sense of our own values.

The permanence of sensibility's legacy is evident by the second decade of the nineteenth century, when Austen wrote and published that very conservative novel *Mansfield Park*. If this novel is any evidence, sensibility had certainly, by that time, been incorporated firmly into educated values, not as an insect is enclosed in amber, but as a habit of thought is assimilated by an intricate consciousness. *Mansfield Park* vindicates both the principle of social order and the principle of an individual conscience that is so attuned to the value of sensibility that it can view people as positively "wicked" if they presume to marry "without affection" (in 1700, this would have been no sin at all).[49] The sensibility movement has done its work so well that Austen's Sir Thomas Bertram, the very embodiment of traditional authority, can notice with disapproval "that independence of spirit, which prevails so much in modern days, even in young women"—and then move toward accommodation with that spirit by encouraging the young woman he is lecturing to take time "for really examining [her] own inclinations."[50]

It has been complained—I myself have complained—that the sensibility movement often encouraged social conformism;[51] it has also been complained that it upheld an ideal of unlimited feeling that could never be fully realized.[52] There is justice in these charges. But the argument of sensibility, which could expose the defects of its own rhetoric, the messiness of its own conceptual apparatus, can also expose the limitations of arguments that are used to criticize it. Because sensibility was so difficult to define and its implications so difficult to work out, its argument very frequently turned on discrimination, on the awareness of fine distinctions, on the importance of seeing beyond rules and formulas and of seeing into states of individual consciousness. As a type of moral and political argument, sensibility was tragically or comically flawed; as a source of education, as a means of imputing value and interest to the individual selves that participate in moral and political systems, it was a remarkable success.

Notes

1. Mary Wollstonecraft, *A Vindication of the Rights of Woman*, ed. Carol H. Poston (New York: Norton, 1975), p. 94.

2. This idea develops throughout Jean Hagstrum's *Sex and Sensibility: Ideal and Erotic Love from Milton to Mozart* (Chicago: University of Chicago Press, 1980).

3. Hannah More, "Sensibility: A Poetical Epistle to the Hon. Mrs. Boscawen," in *Sacred Dramas . . . to which is added Sensibility, A Poem* (London: Cadell, 1782), p. 283. More eventually changed "Pity," in the poem's early editions, to the more general "Feeling"; see *The Works of Hannah More* (New York: Harper, 1851), 1:35.

4. More, "Sensibility" (1782), p. 282; Edmund Burke, *Reflections on the Revolution in France*, ed. Conor Cruise O'Brien (Harmondsworth, England: Penguin, 1968), p. 176. Wollstonecraft, *A Vindication of the Rights of Men*, 2nd ed. (1790; Gainesville: Scholars' Facsimiles, 1960), pp. 68–69, attacks Burke for "advert[ing]," in this way, "to a sentimental jargon" of "*sensibility*" that "has long been current in conversation, and even in books of morals." It is worth noticing that exploitation of sensibility as a device of argument became prominent in a period in which formal study of logic and rhetoric, much of it carried on by writers involved in the sensibility movement, increasingly emphasized experience and intuition rather than syllogistic reasoning and the use of traditional "topics"; on this issue see Wilbur Samuel Howell, *Eighteenth-Century British Logic and Rhetoric* (Princeton: Princeton University Press, 1971).

5. Jane Austen, *The Novels of Jane Austen*, ed. R. W. Chapman, 3rd ed. (London: Oxford University Press, 1933), 1:266–69.

6. Burke, *Reflections*, p. 169.

7. Burke, *Reflections*, p. 168; Francis to Burke, 19 February 1790, Burke to Francis, 20 February 1790, in *The Correspondence of Edmund Burke*, ed. Alfred Cobban and Robert A. Smith (Cambridge: Cambridge University Press, 1967), 6:86–87, 90. O'Brien, *Reflections*, p. 385 n. 63, draws attention to this exchange.

8. Thomas Paine, *Rights of Man*, ed. Henry Collins (Harmondsworth, England: Penguin, 1969), pp. 71–72. Burke, *Reflections*, p. 176, anticipates such objections in his claim that theatrical displays may be perfectly well adapted to evoking people's "natural" and spontaneous moral reactions.

9. Paine, pp. 79, 73; Burke, *Reflections*, p. 281.

10. James T. Boulton, *The Language of Politics in the Age of Wilkes and Burke* (London: Routledge, 1963), p. 121.

11. On the history of sensibility as a concept of self-consciousness and self-awareness, see the important essay by G. S. Rousseau, "Nerves, Spirits, and Fibres: Towards Defining the Origins of Sensibility," in *Studies in the Eighteenth Century III*, ed. R. F. Brissenden and J. C. Eade (Toronto: University of Toronto Press, 1976), pp. 137–57. Hagstrum, p. 172, identifies several connections between sensibility and consciousness. Raymond Williams, *Keywords: A Vocabularly of Culture and Society* (New York: Oxford University Press, 1976), pp. 235–38, also refers to their relationship.

12. Brissenden, *Virtue in Distress: Studies in the Novel of Sentiment from Richardson to Sade* (London: Macmillan, 1974), esp. pp. 56–64. See the long poem on sensibility and other revolutionary virtues in *The Anti-Jacobin; Or, Weekly Examiner* (9 July 1798; reprinted New York: AMS, 1968), pp. 282–87.

13. See esp. "The Friend of Humanity and the Knife-Grinder," with its introduction; "Manners and Character of the Age"; and "Ode to a Jacobin"; in *Anti-Jacobin* (27 November 1797 and 2 July 1798), pp. 15–16, 269–71.

14. David P. Jordan, *The Revolutionary Career of Maximilien Robespierre* (New York: Free Press-Macmillan, 1985), p. 76.

15. See, for example, Wollstonecraft's contrast between natural and unnatural views of motherhood, *Vindication of the Rights of Woman*, pp. 142–43. For a comparison of Burke's rhetoric of sensibility and Wollstonecraft's in her attacks on Burke, see Boulton, pp. 167–76.

16. Michel Foucault, *The History of Sexuality,* trans. Robert Hurley (New York: Pantheon, 1978), vol. 1, *An Introduction*, esp. pp. 20–25, 68–69, 105–6, 120–24. In citing Foucault, I need to register my dissent from some of his most counterintuitive statements, particularly his declaration that "the 'economy' of discourses . . . not a system of representations, is what determines the essential features of what they have to say" (pp. 68–69). It may not be "essential" to Foucault that discourse bears an important relation to the things and ideas it attempts to represent, but discourse would certainly look very different if it were liberated completely from that relation. Discourse shapes concepts, but concepts also shape discourse, as any author consciously selecting forms of representation can discover. Various discourses of sensibility "have to say" a variety of things, not *all* of them "determined" by the "economy" of discourse.

17. Adam Smith, *The Theory of Moral Sentiments*, ed. D. D. Raphael and A. L. Macfie (Oxford: At the Clarendon Press, 1976), pp. 209, 25.

18. Ibid., esp. pp. 109–34.

19. Burke to Francis, 20 February 1790, in *Correspondence*, p. 91.

20. Austen, 1:77, 97.

21. Ibid., 3:33.

22. Williams, p. 236.

23. Thomas Day, *The History of Sandford and Merton* (1783–89; New York: Garland, 1977), 1:4–6.

24. Ibid., 1:11.

25. Ibid., 1:6.

26. In "*The Stranger Within Thee*": *Concepts of the Self in Late-Eighteenth-Century Literature* (Pittsburgh: University of Pittsburgh Press, 1980), pp. 59–81, I discuss this aspect of Clarissa's sensibility.

27. Terry Eagleton, for instance, contends that "spiritual individualism is the acceptable face of the very system which kills Clarissa"—*The Rape of Clarissa: Writing, Sexuality and Class Struggle in Samuel Richardson* (Minneapolis: University of

Minnesota Press, 1982), p. 87. Hagstrum, pp. 173, 204–5, argues against forcing *Clarissa*, or sensibility itself, into a deplorably "bourgeois" mold.

28. Alexander Pope, *An Essay on Criticism*, 2:297–98.

29. Samuel Richardson, *Clarissa*, intro. by John Butt (London: Dent, 1932), 4:499.

30. Ibid., 4:420, 430.

31. Ibid., 4:430.

32. Ibid., 4:429.

33. More, "Sensibility" (1782), pp. 281–88, 276.

34. Ibid., pp. 282, 285, 283.

35. Ibid., pp. 282, 287–88.

36. Day, 3:226–27; 1:75–77.

37. Ibid., 3:64–66.

38. Ibid., 1:28–29.

39. William Blake, *Visions of the Daughters of Albion*, plate 7, 1. 16, in *The Complete Poetry and Prose of William Blake*, ed. David V. Erdman, rev. ed. (Garden City, N.Y.: Anchor-Doubleday, 1982), p. 50. Parenthetical references will cite plate, line, and page numbers in this edition ("E").

40. "A Declaration of Rights is, by reciprocity, a Declaration of Duties also. Whatever is my right as a man, is also the right of another; and it becomes my duty to guarantee, as well as to possess" (Paine, p. 136).

41. Blake, *A Vision of the Last Judgment*, E 564.

42. Ibid.

43. Johann Wolfgang von Goethe, *The Sufferings of Young Werther*, trans. Bayard Quincy Morgan (New York: Ungar, 1957), pp. 126–27.

44. Elizabeth Hamilton, *Memoirs of Modern Philosophers* (1800; New York: Garland, 1974), 3:102–03, 108. Parenthetical references will cite volume and page numbers in this edition.

45. Hagstrum, pp. 11–12.

46. Cf. Burke's accusation that the supposedly liberal revolutionaries had departed so far from real sensibility as to consider "tenderness to individuals . . . as treason to the public" (*Reflections*, p. 161).

47. The idealized Mrs. Fielding had, of course, her activist counterparts in real life, among them Hannah More. For an account of the sensibility movement's positive and negative effects on women's self-assertion, see Katharine M. Rogers, *Feminism in Eighteenth-Century England* (Urbana: University of Illinois Press, 1982), pp. 33–35, 119–47, 217–18.

48. Richardson, 4:506.

49. Austen, 3:324.

50. Ibid., 3:318–19.

51. I make this complaint rather frequently in *The Stranger Within Thee*.

52. This is one of the major arguments urged by Mary Poovey, *The Proper Lady and the Woman Writer: Ideology as Style in the Works of Mary Wollstonecraft, Mary Shelley, and Jane Austen* (Chicago: University of Chicago Press, 1984).

PART II

Expanding Horizons: Sensibility and Literary Transformation

Madness and Lust in the Age of Sensibility

JOHN A. DUSSINGER

Walter Shandy's sage observation on love echoes numerous eighteenth-century writers, ranging from La Rochefoucauld to Jane Austen:

> ———Love, you see, is not so much a SENTIMENT as a SITUATION, into which a man enters, as my brother *Toby* would do, into a corps———no matter whether he loves the service or no———[1]

The loss of reason is a familiar situation associated with eros; and medieval and Renaissance romances abound with examples of desiring subjects who surrender everything to passion.[2] But one situation that seems peculiar to the later eighteenth century involves a tension between a rationally controlled subject and an emotionally abandoned object. Although either sex may fill the roles of subject and object in this scenario, in practice madness seems to be associated with all that is feminine. Sterne's Maria episode in *A Sentimental Journey* and Henry Fuseli's *The Nightmare* both eroticize mental derangement in the woman as a quintessentially defenseless posture, with sado-masochistic implications; and it was precisely this tendency to equate the woman's social, with her psychological, subservience that Austen's novels, *Mansfield Park* above all, consistently repudiate.

To enhance a character's hold on the reader's imagination, Sterne adopts Cervantes's method of alluding to his own text. After Tristram's encounter with the mad Maria in Book IX of *Tristram Shandy*, Yorick, in *A Sentimental Journey*, is meeting someone twice removed from the author's direct encounter and now already canonized among the celebrated sentimental figures of the day. Her change in appearance emphasizes the lachrymose over the lecherous responses: her white dress (recall the violated Clarissa all in white), her loosened hair, and the addition of a green ribbon contribute to the image of distressed innocence; the substitution of the loyal dog, Sylvio, for the faithless goat helps to obviate the wanton thoughts aroused in Tristram. Accordingly, in contrast to his lecherous predecessor, Yorick, cast as a Man of Feeling, is disposed to sympathize as a protective witness: "I look'd in Maria's eyes, and saw she was thinking more of her father than of her lover or her little goat."[3] Although without Tristram's cynical leer, Yorick's rhythm of weeping and wiping, culminating in protestations of spirituality, appears suspicious; and Sterne would surely agree with Diderot about the "instruments of Religion": "Il y a un peu de testicule au fond de nos sentiments les plux sublimes et de notre tendresse la plux epurée."[4] Throughout this exchange of tears and handkerchief, Yorick as narrator remains in control of the situation that he himself has initiated; and his comment, "When Maria had come a little to herself. . . ," implies a journalist's professional detachment.

Maria's repeating the French proverb that God tempers the wind to the shorn lamb arouses in Yorick the idea of her being "shorn" not only of her money and shoes but more significantly of her mental faculties. This situation of her abject surrender melts Yorick into promising her (contingently, as usual) the same terms he had made to Eliza in the *Journal*—shelter in his pastoral cottage, where they could share his bread and cup in peace from this scurvy and disastrous world.[5] Yorick's inquiry about the temperature of her heart touches the right nerve and produces the sentimental tableau: "—she look'd with wistful disorder for some time in my face; and then, without saying any thing, took her pipe, and play'd her service to the Virgin."[6] Muteness, abstract demeanor, and musical expression combine in erotic religiosity without comment by the narrator.

While sublimating his role to that of father and Good Samaritan, Yorick cannot refrain from one last view and measuring her with the eye of a connoisseur: "Maria, tho' not tall, was nevertheless of the first order of fine forms—affliction had touch'd her looks with something that was scarce earthly—still she was feminine—and so much was there about her of all that the heart wishes, or the eye looks for in woman."[7] To the sickly, impotent, and culturally alienated Yorick, this distracted girl epitomizes the wholly non-threatening Other that gives him a measure of power. In his *Treatise of Dreams and Visions*, Thomas Tryon observes: " . . . when men are so divested of their *Rational Faculties*, then they appear naked, having no *Covering*, *Vail*, or *Figg-leaves* before them, to hide themselves in, and therefore they no longer remain under a Mask or Disguise, but appear even as they are, which is very rare to be known in any that retain their Senses and Reason."[8] Madness is the ultimate form of nakedness, the condition of being in society without the normal safeguards for the ego; and thus Maria's innocence is equivalent to her being absolutely attainable as sex object, defenseless before the voyeuristic gaze of the narrator clothed in his black frock coat and in his privilege as storyteller.

In contrast to Sterne, Diderot, and other writers of the Enlightenment who emphasized love as primarily a situation of power and subservience, the Swiss German painter John Henry Fuseli jolted his contemporaries by depicting passion and madness as mysterious phenomena of the unconscious. "One of the most unexplored regions of art are dreams, and what may be called the personification of sentiment," he wrote; and in an age preoccupied with measurement, description, and classification of the material world, his insight into the mysterious depths of the psyche revealed in sleep and in other conditions beyond rational control obviously disturbed his contemporaries.[9] His exhibit in 1782 of *The Nightmare* at the Royal Academy brought him immediate fame throughout Europe as engravings of the painting were widely circulated. Despite his own penchant for Gothic fantasy, Horace Walpole described it as "shocking"; and to judge from the numerous imitations, including one cartoon depicting Lord Nelson about to mount Lady Hamilton in a similar posture, what haunted the spectator was the grotesque blend of pathos and pornography in the woman's utter submission to some monstrous power.[10]

Other than folklore and traditional religious accounts of dreams, rational explanations in the classical period show little interest in what Fuseli so vividly reveals about the mind—its demonic cravings and humiliations that appear uninvited in the darkness. Hobbes, for instance, attributed dreams to the "distemper of some of the inward parts of the Body; divers distempers must needs cause different Dreams."[11] Medical literature stressed simply the bad effects of sleeping on one's back; according to Dr. John Bond, in one of the first English works on the nightmare, the condition "generally seizes people sleeping on their backs, and often begins with frightful dreams, which are soon succeeded by a difficult respiration, a violent oppression of the breast, and a total privation of voluntary motion."[12] In this context, Robert Anthony Bromley ridiculed *The Nightmare* as offering instruction to young people about how to lie in their beds: "*Don't lie on your back, my dear, and no harm will come to you.*"[13]

The dearth of material in Fuseli's cultural milieu, whether in art tradition or in psychological speculation about abnormal states of mind, contradicts Nicolas Powell's view that *The Nightmare* is "very much a product of its period."[14] But Powell does well to point out that "the creature squatting on the sleeper's stomach is the nightmare, not—as many recent writers have assumed—the horse";[15] and he quotes Johnson's *Dictionary* to clarify how the eighteenth-century educated avoided the etymological confusion with the female horse: "NIGHTMARE (*night* and according to Temple, *mara*, a spirit that, in the northern mythology, was related to torment or suffocate sleepers). A morbid oppression in the night, resembling the pressure of weight upon the breast." *Incubus* was another term for the nightmare or night spirit.

Although both sexes are subject to dreams and nightmares, folk legends tended to emphasize the woman's susceptibility, as in Mercutio's Queen Mab speech in *Romeo and Juliet*: "This is the hag, when maids lie on their backs, / That presses them, and learns them first to bear, / Making them women of good carriage."[16] Willoughby, in Jane Austen's *Sense and Sensibility*, alludes to this legend after the Dashwoods decline his gift: " 'But, Marianne, the horse is still yours though you cannot use it now. I shall keep it only till you can claim it. When you leave Barton to form your own establishment in a more lasting home, Queen Mab shall receive you.' " As if associating Queen Mab and the gift horse with Fuseli's traumatic scene, Elinor quite properly believes that Willoughby's sexual innuendoes must indicate a secret engagement to her sister.[17]

Erasmus Darwin, Fuseli's friend, included an engraving of *The Nightmare* in *The Loves of the Plants* (not published completely until 1789) and interpreted its significance in doggerel verse:

> So on his NIGHTMARE through the evening fog
> Flits the squab fiend o'er fen, and lake and bog;
> Seeks some love-wildered Maid with sleep oppress'd,
> Alights, and grinning sits upon her breast.
> —Such as of late by FUSELI'S poetic eye;
> Whose daring tints, with SHAKESPEAR's happiest grace,
> Gave to the airy phantom form and place.—
> Back o'er her pillow sinks her blushing head,
> Her snow-white limbs hang helpless from the bed;
> While with quick sighs, and suffocative breath,
> Her interrupted heart-pulse swims in death.
> —Then shrieks of captur'd towns and widow's tears,
> Pale lovers stretch'd upon their blood-stain'd biers,
> The headlong precipice that thwarts her flight,
> The trackless desert, the cold starless night,
> And stern-eyed Murderer with his knife behind,
> In dread succession agonise her mind.
> O'er her fair limbs convulsive tremors fleet;
> Start in her hands and struggle in her feet;
> In vain to scream with quivering lips she tries,
> And strains in palsy'd lids her tremulous eyes;

In vain she *wills* to run, fly, swim, walk, creep;
The WILL presides not in the bower of SLEEP.
—On her fair bosom sits the Demon-Ape,
Erect, and balances his bloated shape;
Rolls in their marble orbs his Gorgon-eyes
And drinks with leathern ears her tender cries.[18]

Just as Tryon stressed the ultimate nakedness of the mentally deranged, so Darwin describes the rape situation of the nightmare victim, bereft of even the will to resist the hideous "Demon-Ape" that sits "erect" upon her bosom. In contrast to Tryon, however, who valued certain forms of madness as approaching the Christian ideal of innocence, Darwin unabashedly savors the power of the male vampire, who "drinks with leathern ears . . . tender cries" of his helpless female victim.

Fuseli's motive for *The Nightmare*, it now seems generally agreed, was revenge against Anna Landolt, Lavater's niece, with whom he was passionately in love but too poor to marry. Being unable to marry her also meant that he was unable to express his feelings directly to her; but he acknowledged freely his obsession while writing to her friends, as in this letter to Lavater in June 1779: "Last night I had her in bed with me—tossed my bedclothes hugger-mugger—wound my hot and tight-clasped hands about her—fused her body and her *soul* together with my own—poured into her my spirit, breath and strength. Anyone who touches her now commits adultery and incest! She is *mine*, and I am *hers*. And have her I will. . . . I will enforce my first right to her, or else die in the attempt—and perhaps kill somebody too. What God or nature hath joined, let no man—let no business-man sunder."[19] Notwithstanding his claim of ownership, Anna did soon marry the merchant alluded to here, and Fuseli thus set loose the Incubus to prey upon her. On the other side of the canvas is an unfinished portrait of a young woman believed to be that of Anna Landolt.[20] It is of such stuff that dreams—and art—are made!

As his biographers have noted, Fuseli always seemed fascinated with the battle of the sexes, especially after meeting the beautiful and provocative Mary Wollstonecraft.[21] Even if his male figures usually win this battle, we should remember that he also experimented with situations of female dominance over the male, as in his rendering of *Brunhilde and Gunther* (1807), an incident from the *Nibelungenlied* (10.648–50). His sketch of a murderess, her hair adorned with a cluster of baccanal grapes, with dagger in one hand and leg of a sacrificial animal in the other, implies that women as well as men are capable of orgiastic violence; and not surprisingly, his portraits of

Brunhilde and Gunther **(1807). (Copyright to Castle Museum, City of Nottingham.)**

Lady Macbeth leave no doubt about this heroine's will to power over men.

But whether in a state of mastery or submission—whether in portraits of Queen Mab, the voluptuous mischief-maker, or of Mad Kate, the girl in Cowper's *The Task*, crazed after her sailor-lover is lost at sea—Fuseli's woman eroticizes madness.[22] Scenes of dead or dying maidens also have sexual overtones—Celadon holding his limp Amelia after she has been struck by lightning (Thomson's *Summer* 11. 1169–1222) and the death of Dido, which shows the influence of Joshua Reynolds's version, a painting Fuseli admired.[23] Finally, three examples of the *amor pianoforte* provide a useful gloss on the scene in Austen's *Emma*, in which Jane Fairfax plays the Broadwood given to her by Frank Churchill. In these motifs Fuseli endows a domestic situation with depth psychology: in the two sketches the performer is seized, or rather imagines being seized, violently by her lover; by contrast, the painting depicts an autoerotic image—the girl reclining on the sofa is apparently a reflection of the performer's romantic daydream while at the spinet. As Fuseli reveals in uncompromising detail, sensibility is a "civilized" disguise for primal urges toward sexual dominance and surrender; and the reason/madness axis sets the ideal conditions for this struggle.

Like Fuseli's erotic art, Mary Wollstonecraft's sexual politics derived not only from a deeply personal crisis but also from the general social turmoil surrounding the French Revolution. Since at least the time of Wollstonecraft's devastating attack on Burke's feminization of sensibility, in *A Vindication of the Rights of Woman* (1792), moreover, there has been a hypothesis that something called patriarchal hegemony has conspired to imprison women mentally and physically. Political activists from the 1960s to the present, vociferous against this traditional subordination of women, have tended to exaggerate social determinism to the extent of ignoring individual uniqueness and reducing all cultural phenomena to a thinly disguised plot. To press their opinions into an irrefutable dialectic, Sandra Gilbert and Susan Gubar, in *The Madwoman in the Attic*, apply a seesaw mechanism to the whole sweep of English literature:

> for every glowing portrait of submissive women enshrined in domesticity, there exists an equally important negative image that embodies the sacrilegious fiendishness of what William Blake called the "Female Will." Thus, while male writers traditionally praise the simplicity of the dove, they invariably castigate the cunning of the serpent—at least when that cunning is exercised in her own behalf. Similarly, assertiveness, aggressiveness—all characteristic of a male life of "significant action"—are

Young Man Passionately Embracing A Woman Seated at a Spinet. **(Courtesy of Kunsthaus, Zürich.)**

***Nude Playing Piano.* (Courtesy of Öffentliche Kunstsammlung, Basel.)**

> "monstrous" in women precisely because "unfeminine" and therefore unsuited to a gentle life of "contemplative purity."[24]

Predictably, without accounting for the male monsters in romance literature, Gilbert and Gubar attribute any grotesque representation of the female to the author's misogyny; for example, Spenser's Duessa and Lucifera: "Both women use their arts of deception to entrap and destroy men, and the secret, shameful ugliness of both is closely associated with their hidden genitals—that is, with their femaleness."[25]

The trouble with generalizing social and literary history by such behavioral models is that stereotypes of opposite qualities exist simultaneously and hence necessitate an infinite regress of explanation to account for hidden motives. Thus, as Vieda Skultans points out, against the Victorian commonplace that women lack sexual appetite and submit to intercourse only for procreation, there is the reverse image of "sex-craving women" in medical reports, women who entice "the innocent and unsuspecting young physician to an improper and unnecessary use of the speculum."[26] Of course, it will be argued that both stereotypes betray a deep-rooted fear of female assertiveness with the body, the only weapon available to the disenfranchised, who are really fighting for their political *equality*. Perhaps if the man held legitimate power he would not have these neurotic phobias and aggressions. And so on.

An axiom underlying the "male conspiracy" hypothesis is that the "Victorian" social order came about by systematic repression of the woman's sexuality. With Freud's *Civilization and Its Discontents* as prototype, numerous revisionist tracts beginning with Norman O. Brown, Herbert Marcuse, Betty Friedan, Mary Ellmann, Germaine Greer, Kate Millett, and many others incorporate a theory of sexual repression to account for most or all of our social and psychological ills.[27] Against this flood tide, however, Michel Foucault advanced the iconoclasm that exploitation rather than repression denotes the prevailing attitude of the dominant classes since the eighteenth century:

> The new procedures of power that were devised during the classical age and employed in the nineteenth century were what caused our societies to go from *a symbolics of blood* to *an analytics of sexuality*. Clearly, nothing was more on the side of the law, death, transgression, the symbolic, and sovereignty than blood; just as sexuality was on the side of the norm, knowledge, life, meaning, the disciplines, and regulations.[28]

Foucault identifies Sade and the first eugenists "with this transition from 'sanguinity' to 'sexuality.'" Sexuality, in his view, enters discourse when its deployment grows necessary to the bourgeois classes displacing the hereditary castes.

This "analytics of sexuality" may be seen most clearly in the expanded concern over hysteria during the latter decades of the eighteenth century. Since ancient Greece, women were believed to be especially prone to madness because of their reproductive organs. Therefore, when melancholy became a fashionable disease among Elizabethan gentlemen as a positive sign of the contemplative mind, its counterpart in women continued to have the stigma of an inferior constitution, related, as Robert Burton explained, "to those vicious vapours which come from menstruous blood . . . a fulginous exhalation of corrupt seed, troubling the brain, heart and mind. . . . The whole malady proceeds from that inflammation, putricity, black smoky vapours, etc., from them comes care, sorrow and anxiety, obfuscation of spirits, agony, desperation, and the like."[29] Traditionally associated with the uterus, a disease "brought about," William Harvey asserted, "by unhealthy menstrual discharges or from over-abstinence from sexual intercourse when the passions are strong," hysteria was abruptly elevated by the seventeenth-century neurologist Thomas Willis to the brain and nervous system.[30]

Both the uterine and nerve theory of the disease subsisted into the nineteenth century, but the most interesting event for our purpose here is the collapse of the sexual distinction between melancholy or hypochondria, the male disease, and hysteria, the female disease. Identified as similar disorders by Richard Blackmore in 1725, Robert Whytt in 1751 declared them to be equivalent and to be disorders stemming from "a too great delicacy or uncommon sensibility of the nerves in general, or of those of the stomach and intestines, or other organs in particular."[31]

After the disease becomes general, a disposition of the leisured classes, an "ethic of sensibility" gradually displaces a "dynamics of corporeal space." Sexual difference, in other words, diminishes in accordance with Fuseli's *Aphorism* 226: "In an age of luxury woman aspires to the functions of man, and man slides into the offices of woman. The epoch of eunuchs was ever the epoch of viragoes."[32] For both men and women, the discourse of sensibility provides an internal landscape suddenly open to the public gaze, a phenomenon that seems to parallel the increasing acceptance of postmortem autopsies by the latter decades of our period. The mind/body, once conceived of as dualistic but solid and continuous, now becomes victim to predators with uncanny mobility. As Nathaniel Highmore describes it, the animal spirits, "because of their igneous tenuity, can penetrate even the densest, the most compact bodies . . . , and because of their activity, can penetrate the entire microcosm in a single instant."[33] Hysteria is only the extreme case of the "internal body" now open to penetration: given the uncertain motions of the sensibility, no one is safe from madness.

It is this consciousness of the inherent instability of the self that finds a voice in Sade. No raving maniac but thoroughly representative of the Enlightenment—rational and practical, Sade's one main dictum was that "all creatures are born isolated and have no need of one another."[34] Hence, he despised the current benevolism and philanthropy as either naive or hypocritical. Having utterly rejected any a priori relationship between self and Other, Sade embraces solitude as an affirmation of the ego. "Sade repeatedly stresses the point," Simone de Beauvoir remarks, "that it is not the unhappiness of the other person which excites the libertine, but rather the knowledge that he is responsible for it."[35] Paradoxically, the usual master/slave situations become interchangeable and thus sexless; humiliation was for him the ultimate experience of pride: "It was a favorite fantasy of his to be penetrated and beaten while he himself was penetrating and beating a submissive victim."[36] Clearly, this is a long way from Wollstonecraft's relatively naive male conspiracy to dominate the woman because in this game the players are essentially bisexual.

What is most fundamental to Sade, then, is the combination of insatiable sexual appetite and a basic emotional "apartness" while engaging with the Other. He apparently never could or wanted to lose himself in the act of coitus but remained aloof while enjoying his power to inflict pain or pleasure in the Other at will. Without the language to articulate his tortured consciousness, Sade would have been no more than an interesting clinical case for medical history; but by exploding the "ethic of sensibility" in his assertion of schizoidal freedom from the body and from the loss of self in the Other, he illuminates the more sinister motives in the mimetic art of Sterne and Fuseli.

During her entire career as a writer, Jane Austen satirizes the cult of sensibility for its narcissism and like Mary Wollstonecraft attacks in particular its brand of femininity.[37] The early parodies, the dialogical narrative in *Sense and Sensibility*, and the dogmatic ridicule of Sir Edward Denham in *Sanditon* are unequivocal toward the vogue; but in *Mansfield Park* the positive rendering of emotion in a sound mind but infirm body appears to be the most subtle and ambitious reworking of a female stereotype.

Although specifically mentioning gout, contusion, hysteric fits, rheumatism, and the like for her less complex characters, Austen is deliberately vague about Fanny's health except that her disorder appears to be psychosomatically related to her environment and amenable to the solicitous attention of Edmund, Sir Thomas, William, and in a wry way, of both Mrs. Norris and Lady Bertram. On her arrival at Mansfield, the ten-year-old Fanny, we are told, was "exceedingly timid and shy" (12), "[a]fraid of every body, ashamed of herself . . . and could scarcely speak to be heard, or without crying" (13). The "despondence that sunk her little heart was severe" (14), and she "crept about in constant terror of something or other; often retreating towards her own chamber to cry" (15). While Edmund's kindness soon makes her feel at home in Mansfield, nevertheless, five years later Mrs. Norris is being recommended as her guardian to provide a regimen for her same "little heart." Edmund himself favors the idea: "with *her* you will be forced to speak for yourself. . . . she will force you to do justice to your natural powers" (27). Against Lady Bertram's absurd indolence, Mrs. Norris's equally absurd officiousness passes for a model of authority and good sense; and with the first mention of Fanny's horse-riding for health's sake, there may be a hint of what the family suspects to be her constitutional problem—hysteria, a familiar complaint, we have seen, in this period.[38]

If we assume that Fanny is suffering from this sexual disorder, then Edmund's most inspiring act of kindness seems to have been aiding her recovery with the "dear old grey pony" and indirectly giving her more confidence over her own body. Horseback riding was a highly recommended treatment for hysteria and other nervous diseases.[39] Consequently, when Mary Crawford enters the novel, their rivalry over the new mare is metonymic of their qualitatively different attitudes toward the body:

> Miss Crawford's enjoyment of riding was such, that she did not know how to leave off. Active and fearless, and, though rather small, strongly made, she seemed formed for a horsewoman; and to the pure genuine pleasure of the exercise, something was probably added in Edmund's attendance and instructions, and something more in the conviction of very much surpassing her sex in general by her early progress, to make her unwilling to dismount. (66–67)

Besides the predictable enthusiasm of the Bertram sisters over Mary's riding ability, even the old coachman contrasts her zest with Fanny's trembling when Sir Thomas first put her on the old pony:

> "It is a pleasure to see a lady with such a good heart for riding!" said he. "I never see one sit a horse better. She did not seem to have a thought of fear. Very different from you, miss, when you first began, six years ago come next Easter." (69)

With dramatic irony, it is Maria who observes that Mary has the "same energy of character" as her brother and who significantly attributes "good horsemanship" to the mind.

For a character who could jest indelicately about her past, "Of *Rears*, and *Vices*, I saw enough. Now do not be suspecting me of a pun, I entreat" (60), this repeated emphasis on Mary's prowess with horses may serve to contrast the sexually experienced woman to the pubescent heroine. Austen herself, we know, could boast of having detected an adulteress at Bath when others had identified a different woman as the one involved; evidently there was something in the culprit's manner that the author could penetrate.[40] In any case, although Edmund eventually recants his judgment that Mary "is perfectly feminine" (64) and forms quite different criteria of the sexual ideal, his response early in the story, like the old coachman's, is to the erotic spectacle of a vivacious woman on horseback.

One ingenious twist in the plot is the medical benefit actually derived from Mrs. Norris's punitive discipline of the heroine. Notwithstanding the aunt's sadistic pleasure, Fanny's decision to rely more on walking for exercise than on riding Edmund's mare signals not only her improved health but also her increasing moral strength to act alone; and to the end of the story, therefore, the heroine seems actually thankful for her aunt's harsh treatment as the best regimen for a sickly sensibility:

> "If Fanny would be more regular in her exercise, she would not be knocked up so soon. She has not been out on horseback now this long while, and I am persuaded, that when she does not ride, she ought to walk. If she had been riding before, I should not have asked it [cutting the roses] of her. But I thought it would rather do her good after being stooping among the roses; for there is nothing so refreshing as a walk after a fatigue of that kind." (73)

Despite Mrs. Norris's perverse justification of her cruelty, the regimen eventually has psychosomatic value. Far from being impassive toward all the frantic activity around her, the heroine has to suffer bodily as well as mental pain in solitude; and her Stoic "struggling against discontent and envy" is a profound agon that she alone must resolve. In the end, her greatest triumph is in finding a "cure" at Mansfield.

Thanks to her early regimen, Fanny can withstand the greatest threat to her selfhood while exiled to Portsmouth, reduced in health and exposed to Henry's overtures. In contrast to the aunt's outspoken malice, the stuff of fairy tales, the Crawfords belong to a more sophisticated text—to the world of Laclos's *Les Liaisons Dangereuses*, with the Vicomte de Valmont and the Marquise de Merteuil as role models. Just as Mary shares the latter's dread of falling in love like "those giddy women who call themselves women of *feeling*, whose heated imaginations persuade them that nature has placed their senses in their heads; who, having never thought about it, invariably confuse love with a lover,"[41] so Henry imitates his counterpart's desire to seduce a virtuous woman according to a simple law of mechanics: "It has become necessary for me to have this woman, so as to save myself from the ridicule of being in love with her: for to what lengths will a man not be driven by thwarted desire?"[42] When Henry tries to explain his plan to make "a small hole in Fanny Price's heart" (229) because of her physical charms, Mary catches at a more likely reason: "This it is—her not caring about you—which gives her such a soft skin and makes her so much taller" (230). Stimulated by their quarry's resistance, brother and sister collaborate to ensnare Fanny; and although not successful in overcoming her antipathy Henry follows Valmont's course of falling in love—at least temporarily. Again, we see here the project of engaging the Other's emotions and destroying her selfhood while remaining fully clothed and detached.

With the wisdom that love has more to do with situation than with sentiment, Fanny maintains an almost exasperating resistance to the reader's conventional desire for erotic involvement and proves beyond doubt that her physical dependence cannot weaken her will to reject the bogus suitor.[43] No matter how propitious that lovely Sunday in March, the narrative suggests that Fanny's walk with Henry is mainly a session in physical therapy:

> had she been without his arm, she would soon have known that she needed it, for she wanted strength for a two hours' saunter of this kind, coming as it generally did upon a week's previous inactivity. Fanny was beginning to feel the effect of being debarred from her usual, regular exercise; she had lost ground as to health since her being in Portsmouth, and but for Mr. Crawford and the beauty of the weather, would soon have been knocked up now. (409)

For perhaps any young woman other than tough-minded Fanny, the situation would be all to Henry's advantage; and his skillful maneuvering into Edmund's postures of sympathy does have some effect: "They often stopt with the same sentiment and taste, leaning against the wall, some minutes, to look and admire." But at the end of the scene the two retreat separately; Henry goes off to a sumptuous dinner at the best inn in town and Fanny returns to Rebecca's inedible hashes.[44]

To unmask the dangerous seductiveness of sexual dominance and surrender, Austen invokes the discourse of the body—the "dynamics of corporeal space"—and thus undermines the "ethic of sensibility." Feelings matter, but they are always circumstantial. From his standpoint, D. H. Lawrence was right to condemn her "apartness" in rendering sexual love.[45] It is the apartness that Sade understood as the self's best defense against destructive illusion, against the madness that afflicts Sterne's Maria and Fuseli's prostrate victims. It is also the apartness that Hume cultivated throughout his career to overcome a deep-rooted conflict with his Puritan past, an ideal attested shortly before his death: "It is difficult to be more detached from life than I am at present."[46] A strategy of selfhood that eschews commitment to the Other seems intrinsic to the fabled peace of the Augustans.

Notes

1. Laurence Sterne, *The Life and Opinions of Tristram Shandy, Gentleman*, ed. Melvyn New and Joan New, 3 vols. (Gainesville: University Presses of Florida, 1978, 1984), 2:723.

2. See C. S. Lewis, *The Allegory of Love: A Study in Medieval Tradition* (London:

Oxford University Press, 1973) and Denis de Rougemont, *Love in the Western World* (New York: Harper & Row, 1974).

3. Laurence Sterne, *A Sentimental Journey Through France and Italy By Mr. Yorick*, ed. Gardner D. Stout, Jr. (Berkeley and Los Angeles: University of California Press, 1967), p. 271.

4. Denis Diderot, in a letter to Falconet, July 1767. Quoted from R. F. Brissenden, *Virtue in Distress: Studies in the Novel of Sentiment from Richardson to Sade* (London: Macmillan, 1974), p. 279.

5. See *A Sentimental Journey*, n. to 11. 10–11, pp. 275–76.

6. Ibid., pp. 273–74.

7. Ibid., p. 275.

8. Thomas Tryon, *Treatise of Dreams and Visions* (London, 1680), pp. 261–62. Quoted from Michael V. DePorte, *Nightmares and Hobbyhorses: Swift, Sterne, and Augustan Ideas of Madness* (San Marino, Calif.: Huntington Library, 1974), pp. 108–9.

9. John Henry Fuseli, "Aphorism 231," *The Life and Writings of Henry Fuseli*, ed. John Knowles, 3 vols. (1831; rpt. Millwood, N.Y.: Kraus International, 1982), 3:145. According to historians, it was not until well into the nineteenth century that a systematic interpretation of dreams was undertaken. See Franz G. Alexander and Sheldon T. Selesnick, *The History of Psychiatry* (New York and Toronto: New American Library, 1966), pp. 154–56 and 183–84. Michel Foucault, *Madness & Civilization: A History of Insanity in the Age of Reason*, trans. Richard Howard (New York and Toronto: New American Library, 1967), pp. 89–100.

10. Nicolas Powell, *Fuseli: The Nightmare* (New York: Viking, 1973), p. 77.

11. Thomas Hobbes, *Leviathan*, intro. John Plamenatz, Meridian Books (Cleveland and New York: World Publishing, 1966), p. 66.

12. John Bond, *An Essay on the Incubus, or Nightmare* (London, 1753). Quoted from Powell, *Fuseli*, p. 50.

13. *The Collected English Letters of Henry Fuseli*, ed. David H. Weinglass (Millwood, N. Y.: Kraus International, 1982), p. 112.

14. Powell, *Fuseli*, p. 17.

15. Ibid., p. 50.

16. William Shakespeare, *Romeo and Juliet*, I.iv.

17. Jane Austen, *Sense and Sensibility*, in *The Novels of Jane Austen*, ed. R. W. Chapman, 3rd ed., 5 vols. (London: Oxford University Press, 1933, 1960), 1:59–60. Subsequent references to Austen's novels are to this edition and page numbers are included in parentheses within the text.

18. Erasmus Darwin, *The Loves of the Plants*. Quoted from Powell, *Fuseli*, pp. 58–60.

19. Eudo C. Mason, *The Mind of Henry Fuseli: Selections from his Writings with an Introductory Study* (London: Routledge & Kegan Paul, 1951), p. 155.

20. Powell, *Fuseli*, p. 60.

21. Mason remarks: "Fuseli had little sympathy with feminism, and his generalisations on female genius, female affection and on woman aspiring to the functions of man, in Aphorisms 225–7 . . . , can probably be regarded as a veiled commentary on Mary Wollstonecraft's character and mentality," *The Mind of Henry Fuseli*, p. 147.

22. See Gert Schiff, "Fuseli, Lucifer and the Medusa," *Henry Fuseli*, trans. Sarah Twohig (London: Tate Gallery, 1975), esp. pp. 15–20.

23. See Jean H. Hagstrum, *Sex and Sensibility: Ideal and Erotic Love from Milton to Mozart* (Chicago and London: University of Chicago Press, 1980), pp. 280–81.

24. Sandra M. Gilbert and Susan Gubar, *The Madwoman in the Attic: The Woman Writer and the Nineteenth-Century Literary Imagination* (New Haven and London: Yale University Press, 1979, 1984), p. 28.

25. Ibid., p. 30.

26. Vieda Skultans, *English Madness: Ideas on Insanity, 1580–1890* (London, Boston, Henley: Routledge & Kegan Paul, 1979), p. 92. See also Sander Gilman, *Difference and Pathology: Stereotypes of Sexuality, Race, and Madness* (Ithaca: Cornell University Press, 1985).

27. See, for example, Norman O. Brown, *Life Against Death: The Psychoanalytical Meaning of History* (New York: Vintage, 1959); Herbert Marcuse, *Eros and Civilization: A Philosophical Inquiry into Freud* (New York: Vintage, 1955); Mary Ellmann, *Thinking About Women* (New York: Harcourt Brace Jovanovich, 1968); Germaine Greer, *The Female Eunuch* (London: Mac Gibbon & Kee, 1970); and Kate Millett, *Sexual Politics* (London: Virago, 1977).

28. Michel Foucault, *The History of Sexuality: Volume I: An Introduction*, trans. Robert Hurley (New York: Vintage, 1980), p. 148. See Isaac D. Balbus, "Disciplining Women: Michel Foucault and the Power of Feminist Discourse," *Praxis International* 5 (1986): 466–83.

29. Quoted from Skultans, *English Madness*, p. 80.

30. Ibid., p. 84.

31. Robert Whytt, *An Essay on the Vital and Involuntary Motions of Animals* (Edinburgh, 1751), pp. 333–34.

32. Knowles, *The Life and Writings*, p. 144.

33. Quoted from Foucault, *Madness & Civilization*, p. 123.

34. Simone de Beauvoir, *The Marquis de Sade, With Selections from His Writings Chosen by Paul Dinnage* (New York: Grove, 1953), p. 66.

35. Ibid., p. 77.

36. Ibid., p. 39.

37. See Margaret Kirkham, *Jane Austen, Feminism and Fiction* (Sussex: Harvester, 1983), pp. 81–98. For the remarkable parallels between Sade and Austen in their attack on sensibility, see Brissenden, *Virtue in Distress*, pp. 273–93.

38. The symptoms of hysteria and remedies for it are too numerous to review here; but difficulties in speaking and breathing, spasmodic convulsions, fainting fits, and a general drowsiness are mentioned in Dr. Robert James's *Medicinal Dictionary*, 3 vols. (London, 1745) under *Hysterica*.

39. Just as Bernard Mandeville (*A Treatise of the Hypochondriack and Hysterick Passions*, [1711]) had attributed the problem to the deficient number of animal spirits in women and recommended exercise as a means of eliminating the coarser spirits and of aiding digestion, citing swinging, horse-riding, massage, and even marriage for their beneficial effects, so Dr. James, among more questionable cures like the introjection of steel filings in the bowels, emphatically endorses the regimen adopted by the Bertrams for poor Fanny:

> But the best Thing I have hitherto found, for chearing [sic] and strengthening, is a frequent and long-continued Practice of Riding on Horseback: For as this kind of Exercise gives a great Shock to the lower Belly, which is the Seat of the excretory Vessels, appointed, by Nature, to carry off all the excrementitious Parts of the Blood, it should seem, that every Disorder of the Functions, or natural Weakness of the Organs, must be relieved by the often repeated Agitation of the Body in the open Air: Neither can any Person have the innate Heat so extinguish'd, as not to be excited by this Exercise: Nor can there be any preternatural Substance, or vitiated Juice, so intimately lodged in any Cavity of these Parts, which cannot, by the Use of Riding, either be reduced to such a State as it is agreeable to Nature, or dissipated and expelled: And, by this Motion, the Blood, being continually agitated and mixed, is purified and strengthen'd likewise. . . . Vol. 2, under *Hysterica*

Given the sexual nature of the disorder and its treatment by an activity so contrary to the disposition of the victim, Edmund's aiding Fanny toward health using the "dear old grey pony" has an obvious erotic as well as medicinal effect. Indeed, despite his low-keyed manner in contrast to the flamboyant Henry, Edmund seems to have ridden on this pony straight to Fanny's heart. If some readers have wondered why such a timorous creature ever dared to mount a horse, Fanny credits her cousin:

> "when I remember how much I used to dread riding, what terrors it gave me to hear it talked of as likely to do me good;—(Oh! how I have trembled at my uncle's opening his lips if horses were talked of) and then think of the kind pains you took to reason and persuade me out of my fears, and convince me that I should like it after a little while, and feel how right you proved to be, I am inclined to hope you may always prophesy as well." (27)

Dr. James conceded that "this Exercise does not agree so well with Women, who lead an easy and sedentary Life, and may be injured by Motion, especially in the Beginning"; and thus Edmund's service formed an intimate bond that early becomes a source of rivalry with the Crawfords.

40. *Jane Austen's Letters to Her Sister Cassandra and Others*, ed. R. W. Chapman, 2nd ed. (Oxford: Oxford University Press, 1952, 1979), pp. 127–28.

41. Choderlos de Laclos, *Les Liaisons Dangereuses*, trans. P. W. K. Stone (Baltimore: Penguin, 1961), pp. 180–81.

42. Ibid., p. 29.

43. For a sensitive reading of Fanny's love for Edmund and of her immunity to Henry, see Frederick M. Keener, *The Chain of Becoming: The Philosophical Tale, The Novel, and a Neglected Realism of the Enlightenment: Swift, Montesquieu, Voltaire, Johnson, and Austen* (New York: Columbia University Press, 1983), pp. 280–86.

44. "*He* went to while away the next three hours as he could, with his other acquaintance, till the best dinner that a capital inn afforded, was ready for their enjoyment, and *she* turned in to her more simple one immediately" (Austen, 412). Fanny's unabashed interest in good food is a *pro*-vital element that Lionel Trilling overlooked in his notion of her as a "Christian heroine." See "*Mansfield Park,*" *Jane Austen*, ed. Ian Watt, Twentieth Century Views (Englewood Cliffs, N.J.: Prentice-Hall, 1963), esp. pp. 128–32. Trilling is on surer ground, however, in his later interpretation of the "honest soul" (Hegel) in this novel. See *Sincerity and Authenticity* (Cambridge: Harvard University Press, 1972), pp. 75–80.

45. D. H. Lawrence, "A Propos of *Lady Chatterley's Lover,*" *Sex, Literature, and Censorship*, ed. Harry T. Moore (New York: Viking, 1959), p. 109. In his sexist reaction to Austen's manner, Lawrence calls attention to a stylistic trait of many eighteenth-century writers—both male and female.

46. David Hume, "My Own Life," in E. C. Mossner, *The Life of David Hume* (London: Nelson, 1954), p. 615. See my interpretation of Hume's early psychological crisis and his recovery through the ideal of "detachment": "David Hume's Denial of a Personal Identity: The Making of a Skeptic," *American Imago* 37 (1980): 334–50.

What Kind of Heroine Is Mary Wollstonecraft?

CATHERINE N. PARKE

> The creator of a new composition is an outlaw until [she] is a classic there is hardly a moment in between and it is really too bad very much too bad for the enjoyer.
>
> —Gertrude Stein, "Composition as Explanation"

The history of Mary Wollstonecraft's reputation and the narrative renderings that readers have given of her career are a notable instance of Gertrude Stein's observation about the shifting identities of the writer as *outlaw* and the writer as *classic*. Outlaws and classics, so Stein proposes, often hover on the unstable border between these two identities. A writer's position relative to either of these identities ("identity" understood to mean both her developing attitude toward life and the creative cause of her work) is largely determined by the kinds of investments, risks, and returns that readers agree to imagine as characterizing the relationship between the writer's work and her identity.

This essay has two related aims. It intends to suggest a direction that we, as Wollstonecraft's latterday readers, might pursue in attempting to recover for our benefit, more so even than for hers, a degree of the classic Mary Wollstonecraft's outlawry. The essay also aims, by taking Wollstonecraft as both its subject and occasion, to examine some of the challenges for the biographer who attempts to imagine the life of a revolutionary who has been made the heroine of her own life in ways that perhaps blur our perception of her achievement. We shall also discern in the course of our examination that Wollstonecraft herself pondered the same problems and, in her own terms, anticipated our conclusions.

It is paradoxical, but not historically unique, that Wollstonecraft's revolutionary insights are sometimes difficult to see precisely because they have become part of the way we see. Samuel Johnson identified this kind of difficulty in his analysis of why and how readers often fail to discern the qualities of great writers precisely, if ironically, for the very reasons that account for their importance and measure their success: "A writer who obtains his full purpose loses himself in his own lustre. . . . Learning once made popular is no longer learning; it has the appearance of something we have bestowed upon ourselves, as the dew appears to rise from the field which it refreshes."[1]

Just so, Mary Wollstonecraft is in danger of being lost in her own lustre. We may fail sufficiently to imagine her achievement as a writer whose insights were earned rather than simply professed, invented rather than lived out by a kind of necessity that, looking back, we call destiny.[2] For if it is difficult to imagine a time when things were not as they are now, and yet more difficult to imagine that such a past once had a real and hence uncertain future, it follows that such an exercise would be both difficult and necessary for us to undertake. This essay is, in part, an exercise in such imagining with Mary Wollstonecraft serving as the occasion for our thinking along these lines. Not to undertake such imagining is to run the risk of a kind of autism that isolates us in the historical present.

Toward the end of refreshing our perception of Wollstonecraft's revolutionary insights into the politics of sensibility, this essay will track her dynamic and difficult relationship with Rousseau's thinking about sensibility. Her thinking about Rousseau also served as an instrument for testing and revising the current definition of sensibility. By such testing and revision she hoped to redefine sensibility, to move away from its conventional meaning as a "physical and emotional capacity for feeling" understood to be woman's "essential characteristic" and toward a new definition that would combine the qualities of self-definition with justice.[3] We characteristically, if ambivalently, respond to this redefinition by naming Wollstonecraft sometimes an *outlaw*, sometimes a *classic*, depending upon whether we interpret that drama as one that occurred in a real past with an unpredictable future, or as a completed story predictable from the beginning with an implicit ending. Her relationship with Rousseau is also provocative for those who try to imagine her creative temperament, because this drama epitomizes Wollstonecraft's lifelong project of attempting to make autobiography into a suitably objective context and resource for her work.

I should mention, however, to play devil's advocate with my own position, that occasionally there may be good reason for choosing the classic version of this woman's life and work. That choice makes her into a certain kind of heroine ("certain" in both the sense of particular and fixed) whose achievement lies in fulfilling a preordained role or answering to a calling. Sometimes we need such heroines. This essay proposes not to displace but to cross-examine the classic Mary Wollstonecraft, focusing specifically on the notion of her as heroine in ways that Wollstonecraft also examined both explicitly in her writings and implicitly by her example. Such an inquiry intends neither to belittle the idea of a heroine nor to undermine the political force that this concept makes available to women. Rather it aims, if chiefly by indirection, to give the notion of the heroine a renewed strength by reexamining and reimagining its conventional meaning.

Before pursuing this line of thinking, I should perhaps identify what kind of essay this is not: It is not an inquiry into the history of ideas or an influence study, although it may resemble such undertakings. It is rather more precisely (and the distinction is, I think, worth making) an exercise in imagining Wollstonecraft as a creative cause who experimented with different solutions to the paradoxical problem that occupied her throughout her creative life of how simultaneously to get herself both more *into* and more *out of* her work; which is to say, to write both more and less personally.[4]

Her lifelong experiment to yoke these opposites aimed to create a literature that would be sufficiently sympathetic and passionate to accommodate her conception of sensibility as the ground of thinking, but also sufficiently stable and public to incorporate her notion of justice as the primary characteristic of a distinctive and new kind of sensibility that would be both personally and politically satisfying to women. Achieving this balance was crucial for one such as Wollstonecraft for whom the career of writer embodied her early insight that the personal is political. The way her writing career called up and channelled powerful personal forces within her was perhaps as much the disease as the cure. And perhaps in the end she had almost as much at stake in preserving the disease or a facsimile of it as in finding a cure, although this would be the subject of another essay.

The transformation of Mary Wollstonecraft from outlaw into classic was begun by William Godwin. Like Boswell's *Life* for studies of Johnson, Godwin's memoirs and his edition of Wollstonecraft's posthumous works established the terms that his wife's subsequent major critics and biographers have adopted to understand and to evaluate her achievement: namely that there was a marked and unusually active and exemplary relationship between her life and work; and further, that this relationship, as the predominant characteristic of her creative intelligence, was essentially heroic. In this equation by which events are configured into the explanatory narrative that we call history, Wollstonecraft becomes the heroine of her own life. Because the idea of the heroine was throughout her career as attractive to her as it was troubling, it is a subject worth considering when we attempt to come to terms with this writer's creative intelligence.

The parallel between Godwin and Boswell as biographers is apt, however, only up to a point. For, unlike the history of Johnson's critics and biographers who have often disagreed with Boswell's assertion and interpretation of the major terms of his life, Wollstonecraft's readers have generally accepted Godwin's construct. They have agreed that, in the words of Carol H. Poston, Wollstonecraft lived and wrote with an "intensity and vision born of personal experience yet informed by a larger social and aesthetic reality."[5] This marked tendency to see a heroic interrelationship between the life and the work has characterized Wollstonecraft criticism since Godwin. He has substantially determined, so to speak, her life after death, a life that Gary Kelly remarks "has always overshadowed her writings."[6] Virginia Woolf describes the author's life as a daily heroic adventure: "Every day she made theories by which life should be lived; and every day she came smack against the rock of other people's prejudices. Every day too—for she was no pedant, no cold-blooded theorist—something was born in her that thrust aside her theories and forced her to model them afresh."[7] Woolf concludes by asserting that the force of Wollstonecraft's example gives her continued life in the present: "She is alive and active, she argues and experiments, we hear her voice and trace her influence even now among the living." Ralph M. Wardle in his critical biography presents her work as intricately interrelated with her life as Wollstonecraft attempted to create theories she could live with and a life she could respect theoretically.[8] And Moira Ferguson and Janet Todd in their recent study of her life and work comment: "More than for most authors, Mary Wollstonecraft's work reflected her difficult and complex confrontation with life."[9]

While certainly not inaccurate, this consensus that depicts Wollstonecraft as a philosophic heroine, has the liability of going against the grain of her growing uneasiness with the notion of the heroine. She argues explicitly in the *Vindication of the Rights of Woman* (1792), the work in which she made her dramatic break with Rousseau, that we need "fewer heroines and more rational creatures." Thus while her biographers' heroic depiction of her is not false, it is problematic in its implications for approaching her work. Placing a mistaken emphasis on her own conception of herself and her work constitutes a misreading, one that imitates her own early romance with Rousseau. At first she took his revolutionary work as gospel and him as hero, turning him from an outlaw into a classic. But as Wollstonecraft came to rethink that decision, so we might rethink our version of her. For by making revolutionaries into classics, which is to say into heroes of authority, we may betray both them and ourselves.

To read the events of her life as heroic is a plausible construction of the evidence. But it thereby leads us to construe Wollstonecraft as a Rousseauvian romantic heroine of sensibility who, both as artist and as political intelligence, is then defined primarily by her physical and emotional capacity for feeling. It is true that she did believe firmly in feeling as a ground of action. But she also recognized the hazards and liabilities, especially for women, of using the romance of sensibility to give their lives significant form. Although Wollstonecraft never gave up the romance of sensibility, her distinctive accent fell increasingly upon the romance of justice, upon notions that she calls in her last novel, *Maria or The Wrongs of Woman* (1798), "*active* sensibility and *positive* virtue."[10] This new romance may indeed have its heroines, but a new kind whose first duty is to question the very definition of the heroine. The accent of the remainder of this essay will fall upon the story of this romance.

* * *

Wollstonecraft once remarked in a letter to Gilbert Imlay that she had always been "half in love with Rousseau." Her passion for his work began in the late 1770s when, while a governess in Ireland, she read *Emile*. This was an unhappy time for Mary, and Rousseau's novel of education offered her both the image of a model teacher and also a dramatization of sensibility with which she felt an immediate kinship. She wrote that she found Rousseau's sensibility to be "the most exquisite feeling of which the human soul is susceptible: when it pervades us, we feel happy; and could it last unmixed, we might form some conjecture of the bliss of those paradisiacal days, when the obedient passions were under the dominion of reason, and the impulses of the heart did not need correction."[11] Wollstonecraft was delighted to discover that, like herself, Rousseau "rambles into that *chimerical* world in which I have too often [wand]ered—and draws the usual conclusion that all is vanity and vexation of the spirit."[12] They both placed an emotional and philosophical emphasis on the past, an original ideal past that, paradoxically, exists only in the present moment of imagining. Considering that Mary's own future looked unpromising at that time and her past had been disappointing, the model of Rousseau's imaginary ideal past certainly must have had its attractions. Her kinship with Rousseau emerged clearly in 1788 when she published her first novel, *Mary, a Fiction*, and wrote a book of ethical essays for children called *Original Stories* that appeared in the same year.

In *Mary*, as the author's Preface argues, she intends to develop a different kind of heroine from the current model. In this lightly veiled autobiography, she aims to create a heroine who embodies some of her own disappointments. This Mary is raised by parents who do not return her affection and who eventually marry her to a man she does not love. She leaves home while still young and encounters, in the years before she returns with morbid dutifulness to her lawful husband, two delicate, virtuous creatures. The first is Ann, a version of her real life friend Fanny Blood; the second a man named Henry. She cares for each of them. When first Ann and then Henry dies, she transfers her care to his mother. In the end she returns dutifully but with loathing to her husband, dedicating her last years to a variety of good works: She "established manufactories, threw the estate into small farms; and continually employed herself this way to dissipate care, and banish unavailing regret. She visited the sick, supported the old, and educated the young," until death released her into a "world *where there is neither marrying*, nor giving in marriage."[13]

This Mary is a self-sacrificing heroine of feeling, victimized by her emotions because, as the narrative implies, she had no opportunity as a child to express them within the domestic circle. "It is only in the years of childhood that the happiness of a human being depends entirely on others," Wollstonecraft wrote in *Thoughts on the Education of Daughters* (1787).[14] Her clear insight into the significance of this period of absolute emotional dependency takes powerful fictional form in *Mary* in which the novel's namesake lives a life determined and dictated by her early disappointments. Her severance from her family and her search for a new world seem to result directly from the failure of primal family love in her formative years: "Could she have loved her father and mother, had they returned her affection, she would not so soon, perhaps, have sought out a new world."[15] But the new world Mary seeks is peopled with surrogate family (a sister, brother, and mother) who compensate for her own earlier disappointments. She also attempts to correct the failures she observes in our treatment of one another by imagining a scheme of philanthropic power: "If she was ever mistress of a family she would herself watch over every part of it."[16] The urge to goodness that originated in deprivation here takes the form of the will to power.

In *Original Stories*, Wollstonecraft created a heroine of successful and hardy authority. Mrs. Mason is the tutor of the two little girls of the stories, Mary and Caroline. Because they had inadequate teachers while young, the girls are badly educated. After their mother dies, the father hires Mrs. Mason to supervise their training. Like the tutor in *Emile*, she is a benevolent despot, a tyrant of authoritarian sensibility who offers a definitive, confident (one might even say crude) solution to the dilemma of female sense versus female sensibility. Mrs. Mason's methods of organizing and stabilizing the family may have appealed to Wollstonecraft who in her youthful pessimism was searching for some kind of certainty.

In Mrs. Mason she created a surrogate mother, a woman hired to do what Wollstonecraft was coming to recognize was very difficult for mothers to imagine in the current circumstances of her culture: to understand that motherhood is a profession and, like other professions, has significant ethical and moral responsibilities. These responsibilities, she now understood clearly, superseded the patriarchy's demand that women remain child-like. Mrs. Mason, unlike Mary's mother in the novel *Mary*, has no first-born son whom the force of cultural habit leads her to favor; her two charges are girls. Nor is she degraded by the bourgeois life of female self-abnegation that manifests as luxury and laziness. She is a professional who is hired to do a job, and she does it.

In particular, Mrs. Mason works to root out the children's laziness and inattention to their studies and to the serious practical implications for earthly living of the idea of an afterlife. The latter was the major instruction left undone by the girls' previous teachers. By emphasizing such instruction, Mrs. Mason insinuates herself as an awful and indispensable figure into the girls' lives. Perhaps not entirely consciously on the author's part, this becomes the principal aim of her stern heroine's teaching. In experimenting with an alternative to the character of the protagonist's mother in *Mary*, Wollstonecraft created in Mrs. Mason a figure on whom the children are so dependent that they are uneasy whenever she is out of sight. Their greatest hopes and fears revolve around her praise and criticism.

One can discern in *Mary* and *Original Stories*, as well as in other of Wollstonecraft's writings of the late 1780s, a complex of contradictory interpretations of and attitudes toward herself. These contradictions center on the subject of her early emotional disappointments and their relation to her sense of the prospects for future happiness. The protagonist of *Mary* who views herself as one early denied parental affection thus leads to a view of herself as having become thereby prematurely old. In a letter to her friend Miss Arden during this period she writes: "For I am persuaded misfortunes are of the greatest service, as they set things in the light they ought to be view'd in; and give those that are tried by them, a kind of early old age."[17] There appear also in her early correspondence, contemporaneous with these passages, premonitions of early death. Wollstonecraft's pair of notions of a woman, half imagined, half autobiographical, who was forced into the world too young and thereby hurried into "a kind of early old age," leaves no intervening time. The middle years between youth and old age are omitted. But in the later 1780s and on into the 1790s these middle years, newly conceived as both a chronological and imaginative reality, enter Wollstonecraft's thinking and become a new center for her existence. It is surely no coincidence that also during this period her premonitions about dying young disappear from the letters.

At this time, Mary Wollstonecraft did not in any simple sense begin to feel better. Her subsequent suicide attempts are well known. But she did, we can infer from the evidence, begin to feel the real possibility of her own future as a time that would be more satisfactory than the life she had heretofore known. Her thinking enlarged its scope to imagine not just beginnings and endings that are, to be sure, romantic, but also middles that, although perhaps less romantic, are in the long run substantially more interesting and satisfying. Middles give one more to imagine and more time to imagine in.

The questions that Wollstonecraft was coming up against at this time are ones that all heroines of melodrama, if they live long enough, eventually face: "Can a Little Eva or a Little Nell or a Mary live to maturity and remain virtuous?" "Is Christian heroism a quality too good for this world?" "What can the sentimental heroine do in middle age?" "Can having time on your hands be anything but a liability to virtue?" Wollstonecraft found herself in the same situation as people who have been counting on an early death to define the terms of their present life and ensure its heroic, if fragmentary, significance, or those who rely on poverty to arm their virtue. She found herself in the kind of situation that characterized the predicament of first century A.D. Christians who thought that the Apocalypse was just around the corner. Eventually they, like Wollstonecraft, saw that they needed to plan for an earthly future that they had never expected. Because they were not going to be immediate heroines and heroes of the drama of the end of the world, they were obliged to construct a workaday theology. So, too, seventeenth-century Holland experienced " 'an ordeal by prosperity' " in which men and women had to resolve the problem of "how to be rich and moral at one and the same time."[18] Mary Wollstonecraft was still alive, and although not yet rich (nor was she to be), she was making a living, thanks to her publisher and friend Joseph Johnson. Thus in the late 1780s she found she needed to invent a philosophy she could live with while imagining a longer life she could philosophize about.

The two early works that we have considered, *Mary* and *Original Stories*, propose Rousseau's drama of power and powerlessness, authority and victimization as the basis of sexual attraction, family life, and education. At this time in Wollstonecraft's life, such an ethos was the only one she could imagine. But it happened that political circumstance—the French Revolution—provided an occasion for her to clarify her thinking, an occasion larger than and different from an individual influence like Rousseau. Wollstonecraft's thinking had heretofore centered on sensibility understood to be a drama that oscillated between the poles of personal victimization and objective authoritarianism. This drama had served as her model for education that proposed as the key elements in its melodrama the image of an ideal past perfection of which the heroine is cheated in one story and a perfect afterlife to which the characters direct their imaginations in the other.

The revolution in France provided Wollstonecraft with a politically instructive occasion to experience and experiment with, as an imaginative reality, her urge for an actual and present perfection of justice joined with education. She now had the opportunity to experience as a call from the outside what she had heretofore known only as a personal calling. And with that the world suddenly made sense to her as a place she could live and work in. She felt the invigorating challenge to enlarge the boundaries of her ideas beyond mere autobiographical longings and a private agenda that had overleaped the present tense. She felt the need to create an agenda that might actually be lived rather than just imagined. Such a new pattern of movement, in turn, empowered Wollstonecraft with new feelings of confidence. And these feelings, it seems plausible to argue, led directly to her break with Rousseau.

In the *Vindication of the Rights of Woman*, Wollstonecraft identified Rousseau as the epitome of that tribe of male writers who argue that women's education should consist of learning to please. Her critique of Rousseau's educational agenda demonstrates how she had resolved an earlier, nearly paralyzing contradiction in her perception of the world. She expressed this contradiction in a letter to her publisher Joseph Johnson written the same year that the *Vindication* appeared: "I acknowledge that life is but a jest—and often a frightful dream—yet catch myself everyday searching for something serious—and feel real misery from the disappointment."[19] The strain of such self-contradictory perceptions would certainly be difficult to live with. Yet they also seem to promise a distinctive imaginative energy during those times when the "search for something serious" and the capacity for sorrow when that search fails overbalance the sense of life's absurdity. The viewpoint expressed here is the characteristic emotional predicament of the satirist, the wonder of whose life is that she retains her capacity for disappointment. Wollstonecraft's greatest asset was her instinct and skill for laying bare our personal and collective failings. But in the way this talent also accumulated as defensiveness, taking shape as the dream of power to oversee and to direct everything, it was also her greatest liability.

* * *

If *Mary* and *Original Stories* dramatize Wollstonecraft's instinctive, although still latent, comprehension of the authoritarian and victimizing implications of Rousseau's model of sensibility for relations between the sexes, the *Vindication* shows her responding in logical opposition. Although she opposed him, Rousseau continued to figure centrally in her imagination. He was still, if now negatively, a model for her thinking. But while Wollstonecraft still used Rousseau as an adversarial touchstone of her thinking, she also began to write about him in a way that, from our later vantage point, appears to anticipate the new direction of her thought that soon followed as she began to make innovative digressions from his powerful influence. An excerpt from the Preface suggests that new direction: "Rousseau exerts himself to prove that all *was* right originally: a crowd of authors that all *is* now right: and I, that all will *be* right."[20] There is more occurring here than simple dialectic in Wollstonecraft's distinction between the time in which she and Rousseau cast their thinking. Here she allies herself with and casts her thinking toward the future, and thereby suggests the dramatic shift she is beginning to imagine in the way she experiences and understands sensibility.

Such a movement away from the past is, for an amateur of sensibility, a revolutionary decision. It contradicts the conventional historicism of this drama, a historicism that gives priority to an ideal past. Against her self-concept as the child of unsatisfactory parents in *Mary* who spends her life compensating for their failures, or the Mary in *Original Stories* whose tutor makes the child's chief study the afterlife, the Mary Wollstonecraft who argues the *Vindication*, while retaining a commitment to sensibility, now chooses to set her sights on an earthly future. Thus she grants a distinctive and new quality of objectivity to sensibility, which she elaborates throughout the *Vindication* by displacing conventional notions of the heroine and by "seeking to develop not heroines but reasonable creatures."

She thus dramatizes this newly conceived quality of objectivity in a manner that calls into question her earlier presuppositions about the interrelation of sensibility, heroism, and time. The shift in her thought that represents a movement away from the politics of heroism and toward the politics of reason and justice marks a turn in

Wollstonecraft's thinking on the subject of what might legitimately constitute primary and secondary categories of valuable action. The *Vindication* is a full-length exercise in the anti-heroic, a polemic that surely arose from a private but not merely personal self-critique.

For one such as Wollstonecraft who wrote to Joseph Johnson, "Till I can form some idea of the whole of my existence, I must be content to weep and dance like a child," the importance of being able to stand outside her life was the key to her being able to stand squarely within it. For her, the search for an apt vocabulary was the heart of such a project. The pivotal term in the *Vindication* is *justice*, the term that she argues should replace *charity* as our primary category to name what women and men alike truly need. We can see the revisionary ratio for an earthly ideal future Wollstonecraft is constructing by observing that charity is to the heroine what justice is to the reasonable creature.

The plea for justice is a plea for what one is due by virtue of one's humanity; the plea for charity is a plea for what one may manage to extort from a benefactor. The first promises to subvert a social order and arrangement; the second, ironically, confirms and supports the prevailing politics of the relationships between men and women. The conventional heroine nearly always either dispenses or receives charity, and the economy of charity is the defining drama of her life. But for the reasonable creature, justice is the central drama, one that more than makes up for, in passionate dignity and longevity, what it loses in the temporary pleasures of suspense. This shift in her key term measures how substantially Wollstonecraft has revised the tenets of her thinking about sensibility.

This new sensibility is dramatized in the unfinished *Wrongs of Woman*, the story of a woman sent to the madhouse by a husband who has also kidnapped her child. Here she meets another victimized woman, an attendant in the institution; and a fellow inmate, a lovable, but perhaps unreliable man of sensibility, also unjustly imprisoned. Here Rousseau appears again but now presented as neither the beloved teacher nor the devilish antagonist. She now refers to him as "the true Prometheus of feeling," a godlike but damaged figure. Wollstonecraft is now able to incorporate Rousseau into her work as a mythic personage who exists in that aboriginal past that her own thinking and imagining have left behind in order to shape for herself a livably free future. In other words, he is no longer a melodramatic presence for her. He is neither an adored nor a despised lover but rather a figure whom Wollstonecraft can place in a context apart. And this context now no longer fills, either positively or negatively, her present and future.

An explanation of how Wollstonecraft came to this new view of

Rousseau emerges when we turn to her *Letters from Sweden, Norway and Denmark*. In between writing the *Vindication* and *The Wrongs of Woman*, while on a business trip to Scandinavia for her lover Gilbert Imlay, Wollstonecraft wrote a series of letters. Addressed to her publisher Joseph Johnson, but always intended for a larger public, she found in the genre of the travel letter a habitable space for her subjective and objective autobiographical impulses. In her Advertisement to the work she comments on how, in composing these letters, she discovered that she

> could not avoid being continually the first person—"the little hero of each tale." I tried to correct this fault, if it be one, for they were designed for publication; but in proportion as I arranged my thoughts, my letter, I found, became stiff and affected: I, therefore, determined to let my remarks and reflections flow unrestrained, as I perceived that I could not give a just description of what I saw, but by relating the effect different objects had produced on my mind and feelings, whilst the impression was still fresh.[21]

Conscious of the dangers of being the "little hero" of her own writing, Wollstonecraft now also became aware, after her full-length experiment in the anti-heroic of the *Vindication,* that the heroic liabilities of the *I* are sometimes outweighed by the assets of constructing a composite drama of autobiographical sensibility that uses the first person. No longer either so taken with or hostile toward the heroic and its conventional associations, she could at last use this notion fully to her own philosophical advantage.

This undertaking identified as its central task revising what it means to learn by experience. Wollstonecraft was coming to see that the usefulness of past experience is not to be found simply in applying it to guide present conduct by first verifying what situation in the past was "like" the present and then acting in accord with what one has learned from that past. The error in such a procedure lies first in conceiving experience to be essentially an activity of verification and second in narrowly conceiving verification to involve comparing past and present, making plans, and comparing their effects with some preconceived idea learned from that past. What Wollstonecraft was coming to understand was that thought and experience, self and circumstance, are always interweaving.[22]

The outcroppings of this new understanding can be seen in the character of Jemima in *The Wrongs of Woman*. Wollstonecraft introduced the character of Jemima, a poor, lower-class woman, to pair with the beautiful, bold, compassionate, and self-destructive heroine Maria. By her example and the story she tells of her life, Jemima gives Maria an opportunity to think beyond herself and about the plight of woman, and to recognize that in contemporary society women of all classes essentially have no country and are, to all intents and purposes, *outlaws*. The notion of the lone heroine of sensibility is thereby altered in the heroine's mind as it should also be altered in ours: Women, we must realize, are all in the same situation of oppression. Once this truth is perceived, it is no longer meaningful or appropriate to distinguish women according to their delicacy of feeling. When such a perception alters our view of the world so that no woman is seen as less oppressed than any other, we also come to recognize that this is the only fact that matters. In Wollstonecraft's imagination a year before her death, the old notion of the heroine had begun to give way to a new notion of woman.

From an early ideologue of sensibility, then to its antagonist, Wollstonecraft finally entered a period of inventive and confident integration. Perhaps the most radical act is to know when to abandon dialectic that can be resolved only by the quantitative adjustments of unsatisfactory compromise, the bartering of pseudo-power as one side temporarily cedes to the other, hoping the balance of power can be reversed. When the question of the *I* or the *not I*, the heroic or the anti-heroic, is no longer the encompassing issue, then one can begin to imagine genuine power, power *with*, not power *over*.[23] It is but one issue in the larger question of how to identify the grounds and means of human achievement. Around the age of thirty-six, Wollstonecraft seems to have begun to imagine what woman's adulthood might mean. An unhappy child who aged prematurely, she eventually reversed this process, giving herself time for middle age, by discovering adequately large and objective terms for investigating the relationship between thinking and feeling, the subjective and objective, the self and the world.

The contours of her career, particularly her mature thinking about the *I* as neither the hero nor the villain in the drama of philosophical self-expression, would seem to make Wollstonecraft an ideal candidate for the kind of biography recommended by Paul Valéry in his essay on Leonardo da Vinci. In this essay he proposes that there are two kinds of biography: one in which the biographer attempts to live the life of the biographical subject, stitching together anecdotes, facts, and details; the other in which the biographer attempts to construct a life, that is, to write a fiction.[24] The former undertaking is a representational project, a composition. As such, it is always fated to incompletion because it stakes its success on gathering what cannot be gathered completely. The latter is a conscious fiction, an experiment of thought conducted under the highest degree of rational control possible—a synthetic rather than an analytic act that establishes its own criteria of success. As such, this fictional biography could be written completely otherwise. The success of this free invention is measured by its power to compel our imaginative assent rather than by its minute and exacting accuracy. This kind of biography presents neither itself nor its biographical subject as a simple consequence of the circumstances that accompanied its creation. It thus also questions readers' conventional notions of cause and effect in history and frees them from limited notions of what constitutes history and of how to explain what happens.

By her middle and late career, Wollstonecraft was beginning to ask these kinds of questions, as she moved away increasingly from John Locke's notions that men and women are the products of environment alone to notions of our need to invent the future condition of our earthly existence. Wollstonecraft anticipated what eventually became clear to thinkers such as Valéry, William James, and Henri Bergson nearly a hundred years later: that the future belongs as much to the contents of consciousness as does the memory of the past or perception of the present. All are real in a here and now of the mind. If we are to live in the present, we must propel ourselves into the future—a future that Wollstonecraft hoped would be distinguished by the privilege it accords to justice rather than charity, to achievement rather than pity.

To undertake an experimental fictional biography of Leonardo da Vinci, as Paul Valéry did, or a series of fictional autobiographies as Mary Wollstonecraft did, invites the possibility of succeeding paradoxically exactly where other biography fails—namely in convincing us that the past did exist as a present and a future for those who lived it with their own sense and confusion about their past, present, and future. This attempt to make time real, believable, imaginable, was Wollstonecraft's major personal and philosophical problem, and she has arrived ahead of us by inventing a solution to her own problem. The terms of her life and work are an instructive example to the postmodern dilemma of inventing history with a future that we may inhabit in a palpable present. Hers is not a solution as product, but a solution as process, represented dramatically by her series of invented Marys throughout her works: the Mary of *Mary, a Fiction*; the Mary of *Original Stories*; the Mary who is the voice of the *Vindication* and of the *Letters from Sweden*; and the Maria of *The Wrongs of Woman*. Together they are the ancestors of the three Marys in *A Room of One's Own* (Mary Beton, Mary Seton, and Mary Carmichael), the names that Woolf adopted for herself in order to represent all women.

Mary Wollstonecraft's five Marys provide us with rich and ample imaginative biographies of herself as Everywoman. Before Valéry she experimented with constructivist biography. Such thinking and writing are surely the achievement of a writer whom we can name a classic, but whom in order to keep ourselves honest, we had better allow to keep the title of outlaw. This not only gives us an opportunity to better see this author for herself, it also enables us to better see her as an energetic example of a distinctive and successful approach to the writing of history. Her solution to the problem of making an imaginative settlement with her own history by and for the purpose of casting it in several fictional objective forms epitomizes an approach to writing biography that sees its central task to be making the past believable.

Thornton Wilder once described this problem in a way that resembles Wollstonecraft's lifelong project as I have been attempting to describe it:

> The problem of telling you about my past life as a writer is like that of imaginative narration itself; it lies in the effort to employ the past tense in such a way that it does not rob those events of their character of having occurred in freedom. A great deal of writing and talking about the past is unacceptable. It freezes the historical in a determinism. Today's writer smugly passes his last judgment and confers on existing attitudes the lifeless aspect of plaster-cast statues in a museum. He recounts the past as though the characters knew what was going to happen next.[25]

Mary Wollstonecraft's Marys retain their voluntarism by virtue of her writerly craft and her strong belief in both their importance to her own emotional and intellectual survival and their usefulness for drafting a newly plotted relationship between fiction and history grounded in a new politics of just sensibility. She made her Marys believable in order to make herself believable as a free agent in history, responsible, living, and aware of her participation in a historical drama of, at least in part, her own invention.

Notes

1. Samuel Johnson, *Lives of the English Poets*, ed. George Birkbeck Hill, 2 vols. (Oxford: At the Clarendon Press, 1905), 1:411.

2. H. R. James in *Mary Wollstonecraft: A Sketch* (London: Oxford University Press, 1932) refers to the *Vindication of the Rights of Woman* as "the fulfillment, as it were, of her destiny," p. 56. Gary Kelly comments that Wollstonecraft "lived and

wrote in an age of revolution, when character was destiny" in his edition of *Mary, a Fiction and The Wrongs of Woman* (London: Oxford University Press, 1976), p. vii.

3. This definition of sensibility is Gary Kelly's in his introduction to the edition cited in note 2. Here Kelly also notes that Wollstonecraft's "life has always overshadowed her writings" and works toward revising that disproportion.

4. Kelly remarks in his introduction that in order to write *Mary*, Wollstonecraft "had to shape her feelings into the character of her heroine and so see herself from a distance," p. x. Moira Ferguson in the introduction to her edition of *Maria or The Wrongs of Woman* (New York: W. W. Norton, 1975) comments on how Wollstonecraft "rejected her earlier roles as chaperone, seamstress, nurse, teacher, and governess. Writing guaranteed her the degree of autonomy and independence she craved," p. 9.

5. Mary Wollstonecraft, *Letters Written during a Short Residence in Sweden, Norway and Denmark*, ed. Carol H. Poston (Lincoln: University of Nebraska Press, 1976), p. xx.

6. Kelly, p. vii.

7. Virginia Woolf, *The Common Reader: First and Second Series* (New York: Harcourt Brace, 1948), Series Two, "Four Figures," pp. 171–72.

8. Ralph M. Wardle, *Mary Wollstonecraft: A Critical Biography* (Lawrence: University of Kansas Press, 1951).

9. Moira Ferguson and Janet Todd, *Mary Wollstonecraft* (Boston: Twayne, 1984), p. 129. Another particularly notable reading of the relationship between Wollstonecraft's life and writings appears in Chapters 2 and 3 of Mary Poovey's *The Proper Lady and the Woman Writer: Ideology as Style in the Works of Mary Wollstonecraft, Mary Shelley, and Jane Austen* (Chicago: University of Chicago Press, 1984). Poovey proposes that Wollstonecraft was, to cite her own words, "a strange compound of weakness and resolution." By the time she wrote the *Vindication*, Poovey continues, Wollstonecraft found that, to protect herself from considering the implications of women's sexual volatility, she would have to repress her perception of this fact. Poovey also offers the following suggestion: "Perhaps, in fact, the only effective way a woman who thought as well as felt could successfully deal with the issue of feeling was to satirize 'true sensibility,' as Jane Austen did in her juvenilia and in *Northanger Abbey*." My essay offers a different estimate of Wollstonecraft's success in redefining sensibility in a manner that women could justly live with.

10. Kelly, p. 153.

11. Ibid., p. 53.

12. Ralph M. Wardle, ed., *Collected Letters of Mary Wollstonecraft* (Ithaca: Cornell University Press, 1979), p. 145.

13. Kelly, pp. 67, 68.

14. Wollstonecraft, *Thoughts on the Education of Daughters: with Reflections on Female Conduct, in The More Important Duties of Life* (1787; reprint Clifton, New Jersey: Augustus M. Kelley, 1972), p. 7.

15. Kelly, p. 5.

16. Ibid., p. 6.

17. Wardle, p. 69.

18. John Russell, "Dutch Painting Seen in a Sharp New Light," *New York Times* (9 August 1987), p. 31.

19. Wardle, p. 221.

20. Wollstonecraft, *Vindication of the Rights of Woman*, ed. Miriam Brody Kramnick (1792; reprint Harmondsworth, England: Penguin, 1982), p. 95.

21. Wollstonecraft, *Letters*, p. 5.

22. M. P. Follett, *Creative Experience* (London: Longmans, Green, 1924), p. 163.

23. Ibid., p. 189 and passim.

24. Paul Valéry, *Oeuvres*, ed. Jean Hytier, 2 vols. (Paris: Gallimard, 1957), 1:1153–99.

25. From Thornton Wilder's interview in *Writers at Work: The Paris Review Interviews*, ed. Malcolm Cowley (New York: Viking, 1957), pp. 105–6.

Sensibility and the "Walk of Reason"
Mary Wollstonecraft's Literary Reviews as Cultural Critique

MITZI MYERS

> This is a vast commonplace of literature: the Woman copies the Book. In other words, every body is a citation: of the "already-written." The origin of desire is the statue, the painting, the book. . . .
>
> —Roland Barthes, *S/Z*

> I feel all a mother's fears for the swarm of little ones which surround me, and observe disorders, without having power to apply the proper remedies.
> I wish to be a mother to you both.
>
> —Mary Wollstonecraft, *Collected Letters*

Barthes was by no means the first cultural critic to remark the "vast commonplace of literature" that conjoins gender and reading, language and feeling. Virginia Woolf puzzled over the meanings that might reside in the phrase "women and fiction" and wondered how the former's "difference of view" impinged on the structure and style of the latter.[1] Contemporary feminist critics continue to debate the issue of a distinctively female sensibility, language, and fiction with increasingly sophisticated theoretical rigor. As pioneer feminist literary analysis, Mary Wollstonecraft's critiques for the late eighteenth-century *Analytical Review* both illuminate the historical development of these issues and provide an instructive example of a woman writer's struggle to define her "difference of view," to evade the "already-written." Wollstonecraft's reviews illustrate her own development as a theorist of gender. They are documents in the history of sensibility and they offer a case study of how a female journalist, assigned seemingly unpromising "ladies' subjects" like sentimental fiction, managed to create a resonant voice as cultural and literary critic. The gendered perspective that shapes her sociocultural analysis of what she reads and her self-representation as reader offer yet another example of the way the latter eighteenth century's particular dilemma of female identity, of a woman's relation to her culture, takes the form of exploring (and attempting to integrate) the languages of sense and sensibility. Jane Austen's familiar title captures a cultural motif. But whereas Austen mothers a text in which sisters grow up dichotomous and learn from one another's experience, Wollstonecraft as critic assumes a maternal stance toward the imagined girl readers of the fictions she considers, her textual self-construction offering an educative example of the integration she desires. As the epigraphs imply, the rationally responsible yet feelingly protective attitude Wollstonecraft exhibited toward her pupils and sisters is also encoded in her critical commentary and persona. But with a crucial difference: if real life socialization of one's charges (and oneself) is problematic, the reviewer's authority can banish fears, remedy disorders, and textualize a strong self-image in the process of instructing others.[2]

Anticipating the issues and the enlightened maternal stance of her later work, Wollstonecraft's reviews address the nexus of gender-sensibility-language-culture in multiple ways, because her attitudes toward what has been termed the period's "feminization of discourse" or "colonization of the feminine" were complex and problematic. Terry Eagleton argues that feminine values relegated formerly to the private realm returned in the later eighteenth century to the male public sphere, transvaluating the ruling ideologies. However that may be, the female that the century stereotypically defined as a woman of feeling would certainly now be joined by *The Man of Feeling* (1771) that Henry Mackenzie's famous book celebrates, and the "feminine" would be appropriated by male Romantic poets. But as Rousseau—the man of feeling turned sexist philosopher whom Wollstonecraft loved and battled—exemplifies, and as Eagleton observes, this revaluation was bought at a price: "The feminization of discourse prolongs the fetishizing of women at the same time as it lends them a more authoritative voice." Sensibility is woman's glory and her weakness; it liberates and it limits. For the female writer and critic, its overwrought language and behavioral code of extreme emotional responsiveness—a submission to forces outside the self that romanticizes passivity—pose both temptation and threat. Yet if the latter eighteenth century witnessed the transformation of *The Man of Reason* (as Genevieve Lloyd's recent study labels patriarchal discourse) into *The Man of Feeling,* a comparable redefinition of womanly discourse empowered the female pen to include the rational along with the affective. This appropriation of reason most notably informed educational writing by mother-teachers—Wollstonecraft's *Rights of Woman* (1792) is above all a pedagogics critiquing female socialization in sensibility and advocating rational instruction—but late in the century it also modified the feminine narrative tradition hitherto dominated by formulaic fantasies.[3] (Maria Edgeworth and Jane Austen are only the most obvious examples.) It also directs the critical commentary of women of sense who worried about sensibility's effects on the readers of their sex, especially what they liked to call the "rising generation."[4]

As a feminist literary critic, Wollstonecraft the woman of sense predictably resists the model of femininity typically inscribed in the texts she reviews: the linguistic and structural etiquette of powerlessness, of marginalization, of being emotionally and often physically carried away that is the stock-in-trade of even a first-rate popular novelist like Charlotte Smith. (I once heard a male eighteenth-century scholar remark that he did not believe in "gender genres." He could not have been a student of Smith, Ann Radcliffe, or the many other famous or anonymous female fantasists of sensibility: the period's most prolific fictionist was surely "A Lady.") Yet Wollstonecraft was certainly not ready to jettison the positive attributes associated with stereotypically feminine sensibility. No reader could get beyond the early chapters of *Mary, A Fiction* (1788) or of the novel she struggled to complete in the last months of her life without recognizing their kinship with contemporary sentimental narrative. Indeed, her letters, the epigraph from Rousseau that supplies the theme of *Mary,* and several *Analytical Review* essays on his writings testify that she, in common with numerous sister writers, was "half in love" with the seductive philosopher of feeling.[5] Wollstonecraft's whole career might be read as a dialectics of sense and sensibility; here I can examine only her literary reviews for the *Analytical* (her hundreds of contributions also discuss children, education, women, and travel).[6] I want to look at these notices both for their subject, which usually takes the form of a running cultural critique, and for the multi-voiced persona who delivers that commentary and who, I will argue, offers alternative models of reading, selfhood, and female aesthetics.

Wollstonecraft served her literary apprenticeship as a reviewer for the liberal publisher Joseph Johnson's new journal (founded in 1788), and she worked again as a journalist in her latter years when she was on the verge of artistic maturity; interestingly, then, her reviews of poetry and popular romance cluster around the periods when she was herself most intensely involved in creative activity.[7] Her early contributions laid the groundwork for her later achievements—even the earliest show affinities with the themes and language of the *Rights of Woman,* as I shall demonstrate. Clearly, her immersion in contemporary literature and her attempts to correlate models of reading, writing, and selfhood helped her to formulate her own special feminist stance, that peculiarly Wollstonecraftian blend of rational radicalism and precocious romanticism. In particular, demystifying the contemporary feminine specialty—the novel of sensibility so often "told in letters and written by A Lady"—was instrumental in enabling her to evolve her own distinctive voice, making for an aesthetic at once feminist and romantic and an art, as in Wollstonecraft's unfinished last novel, *The Wrongs of Woman: or, Maria* (1798), which aspires to release fictive female experience from tepid conventionalities and endow it with imaginative range and gritty realism. Unlike *Mary* but like the author's literary reviews, this final fiction decenters naive heroinism by overwriting the daughter's with the experienced mother's voice.[8] Along with the "Hints" set down for the unwritten second part of the *Rights of Woman* and with Wollstonecraft's most mature statement of her aesthetics, published in 1797 as "On Artificial Taste" and retitled "On Poetry, and Our Relish for the Beauties of Nature" by her widower William Godwin, Wollstonecraft's reviews both discuss and stylistically enact a poetics of change, an attempt to unite an aesthetic of spontaneity and affect with a morality of reason that is the hallmark of her career.

Wollstonecraft's work as reviewer relates to dual critical contexts—that of her time, with its shifting tastes and romantic trends, and that of our time, for she is not only a pioneer feminist, but also a pioneer feminist critic, whose analysis of the mesh between gender and genre inaugurates the feminist critical project. In reading *as* a historically situated woman, thus grounding her critique in the authority of personal experience, in asserting the continuity of literary and lived response, in insisting on the cultural consequentiality of representations of women, and in thus initiating feminist criticism as a liberating intellectual perspective—a *political* act, aimed not just at interpreting the world but at changing it through changing the consciousness of readers—in these ways and more, Wollstonecraft's critical mode prefigures the spectrum of concerns informing contemporary feminist literary criticism. Maternal, marginal, morally engaged, even moralistic, Wollstonecraft's stance is of her period, yet also familiar.[9] Her enterprise calls to mind Adrienne Rich's now classic linkage of cultural survival and critical revision, the feminist re-entry into textual givens in search of clues as to how women have lived and imagined themselves, so that they may see and live afresh: "Until we can understand the assumptions in which we are drenched we cannot know ourselves. . . . We need to know the writing of the past, and know it differently than we have ever known it; not to pass on a tradition but to break its hold over us."[10]

Thus, defining herself against debased or chauvinist romance, against the flood of anonymous cheap fiction and the tradition that Richardson and Rousseau embodied, Wollstonecraft struggles (not always successfully, as *Mary* and *Maria* demonstrate) to create her own romantic vision, to rehabilitate Georgian romance as a feminist vehicle that will contain, but not confine, female experience. Unwilling to surrender the woman writer's privileged access to feeling, she strains to infuse this cultural ascription with intellectual backbone and revolutionary energy. In the prefaces to both *Mary* and *Maria,* she self-consciously brackets off her protagonists from conventional heroines. *Mary* aims to "develop a character different from those generally portrayed," an adolescent heroine engendered not from Clarissa or Sophie, but from the "soul of the author" herself, and Wollstonecraft amusingly satirizes sentimental fiction within the novel too, even as she struggles to give birth to a different feminine subjectivity. Valorizing originality and self-expression, she tries to display a thinking woman's mind, "whose grandeur is derived from the operations of its own faculties, not subjugated to opinion; but drawn by the individual from the original source." Just as pointedly, *Maria* claims to be, not the typical feminine fiction generated by a "distempered fancy" or a "wounded heart," but a portrayal of woman as she is, a presentation of passions rather than manners, with a mother-heroine who errs and learns from error like a man. The book is intended as a study of female oppression, a contribution to "the improvement of the age." All the same, neither tale escapes the crossed love and fine feelings that are the staples of the period's womanly romance; sensibility is lovingly defined throughout Wollstonecraft's fiction.[11]

Like many women artists past and present, then, Wollstonecraft challenges literary traditions she yet perforce inhabits. And like such modern feminist theorists as Carolyn Heilbrun and Catharine Stimpson, she looks for the sins and errors of the literary past, seeks and romanticizes the "grace of imagination."[12] Finding a literary grid of feminine constraints, Wollstonecraft imagines a literary grammar of human possibilities. And as she matures her feminist aesthetic, the artistic correlative of her alternative ideology, she acts out and appropriates for women's enlargement the rich ideological implications of imagination and genius, formulates what might be called a political aesthetics. If the problematic *Mary* and the inchoate and unfinished *Maria* reveal the themes and shapes of sentimental fiction in the very process of assimilation to feminist forms, if they try to meld critical intelligence and romantic vision in one heroine—"a woman of sensibility, with an improving mind"—the persona and prose of

Wollstonecraft's reviews more smoothly fuse ideological content and artistic expression. These literary notices assert themselves as both explicit discourse about art, especially about women and art, and as implicit exemplification of the values she seeks. Because women who unite "thinking powers" with the "*feeling mind*" are conspicuous by their absence from the works she surveys, Wollstonecraft must—and does—fill the void herself.[13]

Sometimes sportive, sometimes serious, Wollstonecraft as feminist reader displays a lively critical intelligence and, in accordance with her revisionist ideology, a determination to exercise her own independent judgment. Her letters to Johnson sketch the reviewer's routine—returning the batch of books finished, asking whether "you wish me to look over any more trash this month"—and her boredom sometimes surfaces in public laments about the lot of "poor Reviewers, who have lately perused so many bad novels," sometimes in digs at the run-of-the-press witlings who try her patience: "The writer of this Poem, we are informed, is between 15 and 18 years of age. We believe it." Most often and most instructively, however, her irritation focuses on women writers and readers, on the stereotypically feminine tales that these unthinking mothers and lovelorn daughters produce and consume. She takes for granted a growing and predominantly *female* readership hungry for narrative, describing the audience of the very popular Charlotte Smith as "her fair countrywomen," for example.[14] She comments about the growing supply of authoresses eagerly catering to that appetite for spun-sugar fantasies. "The best method, I believe, that can be adopted to correct a fondness for novels is to ridicule them," she later observes in the *Rights of Woman*. The model of reading based on therapeutic mockery she then details recapitulates much of her own critical practice: "if a judicious person, with some turn for humour, would read several to a young girl, and point out . . . how foolishly and ridiculously they caricatured human nature, just opinions" might replace "romantic sentiments."[15] Reading self-consciously *as* an enlightened woman, as mother-teacher, shaping what she reads to serve her own controversialist's purpose, Wollstonecraft criticizes her subjects for writing *like* Woman, for serving as passive channels through which linguistic and cultural codes flow without resistance. She finds oppression and repression inscribed in the feminine texts she reads, never the self-expression her aesthetic demands.

Wollstonecraft's objections to her period's "scribbling women" are at once aesthetic and ideological (for literary artistry and human values are intimately interrelated with her). Literarily, the scribbles are vapid: "pretty nothings," "sweetly sentimental," "milk and water periods," "insipid trifling incidents," "much ado about nothing," "matter so soft that the indulgent critic can scarcely characterize it"—so go her kinder descriptions.[16] "The great number of pernicious and frivolous novels"—"those misshapen monsters, daily brought forth to poison the minds of our young females"—waste the time of readers, plunging them "into that continual dissipation of thought which renders all serious employment irksome"—and of writers, especially schoolgirl romancers who should be improving their minds. Young consumers turn into young producers: "From reading to writing novels the transition is very easy."[17] When she finds a novel written by a *very* young lady, Wollstonecraft repeatedly advises her to "throw aside her pen" or even to "throw her bantling into the fire." Perhaps such an "author will employ her time better when she is married." *Seymour Castle; or, the History of Julia and Cecilia: An Entertaining and Interesting Novel* (1789)—its title, like those of its sister works, weary with cliché—provokes her to even stronger strictures: "This frivolous history of misses and lords, ball dresses and violent emotions . . . is one of the most stupid novels we have ever impatiently read. Pray Miss, write no more!"[18]

Often tart with women writers, Wollstonecraft purposefully counters the indulgent gallantry male reviewers usually reserve for a fair belletrist. Just as she does later in the *Rights of Woman*, she embodies the firm, wise mother brooking no nonsense from the deficient mothers and daughters she instructs. Most female novels, she claims, adapting Pope, have no character at all. Content to copy their predecessors in "this flimsy kind of writing"—Richardson, who modernized romance; Burney, who feminized it; and Sterne, who whipped literary affect into syllabubs of sentimentality—"like timid sheep, the lady authors jump over the hedge one after the other, and do not dream of deviating either to the right or left." Wollstonecraft finds the typical woman's novel both stylistically and morally derivative. She recommends *Clarentine: A Novel* (1796) to "young female readers," who perhaps have more patience than "poor reviewers, condemned to read though dulness, perched on their eye-lids, invites to sleep or forgetfulness"; and though Sarah Harriet Burney's fiction was published anonymously, Wollstonecraft accurately locates the model for the normative lady's heroine "exactly proper, according to established rules. . . . an imitation of Evelina in water-colours."[19]

A work like Mrs. Elizabeth Norman's *The Child of Woe* (1789), "having no marked features to characterize," Wollstonecraft pronounces "a truly feminine novel. . . . the same review would serve for almost all" of these "ever varying still the same productions." She registers her pleasure "when *written by a lady*, is not inserted in the title page" and insists that she can "guess the sex of the writer" by her "tissue of pretty nothings."[20] She even offers a "receipt for a novel" composed of favorite female narrative ingredients: "unnatural characters, improbable incidents, and tales of woe rehearsed in an affected, half-prose, half-poetical style, exquisite double-refined sensibility, dazzling beauty, and *elegant* drapery, to adorn the celestial body, (these descriptions cannot be too minute) should never be forgotten in a book intended to amuse the fair." Add to this framework the usual "decorations, the drapery of woe, grief personified, hair freed from confinement to shade feverish cheeks, tottering steps, inarticulate words, and tears ever ready to flow, white gowns, black veils, and graceful attitudes . . . when the scene is to be pathetic." "Sensibility," she finds, "is the never failing theme, and sorrow torn to tatters, is exhibited in . . . moping madness—tears that flow forever, and slow consuming death." Of course these staples serve woman's one plot: "The ladies are very fond of a dismal catastrophe, and dying for love is the favorite theme." They exalt weaknesses into excellences, and "the passion that should exercise the understanding" becomes "the grand spring of action, the main business of life."[21]

The women's heroines also come from the same mold: "these ladies, for such artificial beings must not be familiarly called women, are something like the cherubim under the organ-loft, soft, simple, and good." Like Austen in her juvenilia, Wollstonecraft satirizes authors' "pulling the wires to make the puppets . . . faint, run mad, &c., &c." And she is equally bored with infallible characters who "love and weep by rule," with "insipid goodness, so imperfect are we!"[22] The "faultless monster" is, like Helen Maria Williams's *Julia* (1790), "viewed with [readerly] respect, and left very tranquilly to quiet her feelings, because," without real passion, too perfect for internal conflict, "it cannot be called a contest." The "most exemplary degree of rectitude in the conduct" of a heroine is not enough for satisfying fiction, which depends on "knowledge of the human heart, and comprehensive views of life." Wollstonecraft then turns her critique, as she often does, into a discussion of the fiction she values and would try to write in *Maria*—"A good tragedy or novel, if the criterion be the effect which it has on the reader, is not always the most moral work, for it is not the reveries of sentiment, but the struggles of passion—of those *human passions*, that too frequently cloud the reason, and lead *mortals* into dangerous errors . . . which raise the most lively emotions, and leave the most lasting impression on the memory; an impression rather made by the heart than the understanding; for our affections are not quite voluntary as the suffrages of reason." Although claiming passion and growth through error for her own heroine, Wollstonecraft can praise the pastel charms of first-rate women writers like Williams and Smith, despite their omitting the "workings of passion" from their tales. To the author of *Almeria Belmore: A Novel, in A Series of Letters*, "Written by A Lady" (1789), she is less generous: "no discrimination of character, no acquaintance with life, nor—do not start, fair lady!—any passion." And with the writer of *The Fair Hibernian* (1789), she is downright irascible: "Without a knowledge of life, or the human heart, why will young misses presume to write?" Such authors fuel Wollstonecraft's outburst in the *Rights of Woman* at "the reveries of the stupid novelists, who, knowing little of human nature, work up stale tales, and describe meretricious scenes, all retailed in a sentimental jargon, which equally tend to corrupt the taste, and draw the heart aside from its daily duties."[23]

Feminine fiction, Wollstonecraft argues, is "sentimental, pumped up nonsense": falsity masking negation. Affectation—phony feelings and incidents cobbled together from books—covers up a void, but strong writing cannot come "merely from reading . . . mocking us with the 'shadow of a shade.'" Because women writers prefer "unnatural sentimental flights" to "catching realities warm with life in the sun-beam that shoots athwart their own path," eschewing the individual and the original to "tread in a beaten track" (a favorite phrase), they warp their own experience, refining and perpetuating damaging stereotypes. She wanted a more serious and thoughtful examination of authentic human emotion and experience, not "artificial feelings, cold nonsensical bombast, and ever varying still the same improbable adventures and unnatural characters." Wollstonecraft was neither the first nor the last critic to lament how popular novels foster escapism and misleading expectations of life: "consequently *adventures* are sought for and created, when duties are neglected and content despised." Paradoxically, she demonstrates, flaccid fiction commands staying power through its very insubstantiality, its capacity to meld into the reader's daydreams and let her play at "becoming a heroine," as a recent study labels the process. However inaccurate as transcripts of life and emotion, the romance's artificial constructs possess a mysterious power to seep back out of literature and shape the life of which they are distortions in the first place, "to infuse insinuating poison into the minds of the inconsiderate."[24]

"No one was harder on women," one biographer justly remarks of Wollstonecraft's reviews, and no one was harder on cultural conditioning agents masquerading as fiction, precisely because she hoped to improve her sex and held the novel in high regard. If, as

Derek Roper suggests in his survey of eighteenth-century reviewing, Wollstonecraft was more exacting than most of her fellow journalists, the reason surely lies in her ideological commitment, her antennae ever alert to "the circumstances that imperceptibly model the manners of a nation." Eighteenth-century conservatives and radicals alike fretted over women and novels; this period's model of the reading experience stresses the exemplary force, for good or ill, of the fiction one imbibes: you are what you read. (Johnson's fourth *Rambler* is the locus classicus.)[25] Wollstonecraft's stories of reading, of the interaction between reader and text, factor gender into this inherited scenario. Her originality is neatly enlisting standard objections to serve the larger purposes of her revisionist social ideology; she makes routine moral cavils shoulder reformist, even radical, values. Wollstonecraft is very much an engaged critic, a contextual critic, a literary *and* cultural critic whose feminist literary critique, like that of her more recent sisters, is undergirded by cultural analysis, a reexamination of the interweave between art and society, a reassessment of prevailing values and female mythology. Literary commentary, she recognizes, is never purely aesthetic but always socially implicated. Her reviews show her forever exercised over how female life gets inscribed in literature and how literature molds life's rules and roles, simultaneously pandering to lovelorn "romantic notions" and prescribing narrow limits. "Why," Wollstonecraft complains of Elizabeth Inchbald's *A Simple Story* (1791), "do all female writers, even when they display their abilities, always give a sanction to the libertine reveries of men? Why do they poison the minds of their own sex, by strengthening a male prejudice that makes women systematically weak?"[26] Systematic weakness, systematic gaps in the texts where real women should be—so goes Wollstonecraft's typical indictment of the feminine novel, which acquires in her work an emblematic value, both a source and symbol of woman's artificiality, of her status as cultural fabrication.

Sweet, soft, and hollow, decorous and passionless mannequins, eighteenth-century images of women in literature yield neither the full-bodied female characters nor the liberating feminist values that Wollstonecraft desires. But if these exist only *in posse* in the fiction she hopes to write, they exist *in esse* in the persona she presents. Unlike the imitative feminine novelists she censures, Wollstonecraft self-consciously exemplifies the mature woman writer with "sufficient courage to think for herself, and not view life through the medium of books." Her critical presence is most obvious as the antithesis of that feminine negation she finds in the texts before her. Her self-confident assertion and decided views, her subjective candor (which again recalls early feminist literary criticism), her down-to-earth common sense, even her rough humor and ready wit function to differentiate her critical voice from the languishing maiden airs she derides and mark her a strong-minded, rational educator attuned to all the ways women have *not* been represented in literature. Indicatively, when Wollstonecraft does offer rare praise for a female character, it is the wise and resilient matron like Charlotte Smith's autobiographical Mrs. Stafford in *Emmeline* (1788) whom she singles out, not the passive romantic lead, the daughter, but the knowledgeable mother figure who has felt and thought deeply, who demonstrates women's "power . . . over themselves" rather than over their lovers called for in the *Rights of Woman.* No copybook tracery of a proper lady, Wollstonecraft reveals herself a real, complex woman with strong feelings and human foibles as well as rational understanding. Irascible, opinionated, enthusiastic, her varied emotional responses contribute to an ongoing dialogue that grants critical detachment and empathic involvement, sense and sensibility, each its due weight. As educative persona and exemplary reader, Wollstonecraft offers her female audience a resistant model of reading that counters their cultural predisposition toward submersion in the events of the text. She asks them to close the gap between their lives and their fantasies, to critique rather than internalize the shopworn images of women in literature, and her strictures on submissive female reading postures slide easily into a broader cultural analysis of female submission.[27]

Take her very first review—of *Edward and Harriet; or, The Happy Recovery: A Sentimental Novel.* "By A Lady" (1788)—with its anticipation of the *Rights of Woman*'s "judicious" reader. Arguing that "ridicule should direct its shafts against this fair game," the "*cant* of sensibility," she pronounces:

> Young women may be termed romantic, when they are under the direction of artificial feelings, when they boast of being tremblingly alive all o'er, and faint and sigh as the novelist informs them they should. Hunting after shadows, the moderate enjoyments of life are despised, and its duties neglected; and the imagination, suffered to stray beyond the utmost verge of probability . . . soon shuts out reason, and the dormant faculties languish for want of cultivation; as rational books are neglected, because they do not throw the mind into an *exquisite* tumult. . . . false sentiment leads to sensuality, and vague fabricated feelings supply the place of principles.[28]

Sentimental fiction is not a negligible literary vogue, Wollstonecraft emphasizes. Novels of sensibility matter because they shape behavior and serve as an index to broader cultural ills. Such reviews point forward to the *Rights'* fully developed analysis of contemporary female socialization in "over exercised sensibility." Woman is "made by her education the slave of sensibility," Wollstonecraft observes. Citing Johnson's definition—"quickness of sensation; quickness of perception; delicacy"—she points out that the "pretty feminine phrases" of sensibility stereotypically denoting the "sexual characteristics of the weaker vessel" are "almost synonymous with epithets of weakness." Novels, music, poetry, and gallantry "all tend to make women the creatures of sensation":

> their understanding neglected, consequently they become the prey of their senses, delicately termed sensibility, and are blown about by every momentary gust of feeling. . . . All their thoughts turn on things calculated to excite emotion; and feeling, when they should reason, their conduct is unstable, and their opinions wavering. . . . Miserable, indeed, must be that being whose cultivation of mind has only tended to inflame its passions! A distinction should be made between inflaming and strengthening them.[29]

The final distinction is characteristic and important. Although Wollstonecraft as a reviewer of commonplace sentimental fiction may stress sense and strategically exemplify how a "judicious" woman must rate "love-lorn tales of novelists," she is not immune to the legitimate charms of sensibility, and she accords it a privileged role in her evolving feminist aesthetic.[30] The weak, false sensibility of cultural stereotype symbolizes imprisonment; the strong, genuine sensibility of romantic genius signifies empowerment.

Wollstonecraft's reviews, then, imply not just alternative models of reading and female selfhood, but also an alternative aesthetics. Most significantly, her favorite critical counters range themselves firmly against the ways of knowing and valuing she attributes to popular literature. The derivative, prescriptive, imitative, and affected—false because copied rather than freshly seen: these are her foils for originality, individuality, independence, spontaneity; for the natural, innovative, imaginative, and real, true feeling—good because uniquely felt at firsthand. These are the characteristics of "genius"—always a standard of value for Wollstonecraft and the heart of the revisionist aesthetics she refines throughout her literary progression: direct observation, independent thought, the primacy of the individual imagination as the source of aesthetic truth. To think and to feel for oneself: such phrases inform her reviews and her whole career, from the preface to her first novel, a neat little piece of expressivist aesthetics which unmistakably enrolls Wollstonecraft among the first English Romantics, to her "Hints" for the *Rights of Woman*, part two, probably written during her reviewing years and packed with maxims about originality, spontaneity, creativity, and imagination; from her personal letters to her final aesthetic manifesto, "On Poetry," initially and more appropriately entitled "On Artificial Taste." Like many of her reviews, the *Hints* connect strong passions and strong minds, "enthusiastic flights of fancy" and individuality: "a writer of genius makes us feel—an inferior author reason"; the "flights of the imagination" grant access to truths beyond the "laboured deductions of reason," necessary though these are.[31]

And much as her reviews critique hackneyed sentimental fiction as a symptom of cultural malaise, of that overrefined "state of civic society . . . in which sentiment takes place of passion, and taste polishes away the native energy of character," "On Poetry" contrasts two styles of feeling and stages of society, the natural and the artificial, into a definitive exposition of Wollstonecraft's aesthetic values. (It is justly described by one biographer as a virtual call for a romantic revival in poetry.) Here she talks again about the natural as the "transcript of immediate sensations, in all their native wildness and simplicity," about "real perceptions" versus bookish declamation, revealing once more how much she values strong feelings, exquisite sensibility, and original genius. The last two are equivalent, she suggests, but she also insists that the "effusions of a vigorous mind" reveal an "understanding . . . enlarged by thought" as well as "finely fashioned nerves" that "vibrate acutely with rapture." Indeed, the understanding, she argues, "must bring back the feelings to nature."[32]

Here she also shows, as she does almost obsessively in so many reviews, a preoccupation with style, a conviction that style, substance, and consciousness indivisibly interconnect. Thus I can argue that Wollstonecraft's critical form and phrasing, to apply her own words, "forcibly illustrate what the author evidently wishes to inculcate." No one was more keenly aware of how ideological substance spills over into style—witness the often-quoted introduction to the *Rights of Woman* with its stress on sincerity, its hatred of "that flowery diction which has slided from essays into novels, and from novels into familiar letters and conversation," and its allegiance to "things, not words!"—and Wollstonecraft's way of scanning artistic expression for its ideological content illuminates her critical practice. In what she says—in the qualities she praises and the recurrent critical counters she deploys—and in the way she says it—in such associated juxtapositions as cold and warm, head and heart, reason and imagination, the "indolent weakness" of "copyists" and the "bold flights of genius," and in her distinctive style, much commented on and seldom analyzed—Wollstonecraft acts out the aesthetics of change she worked at and returned to throughout her career. Very different from the Latinate and often periodic constructions of her colleagues, her loose, informal sentences embody the associative movement of a thinking *and* feeling woman's mind as she strives to integrate the claims and languages of sense and sensibility, giving us, as does her ideal poet, "an image of [her] mind."[33] (Her final assessment of *Julia*, quoted above, is a good example.) Now spontaneously reactive, now reflective; now curt, now sprawling, her sentences enact her critical premises, according feminist issues a formal significance. Like her mix of Yorkshire colloquialisms and abstract philosophy and her attempts to unite imaginative excursus and rational inquiry, her "running" style—with its additive enjambments, its propulsive movement, and its openness to experience—both mirrors her own mind and typifies the free play of the feminist mind as she defines it.[34]

That definition affirms the emotive and imaginative complex that Romantic and feminist critics still accuse Wollstonecraft of devaluing.[35] Her habitual contrasts of "warmth of imagination" and "truth of passion" with "romantic rants of false refinement" or "cold romantic flights" and "false enervating refinement" must be read as the thoughtful cultural critique that they are, as legitimate concern over the impact (especially on women and the young) of sensibility as literary and behavioral cliché. Like Jane Austen, Maria Edgeworth, and other female contemporaries who expose the literary dependence of feminine feelings, Wollstonecraft deplores a congealing of literary language into jargon, a hardening of the emotional arteries so that women feel and act by rote, casting themselves as derivative sentimental heroines and losing touch with cultural realities and their own thoughts and feelings. Wollstonecraft's real quarrel with women writers centers around affectation, falsity, and imitation; it is never with sensibility, passion, imagination, or fiction per se, and certainly not with narrative that feelingly renders female experience. That was her own aspiration in *Maria*: "it is the delineation of finer sensations which, in my opinion, constitutes the merit of our best novels. This is what I have in view," she states in the preface, and the novel values (perhaps even overvalues) the heroine's "true sensibility, the sensibility which is the auxiliary of virtue, and the soul of genius." If Wollstonecraft as reviewer worries about the spurious sensibility of works that "engender false notions in the minds of young persons, who read with avidity such flimsy productions, and imagine themselves *sentimental*, when they are only devoid of *restraining principles*, the sure and solid support of virtue," Wollstonecraft the novelist tries to depict the real thing interacting with rational morality in a woman's mind.[36]

Throughout her career she defined sensibility in glowing terms, repeatedly equating it with genius and forever waxing ardent over Rousseau's ardors; her reviews talk of "that glow of imagination, which constitutes the grand charm of fiction"; and she voices genuine respect for the rare good novel, freshly and imaginatively realized. Praising Robert Bage's *Man As He Is* (1796), she observes that the increasing crop of novels, "the spawn of idleness," might lead "the inconsiderate . . . to conclude, that a novel is one of the lowest order of literary productions; though a very different estimation seems to be suggested by the small number of good ones which appear." She even offers a friendly welcome to romance as a genre (witness her review of the historical *Earl Strongbow* or Ann Radcliffe's Gothic *Italian*). She insisted early in her reviewing career that "to write a good novel requires uncommon abilities," something very different from "exhibiting life through a false medium" or a "sickly veil of artificial sentiment," and the final sentence of her last notice for the *Analytical*, published in May 1797, a few months before her death, makes an appropriate envoi. The story is *Hubert de Sevrac: A Romance of the Eighteenth Century* (1796) by Mary Robinson, a sister feminist who struggled, just as Wollstonecraft was then struggling with *Maria*, to mesh original cultural insights with the exaggerated effusions of feminine romance. All ornamental sentiment, the book has "no centre," Wollstonecraft observes, although "irradiations of fancy flash through the surrounding perplexity, sufficient to persuade us, that she could write better, were she once convinced, that the writing of a good book is no easy task," perhaps especially for a woman.[37]

But although Wollstonecraft's creative work cannot wholly escape from literary conventions, her critical practice demonstrates a surer mastery of these codes, a defter updating of textual femininity, not in the guise of a heroine but of a critical persona, who engenders an alternative selfhood while educating her audience. Embodying the ideal she would teach, this lively voice works against stale, parasitic, adulterated ways of living and feeling. Wollstonecraft explicitly urges women readers to think and feel for themselves; implicitly, she shows them how in a critical discourse that is also a mode of self-definition. Eager to encompass experience, following her consciousness even at the risk of apparent self-contradiction, Wollstonecraft as critic dances nimbly between the flaccid, love-fixated romance she deplores and the romantic genius she valorizes, between a narrative mode that formalizes passive subjection and one that facilitates passionate subjectivity, between fictive conventions and romantic freedoms. Although she emphasizes understanding and gibes at "double-refined sentiments," romantic impulse fuels Wollstonecraft's cultural ideology as much as it does that ideology's aesthetic analogue: individual protest, passion, and perception, as well as an insistence on personal growth, self-definition, and self-realization, undergird everything she wrote. Her social thought, literary criticism, and artistic experiments interplay and explicate one another, and they are all energized by her emergent feminist ideology's catalyzing force. Pursuing reason with emotional intensity, privileging passion while reining in sensibility, subtending a brisk no-nonsense critical posture with self-referentiality, Wollstonecraft the feminist reader shapes the critic's task to her own purposes and converts the bland fodder she reviews to nourish her own political aesthetics.

As a well-rounded woman exemplifying how reviews do indeed offer "points of access to the intellect and sensibility of the reviewer," she demonstrates that a cool head need not preclude a warm heart, that "flights of feelings" are not incompatible with "the slow, orderly walk of reason," that women's heads can "become a balance for our hearts." As woman critic and model mother to her readers, Wollstonecraft borrows the best of two discourses; appropriating reason, distinguishing true from false sensibility, she manages a stance and style that blend the languages of reason and feeling to her own humanist purposes.[38]

Notes

Research for this essay has been supported in part by grants from the American Philosophical Society and the National Endowment for the Humanities.

1. *S/Z*, trans. Richard Miller, 1970 (New York: Hill and Wang, 1974), p. 33; *Collected Letters of Mary Wollstonecraft*, ed Ralph M. Wardle (Ithaca and London: Cornell University Press, 1979), p. 148 (14 April 1787); p. 165 (7 November 1787). In the first instance, Wollstonecraft is speaking of the girl pupils to whom she was governess; in the second, of her two younger sisters; "George Eliot," *Women and Writing*, ed. Michèle Barrett (New York and London: Harcourt Brace Jovanovich, 1980), p. 160.

2. Although *Sense and Sensibility* was not published until 1811, it was drafted in the nineties as one among many contributions to an ongoing cultural debate. Wollstonecraft's reviewing exemplifies the "Maternal Thinking" that Sara Ruddick describes as a revisionist feminist project: "the construction of an image of maternal power which is benign, accurate, sturdy, and sane," *Feminist Studies* 6, no. 2 (Summer 1980), p. 345. I have argued further that Wollstonecraft's educative persona is at once maternal and self-reflexive in "Pedagogy as Self-Expression in Mary

Wollstonecraft: Exorcising the Past, Finding a Voice," *The Private Self: Theory and Practice of Women's Autobiographical Writings*, ed. Shari Benstock (Chapel Hill: University of North Carolina Press, 1988), pp. 192–210. At the same time that I appreciate Mary Poovey's insightful commentary on Wollstonecraft's work in *The Proper Lady and the Woman Writer: Ideology as Style in the Works of Mary Wollstonecraft, Mary Shelley, and Jane Austen*, Women in Culture and Society Series, ed. Catharine R. Stimpson (Chicago and London: University of Chicago Press, 1984), I cannot agree that the paradigm of proper lady versus woman writer adequately accounts for the author's characteristic strengths and weaknesses. Miriam Brody's identification of an alternative "two Mary Wollstonecrafts—one who loved and one who was contemptuous of love"—seems to me provocative in ways beyond what Brody herself has developed, for it suggests that written selfhood is generated from the contestatory discourses of woman historically available to a writer, "Mary Wollstonecraft: Sexuality and Women's Rights (1759–1797)," *Feminist Theorists: Three Centuries of Key Women Theorists*, ed. Dale Spender (New York: Pantheon, 1983), p. 41. Poovey's analysis seems to assume that patriarchal ideology works its repressive will upon a previously existent subjectivity, the transcendent Romantic self that much recent work calls into question; for example, Wendy Hollway, "Gender Difference and the Production of Subjectivity," *Changing the Subject: Psychology, Social Regulation, and Subjectivity*, ed. Julian Henriques et al. (London and New York: Methuen, 1984), pp. 227–63; and Linda Anderson, "At the Threshold of the Self: Women and Autobiography," *Women's Writing: A Challenge to Theory*, ed. Moira Monteith (Sussex: Harvester; New York: St. Martin's, 1986), pp. 54–71. For similar reservations on Poovey's important study, see reviews by Nancy Armstrong, *Modern Language Notes* 100 (1985): 1251–57; and Ellen Pollak, *Eighteenth-Century Studies* 21, no. 2 (Winter 1987–88): 260–63. Poovey also seems to me to neglect increasing evidence attesting to female authorial and maternal power in this period that challenges her somewhat monolithic view of the paternal order; see, for instance, Stuart Curran, "Romantic Poetry: The I Altered," *Romanticism and Feminism*, ed. Anne K. Mellor (Bloomington and Indianapolis: Indiana University Press, 1988), pp. 185–207; Claudia L. Johnson, *Jane Austen: Women, Politics, and the Novel* (Chicago and London: University of Chicago Press, 1988); Nancy Armstrong, "The Rise of Feminine Authority in the Novel," *Novel: A Forum on Fiction* 15, no. 2 (Winter 1982): 127–45, and *Desire and Domestic Fiction: A Political History of the Novel* (New York and Oxford: Oxford University Press, 1987); and Leonore Davidoff and Catherine Hall, *Family Fortunes: Men and Women of the English Middle Class, 1780–1850* (London: Hutchinson, 1987).

3. Terry Eagleton, *The Rape of Clarissa: Writing, Sexuality, and Class Struggle in Samuel Richardson* (Minneapolis: University of Minnesota Press, 1982), p. 13; see also Alan Richardson, "Romanticism and the Colonization of the Feminine," *Romanticism and Feminism*, pp. 13–25; Genevieve Lloyd, *The Man of Reason: "Male" and "Female" in Western Philosophy* (Minneapolis: University of Minnesota Press, 1984). As historians of education have long noted, claims for a more rational female education and emergent feminism travel in tandem; for the most recent explication, see Alice Browne, "Women's Education and Women's Rationality," *The Eighteenth Century Feminist Mind* (Detroit: Wayne State University Press, 1987), pp. 102–21.

4. Earlier twentieth-century studies of Georgian response to fiction typically characterize late-eighteenth- and early-nineteenth-century strictures on the novel as narrow-mindedly moralistic and conservative; see Joseph Bunn Heidler, *The History, from 1700 to 1800, of English Criticism of Prose Fiction, University of Illinois Studies in Language and Literature* 13, no. 2 (Urbana: University of Illinois Press, 1928); Winfield H. Rogers, "The Reaction against Melodramatic Sentimentality in the English

Novel, 1796–1830," *PMLA* 49, no. 1 (March 1934): 98–122; G. Harrison Orians, "Censure of Fiction in American Romances and Magazines, 1789–1810," *PMLA* 52, no. 1 (March 1937): 195–214; W. F. Gallaway, Jr., "The Conservative Attitude towards Fiction, 1770–1830," *PMLA* 55, no. 4 (December 1940): 1041–59; and John Tinnon Taylor, *Early Opposition to the English Novel: The Popular Reaction from 1760–1830* (Morningside Heights, New York: King's Crown Press, 1943). Taylor in particular interprets worries over the young female reader as a displaced critique of women's increased (although still modest) educational privileges: a put-down of sentimental fiction is a put-down of female learning (ch. 3). Obviously, I read Wollstonecraft's concern from a different perspective; many of my arguments about her attitudes would apply to those of other female educational reformers as well, such as Madame de Genlis, Clara Reeve, Catharine Macaulay, Anna Laetitia Barbauld, Priscilla Wakefield, Hannah More, and Maria Edgeworth. (I have explored such educators' attitudes more fully in "Impeccable Governesses, Rational Dames, and Moral Mothers: Mary Wollstonecraft and the Female Tradition in Georgian Children's Books," *Children's Literature*, vol. 14, ed. Margaret Higonnet and Barbara Rosen [New Haven and London: Yale University Press, 1986], 31–59; and in " 'A Taste for Truth and Realities': Early Advice to Mothers on Books for Girls," *Children's Literature Association Quarterly* 12, no. 3 [Fall 1987]: 118–24.) More recently and more perceptively, Gary Kelly has sought to account for the period's disapproval in terms of social and ideological tensions in the professional and upper-middle-class consumers of a genre "associated mainly with the values and culture of the aristocracy and gentry," the customary themes of which were "love, honour, intrigue, gallantry, and property." Clearly, gender needs to be factored into such a class analysis: women reformers characteristically express what I would call enlightened "bourgeois" attitudes in opposition to what Kelly identifies as the "decadent libertine aristocratic" ethos of much Georgian fiction, " 'This Pestiferous Reading': The Social Basis of Reaction against the Novel in Late Eighteenth- and Early Nineteenth-Century Britain," *Man and Nature* 4 (1985): 184, 188. Documentary records of eighteenth-century reading, as opposed to the commentary of moralists and educational reformers, are scarce. For an overview and an account of one rather early example, see Jan Fergus, "Eighteenth-Century Readers in Provincial England: The Customers of Samuel Clay's Circulating Library and Bookshop in Warwick, 1770–72," *Papers of the Bibliographic Society of America* 78, no. 2 (1984): 155–213. Although her work challenges some clichés, it verifies women's taste for fiction, and, as Austen's Henry Tilney points out in *Northanger Abbey*, men's as well. (Although this novel was not published until 1818, it satirizes authors and audiences of the 1790s, just as the 1811 publication date of *Sense and Sensibility* obscures its origins in the same period.) Sentimental narrative writing apparently gratified (probably in different ways) the fantasies of both sexes. The famous bookseller Lackington has much favorable to say about the new woman reader of novels, and contemporary historian Lawrence Stone argues for a correlation between increased consumption of novels and the growth of marriage for love; see *Memoirs of the Forty-five First Years of the Life of James Lackington*, 13th ed. (London: James Lackington, [1791]), esp. pp. 263–66; and *The Family, Sex, and Marriage in England, 1500–1800* (New York: Harper and Row, 1977), pp. 283–87. For a much more casual survey of eighteenth-century readership and circulating libraries than Fergus's, see Devendra P. Varma, *The Evergreen Tree of Diabolical Knowledge* (Washington, D.C.: Consortium Press, 1972). J. M. S. Tompkins, *The Popular Novel in England, 1770–1800*, 1932 (Lincoln: University of Nebraska Bison Books, 1961), remains the best overview of the period's fiction. For more recent criticism, see Roger D. Lund, "The Modern Reader and the 'Truly Feminine Novel,' 1660–1815: A Critical Reading List," *Fetter'd or Free? British Women Novelists, 1670–1815,* ed. Mary Anne Schofield and Cecilia Macheski (Athens: Ohio University Press, 1986), pp. 398–425. Lund's title is from one of MW's reviews.

5. *Collected Letters*, p. 263.

6. Although I do not have space here to rehearse the evidence for MW's contributions, this essay is based on a thorough investigation begun in 1976. For considerations, see Ralph M. Wardle's pioneering article, "Mary Wollstonecraft, *Analytical Reviewer*," *PMLA* 62, no. 4 (December 1947): 1000–9, and biography, *Mary Wollstonecraft: A Critical Biography*, 1951 (Lincoln: University of Nebraska Press Bison Books, 1966); Derek Roper's "Mary Wollstonecraft's Reviews," *Notes and Queries* n.s. 5 (January 1958): 37–38, and *Reviewing before the "Edinburgh," 1788–1802* (London: Methuen, 1978); Eleanor Flexner's *Mary Wollstonecraft: A Biography* (New York: Coward, McCann, and Geoghegan, 1972), Appendix D, pp. 273–74; and Sally N. Stewart's essay, "Mary Wollstonecraft's Contributions to the *Analytical Review*," *Essays in Literature* 11, no. 2 (Fall 1984): 187–99, and dissertation (as Sally Stewart Forrer), "The Literary Criticism of Mary Wollstonecraft" (Ph.D. diss., University of Colorado, 1979). Mixing eternal evidence with stylistic and content analysis, Wardle argues that MW contributed reviews under the signatures of M, W, and T and also the unsigned reviews in a run of short notices ending with such a signature. (He thought T might stand for "teacher" because he first noticed it in an essay on education.) Most of MW's reviews are very short and, in keeping with common practice of the time, would probably have been sent to the printer on a single sheet signed at the end. Key evidence is that the M, W, and T signatures disappear while MW was abroad; after returning from France she picks up only the M. Working independently from unpublished papers, Elbridge Colby, the biographer of Thomas Holcroft, MW's fellow liberal, also identifies T, M, and unsigned reviews followed by M reviews as MW's work in his edition of *The Life of Thomas Holcroft*, 1925, 2 vols. (New York: Benjamin Blom, 1968). Roper's 1958 note severely criticizes Wardle's hypothesis, citing a 1796 review of *The Monk*, which he argues is not as moral as expected from MW. In 1961, however, this review (with three others, all signed only at the end) was identified by Eleanor L. Nicholes from manuscript as MW's work, "*SC* 15," *Shelley and His Circle, 1773–1822*, ed. Kenneth Neill Cameron, vol. 1 (Cambridge: Harvard University Press, 1961), 152–57. Roper also questions attributions that would give MW an occasional brief notice on topics like boxing, but the kinds of reviews and the initials of different reviewers are remarkably consistent, as noted in Gerald P. Tyson's study of the journal's publisher, *Joseph Johnson: A Liberal Publisher* (Iowa City: University of Iowa Press, 1979). Certain reviewers covered certain areas. (MW considered boxing from a humanitarian angle.) Finally, Roper insists that truly anonymous material was part of the *AR*, as evidenced by unsigned final notices, but these are normally the abstracts from foreign periodicals, which were a special feature of the *AR*. Roper's more recent book runs to the opposite extreme, attributing to MW (p. 165) a review even Wardle's generous hypothesis did not countenance, one signed DM, Review of *Henry*, by the Author of *Arundel* [Richard Cumberland], *Analytical Review* 21 (May 1795): 511–16, when MW was still very much romantically entangled with Gilbert Imlay and not reviewing. DM (and MD, its variant) are clearly the insignia of another reviewer. Flexner's appendix is not helpful; she cannot have examined the reviews closely, because the October 1790 review she considers doubtful is not signed W as she says, but M, and is full of characteristic Wollstonecraftisms.

The most thorough published study is Stewart's. She points out some, but far less than all of the parallels between the M, W, and T reviews, indicating that these are indeed by the same person. In addition to very close stylistic echoes and content parallels, these reviews also contain frequent internal cross references, contextual evidence indicating that one person was writing under the three signatures. Still more persuasively, reviews associated with these initials not only sound like one another, but they also dovetail with the style and concerns of MW's known works. The runs of reviews signed only at the end also frequently refer to one another, indicating that they are by the same person; groups of reviews often function as a unit. A computer analysis would resolve all doubts, but the stylistic and content parallels are so marked that readers familiar with MW's work will recognize her hand even in unsigned early reviews. The *AR*'s signature letters follow no single pattern, although some contributors (like Alexander Geddes) used their own initials; two-part reviews sometimes play with initials (O, OS; DM, MD). A hitherto unnoticed way to explain the T is that MW sometimes signs her name M Wt (e.g., *Collected Letters*, p. 210); she may have dropped the W and T after her return because she was primarily going under Gilbert Imlay's name, her usual signature then being Mary Imlay. Interestingly, two previously unnoticed brief reviews signed MI appear in March 1796: Review of *Maria; or, The Vicarage, Analytical Review* 23 (March 1796): 294; and Review of *Angelina: A Novel, in A Series of Letters*, by Mrs. Mary Robinson, *Analytical Review* 23 (March 1796): 293–94. (*Collected Letters*, p. 385, verifies that Wollstonecraft had indeed read *Angelina.*) Shortly thereafter MW had her final break with Imlay; MI henceforth disappears and only M reviews continue until her death. These two reviews, however, are not stylistically distinctive enough to be conclusive.

Because most of MW's reviews are brief, even the longer ones being largely quotation, my references refer to the entire review.

7. The "forward-looking" *Analytical*, as Walter Graham points out, "encouraged . . . the romantic reaction in English literature," reflecting "the romantic or sentimental drift of literature during the 1790's better than any other periodical," *English Literary Periodicals* (New York: Thomas Nelson, 1930), pp. 221, 195, 220. Ironically, as the editor makes clear in the opening issue, the journal was intended originally to be just what its name implies—impartial, objective, devoid of idiosyncratic views, [Thomas Christie], "To the Public," *Analytical Review* 1 (May 1788): i–vi.

8. Cora Kaplan faults Wollstonecraft's "paradigm of women's psychic economy" because "only maternal feeling survives as a positively realized element of the passionate side of the psyche," a somewhat inaccurate but very instructive assessment, "Pandora's Box: Subjectivity, Class, and Sexuality in Socialist Feminist Criticism," *Making a Difference: Feminist Literary Criticism*, ed. Gayle Greene and Coppélia Kahn (London and New York: Methuen, 1985), p. 158.

9. Much recent work considers women and what happens when they read from a variety of perspectives; representative examples include Rachel M. Brownstein, *Becoming A Heroine: Reading about Women in Novels* (New York: Viking, 1982); Jonathan Culler, "Reading as a Woman," *On Deconstruction: Theory and Criticism after Structuralism* (Ithaca: Cornell University Press, 1982), pp. 43–64; Judith Fetterley, *The Resisting Reader: A Feminist Approach to American Fiction* (Bloomington and London: Indiana University Press, 1978); and Elizabeth A. Flynn and Patrocinio P. Schweickart, eds., *Gender and Reading: Essays on Readers, Texts, and Contexts* (Baltimore and London: Johns Hopkins University Press, 1986). Culler's deconstruction of female experience as the ground of reading has provoked dissent from Nancy K. Miller, "Rereading as a Woman: The Body in Practice," *The Female Body in Western Culture: Contemporary Perspectives*, ed. Susan Rubin Suleiman (Cambridge: Harvard University Press, 1986), pp. 354–62; and Robert Scholes, "Reading Like a Man," *Men in Feminism*, ed. Alice Jardine and Paul Smith (New York and London: Methuen, 1987), pp. 204–18.

10. "When We Dead Awaken: Writing as Re-Vision (1971)," *Adrienne Rich's Poetry*, ed. Barbara Charlesworth Gelpi and Albert Gelpi (New York: W. W. Norton Critical Edition, 1975), pp. 90–91.

11. *Mary, A Fiction and The Wrongs of Woman*, 1788; 1798, ed. Gary Kelly (London: Oxford University Press, 1976), *Mary*, pp. 2–3; Advertisement; *Maria*, Author's Preface. Mary writes a long "rhapsody on sensibility," pp. 53–54; it is similarly rhapsodically defined in "The Cave of Fancy" written about the same time, "Extract of The Cave of Fancy: A Tale," *Memoirs and Posthumous Works of Mary Wollstonecraft Godwin, Author of "A Vindication of the Rights of Woman"*, 2 vols. (Dublin: John Rice, 1798), 2: 241. What the author repeatedly terms Maria's "romantic" idealism is central to her character.

12. Carolyn Heilbrun and Catharine Stimpson, "Theories of Feminist Criticism: A Dialogue," *Feminist Literary Criticism: Explorations in Theory*, ed. Josephine Donovan (Lexington: University Press of Kentucky, 1975), p. 64.

13. *Maria*, Author's Preface; *Mary*, Advertisement; Review of *An Excursion to Brighthelmstone, made in the Year 1789*, by Henry Wigstead and Thomas Rowlandson, *Analytical Review* 8 (December 1790): 462 (T review). Commentators on Wollstonecraft's fictions agree on their uncertainties, but vary considerably in explicating their confusions. See, for example, Poovey; Marilyn Butler, "The Woman at the Window: Ann Radcliffe in the Novels of Mary Wollstonecraft and Jane Austen," *Gender and Literary Voice*, ed. Janet Todd, *Women and Literature* n.s. 1 (New York: Holmes and Meier, 1980), pp. 128–48; Mary Jacobus, "The Difference of View," *Women Writing and Writing about Women*, ed. Mary Jacobus (London: Croom Helm; New York: Barnes and Noble, 1979), pp. 10–21, and "Reading Correspondences," *Reading Woman: Essays in Feminist Criticism* (New York: Columbia University Press, 1986), pp. 278–92; Moira Ferguson and Janet Todd, *Mary Wollstonecraft* (Boston: Twayne, 1984); Mitzi Myers, "Unfinished Business: Wollstonecraft's *Maria*," *The Wordsworth Circle* 11, no. 2 (Spring 1980): 107–14; Laurie Langbauer, "An Early Romance: Motherhood and Women's Writing in Mary Wollstonecraft's Novels," *Romanticism and Feminism*, pp. 208–19; and Janet Todd's "The Female Text—Edited," *Studies on Voltaire and the Eighteenth Century: Transactions of the Fifth International Congress on the Enlightenment* 4 (1980): 1949–55, and "Reason and Sensibility in Mary Wollstonecraft's *The Wrongs of Woman*," *Frontiers: A Journal of Women Studies* 5, no. 3 (Fall 1980): 17–20. Also helpful is Lynn Sukenick, "On Women and Fiction," *The Authority of Experience: Essays in Feminist Criticism*, ed. Arlyn Diamond and Lee R. Edwards (Amherst: University of Massachusetts Press, 1977), pp. 28–44.

14. *Collected Letters*, pp. 178–79; Review of *The Young Lady of Fortune; or, Her Lover Gained by a Strategem*, by A Lady, *Analytical Review* 4 (August 1789): 480 (T review); Review of *King Asa: A Poem in Six Books*, by T. May, *Analytical Review* 8 (December 1790): 464–65 (T is next signature); Review of *Ethelinde; or, The Recluse of the Lake*, by Charlotte Smith, *Analytical Review* 5 (December 1789): 484–86 (M is next signature).

15. *A Vindication of the Rights of Woman, with Strictures on Political and Moral Subjects*, 1792, ed. Charles W. Hagelman, Jr. (New York: W. W. Norton, 1967), p. 275. Kathleen McCormack argues that George Eliot's well-known essay "Silly Novels by Lady Novelists (October 1856)"—*Essays of George Eliot*, ed. Thomas Pinney (New York: Columbia University Press; London: Routledge and Kegan Paul, 1963), pp. 300–24—derives from her recent reading of the *Rights* (she especially marked this passage), "George Eliot: Wollstonecraft's 'Judicious Person with Some Turn for Humour,'" *English Language Notes* 19, no. 1 (September 1981): 44–46. Although Eliot was not familiar with MW's reviews, her essay shows many parallels because of the similar approach. For a relevant reassessment of the Wollstonecraft-

Eliot relationship, see Nicholas McGuinn, "George Eliot and Mary Wollstonecraft," *The Nineteenth-Century Woman: Her Cultural and Physical World*, ed. Sara Delamont and Lorna Duffin (London: Croom Helm; New York: Barnes and Noble, 1978), pp. 188–205.

16. Review of *Delia: A Pathetic and Interesting Tale, Analytical Review* 5 (Appendix 1789): 580 (M review); Review of *The Test of Honour: A Novel*, by A Young Lady, *Analytical Review* 4 (June 1789): 223 (M is next signature); Review of *The Parson's Wife: A Novel*, by A Lady, *Analytical Review* 5 (October 1789): 216 (M is next signature); Review of *The Child of Woe: A Novel*, by Mrs. Elizabeth Norman, *Analytical Review* 3 (February 1789): 221–22 (W review); Review of *A Day in Turkey; or, The Ruffian Slaves: A Comedy*, by Mrs. Cowley, *Analytical Review* 13 (June 1792): 147–48 (W review).

17. Review of *Euphemia*, by Mrs. Charlotte Lennox, *Analytical Review* 8 (October 1790): 222–24 (T review); Review of *Henrietta of Gerstenfeld: A German Story, Analytical Review* 1 (June 1788): 209; Review of *Agitation; or, The Memoirs of George Woodford and Lady Emma Melville*, by the Author of *The Ring* and *The False Friends, Analytical Review* 1 (June 1788): 208 (first issues unsigned).

18. Review of *The Vicar of Landsdowne; or, Country Quarters: A Tale*, by Maria Regina Dalton, *Analytical Review* 4 (May 1789): 77 (W is next signature); Review of *The Cottage of Friendship: A Legendary Pastoral*, by Silviana Pastorella, *Analytical Review* 5 (October 1789): 216 (M review); Review of *Almeria Belmore: A Novel, in A Series of Letters*, by A Lady, *Analytical Review* 5 (December 1789): 488–89 (M review); Review of *The Fair Hibernian, Analytical Review* 5 (December 1789): 488 (M is next signature); Review of *Seymour Castle; or, The History of Julia and Cecilia: An Entertaining and Interesting Novel, Analytical Review* 5 (November 1789): 361 (M review).

19. Review of *The Fair Hibernian*; Review of *Juliet; or, The Cottager: A Novel, in A Series of Letters*, by A Lady, *Analytical Review* 3 (March 1789): 345 (M is next signature); Review of *Clarentine: A Novel*, by [Sarah Harriet Burney, Frances Burney's half-sister], *Analytical Review* 24 (October 1796): 404 (M review). Rereading *Clarentine* in 1807, Jane Austen was "surprised to find how foolish it is. . . . It is full of unnatural conduct & forced difficulties, without striking merit of any kind," *Jane Austen's Letters to Her Sister Cassandra and Others*, ed. R. W. Chapman, 2nd ed. (London: Oxford University Press, 1959), p. 180. For this Burney review, see Nicholes, *Shelley and His Circle*, 1:156.

20. Review of *The Child of Woe*; Review of *Agitation*; Review of *The Bastile; or, History of Charles Townly: A Man of the World, Analytical Review* 4 (June 1789): 223 (M is next signature); Review of *Delia*.

21. Review of *The Child of Woe*; Review of *Emmeline, The Orphan of the Castle*, by Charlotte Smith, *Analytical Review* 1 (July 1788): 327–33 (M review); Review of *The Widow of Kent; or, The History of Mrs. Rowley, Analytical Review* 1 (July 1788): 208–9 (first issues unsigned); Review of *The Exiles; or, Memoirs of The Count of Cronstadt*, by Clara Reeve, *Analytical Review* 4 (June 1789): 221 (M is next signature). Commenting on the *Werter* fad, Wollstonecraft writes: "ladies are all so partial to the man, who *could* die for love, that it appears to be high treason against the laws of romance, to allow Charlotte to live, and bring young Alberts into the world:—true, tender hearted ladies—she ought to have *ran mad*, and died.—It was very indelicate to live to fulfil the duties of life!" Review of *Miscellaneous Poems*, by Anne Francis, *Analytical Review* 7 (July 1790): 299–301 (M is next signature). This review's contrast between passive romance and the active citizenship of maternal duty notably anticipates the *Rights of Woman*.

22. Review of *Euphemia*; Review of *Calista: A Novel*, by Mrs. Johnson, *Analytical Review* 5 (September 1789): 98 (M is next signature); Review of *Adriano; or, The First*

of June, A Poem, by the Author of *The Village Curate*, *Analytical Review* 7 (May 1790): 39–42 (M review). Wollstonecraft's satire calls to mind not only Austen's juvenilia, but also her often cited epistolary observation: "pictures of perfection as you know make me sick & wicked," *Jane Austen's Letters*, pp. 486–87. Austen's parodies of the sentimental school are reprinted in *Minor Works*, vol. 6 of *The Works of Jane Austen*, ed. R. W. Chapman, 1954 (London: Oxford University Press, 1963).

23. Review of *Edward: Various Views of Human Nature, Taken from Life and Manners, Chiefly in England*, by [John Moore], *Analytical Review* 24 (January 1797): 23–25 (M review); Review of *Julia, A Novel: Interspersed with Some Poetical Pieces*, by Helen Maria Williams, *Analytical Review* 7 (May 1790): 97–100 (M is next signature); Review of *Ethelinde*; Review of *Almeria Belmore*; Review of *The Fair Hibernian; Rights of Woman*, p. 272.

24. Review of *Heerfort and Clara: From the German, Analytical Review* 5 (December 1789): 487 (M is next signature); Review of *The Revolution: An Historical Play*, by Lieutenant Christian, *Analytical Review* 12 (April 1792): 431–34 (T review); Review of *The Negro Equalled by Few Europeans: Translated from the French, Analytical Review* 7 (August 1790): 462–63 (T is next signature); Review of *The Revolution*; Review of *Doncaster Races; or, The History of Miss Maitland: A Tale of Truth, in A Series of Letters*, by Alexander Bicknell, *Analytical Review* 4 (July 1789): 351 (W is next signature); Review of *Emmeline*; Review of *Doncaster Races*. For modern feminist analyses of women as romance readers that are in many ways analogous to MW's own ambivalence toward the novel of sensibility, see Ann Barr Snitow, "Mass Market Romance: Pornography for Women Is Different," *Radical History Review* 20 (Spring-Summer 1979): 141–61; Kay Mussell, *Fantasy and Reconciliation: Contemporary Formulas of Romance Fiction* (Westport, Ct.: Greenwood Press, 1984); Tania Modleski, *Loving with a Vengeance: Mass-Produced Fantasies for Women* (Hamden, Ct.: Archon, 1982); Janice A. Radway, *Reading the Romance: Women, Patriarchy, and Popular Literature* (Chapel Hill and London: University of North Carolina Press, 1984); Madonne M. Miner, *Insatiable Appetites: Twentieth-Century American Women's Bestsellers* (Westport, Ct.: Greenwood Press, 1984); and Carol Thurston, *The Romance Revolution: Erotic Novels for Women and the Quest for a New Sexual Identity* (Urbana and Chicago: University of Illinois Press, 1987). Depending on whether they align romance with patriarchal ideology or maternal paradigms, modern feminists view the genre negatively or positively, and I believe the same dualisms help explain MW's hostility toward debased romance and her use of romance forms in her own fiction.

25. Emily W. Sunstein, *A Different Face: The Life of Mary Wollstonecraft* (New York: Harper and Row, 1975), p. 172; Roper, *Reviewing before the "Edinburgh"*, p. 168; Review of *Sketches of Society and Manners in Portugal, in A Series of Letters*, by Arthur William Costigan, *Analytical Review* 1 (August 1788): 451–57 (W review); Samuel Johnson, "*The Rambler* No. 4, March 31, 1750," *Rasselas, Poems, and Selected Prose*, ed. Bertrand H. Bronson (New York: Holt, Rinehart and Winston, 1962), pp. 60–69.

26. Review of *A Simple Story*, by Mrs. [Elizabeth] Inchbald, *Analytical Review* 10 (May 1791): 101–3 (M is next signature). In her essay and dissertation on MW's reviews, Stewart (Forrer), following Wardle's early biography, tries to conceptualize MW's aesthetic as a movement from a didactic early orientation to an expressive position in "On Poetry," but MW was always a moral rather than a formalist critic, and parallels to "On Poetry" run through her very earliest reviews. Didactic and expressive modes in style and content intertwine throughout her career; she is always anti-imitation, pro-innovation, and always contrasts the affected and the authentic as standards of value. The best general statements of her position remain Eleanor L. Nicholes's, "Mary Wollstonecraft," *Shelley and His Circle*, 1: 51–55, 178);

and MW's own apologia, *Collected Letters*, p. 345. For weakness as a central component of the sentimental code, see R. W. Brissenden, *Virtue in Distress: Studies in the Novel of Sentiment from Richardson to Sade* (New York: Barnes and Noble, 1974); and Janet Todd, *Sensibility: An Introduction* (London and New York: Methuen, 1986).

27. Review of *Celestina: A Novel*, by Charlotte Smith, *Analytical Review* 10 (July 1791): 409–15 (M review); Review of *Emmeline; Rights of Woman*, p. 107.

28. Review of *Edward and Harriet; or, The Happy Recovery: A Sentimental Novel*, by A Lady, *Analytical Review* 1 (June 1788): 207–8 (first issues unsigned).

29. *Rights of Woman*, pp. 105, 190, 108, 34, 105.

30. *Rights of Woman*, p. 190.

31. "Hints, Chiefly Designed to Have Been Incorporated in the Second Part of the *Rights of Woman*," *Memoirs and Posthumous Works*, 2: 272, 274, 271.

32. Review of *Amusement: A Poetical Essay*, by Henry James Pye, *Analytical Review* 6 (March 1790): 326–27 (M is next signature); Wardle, *Mary Wollstonecraft*, p. 285; "On Poetry, and Our Relish for the Beauties of Nature," *Memoirs and Posthumous Works*, 2: 255, 254, 260, 256, 264. This material was originally published as "On Artificial Taste," *Monthly Magazine and British Register* 3 (April 1797): 279–82, as a "Letter to the Editor" signed W.Q.

33. Review of *Anna St. Ives: A Novel*, by Thomas Holcroft, *Analytical Review* 13 (May 1792): 72–76 (M review); *Rights of Woman*, pp. 34–35; Review of *Earl Goodwin: An Historical Play*, by Ann Yearsley, *Analytical Review* 11 (December 1791): 427–28 (M review); "On Poetry," *Memoirs and Posthumous Works*, 2: 256.

34. Virtually everything MW wrote is stylistically distinctive; two examples (both from M reviews) illustrate the point: "Though several historical tales have been well received by the public, and, in some measure, deserve the reception they met with; yet, we cannot cordially approve of such productions as indirectly weaken the evidence of history, and by confounding truth and fiction in a regular story, mislead young people, who will afterwards, perhaps, find truth in its native dress insipid, or be unable to disentangle matters of fact from the adventitious ornaments that adorn them, or are interwoven so artfully into the very texture of the narration, that matured reason may afterwards vainly endeavour to efface the first lively impression made on the imagination," Review of *Historic Tales: a Novel*, *Analytical Review* 7 (May 1790): 100; "yet, a defence of Rousseau appears to us unnecessary—for surely he speaks to the heart, and whoever reading his works can doubt whether he wrote from it—had better take up some other book. . . . his most enthusiastic admirer must allow that his imagination was sometimes rampant, and breaking loose from his judgment, sketched some alluring pictures, whose colouring was more natural than chaste, yet over which, with the felicity of genius, he has thrown those voluptuous shades, that, by setting the fancy to work, prove a dangerous snare, when the hot blood dances in the veins," Review of *Letters on the Confessions of J. J. Rousseau*, by M. Guigne, trans. from the French, *Analytical Review* 11 (Appendix 1790): 528. MW has been criticized for the supposed disorganization and awkwardness of her style (and for the seeming structural disorder of her work in general). Certainly her discursive, conjunctive style differs from the complexly subordinated linear style typical of the period. The latter lays out ideas *already* classified and arranged; MW's unpremeditated syntactic structure, in accordance with her ethos and aesthetic, mirrors the shifting perspective of the writer's mind, piling up clauses and phrases as they occur. Colloquial, fluid, exploratory, open-ended, immediate, less processed and controlled than standard style, it vividly embodies the subjectivity and the search after wholeness of an active mind. It is the formal analogue of her ideological position, its roughness testifying to the sincerity and artlessness she values. Although Poovey reads Wollstonecraft's style as victim of

paternal ideology, much recent work aligns this style with a female rhetoric and aesthetic; see Josephine Donovan, "The Silence Is Broken," *Women and Language in Literature and Society*, ed. Sally McConnell-Ginet, Ruth Borker, and Nelly Furman (New York: Praeger, 1980), pp. 205–18; Thomas J. Farrell, "The Female and Male Modes of Rhetoric," *College English* 40, no. 8 (April 1979): 909–21; Julia Penelope Stanley and Susan J. Wolfe (Robbins), "Towards a Feminist Aesthetic," *Chrysalis: A Magazine of Women's Culture* 6 (1978): 57–61; and Gary Kelly, "Expressive Style and 'The Female Mind': Mary Wollstonecraft's *Vindication of the Rights of Woman*," *Studies on Voltaire and the Eighteenth Century: Transactions of the Fifth International Congress on the Enlightenment* 4 (1980): 1942–49; but much more feminist criticism is relevant as Nancy K. Miller's title—*The Poetics of Gender*—indicates, Gender and Culture Series, ed. Carolyn G. Heilbrun and Nancy K. Miller (New York: Columbia University Press, 1986). For an insightful analysis of Wollstonecraft's prose from another perspective, see Syndy Conger, "The Sentimental Logic of Wollstonecraft's Prose," *Prose Studies* 10, no. 2 (September 1987): 143–58.

35. See, for example, Michael G. Cooke, *Acts of Inclusion: Studies Bearing on an Elementary Theory of Romanticism* (New York and London: Yale University Press, 1975), pp. 159–63; and Jane Roland Martin, *Reclaiming a Conversation: The Ideal of the Educated Woman* (New Haven and London: Yale University Press, 1985), pp. 70–102. MW herself was fond of observing that "reason and fancy are nearer akin than cold dulness is willing to allow," Review of *Remarks on Forest Scenery, and Other Woodland Views, Relative Chiefly to Picturesque Beauty*, by William Gilpin, *Analytical Review* 10 (July 1791): 396–405 (M review).

36. Review of *Albert de Nordenshild; or, The Modern Alcibiades: A Novel Translated from the German*, by [Carl Gottlob Cramer?], *Analytical Review* 24 (October 1796): 404 (M is next signature); Review of *Euphemia*; *Mary, A Fiction and The Wrongs of Woman*, p. 176; Review of *Original Letters of the Late Mr. Laurence Sterne, Never Before Published*, *Analytical Review* 1 (July 1788): 335 (W review).

37. Review of *New Travels into the Interior Parts of Africa, by the Way of the Cape of Good Hope, in the Years 1783, 84, and 85: Translated from the French of Le Vaillant*, *Analytical Review* 25 (May 1797): 464–75 (M review); Review of *Man As He Is: A Novel in Four Volumes*, by [Robert Bage], *Analytical Review* 24 (October 1796): 398–403 (M is next signature); Review of *Earl Strongbow; or, The History of Richard de Clare and the Beautiful Geralda*, by [James White], *Analytical Review* 3 (February 1789): 343–44 (M is next signature); Review of *The Italian; or, The Confessional of the Black Penitents: A Romance*, by Ann Radcliffe, *Analytical Review* 25 (May 1797): 516–20 (M review); Review of *Arundel*, by the Author of *The Observer* [Richard Cumberland], *Analytical Review* 3 (January 1789): 67–69 (W review); Review of *The Confidential Letters of Albert; from His First Attachment to Charlotte to Her Death: From "The Sorrows of Werter"*, *Analytical Review* 6 (April 1790): 466–67 (M is next signature); Review of *Hubert de Sevrac: A Romance of the Eighteenth Century*, by Mary Robinson, *Analytical Review* 25 (May 1797): 523 (M review).

38. Review of *Zelia in the Desart, from the French*, by the Lady who Translated *Adelaide and Theodore* [by Madame de Genlis], *Analytical Review* 4 (June 1789): 221 (M is next signature); Gerald P. Tyson, Review of *Reviewing before the "Edinburgh," 1788–1802*, by Derek Roper, *Eighteenth-Century Studies* 14, no. 1 (Fall 1980): 71; *Rights of Woman*, pp. 196, 147.

PART III

At the Edge of a New World: The Politics and Aesthetics of Sensibility

Sense and Sensibility: Finance and Romance

JAMES THOMPSON

At the end of *Emma*, readers are told that Emma Woodhouse and Mr. Knightley marry and live happily ever after: "the wishes, the hopes, the confidence, the predictions of the small band of true friends who witnessed the ceremony, were fully answered in the perfect happiness of the union" (*Emma*, 484).[1] Such fairy tale formulae occur at the end of all Austen's novels, and it is difficult to ascertain what relation these promises of perfect happiness have to the often suspicious or even jaundiced view of marriage evident throughout the rest of the novels. Consider Austen's other Emma, the sheltered younger sister of *The Watsons*, whose eldest sister counsels her: "you know we must marry.—I could do very well single for my own part—A little Company, & a pleasant Ball now & then, would be enough for me, if one could be young for ever, but my Father cannot provide for us, & it is very bad to grow old & be poor & laughed at" (*Minor Works*, 317). Is wealth the only thing that separates the perfect happiness of the one Emma from the misery that threatens the other? The stories of the two Emmas were composed ten years apart, in different places, and Austen nowhere asks her readers to reconcile the brutality of *The Watsons* with the gentility of *Emma*. But poverty is felt even in the luxurious world of *Emma*, for the unenviable condition of Miss Bates is ample reminder that "it is very bad to grow old & be poor & laughed at."

In novels, marriage can always perform the formal function of closure, or it can serve as a "mirror of morality," celebrating and marking fruitful union.[2] Marriage can even be seen as the reward of self-knowledge for heroines such as Emma or Elizabeth Bennet.[3] But whatever moral purpose marriage serves in her narrative, Austen never lets her readers forget that marriage is also an economic institution.[4] The complex ways in which the moral or emblematic as well

This essay is a 1985–86 version of material incorporated into *Between Self and World* by James Thompson, pp. 130–57 and nn., pp. 204–8, copyright 1988, The Pennsylvania State University Press, University Park, Pa. 16802. Reprinted by permission.

as emotional and financial dimensions of marriage interrelate need explanation, because the impulses, motives, and needs of marriage in Austen's fiction are complex and contradictory: the desire of romance is inevitably complicated by financial necessity.[5] *Sense and Sensibility* provides the most interesting example for investigation, because Austen's representation of marriage is most hard-nosed and ambivalent there. Her portrayal has softened considerably by the time of *Persuasion*; but although romantic idealism is portrayed more clearly as desirable at the end of her career than at the beginning, Austen never minimizes the illusions that accrue to romantic expectations—in all her fiction, marriage is an endeavor ever fraught with danger and disappointment, closely tied to money as well as to social status.[6] It is often difficult to explain the relationship between the two poles of love and money, whether we call the opposition romantic and pragmatic, idealist and realist, or idealist and materialist. It is particularly difficult to fix their relationship in Austen's fiction because one has not been clearly valorized above the other; the relationship between love and money is neither hierarchical nor dialectical, although they are always found together and affect one another. Austen summarizes the situation of Edward and Elinor in a typically qualified statement: "they were neither of them quite enough in love to think that three hundred and fifty pounds a-year would supply them with the comforts of life" (*Sense and Sensibility*, 369).

No one would deny that a novel such as *Sense and Sensibility* is a comedy that perforce culminates with a celebration of marriage.[7] Yet Austen's novels move toward a climactic marriage by anatomizing its failures along the way; celebrating a handful of individual marriages, Austen's novels do not celebrate the institution per se. To say the least, these novels do not endorse marriage uncritically. As Tony Tanner observes in *Adultery and the Novel: Contract and Transgression*, a double reading of marriage is not uncommon in this period: "although the eighteenth- and nineteenth-century novel may be said to move toward marriage and the securing of genealogical continuity, it often gains its particular narrative urgency from an energy that threatens to contravene that stability of the family on which society depends. . . . [the novel] thus becomes . . . a text that may work to subvert what it seems to celebrate."[8] This paradoxically subversive celebration is historically determined by the function or structure of marriage in bourgeois society. From the early seventeenth century onwards, marriage in England was becoming increasingly regarded as a secular institution, and so was no longer represented, as Tanner puts it, as "a paradigm for the resolution of problems of bringing unity out of difference, harmony out of opposition, identity out of separation, concord out of discord—as it is, for instance, in *A Midsummer Night's Dream*, where marriage is not only social but magical, mythical, metaphysical—but just marriage in all its social and domestic ramifications in a demythologized society." By the end of the eighteenth century, marriage has come to serve different social and ideological functions: "Marriage, to put it at its simplest for the moment, is a means by which society attempts to bring into harmonious alignment patterns of passion and patterns of property."[9]

The comparison between *A Midsummer Night's Dream* and a novel such as *Sense and Sensibility* is an instructive one, for it suggests the vast difference between earlier comic drama and the novel; marriage in Austen is no longer a sacred emblem or sacramental ritual, but rather it has been significantly materialized. Unlike the image of a cosmic dance of harmony in Sir Thomas Elyot's *The Govenour* or the emblematic union of practical and speculative wisdom in *Tom Jones*, marriage for Austen is entirely a matter of earthly choice. Although marriage may refer to or serve or run parallel to other thematic or didactic patterns found in these novels (reward for self-knowledge, for example), it is not represented in emblematic fashion. Marriage in these six novels is presented as a social, domestic, legal, and economic event and condition. This is not to say that it is "natural" or that it is demythologized, for it certainly is not. In order to understand Austen's use of marriage thoroughly, that is, how she manages simultaneously to idealize and to undermine it, one needs to extricate the material and institutional dimensions of marriage from its mythological or emotional dimensions—the myths of rightness, uniqueness, appropriateness—the reward of romantic love. At the heart of her technique lies a presentation of idealized aspiration that resides alongside an often harsh portrayal of marriage's inadequacies. Because it is not possible to explore such questions entirely from within a single text, I shall proceed comparatively, by measuring Austen's representation of marriage in *Sense and Sensibility* with her remarks in her letters, particularly those to her favorite niece Fanny Knight, written when Fanny was considering an offer of marriage. In addition, the reconstruction and interpretation of marriage made possible by historians of the family such as Lawrence Stone in *The Family, Sex and Marriage in England 1500–1800* provide indispensable tools to measure private and possibly idiosyncratic visions against larger social and historical patterns.

The five extant letters of Jane Austen to her niece Fanny Knight compose a remarkably clear statement about the desirability of marriage.[10] These letters are lucid, to the point, and not patronizing; they appear as careful and thoughtful statements presenting a considered opinion on what to look for and expect in a marriage partner. These are the most compelling letters in the whole collection, partly because of their sense of urgency and importance, and partly because they are not composed in the elliptical shorthand more common in Austen's letters to her sister Cassandra. It is apparent from all of the letters (as well as from the later memoirs by family members) that after Cassandra, Fanny Knight was the woman with whom Austen was most intimate.[11] Throughout the collection, from Fanny's childhood, up to the letters just prior to her death, Austen displays a marked affection for Fanny. In 1808, when Jane was thirty-three and Fanny eleven, Austen writes to Cassandra that Fanny is "almost another Sister,—& [I] could not have supposed that a niece would ever have been so much to me. She is quite after one's own heart; give her my best Love, & tell her that I always think of her with pleasure" (*Letters*, 217). Nine years later, in the midst of the debate over Fanny's suitor, Austen writes even more pointedly, "You are the delight of my Life . . . It is very, very gratifying to me to know you so intimately. You can hardly think what a pleasure it is to me, to have such thorough pictures of your Heart.—Oh! what a loss it will be when you are married" (*Letters*, 478–79). I belabor this point not merely to emphasize Austen's sense of responsibility over these matters, but also to suggest the great sense of idealization and desire Austen invested in her niece. Austen seems to have participated in Fanny's courtship as a kind of wish fulfillment.

These letters, then, present Austen's theory of marriage, one that is consistent with her novels and with her other letters.[12] In 1808 Austen writes to Cassandra, "Lady Sondes' match surprises, but does not offend me; had her first marriage been of affection, or had there been a grown-up single daughter, I should not have forgiven her; but I consider everybody as having a right to marry *once* in their lives for love, if they can" (*Letters*, 240). Much like the sentence describing Edward and Elinor, who were not so much in love as to marry without sufficient income, this statement has contrasts and qualifications; Austen sanctions this obviously imprudent match only after weighing questions on propriety (how this reflects on or affects husband and daughter), then ends with that characteristically turned expression: love is a natural right, if you can get it.[13] Such turns characterize all of Austen's pronouncements on marriage.[14] Concerning Fanny's first proposal, Austen writes of this "perfect match," "such a person may not come in your way [again], or if he does, he may not be the eldest son of a Man of Fortune. . . . Anything is to be preferred or endured rather than marrying without Affection" (*Letters*, 409–10). Whether the sentence begins with love or with money, the other is sure to follow by the end. In the last letter of advice to Fanny that we have, Austen ends with this romantic exhortation: "Do not be in a hurry; depend upon it, the right Man will come at last . . . [and then] you will feel you never really loved before" (*Letters*, 483). This sentence, which would not seem out of place in a Harlequin Romance, is found on the same page as the following: "Single Women have a dreadful propensity for being poor—which is one very strong argument in favour of Matrimony" (*Letters*, 483).

The opinions about marriage in the letters are not unlike the view in her novels, nor are they unlike the general pattern of change late in the eighteenth century, which has been detailed by social historians. Lawrence Stone reports a growing "demand" for affection, as Austen counsels Fanny: "nothing can be compared to the misery of being bound *without* Love" (*Letters*, 418), and again, "I could not wish the match unless there was a great deal of Love on his side" (*Letters*, 482). These qualifications to marriage correspond to what Stone labels the "companionate marriage." Of the four possible motives for marriage that Stone distinguishes—monetary gain, personal affection, sexual attraction, and romantic love—Austen regularly portrays the first as common but corrupt.[15] Such marriages abound in *Sense and Sensibility*, from Colonel Brandon's brother's voracious acquisition of the pathetic Eliza, to Willoughby, whose attraction to Miss Grey is reported to lie in her "Fifty thousand pounds" (*Sense and Sensibility*, 194). Alternately, Austen thinks as little of physical attraction, as is evident in Elizabeth's condemnation of Lydia and Wickham: "But how little of permanent happiness could belong to a couple who were only brought together because their passions were stronger than their virtue, she could easily conjecture" (*Pride and Prejudice*, 312). The other two categories, personal affection and romantic love, are not easily separated, but Austen's novels are built around the attempt to distinguish them. Of the latter, she appears to affirm its attraction while she doubts its efficacy, if not its reality. Elinor warns Marianne: "after all, Marianne, after all that is bewitching in the idea of a single and constant attachment, and all that can be said of one's happiness depending entirely on any particular person, it is not meant—it is not fit—it is not possible that it should be so" (*Sense and Sensibility*, 263).

Here Elinor does not deny the attraction of sensibility, only the likelihood that it can be found in ordinary lives. Throughout *Sense and Sensibility*, Austen repeatedly validates the type of attachment that Edward and Elinor develop, with all their reticence to declare love, and their use of the word "esteem" instead, which infuriates Marianne (*Sense and Sensibility*, 21). Elinor and Marianne exemplify this opposition between the gradual development of friendship and affection versus what amounts to romantic "love at first sight." Elinor is disturbed at the rapidity with which Marianne and Willoughby establish their intimacy, a rapidity that is facilitated by romantic expectations: "His person and air were equal to what her fancy had ever drawn for the hero of a favourite story"; "Willoughby was all that her fancy had delineated in that unhappy hour and in every brighter period, as capable of attaching her" (*Sense and Sensibility*, 43, 49).[16]

Austen's letters and novels also convey obvious disapproval of arranged marriages, the type that Stone describes as prevailing. Most of her novels proceed programmatically through a series of variations on marriage arrangements; typically, in *Pride and Prejudice*, Elizabeth passes through her mother's choice of Mr. Collins, Darcy's independent choice, and finally, a successful union of mutual consent with parental approval. Of the four types of arrangement—entirely parental choice, parental with the child's veto, the child's with parental veto, and entirely the child's—Austen shows no sympathy for the first.[17] The long-term plans of Darcy's mother and Lady Catherine to marry their children together come to nothing, and Mrs. Ferrars's plans for her son Edward and Miss Morton are similarly ridiculed. Mrs. Ferrars proceeds on the assumption of "interchangeability," which, although Stone says is characteristic of a much earlier period, is still evident in these novels.[18] Personal affection is so negligible that one son can substitute for the other equally well, as John Dashwood informs his sisters:

> "We think *now*"—said Mr. Dashwood, after a short pause, "of *Robert's* marrying Miss Morton."
>
> Elinor, smiling at the grave and decisive importance of her brother's tone, calmly replied,
>
> "The lady, I suppose, has no choice in the affair."
>
> "Choice!—how do you mean?"—
>
> "I only mean, that I suppose from your manner of speaking, it must be the same to Miss Morton whether she marry Edward or Robert."
>
> "Certainly, there can be no difference; for Robert will now to all intents and purposes be considered as the eldest son." (*Sense and Sensibility*, 296–97)

Although this concern for social status or position over any personal or interior characteristics is clearly represented as outmoded, this attitude is not confined to the Ferrars in *Sense and Sensibility*, for Charlotte Palmer shows a similar confidence in her mother's duty and ability to arrange her marriage. Here she confides to Elinor her indifference to her mother's choice of mate for her:

> "I believe," she added in a low voice, "he [Colonel Brandon] would have been very glad to have had me, if he could. Sir John and Lady Middleton wished it very much. But mama did not think the match good enough for me, otherwise Sir John would have mentioned it to the Colonel, and we should have been married immediately."
>
> "Did not Colonel Brandon know of Sir John's proposal to your mother before it was made? Had he never owned his affection to yourself?"
>
> "Oh! no; but if mama had not objected to it, I dare say he would have liked it of all things. He had not seen me then above twice, for it was before I left school. However I am much happier as I am. Mr. Palmer is just the kind of man I like." (*Sense and Sensibility*, 116–17)

Charlotte Palmer is an unreliable authority on Colonel Brandon's desires, but her expectations concerning marriage arrangements run closer to the norm in *Sense and Sensibility* than do Marianne's ideas of sensibility. In the end, Marianne succumbs to substantially the same process that Charlotte Palmer describes, because the match with Colonel Brandon is arranged largely by her friends.

Although parental tyranny in arranging marriages meets with little approval from Austen, management entirely by children is no more attractive. Edward attributes the mischief of his engagement with Lucy Steele, the chief complication of the plot, to too much leisure and independence: "I returned home to be completely idle, and. . . . I had therefore nothing in the world to do, but to fancy myself in love" (*Sense and Sensibility*, 362). Complete independence is often dangerous in these novels, as seen in the likes of Willoughby and Henry Crawford and Lucy Steele and Isabella. Mutual consent of child and parent is the only arrangement that is likely to succeed in Austen's novels.

One can conclude, then, that some of the changes in attitude that Stone, Trumbach, and other progressivist social historians describe as having occurred by the end of the eighteenth century are not fully evident in Austen's novels. More precisely, the changes that Stone describes as complete appear in Austen's novels as changes in attitude, although perhaps not in practice. Stone writes that "the late eighteenth century sees the full development of the romantic novel, whose central theme was the struggle of love and personal autonomy against family interest and parental control."[19] This pattern, however, does not fit Jane Austen very well (or Fanny Burney, Charlotte Smith, Maria Edgeworth, Elizabeth Inchbald, or Sir Walter Scott, for that matter), whose novels portray personal autonomy as being as dangerous as rigid parental control. Whether this ill-fit occurs because Austen is a conservative social thinker, an anti-Jacobin, as Marilyn Butler states, or because she was particularly attuned to the difficulties unmarried women faced, or because Stone is too optimistic in his conclusions is difficult to determine.[20] Based on the evidence found in Austen's writings, the companionate marriage of affective individualism remained more an ideal than a common social practice.[21] Judging from Austen's view, the actual situation seems to have been one of far more flux and confusion than Stone suggests. Austen's plots, of course, are designed to exploit such confusion, because there can be no story without conflict. Following the example of many eighteenth-century novelists, Austen sets her heroines on their own, with little parental support on which they can rely.

These heroines are not beset by heavy fathers or scheming mothers so much as they are threatened with financial insecurity, because Austen is more concerned with financial than familial conflict. *Northanger Abbey* uses the most conventional romantic plot, with the General as a paternal blocking figure, yet the plot is openly parodic. All of her heroines occupy comfortable social positions (higher, apparently, than Austen's own), and, with the notable exception of Emma, are in straightened, fallen, or threatened circumstances at the story's opening. Only in *Emma* and *Northanger Abbey* are the family fortunes secure, and in *Northanger Abbey* they are threatened by rumor. Readers are given considerable detail about the heroines' personal finances, with the exception of Catherine Morland, about whom we are only given James Thorpe's misinformation: Elinor, Marianne, Elizabeth, and Jane have 1,000 pounds each, Emma has 30,000 pounds, and Anne 10,000 pounds (which her father cannot spare). Fanny has nothing, but presumably Sir Thomas can provide for her. Therefore, only one clearly has sufficient resources to marry into the class into which she was born.[22] Without fortune in the form of a marriage portion (marriage portion is the sum paid by the bride's family at marriage in return for dower or jointure, the compensating widow's annuity), these characters must preserve themselves using their wit and personal beauty, perishable commodities, as the officious John Dashwood observes after being informed that Marianne has been ill:

> "I am sorry for that. At her time of life, any thing of an illness destroys the bloom for ever! Her's has been a very short one! She was as handsome a girl last September, as any I ever saw; and as likely to attract the men. There was something in her style of beauty, to please them particularly. I remember Fanny used to say that she would marry sooner and better than you did; not but what she is exceedingly fond of *you*, but so it happened to strike her. She will be mistaken, however. I question whether Marianne *now* will marry a man worth more than five or six hundred a-year, at the utmost, and I am very much deceived if *you* do not do better." (*Sense and Sensibility*, 227)

On another occasion Charlotte Lucas describes marriage as "the only honourable provision for well-educated young women of small fortune, and however uncertain of giving happiness, must be their pleasantest preservative from want" (*Pride and Prejudice*, 122–23). Austen writes about well-educated young women of small fortune, whose only preservative from want is marriage. The war with France and its blockade resulted in high inflation, one in which the ratio of marriage portion to dower was steadily increasing—in short, a bad market in which to be a marriageable woman.[23] (As many historians note, the father of a son was inherently in a better bargaining position than the father of a daughter; sons brought money into the family, but daughters only took money out.)[24]

Marriage, then, remained a business. Despite the prevalence of romantic novels and a nascent ideology that celebrated personal fulfillment through a marriage of affection, marriage as a financial transaction had not disappeared (or has ever disappeared). Marianne speaks scornfully of an imagined compact between Colonel Brandon and some "woman of seven and twenty" (Anne Elliot's and Charlotte Lucas's age), as a union between nurse and patient: "It would be a compact of convenience, and the world would be satisfied. In my eyes it would be no marriage at all, but that would be nothing. To me it would seem only a commercial exchange, in which each wished to be benefited at the expense of the other" (*Sense and Sensibility*, 38). Marianne's scorn echoes the language of Mary Wollstonecraft, who writes regularly of marriage as a business: "The mighty business of female life is to please."[25] So too, the first page of Maria Edgeworth's *Belinda* announces, "her aunt had endeavoured to teach her [Belinda] that a young lady's chief business is to please in society, that all her charms and accomplishments should be invariably subservient to one grand object—the establishing herself in the world."[26] Although heavily ironic, the concluding passage on Lucy Steele's marriage to Robert Ferrars uses similar vocabulary of business and prosperity as the reward of labor: "The whole of Lucy's behavior in the affair, and the prosperity which crowned it, therefore, may be held forth as a most encouraging instance of what an earnest, an unceasing attention to self-interest, however its progress may be apparently obstructed, will do in securing every advantage of fortune, with no other sacrifice than that of time and conscience" (*Sense and Sensibility*, 376).[27]

The point about this business or market or labor vocabulary is not that marriage had become more of an economic event, but rather that this economic vocabulary seems obtrusive and angry precisely because marriage had come to raise different expectations. In other words, conflicts between love and money, romance and reality, had become more exacerbated and visible than they had been earlier in the century. The metaphor comparing marriage with business or work suggests the degree to which marriage really was a form of labor; therefore examination of this point should expose the antagonism between the economic reality of marriage and the romantic mythology that obscures it.

Julia Prewit Brown has shown how marriage in this period was for women what the choice of profession was for a man, an observation that Mary Wollstonecraft almost comes to in her comparison between men's education to profession and women's education to marriage:[28]

> men, in their youth, are prepared for professions, and marriage is not considered as the grand feature in their lives; whilst women, on the contrary, have no other scheme to sharpen their faculties. It is not business, extensive plans, or any of the excursive flights of ambition, that engross their attention; no, their thoughts are not employed in rearing such noble structures. To rise in the world, and have the liberty of running from pleasure to pleasure, they must marry advantageously, and to this object their time is sacrificed, and their persons often legally prostituted.[29]

Although it does not suit the present needs of Wollstonecraft's argument, which asserts the limiting and degrading nature of women's education, nevertheless the logical extension of her comparison here is that women work toward marriage in the same way that men work toward a profession, as a kind of preferment or sinecure, for she writes elsewhere that "Before marriage it is their [women's] business to please men."[30]

Austen's heroines understand equally well that courtship is female business, particularly if they have mothers such as Mrs. Bennet for whom "The business of her life was to get her daughters married" (*Pride and Prejudice*, 5). Mrs. Bennet, however, does not get her daughters married—they have to do the work for themselves; if marriage or courtship is a business, late eighteenth-century women are more self-employed than they are employed by others. That is, affective individualism and the rise of personal autonomy in choosing mates meant that young women had to do work that, in their mothers' time, would have been done for them. At the least, the limits of responsiblity were unclear. Austen's heroines are sent out to do business in a bad market, without adequate direction or training, on the shifting ground between a compact of affection and a transfer of property. Such uncertainty may be seen as the primary cause of Elizabeth Bennet's trouble and anxiety: although she is raised by her father to respect her own intelligence and worth, she is in a marriage market in which she is not evaluated for her intelligence or individual or inner worth but for her wealth and beauty. These characters are unwillingly thrust into a marriage market even before they seem to be aware that they are there. Everyone Elinor and Marianne meet from Fanny Dashwood to Sir John Middleton to Mrs. Jennings, assumes they are angling for husbands. Sir John tells them that Willoughby "is well worth catching," a phrase that Mrs. Dashwood finds objectionable: " 'I do not believe,' said Mrs. Dashwood, with a good humoured smile, 'that Mr. Willoughby will be incommoded by the attempts of either of *my* daughters towards what you call *catching him*. It is not an employment to which they have been brought up. Men are very safe with us, let them be ever so rich' " (*Sense and Sensibility*, 44). This denial has no effect, because shortly thereafter Sir John insists to Marianne,

> "You will be setting your cap at him now, and never think of poor Brandon."
>
> "That is an expression, Sir John," said Marianne, warmly, "which I particularly dislike. I abhor every commonplace phrase by which wit is intended; and 'setting one's cap at a man,' or 'making a conquest,' are the most odious of all. Their tendency is gross and illiberal; and if their construction could ever be deemed clever, time has long ago destroyed all its ingenuity." (*Sense and Sensibility*, 44–45)

Despite their objections, the women of Austen's fiction are considered "out" or nubile whether they will or no. When Emma is suddenly wooed by Mr. Elton, although it is comic testimony to her social blindness, it also testifies that she is considered available for marriage. Elizabeth is similarly pursued by Mr. Collins. Although many claim there is no real work nor any real laborers in Austen's fiction, her novels are full of both—young women working at courtship, laboring towards marriage, their pleasantest preservative from want.

It is clear from the remarks of Mary Wollstonecraft that the work of courtship had become more burdensome than it had been a few generations earlier. Although one might expect her to be sympathetic to the conflicting pressures felt by young women, at times she blames them for the same prudence and circumspection that parents had exercised earlier: "Girls marry merely to *better themselves*, to borrow a significant vulgar phrase, and have such perfect power over their hearts as not to permit themselves to *fall in love* till a man with a superiour fortune offers."[31] This is the sort of prudence that Austen recommends to her niece Fanny. During this period children of the propertied classes seem to have been taught both contradictory sets of values, sense and sensibility, finance and romance, told to expect or hold out for affection in a world largely ruled by commodity. If the "finishing" education to female accomplishments was, as Wollstonecraft insists, directed toward the "business to please men," then female education remained focused on courtship while the ideology of romantic attachment, which is supposed to be natural and spontaneous, necessarily contradicted the need for rules and instruction, art and artifice:[32]

> Women are told from their infancy, and taught by the example of their mothers, that a little knowledge of human weakness, justly termed cunning, softness of temper, *outward* obedience, and a scrupulous attention to a puerile kind of propriety, will obtain for them the protection of man; and should they be beautiful, every thing else is needless, for, at least, twenty years of their lives.[33]

Therefore, women were expected to follow strict rules of propriety, exert their training in pleasing, while living in both ideal and material worlds of romance and commodity. For characters such as Elinor Dashwood or Elizabeth Bennet, who are presented as being intelligent, it is no wonder that they find "setting one's cap" abhorrent. Neither one is comfortable, happy, or at ease displaying herself as available, being "out." Both Stone and Wollstonecraft liken being displayed in Bath or London to marketing: "what can be more indelicate than a girl's *coming out* in the fashionable world? Which, in other words, is to bring to market a marriageable miss, whose person is taken from one public place to another, richly caparisoned."[34] In such a market, where women are no longer valued solely by family connections or portion, stress on beauty tends to exacerbate the tendency to reify or objectify women into commodities. The best example of commodification in Austen's fiction is Marianne Dashwood: as her brother clearly sees, in sickness she is scarcely worth 400 or 500 pounds a year. This estimate of her worth has nothing to do with her character, her nature, or any internal quality, but only with her looks, her "bloom." Thus it is easy to see why Elinor Dashwood, Elizabeth Bennet, Emma Woodhouse, and the others are so alienated from the work of courtship: when the process objectifies one into a commodity and results in loss of self-determination or autonomy, the whole event is dispiriting and dehumanizing—"the worker sinks to the level of a commodity"; "the worker is related to the *product of his labor* as to an *alien* object."[35]

In this respect, marriage is no different from other social relationships that were going through extreme changes under industrial capitalism, which Marx described as a " 'reification' of human relationships," in which patriarchal and feudal traditions of authority, structure, stability, and hierarchy seemed to be reduced to their exchange value.[36] As Wordsworth complains in a famous letter, "Everything has been put up to market and sold for the highest price it would bring."[37] That is, objects became valued, not for traditional values or natural, inalienable properties they possess—use value—but rather for their exchange value, for what they will fetch. The object itself becomes meaningless, except for its market value, much as in the real estate boom in California in the 1970s. As Clifford Siskin argues, mass production transformed the value of exclusivity: "the object of desire as value is transferred from the product, *whatever* its associations, to the act of possession."[38] Austen acknowledges these changes in *Mansfield Park*, in which Mary Crawford celebrates that "true London maxim, that every thing is to be got with money" (*Mansfield Park*, 58).[39] In their most extreme form, these new practices of consumption seem to narrow down from possession to the single act of acquisition. For example, to John Dashwood, land has been divorced from estates and inheritance and is now merely a commodity to be bought and sold. Here he is complaining to Elinor of his cash flow problems:

> "And then I have made a little purchase within this half year; East Kingham Farm, you must remember the place, where old Gibson used to live. The land was so very desirable for me in every respect, so immediately adjoining my own property, that I felt it my duty to buy it. I could not have answered it to my conscience to let it fall into any other hands. A man must pay for his convenience; and it *has* cost me a vast deal of money."
>
> "More than you think it really and intrinsically worth."
>
> "Why, I hope not that. I might have sold it again the next day, for more than I gave: but with regard to the purchase-money, I might have been very unfortunate indeed; for the stocks were at that time so low, that if I had not happened to have the necessary sum in my banker's hands, I must have sold out to very great loss." (*Sense and Sensibility*, 225)

Despite the vestiges of the aristocratic values exemplified by the hereditary estate, Dashwood's interest is that of a speculator; land is purchased, not to expand or buttress the hereditary estate, but to make a cash profit, because it can be exchanged for more than he paid for it.[40]

This attitude toward the land is analyzed by Marx in the *Economic and Philosophical Manuscripts of 1844:*

> It is necessary that this appearance [the idealized view of feudal allegiance to the hereditary estate and its master] be abolished—that landed

> property, the root of private property, be dragged completely into the movement of private property and that it become a commodity; that the rule of the proprietor appear as the undisguised rule of private property, of capital, freed of all political tincture; that the relationship between proprietor and worker be reduced to the economic relationship of exploiter and exploited; that all personal relationship between proprietor and his property cease, property becoming merely *objective*, material wealth; that the marriage of convenience should take the place of the marriage of honor with the land; and that the land should likewise sink to the status of a commercial value, like man.[41]

Agrarian capitalism leads to a general dissociation of possession from acquisition, which can be seen in marriage practices as well. If wives are chosen only for their portion or beauty and not on the basis of their lasting family connections and power, then marriage also comes to be regarded as acquisition but not possession: that is, as an act but not as a condition—marriage is performed once, not as an ongoing responsibility. A wife chosen for her beauty (a wife who cannot, of course, be discarded or exchanged for another) may become like Lady Middleton, purely ornamental. Unlike a valuable painting that can be exchanged for more than was given, a wife is like wallpaper; attractive, perhaps, but having no exchange value, as Mr. Bennet finds when he marries solely on the basis of appearance.[42] If, however, a wife is chosen for her portion, as Willoughby is supposed to do with Miss Grey's 50,000 pound portion (*Sense and Sensibility*, 194), then the object, Miss Grey, is valueless from the start. As he complains later, "She knew I had no regard for her when we married" (*Sense and Sensibility*, 329). Unlike conditions in laboring classes, where mates may be attractive for tangible, lasting skills such as weaving, spinning, or household economy, besides their looks and/or possessions, or unlike the upper classes, in which birth and title remained substantial values, conditions from the middle classes to the lower gentry seem to conspire to make a wife useless after marriage, as is clear from this bizarre exchange between Mrs. Jennings and her son-in-law:[43]

> "Aye, you may abuse me as you please," said the good-natured old lady, "you have taken Charlotte off my hands, and cannot give her back again. So there I have the whip hand of you."
>
> Charlotte laughed heartily to think that her husband could not get rid of her; and exultingly said, she did not care how cross he was to her, as they must live together. It was impossible for any one to be more thoroughly good-natured, or more determined to be happy than Mrs. Palmer. The studied indifference, insolence, and discontent of her husband gave her no pain: and when he scolded or abused her, she was highly diverted. (*Sense and Sensibility,* 112)

Thus, during this period young women apparently had to endure the duties, responsibilities, and blame of courtship, without much of the benefits. A general analogy can be drawn between women working toward marriage and the laboring classes. The latter may eventually have benefited from the industrial and capitalist revolutions, but patriarchy and the sense of moral responsibility was disintegrating, and with the loss of responsibility went the patronizing institutions of patriarchy. Consequently, between 1790 and 1820 (the years during which Jane Austen was writing novels) conditions for the laboring classes got much worse before they got better (without any poor relief in some cases, or extremely miserable conditions in the work and poor houses).[44] Austen focuses on this period in which the working conditions also declined for young women working at courtship.

These issues concerning courtship and marriage are so deeply infused in *Sense and Sensibility* that it almost seems as if the novel proceeds as a systematic exploration of the possibilities. With so many contrasting pairs, the novel suggests a couplet structure of balance and antithesis; yet, as has been argued over the thematic contrast in the title, pairs do not necessarily lead to neat, valorized oppositions or to any happy syntheses. In terms of marriage, the multiplicity of contrasting examples confuses and distracts more than it suggests any clear recommendation. Elinor's sense and Marianne's sensibility are not finally reducible to restraint and excess nor to prudence and folly, nor does Austen offer any easy Horatian mean between the two.

The many marriages anatomized in *Sense and Sensibility* are not set into simple oppositions of approved and disapproved behavior, but rather they are arranged in increasing complexity of choice. Elinor and Marianne form one of the contrasting pairs around which the story is built, for these two sisters are matched by the two brothers, Edward and Robert Ferrars. As further contrast, Austen includes the two Steele sisters, the two daughters of Mrs. Jennings, Mrs. Palmer and Lady Middleton, and the two Elizas. This pattern seems to indicate that Austen chooses to focus on the family rather than individual choice, so that marriage remains a familial, not an individual, affair. Readers are invited to examine marriage possibilities, not necessarily as separate marriages, but by contrasting five family situations and five different kinds of parental pressure: the Dashwoods, the Ferrars, the Jennings, the Steeles, and the Brandons. From this perspective, it is not surprising that the marriages of the Dashwood sisters end up similar, as do the Jennings sisters', and so on. The multiplicity of contrasts removes the motives for marriage from an individual plane onto a familial or social plane: that is, the various choices do not represent individual styles or decisions as much as they represent the range of available forms.

In *Sense and Sensibility*, although their beginnings may be different, the matches made by Elinor and Marianne in the end are similar, in contrast to the matches made by Mrs. Jennings's daughters, which also resemble each other. For the former we are told, "It was contrary to every doctrine of her's [Mrs. Dashwood's] that difference of fortune should keep any couple asunder who were attracted by resemblance of disposition" (*Sense and Sensibility*, 15). Judging from the results of her matchmaking, it appears that it was contrary to Mrs. Jennings's principles that difference of disposition should keep any couple asunder who were attracted by resemblance of fortune. Neither the Palmers nor the Middletons have anything in common except similar economic status. Yet compared with the undisguised greed of Fanny and Robert Ferrars, whom the narrator continuously exposes to satiric ridicule, the marriages of Mrs. Jennings's daughters are presented not as corrupt or disgraceful or even regretful, but rather as normative. That is, if the Dashwoods are idealized in matters of love and marriage, and the Ferrars and Steeles satirized, the Jenningses may represent Austen's sense of ordinary practice. Furthermore, within these contrasts and oppositions, the choices seem governed by parental control, which is environmental or educational (the Dashwoods of one mother are romantic, of another are pragmatic). The Dashwoods, Jenningses, Steeles, and Ferrars all follow a familial pattern with the exception of Edward Ferrars, who has been educated differently from his foppish brother.

Because Marianne's romantic notions of attachment most conform to our own, readers are liable to identify hers as the central values of the novel, the ones by which the others should be judged. Even when readers accept the authority of Elinor's more prudent and practical view, it is common to find muted expressions of disappointment at what happens to Marianne, disappointment that she has to be penalized with Colonel Brandon and chastised under a policy of reduced expectations. It would be a mistake, however, to evaluate all these marriages by the standard of the most idealized vision. We may judge that few are shown to be successful, in our narrow sense of leading to domestic comfort or variety of happiness, yet on her terms of acquisition and social mobility, Lucy Steele's marriage to Robert Ferrars is wildly successful. Willoughby is the only one to complain that his marriage is a failure, and he only does so to elicit sympathy from Elinor and also indirectly from Marianne. Only the marriage of the first Eliza breaks down into public scandal and divorce: again, the marriages of the Middletons and the Palmers are more typical. The

Middletons have nothing in common and seem ill-suited to one another, yet there is no indication of discontent. The Palmers hardly fulfill romantic expectations of companionate union, but they are not unhappy, and Mrs. Palmer appears content with her lot. Although Marianne obviously is forced to soften her harsh judgment of Mrs. Jennings and family, it is significant that Austen also has Elinor change her view of Mr. Palmer; when Elinor observes him at his home, he too is not displeased with his domestic lot.

Sense and Sensibility argues that romantic expectations have little likelihood of producing domestic tranquility or personal happiness. Marianne's attraction to Willoughby, a restrained version of "love at first sight," is viewed with suspicion from the first. Austen represents love at first sight not as some natural or spontaneous action, but a result of mediated desire, the result of romantic longing or expectation for "something evermore about to be," in Wordsworth's phrase. Austen makes it clear that Willoughby conforms to what Marianne's "fancy had delineated." Marianne's precipitous attraction to Willoughby, therefore, contrasts explicitly with the slow growth of Elinor's esteem for Edward. Elinor's courtship is characterized by labor or exertion—work—while her sister's is characterized by laxity and lassitude. One method leads to security and happiness, the other to disappointment, which is followed by exertion, security, and happiness. All of this returns the reader to Austen's view that courtship must involve work to develop affection and respect.

From *Northanger Abbey* to *Persuasion*, Austen makes it clear that it is not enough that the two protagonists like or even love each other. In several of the novels, including *Northanger Abbey* and *Mansfield Park*, the heroine's affection for the hero is established early, from childhood in the case of Fanny Price. In others, including *Pride and Prejudice* and *Emma*, the male protagonist's affection develops first; in *Emma*, of course, it is not revealed until near the end. Either way, both characters spend the entire novel learning enough about the other to venture into a lifelong compact of dependence. In *Northanger Abbey*, Austen states explicitly that Catherine and Henry do not know one another well enough to marry safely; his father's "unjust interference [and the delay occasioned by it], so far from being really injurious to their felicity, was perhaps rather conducive to it, by improving their knowledge of each other, and adding strength to their attachment" (*Northanger Abbey*, 252). Austen returns to this idea again at the end of her life in *Persuasion*, in which Anne Elliot and Captain Wentworth "returned again into the past, more exquisitely happy, perhaps, in their re-union, than when it had been first projected; more tender, more tried, more fixed in a knowledge of each other's character, truth and attachment; more equal to act, more justified in acting" (*Persuasion*, 240–41). If the romance plot of these works is based on a trial or agon, that trial turns on thorough knowledge of the other, the sine qua non of successful marriage according to Austen. In *Sense and Sensibility*, Willoughby's confession shows that Marianne was not deceived by his affection for her, but she had no adequate knowledge of his character. In this novel, the issue of knowledge is underscored by the emphasis on mystery and secrecy.[45] Lucy Steele hoards and selectively (and punitively) divulges secrets about Edward. Mrs. Jennings has an unseemly interest in Colonel Brandon's unknown "business" that mysteriously takes him away to London. Marianne seems to conceal a secret engagement to Willoughby, and Elinor spies on her sister and her correspondence when they are in town (e.g., *Sense and Sensibility*, 156–57, 167).

Within the highly constrained and structured rituals of courtship, both man and woman (but mostly the woman because she gives up the most) must find out enough about the other to venture her independence. As with any important investment, but especially with this one in which one's self is invested, one does as much research as possible to minimize risk, which is what the labor of courtship involves for Austen's heroines: not only angling or setting one's cap in the business of pleasing, but rather more the research into a potential, all-important investment. However much research one does, Austen still makes it clear that marriage is a high-risk investment, because it is by definition a bad business practice—sinking all of one's working capital into a single venture. Nevertheless, courtship and marriage remain the only real work open to women in this period and class. As Mary Crawford observes to Fanny Price after recounting a horrific series of marital histories among her London acquaintances ("I look upon the Frasers to be about as unhappy as most other married people"), "This seems as if nothing were a security for matrimonial comfort!" (*Mansfield Park*, 361).

In all of her novels, Austen insists that affection is not sufficient means on which to marry. This insistence is perhaps more forcefully asserted in *Persuasion* than in any other of the novels, because any romantic plot with its idealization of marriage in a realistic treatment is bound to make normative practice seem worse—the grander the expectations, the worse common practice will appear. On the one hand, the harsh judgment of "ordinary" marriage is the direct consequence of idealization; on the other hand, however, the idealization is also always questioned. Unlike more traditional comedy, such as Goldsmith's *She Stoops to Conquer*, love and money are not opposites around which a plot is fashioned. To read Austen's work aright, readers must rid themselves of the romantic preconception that only love matters, that love conquers all and is transcendent. Although it is important to recognize the demands of both, love is neither privileged over money in a hierarchy, nor are they synthesized in a dialectic. Love and money are not presented as antimonies, enemies, or antitheses: in Jane Austen's novels they are simply unrelated; or, they are related only because individuals must deal with both, by consequence or effect but not by mythological, ideological, or even narrative structure. The assertion that money and love are antithetical or that one is the enemy or nemesis of the other implies a structure that is not of Austen's making or even her reflecting: that is, to call money the antithesis of love is to endorse an ideology of romantic love. One affects or qualifies the other, and they both have to be dealt with; but in and of themselves they are not related, except in accidental or incidental ways, no more than love and health or love and work are related.

Although Austen can present love and money in this parallel fashion, it is not clear that she either resists or is fully conscious of the ideology of romantic love. Austen is unwilling or unable to recognize alternatives to marriage. In all her works, she sets marriage for security against the single life of poverty, but nowhere in her letters or her novels does Austen seriously consider the obvious alternative, one she may have enjoyed toward the end of her life: a single life of financial independence. On this point, we can compare Anne Elliot, the one character who comes closest to living alone and faces it with considerable distress, with Charlotte Brontë's Lucy Snowe, whose independence is painfully but triumphantly achieved at the close of *Villette*. Austen comes closest to considering the alternative in *Emma*, in which Emma amusingly, if cruelly, distinguishes for Harriet the difference between poor and wealthy old maids:

> Never mind, Harriet, I shall not be a poor old maid; and it is poverty only which makes celibacy contemptible to a generous public! A single woman, with a very narrow income, must be a ridiculous, disagreeable, old maid! the proper sport of boys and girls; but a single woman, of good fortune, is always respectable, and may be as sensible and pleasant as anybody else. (*Emma*, 85)

Yet this distinction is repudiated explicitly in several ways: most obviously, Emma herself cannot resist the lure of marriage, and poor spinsters are declared exempt from sport, Emma's in particular. In a more telling category, content widows are not very common in Austen's work.[46] Perhaps one can only conclude that the ideological pressure toward marriage is so powerful and pervasive that Austen can neither recognize nor resist it.

Still, in those passages where Austen recommends marriage, financial security is often offered as the most pressing reason. She does not say that unmarried women will be lonely or unfulfilled or inadequate—she only says that they are likely to be poor. Although Austen never states this directly (and the structure of *Emma* actively belies it), the logical, silent, conclusion is that a secure single life might be just fine. Given the social role of women, however, which is practically defined by dependence, it seems that happily unmarried women are as rare in fact as in her fiction.[47] But happily married women also are rare in Austen's fiction, leaving the companionate marriage of affection a longed-for ideal, infinitely desirable and infinitely rare.

Marriage in Austen is representative of her technique of simultaneously undermining and idealizing, a satiric apposition between the depressingly debased common run of things and an idealization of one exceptional alternative: the many versions of Mr. and Mrs. Bennet versus the singular match of Darcy and Elizabeth. In this respect, marriage lies at the heart of ideological contradiction in Austen's fiction, for it is simultaneously problem and solution. In Austen's class, the practices and procedures of marriage reveal the objectification of social relations unusually clearly.[48] Prospective mates are chosen as if they were objects, as if marriage itself is not a relation between people but rather assumes "the fantastic form of a relation between things." The opening of *Pride and Prejudice* dramatizes the humiliation involved in this process, where Austen shows Darcy first responding to Elizabeth, "quizzing" her as if she were a horse or other animal on show: "She is tolerable; but not handsome enough to tempt *me*" (*Pride and Prejudice*, 12). Like a shopper in the market, the men look over the women at the assembly as if they were all on display for purchase. Through the course of this novel, Austen attempts the difficult task of transforming Darcy from a jaded shopper who sees only the physical object before him, to one who can see *within* Elizabeth, beyond exchange value, to see finally what she really is. This process spans the two poles of marriage in Austen, from the angry exposure of the courtship as a relation not between people but between things, to the idealization of romantic intimacy. If middle-class marriage practices do not seem quite the same as the worker's sale of her labor for wages, many conditions are similar. The nubile female must part with her independence on the open market, taking what the market will bear, thus the marriage market is like all other social institutions in that it has become externalized and objectified, transformed into an institution that always precedes the individual, is external to and alienated from her, such that she seems to have no say in its rules or organization, but is merely subject to it. As Georg Lukács writes of the worker entering the labor force and the monolithic factory, "the personality can do no more than look on helplessly while its own existence is reduced to an isolated particle and fed into an alien system."[49]

Yet despite suggestions of these practices in Austen, marriage is never fully represented as an institution but rather as an individual practice, something at which Mr. and Mrs. Bennet have failed, and not something that is at its very heart corrupt. Herein lies the other side of the contradiction. Whenever marriage is imaged as an institution (as, very briefly, in Charlotte Lucas's statement about preservatives from want), a system or "factory" in which women must enter and work for others, it is always seen as cruel and unjust. At the same time, however, rather than dwell on its institutional and social nature, Austen portrays marriage as a flight and refuge from commodification and the objectification of social relations. If, as in other realms, men and women come to interact as if they were things, then the romantic conception of marriage serves as the solution to this alienation, providing love, support, and presence in the face of the terrible reification in all other social realms. The problem, the reifying, objectifying, dehumanizing nature of marriage as capital exchange, thus by the process of ideological contradiction becomes the solution, the refuge from a terrifyingly externalized world. Austen thus portrays marriage, on the one hand, as cruel, brutal, and inevitably disappointing, and, on the other hand, as the ideal and only solution to all social and individual ills. Finally in Austen, despite the myriad examples of failed and brutal marriages, what gets emphasized is only its private and personal side, not its institutional, public, or ideological nature, and so each marriage portrayed remains personal and individual rather than prototypical, and its larger social, public, and institutional nature is obscured or mystified. The particular shape of its individual form can only be understood here, however, by restoring and understanding its institutional nature.

Notes

1. Austen's fiction is quoted from *The Novels of Jane Austen*, 5 vols., ed. R. W. Chapman (1923, Oxford: Oxford University Press, 1978) and *Minor Works*, ed. R. W. Chapman (1954, London: Oxford University Press, 1975). Subsequent references

to Austen's novels are to these editions and page numbers appear parenthetically in the text.

2. On marriage used as a device for closure, see Northrop Frye, *Anatomy of Criticism* (Princeton: Princeton University Press, 1957), pp. 163–64; on marriage as an emblem of morality, see Murial Brittain Williams, *Marriage: Fielding's Mirror of Morality* (University: University of Alabama Press, 1973); on the emblematic nature of Fielding's marriages, see Martin Battestin, *The Providence of Wit* (Oxford: At the Clarendon Press, 1974), pp. 179–92.

3. Mary Poovey, *The Proper Lady and the Woman Writer* (Chicago: University of Chicago Press, 1984), p. 201.

4. Marriage is, of course, an important subject in Austen, and it has attracted especially excellent commentary from, among others, Lloyd Brown, "The Business of Marrying and Mothering" in *Jane Austen's Achievement*, ed. Juliet McMaster (New York: Harper and Row, 1976), pp. 27–43; Julia Prewit Brown, *Jane Austen's Novels—Social Change and Literary Form* (Cambridge: Harvard University Press, 1979); and, most recently, Karen Newman, "Can This Marriage Be Saved; Jane Austen Makes Sense of an Ending," *ELH* 50 (1983), pp. 693–710. This essay covers some of the topics treated in Catherine Sobba Green's unpublished dissertation, "The Courtesy Novel (1740–1820): Women Writing for Women" *DAI* 1984.

5. Jean H. Hagstrum discusses the role of passion in *Sense and Sensibility*: *Sex and Sensibility, Ideal and Erotic Love from Milton to Mozart* (Chicago: University of Chicago, 1980), pp. 268–74.

6. As has been pointed out several times, *Persuasion* contains Austen's only use of the word "romance" in the sense of love: because Anne Elliot "had been forced into prudence in her youth, she learned romance as she grew older" (p. 30).

7. See, for example, Tony Tanner, *Adultery and the Novel: Contract and Transgression* (Baltimore: Johns Hopkins University Press, 1979), p. 144.

8. Ibid., p. 4.

9. Ibid., p. 15.

10. Austen's letters are quoted from *Jane Austen's Letters,* ed. R. W. Chapman (1932, Oxford: Oxford University Press, 1979). Subsequent references to the letters appear in the text with page numbers in parentheses. The letters to Fanny Knight are numbers 103, 106, 140, 141, and 142.

11. On Jane Austen's relationship with Cassandra and Fanny, see Janet Todd's insightful discussion in *Women's Friendship in Literature* (New York: Columbia University Press, 1980), pp. 396–402.

12. In "The Business of Marrying and Mothering," Lloyd Brown rightly observes some important distinctions between Austen's presentation of marriage in her fiction and her attitude toward marriage in the letters, and that the former is obviously more idealized. Although this observation is true, here I am trying to show the underlying similarity of financial pressure in both life and fiction.

13. Lest we misinterpret this letter to cover solely emotional matters, its central concern is likely to be complicated by property. For a discussion of how property can be alienated from the patrilineal estate by the widow's remarriage, see Randolph Trumbach, *The Rise of the Egalitarian Family: Aristocratic Kinship and Domestic Relations in Eighteenth-Century England* (New York: Academic Press, 1978), pp. 50–61.

14. Similar qualification is commonly found in other correspondence from the period: Mrs. Delaney writes, "I have no notion of love in a knapsack, but I cannot think riches the only thing that ought to be considered in matrimony." *Delaney* (1861) I: 173. Quoted from Randolph Trumbach, *The Rise of the Egalitarian Family*, p. 105; see also pp. 93 and 99 for similar statements.

15. Lawrence Stone, *The Family, Sex and Marriage in England 1500–1800* (New York: Harper and Row, 1977), pp. 271–72.

16. The idea of love as mediated desire comes from René Girard, *Deceit, Desire, and the Novel*, trans. Yvonne Feccero (Baltimore: Johns Hopkins University Press, 1965).

17. Stone, pp. 270–71.

18. Ibid., pp. 257–58.

19. Ibid., p. 228.

20. See Marilyn Butler, *Jane Austen and The War of Ideas* (Oxford: At the Clarendon Press, 1975).

21. Susan Moller Okin argues that Stone overestimates the legal powers of women in the latter part of the century. "Patriarchy and Married Women's Property in England: Questions on Some Current Views," *Eighteenth-Century Studies* 17 (1983): 121–38.

22. Igor Webb observes that most of Austen's families have to contend with financial difficulties. *From Custom to Capital, The English Novel and the Industrial Revolution* (Ithaca: Cornell University Press, 1981), pp. 43–44.

23. For a clear explanation of portion, jointure, and dower, see Alan Macfarlane, *Marriage and Love, Modes of Reproduction 1300–1840* (Oxford: Basil Blackwood, 1986), pp. 263–90.

24. Stone, pp. 392–404. Cf. Miriam Slater: "the father of the prospective bride negotiated under the disadvantage of a buyer's market whereas the father of the prospective groom normally enjoyed the advantage of a seller's market," *Family Life in the Seventeenth Century: The Verneys of Claydon House* (London: Routledge and Kegan Paul, 1984), p. 82.

25. Mary Wollstonecraft, *A Vindication of the Rights of Woman*, ed. Carol H. Poston (New York: Norton, 1975), p. 183. Austen's relation to Wollstonecraft has been explored by Lloyd Brown, "Jane Austen and the Feminist Tradition," *Nineteenth-Century Fiction*, 28 (1973): 321–38; Alison Sulloway, "Emma Woodhouse and *A Vindication of the Rights of Woman*," *Wordsworth Circle*, 7 (1976): 320–32; and most fully in Margaret Kirkham, *Jane Austen: Feminism and Fiction* (Totowa, NJ: Barnes and Noble, 1983).

26. Maria Edgeworth, *Belinda*, 2 vols. (London: Baldwin & Cradock, 1833), p. 1. The aunt here is ridiculed for her obsession with the mercantile tactics of courtship, while the heroine goes off in prudent pursuit of the companionate marriage.

27. The language and economy of self-interest in this passage should be connected with the relatively recent history of the political justification of self-interest. See Albert O. Hirschman, *The Passions and the Interests: Political Arguments for Capitalism before Its Triumph* (Princeton: Princeton University Press, 1977), pp. 31–48.

28. Julia Prewit Brown, pp. 8–9.

29. Wollstonecraft, p. 60.

30. Ibid., p. 187. Slater writes of an earlier period: "marriage was considered to be the most important endeavor in a woman's life. In the society of the upper-gentry there were few career options for younger sons, but there was only one for daughters. The prospect of marriage was in fact and for good reason referred to as a woman's 'preferment,' because it was viewed and assiduously sought after as her only possibility for advancement" (pp. 79–80).

31. Ibid., p. 75.

32. Ibid., p. 187.

33. Ibid., p. 19.

34. Ibid., p. 170; Stone, pp. 316–17. "A Young Lady's Entrance into the World," Burney's phrase for the prototypical female plot, is accompanied in the fiction of this period, with grandmothers in Burney, aunts in Edgeworth, and the likes of Mrs. Jennings in *Sense and Sensibility*, who, like real estate agents, superintend their charges' entrance onto the marriage market.

35. Karl Marx, *The Economic and Philosophical Manuscripts of 1844,* ed. Dirk J. Struik (New York: International Publishers, 1964), pp. 106, 108.

36. See István Mészáros, *Marx's Theory of Alienation* (New York: Harper and Row, 1970), pp. 33–36.

37. *The Letters of William and Dorothy Wordsworth*, ed. Ernest De Selincourt, 2nd ed. (Oxford: At the Clarendon Press, 1970), #440, 7 April 1817, to Daniel Stuart, 3: 375.

38. Clifford Siskin, "High Wages and High Arguments: The Economics of Mixed Form in the late Eighteenth Century," in *The Historicity of Romantic Discourse* (Oxford: Oxford University Press, 1988). For an exemplary history of Josiah Wedgwood's's central role in the transformation via mass production, from exclusivity to emulative spending, see Neil McKendrick, "Josiah Wedgwood and the Commercialization of the Potteries," in Neil McKendrick, John Brewer, and J. H. Plumb, *The Birth of a Consumer Society, The Commercialization of Eighteenth-Century England* (Bloomington: Indiana University Press, 1982), pp. 100–45.

39. This episode concerns the farmer's cart that Mary Crawford is unable to hire in harvest time. Similarly, Marx argues in the *1844 Manuscripts* that money is "men's estranged, alienating and self-disposing *species nature*. Money is the alienated *ability of mankind*. That which I am unable to do as a *man*, and of which therefore all my individual essential powers are incapable, I am able to do by means of *money*" (p. 168).

40. Raymond Williams observes that land in Austen's novels is represented as something to own rather than as something to work. *The Country and the City* (New York: Oxford University Press, 1973), pp. 108–19.

41. Marx, *Manuscripts of 1844*, pp. 101–2.

42. Macfarlane observes that the market analogy to marriage was common at this time, with the exception that marriage allowed for no resale (*Marriage and Love*, pp. 165–66). See also M. Dorothy George, *London Life in the Eighteenth Century* (1925; rpt. Chicago: Academy Chicago, 1984), p. 171.

43. In his *Advice to a Lover* (1837), p. 10, for example, William Cobbett recommends these desirable qualities in a wife: "1. Chastity. 2. Sobriety. 3. Industry. 4. Frugality. 5. Cleanliness. 6. Knowledge of domestic affairs. 7. Good temper. 8. Beauty" (Quoted from Macfarlane, p. 163).

44. For the conditions of the working class in this period, see E. P. Thompson, *The Making of the English Working Class* (1963; New York: Vintage, 1966).

45. As Joseph Wiesenfarth notes, both sisters are attracted to men with secrets or enigmas that must be solved. *The Errand of Form* (New York: Fordham University Press, 1967), p. 42.

46. Mrs. Jennings, Mrs. Dashwood, and Lady Russell seem content, if not fully sketched in, but more common are the Mrs. Bateses in Austen, Mrs. Thorpe, Mrs. Smith, Lady Catherine de Bourgh, and Mrs. Norris. Widowers, who include General Tilney, Sir Walter Elliot, Captain Benwick (of a sort), Mr. Weston, and Mr. Woodhouse, obviously have a better time of it than do the likes of Mrs. Smith from *Persuasion*.

47. Austen's letters everywhere make it clear that what is most distressing about the single life for women is the perpetual state of dependence; as Slater writes of seventeenth-century women, "the unmarried woman became a perennial supplicant

who had little possibility of returning favors; this placed her in an untenable position in a society which placed high priority on reciprocation." *Family Life*, p. 85.

48. The degree to which Austen recognizes this situation as contradictory remains an open and important question, one to which feminist revision of Austen returns again and again. Karen Newman makes a persuasive but, I think, finally unconvincing argument that Austen leaves the contradictions between love and money in her novels as a kind of tense and unresolved silence, "the true place of women in a materialist culture in which men control money." "Can this Marriage be Saved," p. 699.

49. Georg Lukács, *History and Class Consciousness*, trans. Rodney Livingstone (1968; reprint, Cambridge: MIT Press, 1972), p. 90.

The Role of Feeling in the Formation of Romantic Ideology
The Poetics of Schiller and Wordsworth

LORE METZGER

1

In this essay I reread two familiar critical texts, two seminal manifestoes of Romantic aesthetics: Schiller's *Über naive und sentimentalische Dichtung* (1795) and Wordsworth's Preface to the *Lyrical Ballads* (1800). My rereading does not aim at constructing or construing their essential coherence—that has been done successfully by critics from Lovejoy to Abrams—but aims rather at revealing intriguing moments of contradiction, discontinuity, and reversal. It attempts to raise questions rather than to offer definitive answers; it aims at practicing the kind of acuity Foucault ascribes to Nietzschean genealogy: "the acuity of a glance that distinguishes, separates, and disperses, that is capable of liberating divergence and marginal elements."[1] Such a rereading acknowledges yet questions the widely held assumption that these Romantic manifestoes translate the political ideals of the French Revolution into a theory of poetry, that they participate in the revolutionary upheavals of the times by replacing hierarchic with egalitarian poetics. This received tradition further emphasizes that the Romantics' focus on the transformational power of the individual imagination, their achievement of (in Abrams's words) "Apocalypse by Imagination," was a means of salvaging, not abrogating, revolutionary ideals, even as they became disillusioned with the violent events of the Terror of 1793–94. Thus Abrams, the premier spokesman of this critical tradition, argues that Wordsworth salvaged his millennial hopes by turning from "mass action to individual quietism, and from outer revolution to a revolutionary mode

An earlier version of this essay was presented as the Eberhard L. Faber Memorial Lecture at Princeton University, 5 March 1987.

of imaginative perception which accomplishes nothing less than the 'creation' of a new world."[2]

My critical glance at this interpretation does not contradict the hypothesis that the Romantics' recourse is "from mass action to individual quietism" but rather questions its evaluation as an unequivocally revolutionary achievement. That is, it uncovers in this Romantic turn from political goals to the redemptive individual imagination something more than an innocent "shift in the agency" that would bring about the regeneration of the world.[3] A critical glance sees some inherent contradictions in this Romantic ideology, which privileges the cultivation of the sensibility and imagination of the individual over collective political action. Whereas the Romantic language of reform, regeneration, and perfectibility appears highly charged with the epochal ideology of the French Revolution, its underlying commitment is to achieve reform through aesthetic imperatives and to bring about (in Lukács's memorable words) the social results of the French Revolution without a revolution.[4]

To uncover some of the explicit or implicit contradictions, displacements, or ruptures in the Romantic aesthetics, I limit myself here to a few key passages in Schiller's and Wordsworth's programmatic apologetics for a new poetry. And I find support in Pierre Macherey's statements that "like a planet revolving around an absent sun, an ideology is made out of what it does not mention; it exists because there are things which must not be spoken of." Furthermore "the work cannot speak of the more or less complex opposition which structures it. . . . In its every particle, the work *manifests*, uncovers, what it cannot say."[5] In Schiller's and Wordsworth's manifestoes, we need to modify Macherey's project to uncover not what they cannot say but rather what they strategically evade, disguise, or marginalize by their key syntheses.

Disguise, evasion, and contradiction are inherent in the functioning of all ideology, not just Romantic ideology. I have followed the practice of many recent scholars who use *ideology* to mean a system of beliefs, ideas, or fictions, which is taken to be so self-evident that individuals readily use it without questioning its universal validity, whether they are describing their views on poverty or on poetry. But if ideological representations at once appear as obvious and natural truths, they obscure and displace inconvenient socioeconomic details. Ideology, in the recent Althusserian formulation of Catherine Belsey, "obscures the real conditions of existence by presenting partial truths. It is a set of omissions, gaps rather than lies, smoothing over contradictions, appearing to provide answers to questions which in reality it evades, and masquerading as coherence in the interests of the social relations generated by and necessary to the reproduction of the existing mode of production."[6]

No one, of course, functions outside of ideology, although we like to talk as if ideological discourse were only what others, but never we, produce—especially not we, literary critics. Thus it is especially remarkable when a distinguished critic like Henry Nash Smith publicly unmasks an earlier ideological bias, providing us with a casebook example of ideology at work in literary criticism. More than fifty years after publishing *Virgin Land*, Henry Nash Smith writes that he failed to consider the "tragic dimensions of this Westward Movement" because they were cloaked in ideas so familiar as to be "almost inaccessible to critical examination." The same slogans (civilization, free land, frontier-initiative, manifest destiny) also obscured the views of the writers he was studying, as well as having served to rationalize the actual atrocities committed by the settlers against the native Indian population.[7]

Such complicity between the ideology inscribed in the literary text and that informing the critic's commentary is not limited to American cultural studies. As Jerome McGann has observed recently, Romanticists have too often accepted uncritically the Romantic view that poetry has a "special insight and power over truth"; they have also uncritically perpetuated the Romantic ideology that the age's crises and dislocations could be resolved in the realm of transhistorical, universal ideas. "Literary criticism," he concludes, "likes to transform the critical illusions of poetry into the worshipped truths of culture."[8] Although this charge is certainly well founded, a critic must also bear in mind that even if she subjects Romantic ideologies to critical analysis, it is impossible, as Gayatri Spivak reminds us, to analyze the ideology of any group "without sharing complicity with its ideological definition. A persistent critique of ideology is thus forever incomplete."[9] An incomplete uncovering of the ideological subtext of Schiller's and Wordsworth's manifestoes is therefore all I attempt in this essay.

2

Schiller's *Über naive und sentimentalische Dichtung* is the first philosophical exploration of the problematic of Romantic poetics, although it uses the term *sentimental* and not *romantic* to legitimate modern against classical literary practice. This treatise lays the groundwork for Romantic poetry as an authentic mode (*echte Art*) that enlarged the horizon of poetry, rather than as a mere aberration

(*Abart*) of classical models. It articulates the aesthetic judgments that proved seminal for European Romanticism.

Schiller's case for emancipating modern poetics from the shackles of classical norms proceeds cautiously. Its radical potential is defused by his repeated assurance that his categories are not intended to supplant but only to supplement traditional genres. His strongest anti-classical, anti-authoritarian move consists in his installing modalities of feeling (*Empfindungsweisen*) as the mainspring of his theoretical distinctions, displacing the neoclassic norm of social decorum. Specifically, Schiller investigates the differences that result from the modes of feeling informed by a unified sensibility on the one hand and a divided sensibility on the other. He interweaves aesthetic, psychological, epistemological, moral, and social filaments in his intricate argument. Its key affiliations can be identified by the terms: *nature*, *sensation*, *feeling*, *thought*, *idea*, *ideal*, *idyll*. This progression of terms reveals the dialectical subsumption of empirical, particular, time-and-place specific experience under transhistorical, typical, and universal ideas and ideals.

Schiller begins from the specific historical moment in which he finds himself in 1795, as is clear from the basic issue he formulates in a letter to Herder written while he was working on the middle section of his treatise, which dealt specifically with sentimental (modern) poetry.[10] His essay, he tells Herder, addresses the crucial question: "What road should the poet take in an age and under conditions like ours?"[11] Far from agreeing with Herder's premise that poetry should originate from, merge with, and flow back into the real life of its time, Schiller argues that it is so totally threatened by real conditions that it must secede from them. Because this letter sketches the problematic of *Naive and Sentimental Poetry* more explicitly than the treatise itself does, it is worth considering for a moment.

Schiller posits two unequal, opposing forces: prose and poetry. On the side of prose he sees arraigned the all-powerful resources of all civil, political, religious, scientific life and action; on the other side he places the embattled poetic spirit. And he defines the only possible defense for the poet: total withdrawal into an autonomous world of his own creation to effect a "rigorous separation from the real world instead of a coalition with it which would endanger the poetic spirit."[12]

Whereas earlier in the century such a stand for the autonomy of art could have been a political gesture for emancipating art from aristocratic patrons, by 1795, six years after the outbreak of the French

Revolution, Schiller's declaration of a strict separation of the artist's cause from all empirical thought and action suggests at best a compromising withdrawal from the political arena on the part of this honorary citizen of the French Republic. He also dissociates himself from his own earlier Jacobin sympathies to devote himself to a bourgeois cultural politics that conflates the private with the public realm. Schiller sought to constitute a socio-aesthetic realm of elite readers by precisely the means he had recommended to poets in his review of Matthison's poems in December 1794. There he prescribed that the poet should disregard feelings that were contingent on specific occasions and specific times and so constitute his subject that it necessarily determined the reader's emotional state (*Empfindungszustand*). This, he argued, could only be done if the poet addressed himself to what is universal rather than what is individual in the reader.[13]

Schiller's aesthetic strategy of strict separatism from the prosaic, contingent particulars of the real world clearly informs his project of gaining a legitimate homeland for sentimental (modern) poetry: he claims for it the territory of the mind, an ideal spot in ideal time. Schiller did not need to present this aesthetic ideology as explicitly in *Naive and Sentimental Poetry* as in his letter to Herder, because he published the treatise in his journal, *Die Horen*, whose stated policy was to avoid all involvement in current socio-political events and debates. At a time when war threatened to engulf Germany and political battles encroached on every corner of cultural life—as the announcement (*Ankündigung*) reprinted in the first issue of the journal proclaimed—Schiller's *Horen* maintains strict silence on the turmoil of current events. Schiller deploys his *Ecclesia militans*, as he called the *Horen* in a letter to Goethe, 1 November 1795, to war against the furies of political criticism—"[den] allverfolgenden Dämon der Staatskritik"[14]—the oppressive, divisive, inflammatory demon of partisan interests. He invites his readers to form an intimate circle rigorously engaged in a purifying, liberating dialogue dedicated to the higher, dispassionate, non-partisan interests of true humanity. Thus the *Horen* was to become the guardian of those "better ideas, purer principles, and nobler morals, on which all true improvement of the social condition ultimately depends."[15] *Ultimately* is the key word for this ideology that sets its sights on the unchanging horizon of universal ideas, abandoning all concerns with the prosaic immediate social conditions.

Naive and Sentimental Poetry observes the *Horen's* strategic silence on divisive contemporary events and implements its policy of orienting all discourse by the transhistorical lode-star of the ideal of noblest humanity—"das Ideal veredelter Menschheit."[16] Thus in a central formulation the treatise declares that the shared task of all poets—naive or sentimental—is to give human nature its full expression (*völligen Ausdruck*), if they are to be worthy of being called poets. The *Horen* ideology echoes even more clearly in Schiller's central distinction between the means by which naive and sentimental poets can achieve this shared task of embodying in their literary works a model of human perfection. Schiller theorizes that because naive poetry reflects human wholeness and harmony within the self and between the self and the external world, the naive poet's task is the perfect mimesis of reality (*die möglichst vollständige Nachahmung des Wirklichen*). Because sentimental poetry, on the contrary, is grounded in the human condition of divided sensibility, in which the naive state of harmonious wholeness exists only as an idea or goal, the sentimental poet's task is "the elevation of the real to the ideal, or, what amounts to the same thing, the *representation of the ideal*."[17] In other words, the modern poet must save himself from contamination with prosaic reality by dematerializing this discordant reality and by deriving from normative ideas (ideals) all intensity of feeling and dynamic force.

Having made this basic distinction between ancient and modern, naive and sentimental poetry, Schiller develops sub-genres of the sentimental mode. In supplementing the neoclassical hierarchy of genres, Schiller now develops his own hierarchy, based on modalities of feeling (*Empfindungsweisen*) rather than subject matter and literary form. Subject matter is immaterial for this hierarchy: its rungs are marked by the perspective on the real/ideal opposition that generates the feeling communicated by the given literary work of art. Thus satire in Schiller's poetics focuses on the conflict between the real and ideal, in which reality is depicted as an object of antipathy. In the satiric modes, as in all other modes discussed in the treatise, the poet is advised to transcend flawed, deficient reality and move the reader through sublime feelings rather than through bitter pathos, to cultivate feelings for noble ideas that lift us out of the confining limits of experience.[18] In the elegiac mode, the poet is advised to privilege nature and the ideal in confronting the nature/art, ideal/real opposition and to derive from idealized nature the poetic work's dominating feelings. I need not dwell here on the famous distinction that Schiller makes between the backward-looking lament and the forward-looking idyll, between the nostalgia for Arcadia and the anticipation of Elysium. Needless to say the Elysian idyll, which joyfully celebrates the ideal as real, as all contradictions and conflicts have been resolved in a dynamic transcendent synthesis, emerges as the highest possible poetic achievement.[19]

Thus Schiller's anti-authoritarian poetics ends in its own prescriptive hierarchy. And while its emphasis on modalities of feeling seems initially to privilege a subjectivist, individualistic aesthetic, Schiller's argument insists conversely that the modern poet should always address the individual's universal feelings. This means that feelings should never directly reflect experience. Schiller states categorically that the sentimental poet "reflects about the impression things make on him and only this reflection is the basis of the emotion they induce in him and he induces in us." Even when the subject of the poetry is the poet's own feelings, he does not communicate them as firsthand experience but rather as he has reflected on them as a spectator of himself.[20] It is precisely for his subjectivist, expressive poetry that Schiller criticized the popular poet Bürger because he failed to express idealized feelings with which everyone could identify. What makes the depiction of passion significantly human, Schiller instructs Bürger, is not its representation as "what an individual person has actually felt, but what *all men* without exception *must empathize with*."[21] To avoid debasing feelings from their "ideal universality" to an "imperfect individuality," the poet must distance himself from his own experience, informing his poetry with "emotion recollected in tranquility," as Wordsworth so seminally reformulated Schiller's dictum that the poet should write "from a calming and distancing recollection" (*aus der sanftern und fernenden Erinnerung*).[22]

Throughout Schiller's defense of modern poetry runs a thinly veiled political imperative: to save poetry from contamination with empirical reality, on the one hand, and to save political ideals by inscribing them in poetry, on the other. That is the consistent subtext of the discussion of naive and sentimental poetry. Yet although Schiller deliberately excludes any reference to unsettling contemporary events, their excluded chaotic presence exerts an unhinging pull against the tightly woven non-partisan, transhistorical imperatives of his poetics. At two key moments the pull becomes so strong that Schiller can or will no longer displace it but now directly inscribes his fear of being swept up in the maelstrom or—to use his own metaphor—of sinking into the abyss. The two moments occur in the introductory and concluding sections of the treatise.

The first passage I focus on is part of the discussion of naive sentiment, in which Schiller is interested in the way we frequently transfer free will to animals or landscapes, using catachresis, attributing to them a conscious choice. Schiller ascribes the reason for this projection of free will into nature to our own abuse of moral freedom. Although he leaves the abuses unspecified, his indictment suggests the moment in which, as he stated explicitly in his *Aesthetic Letters*, the people proved unready and unreceptive for the seed of freedom and the revolution that would restore their inalienable rights.[23] Therefore, as Schiller argues in *Naive and Sentimental Poetry*, men regard the "prerogative of reason as a curse" and long for nonrational nature's (*unvernünftigen Natur*) happiness and perfection. To probe further this longing for an irrecoverable state of nature, Schiller resorts to the rhetorical strategy of direct address to a sympathetic auditor he identifies as a "sensitive friend of nature" (*empfindsamen Freund der Natur*).[24] He invokes a surrogate reader, whose Rousseauistic sensibility alienates him from his society, and he interrogates him as a subject subjected to all the evil and dissociation of modern civilization that drive him to seek nature's healing power. That is to say: the author here constitutes as the subject of his discourse both a generalized psychological problem (with implied aesthetic consequences) and a concretized individual whom he can interrogate. The addressed "sensitive friend of nature" is an alter ego of the sentimental poet who indulges in the elegiac mode of feeling, longing to escape from society's discord into Arcadian harmony. It is worth remembering that Schiller had taken the epigraph for his *Aesthetic Letters* from *La Nouvelle Héloise*: "If it is reason that makes man, it is feeling [*sentiment*] that guides him."[25] But in *Naive and Sentimental Poetry*, he criticizes Rousseau, on the one hand, for an imbalance between feeling and thought and for indulging in pathological feeling, and on the other for inhibiting his imagination by excessive reasoning. His excessive sensibility makes him wish to cure mankind's self-division by retreating to the uniformity of nature and makes him lower his sights for the human ideal so he can secure it more readily.[26]

The imperative to examine closely this nostalgia for nature is central to the discourse addressed to the Rousseauistic friend. The author rhetorically distances this *Sehnsucht*, this forbidden desire for an irrecoverable ideal, yet authors this unauthorized mode of feeling. "Ask yourself," he insists, "when art disgusts you and the abuses of society drive you to solitary, lifeless nature, whether you loathe society's deprivations, burdens, hardships, or its moral anarchy, arbitrariness, disorder. The former you must joyfully and courageously embrace and your compensation shall be freedom itself. . . ."[27] The author instructs his "sensitive friend of nature" in the correct reaction to this disgust with civilization: "No more complaints about the difficulty of life, about the inequality of conditions, about the pressure of circumstances, about the insecurity of possessions, about ingratitude, oppression, persecution. You must resign yourself freely to all the necessary evils of civilization, respecting them as the natural conditions of the Only Good. . . . Take heed rather that even in the midst of this pollution you remain pure, that in this slavery you remain free . . . that in this anarchy you act lawfully."[28]

Among the many noteworthy points in this passage, I focus on the antithesis between its implication for avant-garde poetics and rearguard politics. The questions followed by imperatives recall the sensitive nature-lover—whether a budding poet or another member of the *Horen's* circle of elect readers—from yearning for nature's peace and quiet and escaping society's disorder and distress. Imperiously the author demands that his interlocutor relinquish such nostalgia and aspire to the worthier goal of moral autonomy, which must serve him as the *Ersatz* for the happy state of Nature. This argument lays the groundwork for Schiller's most original contribution to the theory of pastoral, his distinction between elegiac and idyllic modes of feeling, between nostalgic longing for a lost past and enthusiastic projection of an ideal future community. Yet at the same time this passage buttresses Schiller's dissociation of aesthetics from the prosaic realities of his time. His avant-garde equation of a moral ideal with a poetic mode in the form of the idyll also reinforces in his reader-subject the acceptance of an aesthetic solution to the backward socioeconomic institutions of Germany's petty principalities. How else can one read the catalogue of evils to which, so the author insists, his sensitive addressee must submit to surpass them through the exertion of his autonomous will?

Nowhere else in the treatise does Schiller anchor his argument so explicitly in a social context as when he itemizes the necessary evils of civilization—inequality of conditions, insecurity of possessions, ingratitude, oppression, persecution. Schiller admits this indictment of civilization while removing from it all contemporary historical specificity. His sensitive nature-loving friend is allowed the comforting illusion that he is above all suspicion of complicity with the exploitation and dehumanization of specific socioeconomic institutions in Germany during the last decade of the eighteenth century. He is allowed the comfortable illusion that the only thing at stake is the polity of his psyche and not the polity of the state. "You must freely resign yourself to all the necessary evils of civilization," the author commands, "you must respect them as the natural conditions of the Only Good." His sole concern must be to preserve his own integrity in the midst of corruption and slavery. Freely subjecting himself thus to his subjection, the addressee can maintain the illusion of his autonomous will. The subject in his discourse illustrates the paradox so brilliantly explicated by Althusser in terms of ideology's functioning in such a way that it transforms individuals into subjects by interpellation: "the individual is interpellated as a (free) subject in order that he shall submit freely to the commandments of the Subject, i.e. in order that he shall (freely) accept his subjection, i.e. in order that he shall make the gestures and actions of his subjection 'all by himself.' " And Althusser concludes: "There are no subjects except by and for their subjection. That is why they 'work all by themselves.' "[29]

Perhaps what surfaces in and through Schiller's interpellation of the sensitive friend of nature is the bourgeois ideology of laissez faire, an ideology that promised enterprising individuals unprecedented socioeconomic opportunities exactly when capitalist production forced individuals into the unenterprising, subordinate role of cheaply selling their labor. Schiller averted his eyes from the specific conditions of his time to focus on the moral psychodrama being enacted: "Man portrays himself in his actions. And what a figure he cuts in the drama of the present time! On the one hand, a return to the savage state; on the other, to complete lethargy: in other words, to the two extremes of human depravity, and both united in a single epoch!"[30] Even though this vision of civilization is bleak enough to drive a sensitive Rousseauist to dream of harmonious nature, Schiller urges that he should relinquish such escapism. This is his parting injunction: "The irrational nature which you envy is not worthy of your respect or desire [*Sehnsucht*]. It lies in the past and will always lie in the past. Abandoned by the ladder which supported you, you now have no other choice than to exercise your free will and pure consciousness to embrace the law or to sink hopelessly into a bottomless pit [*bodenlose Tiefe*]."[31]

Here in his conclusion the fissure in Schiller's self-styled nonpartisan poetics becomes visible. His addressed subject is given a choice between the abyss of freely submitting to the enslavement of civilization as the price for theorizing a future ideal (in the form of pure consciousness or pure poetry) or the abyss of having no ground on which to build his visions. The Kantian imperative of self-determination—"Bestimme Dich aus Dir selbst"—is offered as the moral life preserver to the subject who, as Schiller states clearly, has no choice that does not involve his subjugation.

Schiller's counsel of despair remains a remarkable subtext that surfaces again in the concluding section of the treatise. And it puts into question the confident intervening legitimation of the ways in which the modern (sentimental) poet's divided sensibility and perspective can triumph over the ancient (naive) poet's harmony. The abysmal imperatives developed in the address to the nature-lover make one doubt Schiller's confident proclamation that the direction chosen by the modern poet is that which every individual, indeed, mankind in general, must take: through the ideal the divided sensibility returns to the unity lost in the fall from nature.[32] It makes one suspect the claim that to restore to modern man the wholeness lost through civilization's fragmenting of human potentiality is the modern poet's distinctive achievement; that he can show the way to the ultimate Elysium, the reintegration that heals all divisions, rifts, and corruptions of modern society. One cannot forget that because Schiller prescribes that this reintegration must take place in and through the developments of modern civilization, this path is also the one that leads to the abyss. As indeed Schiller reminds readers once more at the conclusion of his treatise.

Idealist though he was, Schiller concludes his speculations on naive and sentimental poetry with a remarkable negation of his earlier "poetically exalted" projection of an ultimate synthesis of naive and sentimenal modalities of feeling—a synthesis constituting the ideal of sublime humanity. As he concludes his discourse, he leaves his poetic typology to extract from it the purely psychological typology of idealists and realists. He ends this digression with a further digression on the aberrations, indeed caricatures, of these two types, reserving his most caustic strictures for the excessive idealist. The treatise, which has already offered a recapitulation of his idealist poetic typology, now offers a second conclusion in the form of a psychological deterrent, a Gothic horror story. Like Mary Shelley's Frankenstein, the idealist author now confronts his own creation as a grotesque caricature of his sublime ideal:

> [If] the effects of even true idealism are unsettling and frequently dangerous, the effects of false idealism are horrifying. The true idealist abandons nature and experience only because he does not find in them the immutable and unconditional necessity for which reason bids him strive. The fantast abandons nature out of mere caprice [*Willkür*], in order to give free rein to his willful desires [*dem Eigensinne der Begierden*] and to the whims of his imagination. . . . But precisely because fantasticality [*Phantasterei*] is not an extravagance of nature but an excess of freedom, resulting from an intrinsically admirable and infinitely perfectible disposition, it leads to an infinite fall into a bottomless abyss [*bodenlose Tiefe*] and can end only in total annihilation.[33]

Thus twice, at critical moments of his idealist poetics, Schiller cautions his reader-subject to beware of the abyss lurking in the excesses of idealism. His own reexamination of the psychological premises of his argument does not, however, lead him to re-view the premises on which his whole aesthetics is built: the strictly imposed silence on the prosaic events of his time, which included the repercussions in Germany and throughout Europe of the successive stages of the French Revolution. Schiller told Goethe explicitly in 1794 that in his journal *Die Horen* he had not capitulated to the public, had never put pen to paper about the current political calamity [*Jammer*] except in the first *Letters on the Aesthetic Education of Man*, and then only in order never again to speak on the subject.[34] Silent on contemporary political events and on the political implications of aesthetics, Schiller sought to promote through art the prior aim of effecting a revolution in the individual sensibility. Brecht as usual hit the nail on the head when he spoke of Goethe and Schiller, who, having digested the French Revolution in their own way, then engaged in a "highminded conspiracy against the public" that forced an elitist literature on the bourgeoisie "like a civil code of law."[35] Yet, when applied to *Naive and Sentimental Poetry,* such an unsympathetic diagnosis leaves out of account—just as the empathetic interpretations of many recent Romanticists do—that Schiller's text enforces not only an elitist aesthetics but also disrupts its own aesthetic imperatives in moments in which a radical skepticism creates fissures in the carefully structured argument.

3

Wordsworth's Preface to the *Lyrical Ballads* shares, in many places, the ideological subtext of Schiller's treatise although it is much more explicitly anti-elitist in its declaration of an experimental poetics based on the language of ordinary men and "incidents of common life." But against this emphatic affirmation of a revolutionary poetics there also emerges an unacknowledged conflicting ideological commitment to severing the relation between poetry and society, in the service not of revolution but rather of stable social relations. Overtly, Wordsworth defends the overturning of poetic conventions; covertly, he warns against overturning the social order by appealing to transhistorical, permanent interests. His emphasis on feeling plays a crucial role both in revolutionizing poetics and in displacing political issues.

Wordsworth's defense of an experimental poetics, which was immediately recognized even by his hostile critic Francis Jeffrey as the manifesto of a new school of poetry, had as its stated aim (in the language of the 1798 Advertisement) "to ascertain how far the language of conversation in the middle and lower classes of society is adapted to the purposes of poetic pleasure."[36] Wordsworth challenges his readers to judge his poems for themselves, to disregard "pre-established codes of decision," authoritarian rules that prevent readers from enjoying art that does not meet with official approval. Wordsworth's anti-authoritarian stance in experimenting with the language and incidents drawn from the lower classes of society—his cardinal statement as he elaborates it in the preface of the 1800 edition of the *Lyrical Ballads*—supports the inference that Wordsworth's manifesto translates radical democratic convictions into a theory of poetry. His justification for writing about subjects not previously thought fit for serious poetry—peasants, beggars, gypsies, madmen, thieves, idiots, and other outcasts—is a subversion of the literary ancien régime. This subversion, however, does not abolish hierarchical order; it dismantles the neoclassic hierarchy to replace it with a subjectivist hierarchy, centered, like Schiller's, not on decorum but on feeling.

In restating the nature of his experimental poetics for the full-fledged preface of 1800, Wordsworth deemphasizes the social nature of his experiment and elaborates the notions of subjective sensation and aesthetic pleasure. He now says that he tried to "ascertain, how far, by fitting to metrical arrangement a selection of the real language of men [note the erasure of all references to social classes] in a state of vivid sensation, that sort of pleasure . . . may be imparted, which a Poet may rationally endeavour to impart."[37]

The term *vivid sensation* becomes the central link in a chain of interrelated psychological terms deployed in predicates defining "the principal object" of Wordsworth's experiment. He shifts his emphasis from the "real language of men" to the problem of giving interest to incidents drawn from "common life" by "tracing in them . . . the primary laws of our nature: chiefly as far as regards the manner in which we associate ideas in a state of excitement."[38] Wordsworth moves from a specific social experiment to a psychological generality: the primary laws of human nature. He proposes to trace in his poems the laws governing the association of ideas in a state of excitement. And thus he severs his poetics from the historical moment.

At this point Wordsworth reintroduces the reference to social class, but now subordinates it to his principal psychological purpose; he has chosen to depict "low and rustic life" (again this formulation mutes the earlier reference to class structure) "because in that situation the *essential passions of the heart* find a better soil in which they can attain their maturity . . . [and] because in that situation our *elementary feelings* exist in a state of greater simplicity . . . and lastly, because in that situation the *passions of men* are incorporated with the beautiful and permanent forms of nature."[39]

In his note to *The Thorn* (1800), Wordsworth elaborated further this central emphasis on feeling: "Words, a Poet's words more particularly, ought to be weighed in the balance of feeling, and not measured by the space which they occupy upon paper. For the Reader cannot be too often reminded that Poetry is passion: it is the history or science of feelings. . . ."[40] Poetry as the "science of feelings" clearly serves the purpose of disabusing the reader of a passionate interest in contemporary events and in elevating his taste to the "essential passions" and "elementary feelings" connected with the "beautiful and permanent forms of nature." Wordsworth, like Schiller, does not weigh in the balance whose interests are served by directing his community of readers to universal and essential emotions. In our own time Brecht was quick to recognize a grotesque Romantic aberration in the fascist revival of the cult of feeling. But he was also quick to reveal an aspect of the "science of feelings" that the Romantics had thoughtfully overlooked: "The emotions always have a quite definite class basis; the form they take at any time is historical, restricted and limited in specific ways. The emotions are in no sense universally human and timeless." And he goes on to observe that the "linking of particular emotions with particular interests is not unduly difficult so long as one simply looks for the interests corresponding to the emotional effects of works of art. Anyone can see the colonial adventures of the Second Empire looming behind Delacroix's paintings and Rimbaud's 'Bateau Ivre.' "[41]

Vivid sensation, state of excitement, essential passions, elementary feelings—this chain of psychological terms is symptomatic of Wordsworth's strategic move to elevate feeling to absolute prominence in his revolutionary project while totally averting his eyes from the specific material conditions ("that situation") in which his subjects in "low and rustic life" struggle daily. From the sublime height of the poet who is superior to all other men in degree though not in kind, he bestows the grace of his meditative pathos on the lower classes to show "that men who do not wear fine cloaths can feel deeply."[42] This phrase from Wordsworth's well-known letter to Charles James Fox of January 1801, accompanying his inscribed copy of *Lyrical Ballads*, shows how Wordsworth's aesthetic ideology displaces all interest in the plight of rural and urban wage laborers at a time when the capitalist system of production rapidly expanded to engulf commercial activities from weaving stockings to producing food. In his letter Wordsworth notably enumerates some of the recent economic developments and government measures that had an adverse effect on the working poor: "the spreading of manufactures through every part of the country, . . . the heavy taxes upon postage, . . . workhouses, Houses of Industry, and the Invention of Soupshops &c&c superadded to the encreasing disproportion between the price of labour and that of the necessaries of life."[43] Wordsworth, however, does not notice that these measures help preserve a cheap supply of labor and help keep the poor in their place. What he regards as the "most calamitous effect" of such exploitation is the "rapid decay of the domestic affections" among the lower orders of society. He appeals to Fox to intervene on this issue as a man he admires not so much for exercising political acumen as for exhibiting in his character a "constant predominance of sensibility of heart." And this "sensibility of heart" as manifested in the domestic relations is the cause for which he himself sought to elicit sympathy through such poems as "The Brothers" and "Michael." He tells Fox that no greater curse can befall the land than the erosion of the "blessings of independent domestic life": "parents are separated from their children, and children from their parents; the wife no longer prepares with her own hands a meal for her husband, the produce of his labour; there is little doing in his house in which his affections can be interested."[44]

Just as this letter to the Whig leader in Parliament is remarkable for its obfuscation of economic conditions, the Preface to the *Lyrical Ballads* is remarkable for its exclusion of the material conditions of the "rustic life" whose virtues it extols. These conditions do not intrude on the poet's contemplation of his subjects' feelings. Also excluded from Wordsworth's purview is the possibility that his casting marginal individuals as subjects in his dramatic lyrics may be a poetic innovation, yet it confirms them in rather than liberates them from the system of social relations in which they struggle to survive, in which their subjection is a given. The author as autonomous subject recognizes the lowly subjects in his poems because their rank placing them "less under the action of social vanity [,] they convey their feelings and notions in simple and unelaborated expressions."[45] His deliberate extension of the subject matter of poetry beyond the norms of neoclassic decorum, which would not have countenanced an idiot boy as a subject appropriate for a serious poem, camouflages his legitimation of the socioeconomic system that requires "lower orders of society" for its continued functioning. Attention to their domestic affections, to their feelings expressed in unpretentious and unelaborated simplicity displaces effectively the material existence of Wordsworth's subjects of which his text will not or cannot speak.

Wordsworth's humanitarian sympathy with outcasts reflects the widespread sentimental desire among writers of the second half of the eighteenth century to use literature to reform and ennoble readers and spectators. Richard Cumberland, for example, the author of the successful stage play *The West Indian* (1771), explained that he chose to depict victims of society, those who had been usually ridiculed or abused on the stage, and "endeavored to present them in such lights, as might tend to reconcile the world to them, and them to the world." He also saw in such characters an opportunity for greater originality and variety than found in polished society. He therefore resolved "either to dive into the lower class of men, or betake [him]self to the out-skirts of the empire; the center is too equal and refined for such [comic] purpose."[46]

Wordsworth, like Cumberland, probably hoped to reconcile society and its victims while also introducing novelty and variety into his lyrical ballads. His compassionate choice of society's outcasts gave prominence to the sovereign author-subject who displays in his subjects "the essential passions of the heart" in the "plainer and more emphatic language" found in "low and rustic life." Having discovered "what is really important," the poet-author nourishes the feelings connected with important subjects, certain that "the understanding of the being to whom we address ourselves . . . must necessarily be in some degree enlightened, his taste exalted, and his affections ameliorated." Thus the poet is a man speaking to men of the "great and universal passions of men, the most general and interesting of their occupations, and the entire world of nature."[47] This then is the "worthy purpose" for which he chooses his subjects from "low and rustic life," erasing all class differences and specific socioeconomic conditions that were the byproducts of England's unprecedented industrial and territorial expansion.

In Wordsworth's aesthetic ideology, the distinction between poetry that privileges feeling from poetry that privileges incident generates his central shift from the poem to the poet in the most familiar statement of the entire preface. His claim is moreover not limited to the creative act that produced the specific volume, *Lyrical Ballads*, but has become all-inclusive: "all good poetry is the spontaneous overflow of powerful feelings." *Good poetry* is thus distinguished from bad or indifferent poetry that would not exhibit *all three* of the necessary criteria: the poet's *spontaneity* producing a *surplus* (overflow) of *powerful feelings*. Although Wordsworth immediately qualifies his normative assertion by stressing thought, he repeats it without this qualification later in the preface.[48] On this key statement, this "ground-idea," according to M. H. Abrams, Wordsworth "founded his theory of the proper subjects, language, effects and value of poetry." It signals "the displacement of the mimetic and pragmatic by the expressive view of art in English criticism."[49] Or, put another way, it signals the displacement of art anchored in the social relations of a specific time and place by an autonomous art anchored in the individual situated in mental space, in an ideal spot of time. This displacement of mimetic-pragmatic poetics by expressive-subjective poetics takes place in Wordsworth's elaboration of the 1798 Advertisement into the text of the 1800 Preface and achieves its fullest formulation in the passages added to the 1802 version that border on solipsism. (I have in mind especially the passages addressing the two questions: "What is a Poet?" [Poet with a capital *P*] and "What does the Poet?") Such displacement is not politically neutral or innocent.

In a single important moment Wordsworth allows his suppressed socio-political themes to enter overtly into his preface as he explains what he is *not* undertaking, what he is excluding from the purview of his discourse: namely, a "systematic defense" of the theory in which his poems are grounded. Such a systematic treatment, he says, would have to account for the manner in which "language and the human mind act and react on each other." He recognizes that this project could not be accomplished without "retracing the revolutions not of literature alone but likewise of society itself."[50] This moment of recognition is thus the moment of exclusion from his discourse of the investigation of the ways in which the language of poetry (like the language of all social texts) reflects changes not only in literary tradition but also in social relations. Wordsworth's deliberate suppression of the project of retracing the revolutions of literature *and* society in his allegedly revolutionary manifesto contributes to his effectively enshrining a subjectivist individualism that reverberates with an apologetics for silently preserving the existing institutions and class relations.[51]

Of special interest for understanding the conflict between Wordsworth's acknowledged and unacknowledged ideologies is the argument he produces to justify his privileging feeling over action. It is a long but important passage:

> I will not suffer a sense of false modesty to prevent me from asserting, that I point my Reader's attention to this mark of distinction far less for the sake of these particular Poems than from the general importance of the subject. The subject is indeed important! For the human mind is capable of excitement without the application of gross and violent stimulants; and he must have a very faint perception of its beauty and dignity who does not know this, and who does not further know that one being is elevated above another in proportion as he possesses this capability.

From these premises Wordsworth draws the conclusion that his own task

> to produce or enlarge this capability is one of the best services in which, at any period, a Writer can be engaged; but this service, excellent at all times, is especially so at the present day. For a multitude of causes unknown to former times are now acting with a combined force to blunt the discriminating powers of the mind, and unfitting it for all voluntary exertion to reduce it to a state of almost savage torpor. The most effective of these causes are the great national events, which are daily taking place, and the encreasing accumulation of men in cities, where the uniformity of their occupations produces a craving for extraordinary incident which the rapid communication of intelligence hourly gratifies.[52]

Wordsworth concludes that in his efforts to counteract this "general evil" he would be "oppressed with no dishonorable melancholy" had he not "a deep impression of certain *inherent* and *indestructible* qualities of the human mind, and likewise of certain powers in the *great* and *permanent* objects that act upon it which are equally *inherent* and *indestructible.*"[53]

There are three noteworthy points in this remarkable passage. First, Wordsworth implies that his earlier string of positive predicates elevating feeling—vivid sensation, essential passions, elementary feelings—that these states of proper excitement that ennoble the "sensibility of heart" must be distinguished from states of improper excitement that debase the discriminating powers of the mind. He accordingly establishes a hierarchy of sensibility in which "one being is elevated above another" (and, even more importantly, one poet above another) proportionally to his "capability of excitement without the application of gross and violent stimulants." Thus while demoting the old hierarchy that places at its apex literary works depicting noble men engaged in heroic action, Wordsworth promotes a new hierarchy that elevates works cultivating sensibility of heart.

What must the poet-custodians of true feeling guard against so that their minds and the minds of their readers will not be reduced to a "state of almost savage torpor"? The answer leads me to the second point worth noting in Wordsworth's argument. Among a "multitude of causes unknown to former times . . . now acting with a combined force to blunt the discriminating powers of the mind," Wordsworth singles out the most powerful causes as the "great national events, which are daily taking place, and the encreasing accumulation of men in cities." Just when he seems to situate his poetics in the historical moment, Wordsworth emasculates the force of contemporary political events while dwelling only on their impact on mental processes. He leaves unspecified the great national events of the day, presumably so as not unduly to excite the reader's imagination. Thus such contemporary events as battles against the Napoleonic armies abroad, conflict at home over the government's repressive measures to block the spread of revolutionary agitation—the kind of measures that had engaged Coleridge in political lectures and in the publication of the periodical *The Watchman*—these Wordsworth transforms into mass media events that gratify the public's "thirst after outrageous stimulation." Aristocrats of fine feeling among poets and their proper audience are not caught up in social upheavals but concern themselves solely with the "inherent and indestructible qualities of the human mind."

This leads me to my third point about Wordsworth's long passage in defense of the primacy of feeling: namely, that this defense involves him in a dichotomy between high art and low art, between those poets who, like himself, dedicate their efforts to cultivating the "indestructible qualities of the human mind" through "great and permanent objects" and those other vulgar writers, like Monk Lewis, who pander to the readers' taste for "outrageous stimulation." Like all of Wordsworth's dichotomies and distinctions in the Preface, this dichotomy is between asymmetrical alternatives in which one is of infinitely higher value than the other. With telling vehemence Wordsworth unleashes his invective against "frantic novels, sickly and stupid German tragedies, and deluges of idle and extravagant stories in verse" that have driven the "invaluable works of our elder writers" into neglect.[54]

Wordsworth's project, then, may be understood as one of containment, as the construction of a dike against the tide of sensationalist art (low art) whose plots displayed the violent rifts in the "moral cement" of social and familial relations. Popular literature stands condemned while genuine poetry withdraws into the rarified sphere of the inherent and indestructible qualities of the human mind. "If the object which I have proposed to myself were adequately attained," Wordsworth writes, "a species of poetry would be produced, which is genuine poetry; in its nature well adapted to interest mankind permanently. . . ."[55] Wordsworth thus paradoxically distances his new poetics from the lower classes from whom, as a revolutionary move, he proposed to draw his literary subjects.

In short, Wordsworth's acknowledged ideology commits him to the antihierarchical, antiauthoritarian stance of democratizing poetry by assigning feeling the key role in the poet's act of creation, the selection of subject matter, and the effect on the reader. The gaps, dissonances, and contradictions in his discourse, however, reveal his unacknowledged ideology that promotes a hierarchy of feeling that masks his complicity with a repressive and exploitative socioeconomic system. To pay attention to the covert as well as the overt details of his argument shows how conflict-laden was Wordsworth's production of what Romantic critics have generally regarded as a cohesive revolutionary manifesto announcing the new poetics of English Romanticism.

4

Both Wordsworth and Schiller assign a key role to the poet in effecting (in Schiller's words) a "complete revolution" in man's "whole way of feeling" ("einer totalen Revolution in seiner ganzen Empfindungsweise") without which "he could not even find himself *on the way* to the ideal."[56] But let us not overlook a significant difference: Schiller defines the poet's vocation for his time as elevating the real to the ideal, whereas Wordsworth defines it in depicting the ideal within the real, believing that it is "in the very world which is the world/ Of all of us," that "in the end,/ We find our happiness, or not at all."[57] Despite this difference, both *Naive and Sentimental Poetry* and the Preface to the *Lyrical Ballads* can be seen as complementary defining statements of Romantic aesthetics. The language of both texts displays the ideological tension between their commitment to revolutionizing the individual sensibility and to maintaining the social equilibrium that their arguments reinforce.

Notes

1. Michel Foucault, *Language, Counter-Memory, Practice*, trans. Donald F. Bouchard and Sherry Simon (Ithaca: Cornell University Press, 1977), p. 153.

2. M. H. Abrams, *Natural Supernaturalism: Tradition and Revolt in Romantic Literature* (New York: Norton, 1971), p. 338. "Apocalypse by Imagination" is Abrams's subheading of chapter 6, section 2.

3. Ibid, p. 338.

4. Georg Lukács, *Probleme der Ästhetik* (Neuwied and Berlin: Luchterland, 1969), p. 47.

5. Pierre Macherey, *A Theory of Literary Production*, trans. Geoffrey Wall (London: Routledge and Kegan Paul, 1978), p. 84.

6. Catherine Belsey, "Constructing the Subject: Deconstructing the Text," in *Feminist Criticism and Social Change*, ed. Judith Newton and Deborah Rosenfelt (New York: Methuen, 1985), p. 46. It is worth noting that Destutt de Tracy first coined the

term *idéologie* in 1796 as a synonym for "science of ideas" and developed the concept fully precisely during the period that Schiller and Wordsworth were formulating their Romantic manifestoes. Because of their ideological commitment to the liberalism of a free press, individual liberties, and representative assemblies, Tracy and his circle were attacked by Napoleon as "Windbags and ideologues who have always fought the existing authority" (Emmet Kennedy, "'Ideology' from de Tracy to Marx," *Journal of the History of Ideas* 40 [1979]: 358). For other recent discussions of ideology, see especially the full-length studies of Jorge Larrain, *The Concept of Ideology* (Athens: University of Georgia Press, 1979); David McLellan, *Ideology*, Concepts in Social Thought (Minneapolis: University of Minnesota Press, 1986); John B. Thompson, *Studies in the Theory of Ideology* (Cambridge: Polity Press, 1984).

7. Sacvan Bercovitch, "The Problem of Ideology in American Literary History," *Critical Inquiry* 12 (1986): 637.

8. Jerome J. McGann, *The Romantic Ideology: A Critical Investigation* (Chicago: University of Chicago Press, 1983), pp. 70, 135.

9. Gayatri Chakravorty Spivak, "Politics of Interpretation," *Critical Inquiry* 9 (1982): 259.

10. The treatise first appeared in Schiller's journal *Die Horen* in three installments: the first on the naive in November 1795, the second on sentimental poets in December 1795, and the conclusion in January 1796.

11. Friedrich Schiller, *Werke*, Nationalausgabe, ed. Julius Petersen et al., 17 vols. to date (Weimar: Hermann Böhlaus Nachfolger, 1943–), 28:98.

12. Ibid.

13. Ibid., 22:268.

14. Ibid., 22:1066.

15. Ibid., 22:107.

16. Ibid., 22:106.

17. Ibid., 20:437.

18. Ibid., 20:433–44.

19. For a fuller explication of Schiller's argument, see Lore Metzger, *One Foot in Eden: Modes of Pastoral in Romantic Poetry* (Chapel Hill: University of North Carolina Press, 1986), chapter 1.

20. *Werke*, 20:441, 452.

21. Ibid., 22:260.

22. Ibid., 22:256. Leonard Willoughby, who first drew attention to this connection between Wordsworth and Schiller in 1937, has shown that Wordsworth probably had his attention drawn to Schiller's review of Bürger's *Gedichte* by Coleridge, who read the *Jenaische Allgemeine Zeitung* in which it appeared in 1791 (Willoughby, "English Romantic Criticism or Fancy of the Imagination," in *Weltliteratur, Festgabe für Fritz Strich*, ed. Walter Muschg and Emil Staiger [Bern: Francke Verlag, 1952], pp. 155–76).

23. Friedrich Schiller, *On the Aesthetic Education of Man, in a Series of Letters*, ed. and trans. Elizabeth M. Wilkinson and Leonard A. Willoughby (Oxford: At the Clarendon Press, 1967), 5.2. (Hereafter cited as *Aesthetic Letters*. Numerals refer to letter and paragraph, as numbered in this edition.)

24. *Werke*, 20:428.

25. Schiller's motto appeared only in the first installment of the *Aesthetic Letters* published in the *Horen* in January 1795 and was omitted in his later republication of the treatise in *Kleinere prosaische Schriften* (1801).

26. *Werke*, 20:451–52.

27. Ibid., 20:428.

28. Ibid.

29. Louis Althusser, "Ideology and Ideological State Apparatuses," in *Lenin and Philosophy*, trans. Ben Brewster (New York: Monthly Review Press, 1971), p. 182.

30. *Aesthetic Letters*, 5.3.

31. *Werke*, 20:428.

32. Ibid., 20:438.

33. Ibid., 20:503.

34. Ibid., 27:67.

35. Bertolt Brecht, *Arbeitsjournal, 1938–1955*, ed. Werner Hecht ([Berlin]: Aufbau-Verlag, [1977]), pp. 436–37.

36. *The Prose Works of William Wordsworth*, ed. W.J.B. Owen and Jane Worthington Smyser, 3 vols. (Oxford: At the Clarendon Press, 1974), 1:116.

37. Ibid., 1:118.

38. Ibid., 1:122, 124.

39. Ibid., 1:124; emphasis added.

40. *The Poetical Works of William Wordsworth*, 2nd ed., Ernest de Selincourt, 5 vols. (Oxford: At the Clarendon Press, 1952), 2:513.

41. *Brecht on Theatre*, ed. and trans. John Willett (New York: Hill and Wang, 1964), p. 145.

42. *The Letters of William and Dorothy Wordsworth: The Early Years, part 1, 1787–1805*, 2nd ed., ed. Ernest de Selincourt, rev. Chester L. Shaver (Oxford: At the Clarendon Press, 1967), p. 315.

43. Ibid., p. 313.

44. Ibid., p. 314.

45. *Prose Works*, 1:124.

46. Joseph W. Donohue, Jr., *Dramatic Character in the English Romantic Age* (Princeton: Princeton University Press, 1970), pp. 99–100.

47. *Prose Works*, 1:126, 144.

48. See *Prose Works*, 1:148.

49. M. H. Abrams, *The Mirror and the Lamp: Romantic Theory and Critical Tradition* (1953; rpt., New York: Norton, 1958), pp. 21–22.

50. *Prose Works*, 1:120.

51. Cf. Wordsworth's interesting comparison of the danger of revolution in the England of 1817 with that of 1794. Wordsworth is confident in 1817 that a workers' rebellion can be suppressed and defends the government's renewed suspension of the Habeas Corpus Act. He attributes the increasing polarization of classes to the attrition of "moral cement" and "personal feeling" that in the idyllic days of his youth had attached "Farmers to their Landlords, and labourers to their Farmers who employed them." In 1817 he is an "alarmist" because he sees clearly that "the principal ties which kept the different classes of society in a vital and harmonious dependence upon each other have, within these 30 years either been greatly impaired or wholly dissolved. Everything has been put up to market and sold for the highest price it would bring" (*The Letters of William and Dorothy Wordsworth: The Middle Years, part 2, 1812–1820*, 2nd ed., ed. Ernest de Selincourt, rev. Mary Moorman and Alan G. Gill [Oxford: At the Clarendon Press, 1970], p. 375). By focusing on the universal desire for material possessions rather than on specific class relations, Wordsworth could propose a moral solution to the socioeconomic crisis he diagnosed which, like disinterested aesthetic solutions, unwittingly provided, then as now, a humanistic veneer for exploitative institutions.

52. *Prose Works*, 1: 128.

53. Ibid., 1:130; emphasis added.

54. Ibid., 1:128.
55. Ibid., 1:158.
56. *Aesthetic Letters*, 27.1.
57. *The Prelude*, ed. Ernest de Selincourt, 2nd ed. rev. Helen Darbishire (Oxford: At the Clarendon Press), 1805 text, 10.726–728.

"Persecutions of the Infinite"

De Quincey's "System of the Heavens as Revealed by Lord Rosse's Telescopes" as an Inquiry into the Sublime

ROBERT PLATZNER

In the history of creative misreadings, none, I think, is more spectacular (in a very literal sense) or more revealing than that provided by Thomas De Quincey in an essay entitled "System of the Heavens as Revealed by Lord Rosse's Telescopes." De Quincey's essay purports to be a review of a contemporary work of popular astronomy, one that surveys the achievements of the two Herschels and describes the present state of astronomical projections of galactic dimensions and velocities. De Quincey had little direct knowledge of his subject—most of what he relates is clearly derived from reading the book under review—but he does convey its principal message clearly enough: namely, that the perfected telescope has revealed a universe more vast and more perfectly visualisable than that of Galileo or Newton. What De Quincey really wants to communicate to his readers, however, and succeeds in doing only by setting aside the data that form the basis of his exposition, is a contrary hypothesis: that in imaginative terms the universe has grown far beyond human powers of mensuration, that it has become once again what it was for Burnet's contemporaries, an alien monstrosity that human consciousness labors in vain to comprehend or represent. By altering his received "text" De Quincey has done more than simply expropriate and then misrepresent his sources, however; he has also, and more importantly, afforded us a glimpse of an aesthetic and a genre undergoing radical change. This genre is that of the meditative lyrical essay, as it descends to De Quincey from two of his favorite authors, Sir Thomas Browne and Jeremy Taylor; the literary esthetic I have in mind is that of the Sublime, as interpreted for De Quincey by both Burke and Kant. In each instance, De Quincey's departures spring from a strategy of psychological and linguistic inversion (and perhaps subversion), through which all direct or extrapolative data are seen as artifacts of consciousness and language. De Quincey is not alone, of course, among Romantic visionaries, in a commitment to the internalization of narrative or the transformation of subject-object relations.[1] What is peculiar to this essay, as well as many of De Quincey's experiments in "impassioned" prose, is an apparent determination to present the universe of the "new philosophy" and the complex ideology of the Sublime as a single and deeply personal act of heightened consciousness and rhetoric, a construct as unstable as it is subjective.

De Quincey's point of imaginative departure from his expository subject, and his principal emblem of the imagination's "esemplastic" powers, is the telescope—the third Earl of Rosse's new and improved two-ton telescope—through which previously imperceptible, or blurred nebulae could now be sighted with increased resolution, and the number of stars computed with greater accuracy. Comparing Lord Rosse to Columbus and Augustus Caesar, De Quincey concludes that astronomy has uncovered the existence of "immeasurable worlds," of a sidereal universe, whose "frightful magnitude" at first stuns, then elevates the beholding mind:

> Great is the mystery of space, greater is the mystery of time; either mystery grows upon man as man himself grows, and either seems to be a function of the godlike which is in man. In reality, the depths and the heights which are in man—the depths by which he searches, the heights by which he aspires—are but projected and made objective externally in the three dimensions of space which are outside of him. He trembles at the abyss into which his bodily eyes look down or look up, not knowing that abyss to be, not always consciously suspecting it to be, but, by an instinct written in his prophetic heart, feeling it to be, boding it to be, fearing it to be, and sometimes hoping it to be the mirror to a mightier abyss that will one day be expanded in himself. Even as to the sense of space, which is the lesser mystery than time, I know not whether the reader has remarked that it is one which swells upon man with the expansion of his mind, and that it is probably peculiar to the mind of man. An infant of a year old, or oftentimes even older, takes no notice of a sound, however loud, which is a quarter of a mile removed or even in a distant chamber; and brutes, even of the most enlarged capacities, seem not to have any commerce with distance: distance is probably not revealed to them except by a *presence*,—viz., by some shadow of their own animality,—which, if perceived at all, is perceived as a thing *present* to their organs. An animal desire or a deep animal hostility may render sensible a distance which else would not be sensible, but not render it sensible as a distance. Hence perhaps is explained, and not out of any self-oblivion from higher enthusiasm, a fact that often has occurred, of deer, or hares, or foxes, and the pack of hounds in pursuit, chaser and chased, all going headlong over a precipice together. Depth or height does not readily manifest itself to *them*; so that any *strong* motive is sufficient to

overpower the sense of it. Man only has a natural function for expanding on an illimitable sensorium, the illimitable growths of space. Man, coming to the precipice, reads his danger; the brute perishes; man is saved, and the horse is saved by his rider.[2]

It is at this moment that De Quincey's reflections cease to have any direct connection to nineteenth-century astronomical technology; the lens through which he is gazing upon the galaxies is almost entirely internal, and as a consequence his meditation of the stars takes on another more fearful life of its own. The anxiety evident in the passage quoted above—a recurrent note, incidentally, and expressed intensely—is not simply a reflex of intellectual dislocation brought on by the scientific revolution. Admittedly, the sight of astronomical bodies, whose size and position in space can be measured only in relative terms, does disconcert De Quincey, but the focal point of his anxiety lies elsewhere. What arouses De Quincey's mind to the point of metaphysical terror—and not coincidentally to the point of sublime vision—is the sudden appearance of an "abyss" where the divine sensorium of Newton once stood. The final absence from this newly perceived cosmos of any determinate frame or limit to perception and the internal reflection of that abyss within, a nightmare of the infinity of both space and consciousness, turns De Quincey's initially exultant response to this sudden expansion of human knowledge toward despair. The "precipice" before the abyss toward which the enlightened imagination proceeds almost irresistibly is just one of a number of threshold images De Quincey projects onto the beckoning void, but each time this image or its cognate appears one senses an enormous fear that the threshold will not deter the mind in flight, that at some point consciousness will pass over the brink into an unconditioned world where the "shadow" of our own animality will no longer provide a mooring point to identity.

As any reader of the *Confessions of an English Opium Eater* can testify, this is not the first time De Quincey has been assailed by a vision of "illimitable" space; one of the chief "pains" of opium is a shattered or infinitely expansive sense of space-time, registered upon the senses as an endless sequence of ballooning structures or a dizzying passage through labyrinthine dream-chambers.[3] The magnificence of such dreams readily lends itself to the experience of the Sublime, as well as a necessary (from the Burkean point of view) element of terror, what is peculiar to "System of the Heavens" and its escalating dream structures, however, is that within the essay itself (or within the authorial consciousness) no external inducement—recollections of childhood grief, physical deprivation, or drugs—to sublimity is provided for. The mind itself has now become its own stimulant, and the reflexive process a source both of excitement and, increasingly, torment. By discovering an abyss within that parallels and deepens the abyss without, De Quincey displaces the Pascalian horror of infinite space into the more problematic world of epistemological relation.

Within the relationship of the subliming self and the object-world, the Sublime acquires a degree of imaginative autonomy it did not possess for Burke or his near contemporaries. De Quincey achieves this relative autonomy only by theatrically exploiting the possibilities of extrapolation and free association inherent in the deep fear that nearly all exponents of the Sublime, from Burke through Kant and Wordsworth, have found in images of colossal size and impossible distance.[4] De Quincey is particularly successful in the evocation of sublime emotions that are self-generated and of images that spawn in a dream-like sequence:

> It is the famous *nebula* in the constellation of Orion; famous for the unexampled defiance with which it resisted all approaches from the most potent of former telescopes; famous for its frightful magnitude and for the frightful depth to which it is sunk in the abysses of the heavenly wilderness; famous just now for the submission with which it has begun to render up its secrets to the all-conquering telescope; and famous in all time coming for the horror of the regal phantasma which it has perfected to eyes of flesh. Had Milton's "incestuous mother," and her fleshless son, and with the warrior angel, his father, that led the rebellions of heaven, been suddenly unmasked by Lord Rosse's instrument, in these dreadful distances before which, simply as expressions of resistance, the mind of man shudders and recoils, there would have been nothing more appalling in the exposure; in fact, it would have been essentially the same exposure—the same expression of power in the detestable phantom, the same rebellion in the attitude, the same pomp of malice in the features to a universe seasoned for its assaults.
>
> The reader must look to Dr. Nichol's book, at page 51, for the picture of this abominable apparition; but then, in order to see what I see, the obedient reader must do what I tell him to do. Let him, therefore, view the wretch upside down. If he neglects that simple direction, of course I don't answer for any thing that follows: without any fault of mine my description will be unintelligible. This inversion being made, the following is the dreadful creature that will then reveal itself:—
>
> *Description of the Nebula in Orion, as forced to show out by Lord Rosse.*— You see a head thrown back, and raising its face, (or eyes, if eyes it had,) in the very anguish of hatred, to some unknown heavens. What *should* be its skull wears what might be an Assurian tiara, only ending behind in a floating train. This head rests upon a beautifully developed neck and

> throat. All power being given to the awful enemy, he is beautiful where he pleases in order to point and envenom his ghostly ugliness. The mouth, in that stage of the apocalypse which Sir John Herschel was able to arrest in his eighteen-inch mirror, is amply developed. Brutalities unspeakable sit upon the upper lip, which is confluent with a snout; for separate nostrils there are none. Were it not for this one defect of nostrils, and, even in spite of this defect, (since, in so mysterious a mixture of the angelic and the brutal, we may suppose the sense of odor to work by some compensatory organ,) one is reminded by the phantom's attitude of a passage, ever memorable, in Milton—that passage, I mean, where Death first becomes aware, soon after the original trespass, of his own future empire over man.[5]

De Quincey's stratagem proposes a succession of imaginative surrogates, self-consciously artifacted images of a sublime "entity" that cannot be "resolved" into any single or stable image. What De Quincey definitely is not doing is simply peopling the void or creating his own sub-Miltonic mythology of Space and Death. Instead, he alludes to Milton's horrific figure as a means of establishing, at this moment, what the entire essay reminds us of repeatedly: namely, the mythological character of all images, from whatever source, projecting onto and out of the "abyss."

To avoid confusion between the imaged construct and the thing, De Quincey notes with particular emphasis how the mind recoils in the presence of such "power" and such "dreadful distances." De Quincey discerns a reflex of imaginative dissociation here, as surely as an impulse of identification. Because such an image can arouse feelings of dread and persecution, it raises some interesting psychoanalytic questions about the role of the Sublime in the "economy" of De Quincey's emotional life, but for the present it will suffice to identify this death's-head phantasm as a figured displacement of a reality whose transcendence is experienced as distance and fear. Therefore, the sense of the Sublime is partly a function of that resistance which the authorial consciousness displays in the presence (portrayed, paradoxically, as a malicious mask without a face) of that transcendence. In an earlier paragraph, De Quincey had noted that before seeing Lord Rosse's diagram of the Orion constellation—the putative "object" of De Quincey's free associations—his most forceful mental picture of the Sublime centered on a Memnon's head, in whose gaze he had found an eternal peace and love too vast and formless to be comprehended. Now, a new and even more visionary "head" has taken Memnon's place, and accompanying that shift in imagery is a perceptible shift in feeling-tone. It is "malice," more than any other imagined attribute, that characterizes this new surrogate of the ineffable; that much De Quincey intuits almost immediately, and by repeating that notion over and over again and describing this figure as poised for an "assault," he accustoms us to the correlative notion of its final unintelligibility. For whatever this sublime entity may be in ontological fact, its phenomenal character alienates the very consciousness that seeks to grasp it. Confined to the intermediate data of that consciousness, we are not permitted the privilege of peering behind the mask. We are compelled to acknowledge the inadequacy of the contrived rhetorical trope by which this constellation of fear is made evident. De Quincey offers no escape from this spectre, either, because its existence is a function of the same reflexive process by which it might be dispelled.

Thus, the metamorphosis of this figure in the passage that follows, reminds us that the power to invoke images of sublimity is never, for De Quincey, equal to the power to control them:

> But the lower lip, which is drawn inwards with the curve of a conch shell,—O, what a convolute of cruelty and revenge is *there*! Cruelty!—to whom? Revenge!—for what? Ask not, whisper not. Look upwards to other mysteries. In the very region of his temples, driving itself downwards into his cruel brain and breaking the continuity of his diadem, is a horrid chasm, a ravine, a shaft, that many centuries would not traverse, and it is serrated on its posterior wall with a harrow that perhaps is partly hidden. From the anterior wall of this chasm rise, in vertical directions, two processes—one perpendicular, and rigid as a horn, the other streaming forward before some portentous breath. What these could be seemed doubtful; but now, when further examinations by Sir John Herschel, at the Cape of Good Hope, have filled up the scattered outline with a rich umbrageous growth, one is inclined to regard them as the plumes of a sultan. Dressed he is, therefore, as well as armed. And finally comes Lord Rosse, that glorifies him with the jewelry of stars. He is now a vision "to dream of, not to tell;" he is ready for the worship of those that are tormented in sleep; and the stages of his solemn uncovering by astronomy, first by Sir W. Herschel, secondly by his son, and finally by Lord Rosse, is like the reversing of some heavenly doom, like the raising of the seals that had been sealed by the angel in the Revelation.[6]

As this nightmare figure emerges in all its splendor, the reader becomes increasingly, disconcertingly aware of its fictitious character. This is neither a physiognomical nor a topographical metaphor of the cosmic sublime; it is the absence rather than the presence of form that we respond to. Once again, the sublimated image of the abyss appears, in the form of "a horrid chasm, a ravine, a shaft," and once again the mind is out of its depth. Where consciousness falls far short of any reliable apprehension of the objects of perception, acute anxiety follows, and for De Quincey the supreme expression of anxiety is the Apocalypse—but here with a difference. The "raising of the seals" signals not the end of the material world but rather the revulsive awakening of consciousness to an ambivalent state of *agnosis*. For what repels the authorial imagination, as this vision unfolds, is not the stellar "reality" of Orion, but instead its prefiguration in the mind, its "textualized" image, and one that can be achieved only by holding the astronomer's drawing upside down! Such inversion and internalization of the object of sublimity is never experienced by De Quincey as a release from the object-world and its varied persecutions—quite the opposite. By drawing this object of hideous grandeur within, De Quincey merely sets the stage for an involuted drama of phenomenological pursuit and recoil, but where the object of attraction and repulsion is a "phantasm," or simply consciousness itself. Having extracted this image from its extrinsic context, having made it his own, so to speak, De Quincey has no choice, seemingly, but to make it a part of the larger dream-world (revealed fragmentedly in both *Confessions* and *Suspiria de Profundis*) that constitutes his interior universe.

Within *that* world, De Quincey's half-personified abyss is quickly absorbed into a larger "mythological" frame of reference, in which distance is translated into "exile" and personification of will is attributed to an absent Father, a *Deus absconditus*, whose withdrawal leaves the cosmic voyager in a state bordering on metaphysical despair:

> In taking leave of a book and a subject so well fitted to draw out the highest mode of that grandeur which *can* connect itself with the external, (a grandeur capable of drawing down a spiritual being to earth, but not of raising an earthly being to heaven,) I would wish to contribute my own brief word of homage to this grandeur by recalling from a fading remembrance of twenty-five years back a short *bravura* of John Paul Richter. I call it a bravura, as being intentionally a passage of display and elaborate execution; and in this sense I may call it partly "my own," that, at twenty-five years' distance, (after one single reading,) it would not have been possible for any man to report a passage of this length without greatly disturbing[12] the texture of the composition. By altering, one makes it partly one's own; but it is right to mention that the sublime turn at the end belongs entirely to John Paul.
>
> "God called up from dreams a man into the vestibule of heaven, saying, 'Come thou hither and see the glory of my house.' And to the servants that stood around his throne he said, 'Take him and undress him from his robes of flesh; cleanse his vision and put a new breath into his nostrils; only touch not with any change his human heart—the heart that weeps and trembles.' It was done; and, with a mighty angel for his guide, the

man stood ready for his infinite voyage; and from the terraces of heaven, without sound or farewell, at once they wheeled away into endless space. Sometimes with the solemn flight of angel wing they fled through Zaarahs of darkness, through wildernesses of death, that divided the worlds of life; sometimes they swept over frontiers that were quickening under prophetic motions from God. Then from a distance that is counted only in heaven, light dawned for a time through a sleepy film: by unutterable pace the light swept to *them*, they by unutterable pace to the light: in a moment the rushing of planets was upon them; in a moment the blazing of suns was around them. Then came eternities of twilight, that revealed, but were not revealed. To the right hand and to the left towered mighty constellations, that by self-repetitions and answers from afar, that by counter positions, built up triumphal gates, whose architraves, whose archways,—horizontal, upright,—rested, rose,—at altitudes, by spans,—that seemed ghostly from infinitude. Without measure were the architraves, past number were the archways, beyond memory the gates. Within were stairs that scaled the eternities above, that descended to the eternities below: above was below, below was above, to the man stripped of gravitating body: depth was swallowed up in height insurmountable, height was swallowed up in depth unfathomable. Suddenly, as thus they rode from infinite to infinite, suddenly, as thus they tilted over abysmal worlds, a mighty cry arose, that systems more mysterious, that worlds more billowy,—other heights and other depths,—were coming, were nearing, were at hand. Then the man sighed and stopped, shuddered and wept. His overladen heart uttered itself in tears; and he said, 'Angel, I will go no farther; for the spirit of man aches with this infinity. Insufferable is the glory of God. Let me lie down in the grave from the persecutions of the infinite; for end, I see, there is none.' And from all the listening stars that shone around issued a choral voice, 'The man speaks truly; end there is none, that ever yet we heard of.' 'End is there none?' the angel solemnly demanded. 'Is there, indeed, no end? and is this the sorrow that kills you?' But no voice answered, that he might answer himself. Then the angel threw up his glorious hands to the heaven of heavens, saying, 'End is there none to the universe of God? Lo, also, there is no beginning.' "[7]

De Quincey's coyness in attributing this concluding vision to Jean Paul, or rather in portraying it as a subtext with respect to the original, is an understandably defensive gesture. De Quincey's sense of the indiscretion he is committing at this climactic point in his argument—an indiscretion that is both personal and philosophical—must have necessitated the forging of a creative alibi. This bravura exercise in rhetorical sublimity is more than half his own; he has transposed, condensed, re-written and (most importantly) rethought Jean Paul's fable—as anyone can tell by comparing De Quincey's earlier and more literal translation with this version—

reshaping it to his own visionary argument.[8] The essence of that argument is distilled for us at the very end of this "flight:" there is neither beginning nor ending, there is no finite understanding at all, in our quest of the infinite (whether of Nature or of the Mind). The cry that escapes the lips of the visionary is either expressive of or similar to the anguish that mystics of virtually every culture experience in their longing to confront, or achieve identity with, the imagined source of their being. Drawing upon a rhetoric that is both scriptural and kabbalistic, De Quincey thus rehearses the deepest inner fear that can possibly assail the contemplative mind: that no exertion of intellect or imagination will guarantee our entry into the Father's mansion.[9] Indeed, that mansion is represented here through a montaged sequence of Piranesi-like fragments, a dream-structure of mass without definitive form, and one whose dimensions are designed to swallow up the mind that first conceives them. In a mental universe that is both self-replicating and self-alienating, no unity or intimacy can be posited between thought and being; the expansive sublimity of an imagined world, at last, threatens consciousness with dissolution as it is drawn repeatedly to the brink of "unfathomable" and "abysmal" voids. De Quincey's dream of the universe has become a painful sublimate of the unintelligibility of consciousness *to itself*, and every trope or figurative device used to structure thought shatters into a terrifying sensation of weightlessness and sensory deprivation.

Framing this imaginary voyage into the vacuity of internalized sublimity, however, are two ancient literary conventions—the dream vision and the angelic dialogue—that introduce a note of imaginative duplicity into De Quincey's discourse, an intentional duplicity meant to distance its audience from both the authorial consciousness and its inventions, almost like a telescope. While spinning his fable, De Quincey has imposed upon the unfathomable a rudimentary narrative structure of concatenation, image following image, culminating in an exchange between two voices, one expressive of the despair of pursuing the transcendent, the other exultant over its knowability. Both voices are the author's, of course, although not weighted equally, because the dramatic design of this fable encourages identification with only the human, the mortal consciousness. But in literary fact both coexist within the same imaginative frame, and their coexistence defines that transaction upon which the De Quincean form of the Sublime relies. What De Quincey has done here and throughout this essay is make it possible, through a kind of "magnification," to imagine the unimaginable and to observe consciousness "in the act" through a series of self-disintegrating schematizations.

The only "face" the universe possesses, De Quincey insists, is our own; its dimensions are coterminous with the expansion (or explosion) of consciousness or with whatever time-lapse schema language imposes on the process of retelling the experience of that expansion. We can no more speak the language of the unmediated Sublime than we can think the ontology of an unmediated transcendence. In either case, the rhetoric of grandeur is a "raid upon the inarticulate" (in Eliot's phrase) that presupposes the permanent separation of consciousness from the "objects" it desperately invokes.

The power to invoke, however, is also the power to retain, if only for a moment of Coleridgean "suspension"; De Quincey's foray into an imagined cosmos is not simply the voyage of a monad moving about in purely mental seas of thought. There is a perceptible nostalgia for the referent, an "aching" sense of an absent presence whose absence is the occasion of sublime speech and thought. The tension here generates and sustains the incredible proliferating machinery of De Quincean discourse and keeps it from becoming merely eloquent babble. Each successive redrawing of the map of an imaginary heaven, every cartoon projection of the cosmos De Quincey flashes by us, carries the implicit semiological fiction of the "other." Each cosmic fiction attests to the ungrounded conviction that there is *not nothing* "out there," beyond the reach of the last rhetorical sublimation, but rather a formless intuition of being, perceptible only to those who, like De Quincey, possess what might be termed a sensibility of the absolute.[10] God may no longer be in His heaven—Lord Rosse's telescopes appear to have dispelled that fiction as effectively as Galileo's—but at least His attenuated presence can be felt in verbal constructs we erect to contain and memorialize the sensation of metaphysical elusiveness, of a presence experienced as absence. In De Quincey these constructs consist of non-signification, hypertrophic negative modifiers like "unutterable," "insurmountable," and "unfathomable," which, used often enough, endow almost any substantive they come near with a negative valence. It is not the dialectical intervention of Kantian reason, through which critical intelligence seizes upon the essential fictitiousness of sublime discourse, however, that alone provokes a "negative" response to the conventions of sublimity, as much as the exhaustion of a rhetoric designed to feed on immanence and dependent on terms conveying intimacy and interchange between the perceiving, verbalizing mind and the silent but emotive universe. What M. H. Abrams calls the theodicy behind the sublimating movements of Wordsworthian lyricism is simply not there in De Quincey; consequently De Quincey's "usurpation" or interventions of consciousness overriding the evidence of the senses provoke no renovating or unifying response within the imagination.[11] The language of natural grandeur and self transcendence no longer seems appropriate when every metaphor of sublimity that is invoked reveals at last a type of cognitive dissonance that language alone can neither overcome nor conceal successfully. At most, De Quincey can only intimate or cast the shadow of a noumenal realm he, perhaps alone among the major visionaries of the Romantic era, cannot re-enter. At worst, all the experience of the Sublime can precipitate within the subliming consciousness is self-reflexive paranoia in which the imagined object of mental pursuit forever taunts and eludes the mind that first conceived it.

Within this system of self-inflicted persecutions one cannot turn toward the heavens or the phenomenal world at all in hopes of tranquil restoration. Instead, there is only a post-Kantian "turn" toward a radicalized sensibility in which the intense feelings aroused by peering at the universe through Lord Rosse's telescope return to consciousness itself, unable to connect, cognitively or affectively, with the object-world. The rhetoric of sublimity, therefore, has nothing to adhere to in a universe in which the imagination moves "from infinite to infinite"; indeed, once the very sense of magnitude has imploded under the weight of a feeling for infinity, it is no longer possible to encode things or to incorporate them into a system of renovative reflections. In such a universe, Kant's shopping list of sublime effects and occasions appears arbitrary or beside the point,[12] and even when (as in "System of the Heavens") the putative object of sublime contemplation is a conventional "numen"—the heavens—the anxiety that attends all subject-object relations in the sublime "moment," as Thomas Weiskel has argued, attends upon De Quincey's perceptions and induces heightened sensory negation.[13] The extended image with which "System of the Heavens" concludes, that of a mind hurtling through the abyss of space, was not only the most compelling image of metaphysical terror he was capable of invoking but also the most accessible image of negative space or inverse movement his mind was capable of forming. Certainly the frequency of free-fall and flight images in his narratives suggest the presence, in all of De Quincey's literary transactions with dreams, visions, and reveries, of a thoroughly shattered ego whose ambivalence toward all object-relations constantly spawned images of spatial or temporal weightlessness and regression.[14]

Whatever the source of De Quincey's anxiety, however, it alters irreversibly the balance of awe and terror that sustains the cult of Sublime throughout the Age of Sensibility. The comparable shift in psychological focus and aesthetic balance that occurs in the Gothic romance at least a generation before De Quincey's own must suggest that "System of Heavens" is revelatory of something more than one late Romantic's nightmares. This bravura narrative makes it possible to relate De Quincey, philologically as well as psychologically, to that shifting of the philosophical center of gravity which, in Germany as in England, precedes and facilitates the creation of Romantic literature.

Notes

1. The strongest and most consistent case for an internalized mode of narrative as the quintessential form of Romantic discourse is found in Harold Bloom's essay, "The Internalization of Quest Romance" in *Romanticism and Consciousness: Essays in Criticism* (New York: W. W. Norton, 1970), pp. 3–23.

2. *The Collected Writings of Thomas De Quincey* (Edinburgh, 1890), 8:15–16. All quotations from "System of the Heavens" are from this text.

3. For J. Hillis Miller, *The Disappearance of God* (Cambridge: Mass.: Harvard University Press, 1963), pp. 17–80, such passages mark De Quincey as a "post-Romantic" for whom time and space have undergone a radical expansion after the withdrawal of God from a universe of perceptually and metaphysically intelligible dimensions. The object of the present essay is not to prepare a taxonomical label for De Quincey, but rather to offer a phenomenologically precise outline of his imaginative cosmology.

4. See Samuel H. Monk, *The Sublime* (Ann Arbor: University of Michigan Press, 1960), pp. 84–93, 146–47, 158–59, 216. Monk stresses the crucial role played by the concepts of grandeur and infinity in the emergence of a Sublime aesthetic. De Quincey's own familiarity with the classical (as well as Burkean) tradition of *peri hupsous* is well documented. See Frederick Burwick, ed., *Selected Essays on Rhetoric by Thomas De Quincey* (Carbondale: Southern Illinois University Press, 1967), pp. 300–302.

5. "System of the Heavens," pp. 17–20.

6. Ibid., pp. 20–21.

7. Ibid., pp. 32–34.

8. V. A. Deluca, *Thomas De Quincey: The Prose of Vision* (Toronto: University of Toronto Press, 1980), pp. 94–95, briefly discusses De Quincey's reversal of Jean Paul's culminating vision of a Madonna and Child, from which the space voyager derives consolation for the oppressions of the stellar void. De Quincey had translated this piece years before writing "System of the Heavens" and had already assimilated it to his own experience of what Deluca calls the pursuit of "the ever-soaring throne of God" (p. 85).

9. It is this constant separation anxiety that distinguishes De Quincey's nervous effusions of quasi-religious "enthusiasm" from those of a sentimental writer like Sterne, for whom, in *Sentimental Journey*, the sensation of "divinity" that stirs the heart leads irresistibly to a vision of the divine residing in the "great Sensorium of the world." Put another way, for Sterne the power of sensibility is such that the feeling of benevolence and intimacy with the world is a sufficient validation of religious conviction. For De Quincey, conviction and perception have ceased to have any certain correlation.

10. In *Sex and Sensibility: Ideal and Erotic Love from Milton to Mozart* (Chicago: University of Chicago Press, 1980), pp. 260–63, Jean Hagstrum observes, in the context of his discussion of *Die Leiden des jungen Werthers*, just how sensibility—in what he terms its "post-meridian" or decadent form—can be linked to feelings of spiritual "transcendence" and even terror, the very emotions that formed the affective nucleus of the Burkean Sublime. Thus, Werther's morbid excitement in the presence of a "devouring" and emotionally destructive universe finds its erotic parallel in a relationship with death and in a tragic-sentimental love affair. In "System of the Heavens" no such parallelism is possible.

11. See M. H. Abrams, *Natural Supernaturalism: Tradition and Revolution in Romantic Literature* (New York: W. W. Norton, 1971), pp. 88–117.

12. See Immanuel Kant, *Critique of Judgment*, translated by J. H. Bernard (New York: Hafner Press, 1951), p. 100. One should note, however, that Kant's inventory of Sublime images is linked directly to his epistemology of aesthetic experience by a principle of proportionality and by the reflective agency of Reason as it contemplates both infinity and the "insufficiency of our faculties."

Similarly, James Twitchell, *Romantic Horizons: Aspects of the Sublime in English Poetry and Painting, 1770–1850* (Columbia: University of Missouri Press, 1983), argues that a dialectical confrontation with what he terms "liminal" (or perceptual) thresholds lies at the core of the Sublime. The iconography that sustains such moments of threshold consciousness reflects, Twitchell insists, the "shock" of discovering that the limits of the perceivable always stop short of the imaginable, generating in turn a heightened awareness of the incommensurable in Nature and in human thought.

13. See Thomas Weiskel, *The Romantic Sublime: Studies in the Structure and Psychology of Transcendence* (Baltimore: Johns Hopkins University Press, 1976), pp. 23–25, 83–85.

14. See Deluca's diagnosis of De Quincey's psychic myth-world in *The Prose of Vision*, pp. 3–5.

Sensibility
A Select Bibliography of Secondary Sources

SYNDY McMILLEN CONGER
AND PETER V. CONROY, JR.

In compiling this bibliography, we chose works, whatever their specific focus, that seem to contribute to a better general understanding of the concept of sensibility. Most of the works in the list are twentieth-century studies, but we made no decision to exclude earlier items of importance. We did, however, make a conscious effort to present English, French, and German studies in a single list to emphasize the cross-cultural nature of both the original phenomenon and the continuing scholarly attention it attracts. Works by Jean Hagstrum of special significance to the study of sensibility are listed here as well as in the more complete, chronological bibliography of his works that concludes this volume.

Alderman, William. "Shaftesbury and the Doctrine of Benevolence in the Eighteenth Century." *Transactions of the Wisconsin Academy of Sciences, Arts, and Letters* 26 (1931): 137–60.

———. "Shaftesbury and the Doctrine of Moral Sense in the Eighteenth Century." *PMLA* 46 (1931): 1087–94.

Allen, Richard. "Sentimentalism as Soft Romanticism." *Genre* 8 (1975): 119–45.

Appell, Johann Wilhelm. *Werther und seine Zeit*. 4th ed. Oldenburg: Schulze, 1896.

Arciniegas, Germán. "Le Bon Sauvage." *Revue de Paris* 71 (1964): 85–90.

Aron, A. W. "The Mature Goethe and Rousseau." *Journal of English and Germanic Philology* 35 (1936): 170–82.

Atkinson, Geoffroy. *Le Sentiment de la nature et le retour à la vie simple (1690–1740)*. Geneva: Droz; Paris: Minard, 1960.

———. *The Sentimental Revolution: French Writers of 1690–1740*. Edited by A. C. Keller. Seattle: University of Washington Press, 1966.

———. and Abraham C. Keller. *Prelude to the Enlightenment: French Literature 1690–1740*. Seattle: University of Washington Press, 1970.

Auserve, Philippe. "Delille préromantique?" In *Le Préromantisme: Hypothèque ou hypothèse?*, edited by Paul Viallaneix, pp. 114–28. Paris: Klincksieck, 1975.

Avice, Robert. "Le XVIIIe siècle, siècle de la sensibilité." *L'Ecole des Lettres* (9 November 1974): 2–4, 49–51.

Babbitt, Irving. *Rousseau and Romanticism*. New York: Houghton Mifflin, 1919.

Badinter, Elisabeth. *Emilie, Emilie: L'Ambition feminine au XVIIIe siècle*. Paris: Flammarion, 1983.

Baker, Ernest. *The Novel of Sentiment and the Gothic Romance*. Vol. 5. *The History of the English Novel*. 5 vols. 1929. Reprint. New York: Barnes and Noble, 1969.

Baker, Susan Read. "Sentimental Feminism in Marivaux's *La Colonie*." In *To Hold a Mirror to Nature: Dramatic Images and Reflections,* edited by Karelisa Hartigan, pp. 1–10. Washington, DC: University Presses of America, 1982.

Baldensperger, Fernand. *Goethe en France*. Paris: Hachette, 1904.

———. *Bibliographie critique de Goethe en France*. Paris: Hachette, 1907.

Barker, Gerard A. "*David Simple*: The Novel of Sensibility in Embryo." *Modern Language Studies* 12.2 (1982): 69–80.

Bascoul, Abbé Louis. "Femmes sensibles et tendres coeurs au XVIIIe siècle." In *Lectures d'un ignorant*. Paris, 1892.

Bäumler, Alfred. *Das Irrationalitätsproblem in der Asthetik und Logik des 18. Jahrhunderts bis zur Kritik der Urteilskraft*. 1923. Reprint. Darmstadt: Wissenschaftliche Buchgesellschaft, 1967.

Bate, Walter Jackson. *From Classic to Romantic: Premises of Taste in Eighteenth-Century England*. 1946. New York: Harper & Row, 1961.

Bayne, Sheila Page. "Le Siècle en pleurs: L'Emotivité au service de la société." In *Das weinende Saeculum*, pp. 25–30. Arbeitsstelle Achtzehntes Jahrhundert, Gesamthochschule Wuppertal. Edited by Rainer Gruenter. Heidelberg: Winter, 1983. Beiträge zur Geschichte der Lit. und Kunst des 18. Jahrhunderts 7.

Beasley, Jerry. "Romance and the 'New' Novels of Richardson, Fielding, and Smollett." *Studies in English Literature* 16 (1976): 437–50.

Beaujean, Marion. *Der Trivialroman im ausgehenden 18. Jahrhundert*. Bonn: Bouvier, 1964.

Beaunier, André. "Julie, ou les périls de la sensibilité." *Revue Universelle* 19 (1924): 641–65.

Bellessort, André. *Dix-huitième Siècle et romantisme*. Paris: A. Fayard, 1941.

Bernbaum, Ernest. *The Drama of Sensibility*. Gloucester, Mass.: Peter Smith, 1958.

Bernstein, John A. *Shaftesbury, Rousseau, and Kant: An Introduction to the Conflict between Aesthetic and Moral Values in Modern Thought*. Madison, N.J.: Fairleigh Dickinson University Press, 1980.

Birkhead, Edith. "Sentiment and Sensibility in the Eighteenth-Century Novel." *Essays and Studies* 11 (1925): 92–116.

Bloom, Harold. "From Topos to Trope, from Sensibility to Romanticism: Collins's 'Ode to Fear.' " In *Studies in Eighteenth-Century British Art and Aesthetics*, edited by Ralph Cohen, pp. 182–203. Berkeley: University of California Press, 1985.

Boiteux, L. A. *Au temps des coeurs sensibles*. Paris: n.p., 1948.

Böschenstein, Hermann. *Deutsche Gefühlskultur: Studien zu ihrer dichterischen Gestaltung*. Bern: P. Haupt, 1954–66.

———. "Madame de Staël, Goethe und Rousseau: Anmerkungen zu De l'Allemagne." In *Goethezeit: Studien zur Erkenntnis und Rezeption Goethes und seiner Zeitgenossen*, edited by Gerhart Hoffmeister, pp. 145–55. Bern: Francke, 1981.

Boucé, P.-G. *Sexuality in Eighteenth-Century Britain*. Manchester: Manchester University Press, 1982.

Bourgeois, Susan D. *Nervous Juyces and the Feeling Heart: The Growth of Sensibility in the Novels of Tobias Smollett*. New York: Peter Lang, 1986.

Brant, Helmut. "The Emancipation of the Individual in the *Sturm und Drang* Period as a Contribution to European Enlightenment." In *Proceedings of the Eighth Congress of the ICLA*, edited by Bela Köpeczi and György Vajda, pp. 355–60. Stuttgart: Bieber, 1980.

Brassner, Frank. "The Changing Meaning of 'Sensibilité': 1654–1704." *Studies in Eighteenth-Century Culture* 15 (1986): 77–96.

———. "L'Amour, l'esprit, et le coeur: Les Origines de la sensibilité des Lumières au XVIIième siècle." *PFSCL* 1984; 14 (26): 235–52.

Braudy, Leo. "The Form of the Sentimental Novel." *Novel* 7 (1973): 5–13.

Bredvold, Louis I. "Some Basic Issues of the Eighteenth Century." *Michigan Alumnus Quarterly Review* 64.10 (7 December 1957): 45–54.

———. *The Natural History of Sensibility*. Detroit: Wayne State University Press, 1962.

Brenner, Peter J. *Die Krise der Selbstbehauptung: Subjekt und Wirklichkeit im Roman der Aufklärung*. Tübingen: Niemeyer, 1981.

Brissenden, R. F. "'Sentiment': Some Uses of the Word in the Writings of David Hume." In *Studies in the Eighteenth Century*, edited by R. F. Brissenden, pp. 89–107. Toronto: University of Toronto Press, 1968.

———. "The Task of Telling Lies: Candor and Deception in *Sense and Sensibility*." In *Greene Centennial Essays*, edited by Paul J. Korshin and Robert R. Allen, pp. 442–57. Charlottesville: University Press of Virginia, 1984.

———. *Virtue in Distress: Studies in the Novel of Sentiment from Richardson to Sade*. New York: Harper & Row, 1974.

Bronson, Bertrand H. "The Retreat from Reason." In *Irrationalism in the Eighteenth Century*. Vol. 2. *Studies in Eighteenth Century Culture*, edited by Harold E. Pagliaro, pp. 225–38. Cleveland: Case Western Reserve University Press, 1972.

Brown, Marshall. "The Pre-Romantic Discussion of Consciousness." *Studies in Romanticism* 17 (1978): 387–412.

Brüggeman, Fritz. "Der Kampf um die bürgerliche Welt und Lebensanschauung in der deutschen Literatur des 18. Jahrhunderts." *Deutsche Vierteljahrsschrift* 3 (1925): 94–127.

Brunet, G. "Les Thèmes littéraires du préromantisme." *Renaissance* (January 1927): 6–15.

Bystrom, Valerie Ann. "The Abyss of Sympathy: The Conventions of Pathos of Eighteenth and Nineteenth Century British Novels." *Criticism* 23.3 (1981): 211–31.

Campagnac, E. T., ed. *The Cambridge Platonists*. Oxford: At the Clarendon Press, 1901.

Carnochan, W. B. *Confinement and Flight: An Essay on English Literature of the Eighteenth Century*. Berkeley: University of California Press, 1977.

Cassirer, Ernst. *Rousseau, Kant, Goethe: Two Essays*. Princeton: Princeton University Press, 1945.

Chapin, Chester. "Shaftesbury and the Man of Feeling." *Modern Philology* 81.1 (1983): 47–50.

Chérel, Albert. "XVIIIe Siècle et romantisme." *Revue bleue* (1933): 533–37.

Cleary, John. "Madame de Staël, Rousseau, and Mary Wollstonecraft." *Romance Notes* 21.3 (1981): 329–33.

Cohen, Murray. *Sensible Words: Linguistic Practice in England 1640–1785*. Baltimore: Johns Hopkins University Press, 1977.

Columbi, P. "Autant de mouchoirs que de spectateurs. Sensibilita e lacrime nel teatro francese del Settecento." *Atti dell'Academie delle scienze dell'Instituto di Bologna* (1977–78): 237–79.

Conger, Syndy M. "Austen's Sense and Radcliffe's Sensibility." *Gothic* New Series 2 (1987): 16–24.

———. "The Sentimental Logic of Wollstonecraft's Prose." *Prose Studies* 10.2 (1987): 143–58.

———. "The Sorrows of Young Charlotte: Werther's English Sisters 1785–1805." *Goethe Yearbook* 3 (1986): 21–56.

Cotoni, Marie-Hélène. "Images, esprit, sensibilité dans quelques lettres de Voltaire (Août-Septembre 1749)." In *Hommage à Pierre Nardin*, edited by Jean Granarolo, pp. 137–46. Monaco: Belles Lettres, 1977.

Coward, D. A. "Laclos et la sensibilité." *Studies on Voltaire and the Eighteenth Century*. 87 (1972): 235–51.

Cox, Stephen D. *"The Stranger Within Thee": Concepts of the Self in Late-Eighteenth-Century Literature*. Pittsburgh: University of Pittsburgh Press, 1980.

Crane, R. S. "Suggestions Toward a Genealogy of the 'Man of Feeling.'" *ELH* 1.3 (1934): 205–30.

DeBruyn, Frans. "Latitudinarianism and Its Importance as a Precursor of Sensibility." *Journal of English and Germanic Philology* 80 (1981): 349–68.

Dédéyan, Charles. *Jean-Jacques Rousseau et la sensibilité littéraire à la fin du XVIIIe siècle*. Paris: Centre de Documentation Universitaire, 1963.

Deloffre, Frédéric. "Un Mode préstendhalien d'expression de la sensibilité à la fin du 17ième siècle." *Cahiers de l'Association Internationale d'Etudes françaises*. 11 (May 1959): 9–32.

Delon, Michel. "Le Préromantisme en question à Clermont-Ferrand." *Europe* (Février 1973): 209–12.

Dewey, Pascale. "Mesdames de Tencin et de Graffigny: Deux romancières oubliées de l'école des coeurs sensibles." *DAI* 37 (1976): 2218A (Rice University).

Diktor, Wolfgang. *Die Kritik der Empfindsamkeit*. Regensburger Beiträge zur deutschen Sprach- und Literaturwissenschaft. Vol. 5. Bern, Frankfurt/Main: Herbert Lang, 1975.

Donaldson, Ian. "Cato in Tears: Stoical Guises of the Man of Feeling." In *Studies in the Eighteenth Century*, vol. 2, edited by R. F. Brissenden, pp. 377–95. Toronto: University of Toronto Press, 1973.

Doody, Margaret Anne. *A Natural Passion*. Oxford: At the Clarendon Press, 1974.

Dorbec, Prosper. "La Sensibilité plastique et picturale dans la littérature du XVIIIe siècle." *Revue d'Histoire Littéraire de la France* 26 (1919): 374–95.

Doumic, René "Lettres d'un philosophe à une femme sensible; Condorcet et Mme Suard, d'après une correspondance inédite." *Revue des Deux Mondes* 5 (September 1911): 302–25; 5 (October 1911): 835–60; 7 (January 1912): 57–81.

Duffy, Edward. *Rousseau in England: The Context for Shelley's Critique of the Enlightenment*. Berkeley: University of California Press, 1979.

Durant, David. "The Vicar of Wakefield and the Sentimental Novel." *Studies in English Literature* 17 (1977): 477–91.

Dussinger, John A. *The Discourse of Mind in 18th Century Fiction*. The Hague: Mouton, 1974.

———. "The Sensorium in the World of *A Sentimental Journey*." *Ariel E* 13.2 (1982): 3–16.

Dutchie, Elizabeth. "The Genuine Man of Feeling." *Modern Philology* 78 (1981): 279–85.

Dutoit, Marie. "De la sensibilité chez Mme Goeffrin." *Revue Chrétienne* 1 (1898): 357–62.

Eagleton, Terry. *The Rape of Clarissa: Writing, Sexuality, and Class Struggle in Samuel Richardson*. Minneapolis: University of Minnesota Press, 1982.

Ehrard, Jean. *L'Idée de la nature en France dans la première moitié du XVIIIe siècle. 2 vols. Paris: SEVPEN, 1964.*

Empson, William. The Structure of Complex Words. London: New Directions, 1951.

Engelberg, Karsten. "The Sentimental Appeal in Criticism of Shelley, 1822–1860." In *The Romantic Heritage: A Collection of Critical Essays*, edited by Karsten Engelberg, pp. 153–72. Copenhagen: University of Copenhagen Press, 1983.

Erämetsä, Eric. "Sentimental-Sentimentalisch-Empfindsam." In *Annales Academiae Scientiarum Fennicae*, vol. 84, pp. 659–66. Helsinki, n.p., 1954.

———. *A Study of the Word "Sentimental" and of Other Linguistic Characteristics of the Eighteenth Century Sentimentalism in English Literature*. Helsinki: Helsingen Liike Kinjapaino Oy, 1951.

Estève, Edmond. *Etudes de littérature préromantique*. Paris: Champion, 1923.

Etienne, Servais. *Le Genre romanesque en France depuis l'apparition de la 'Nouvelle Héloise' jusqu'aux approches de la Révolution*. Paris: Colin, 1922.

Fabre, Jean. "L'Abbé Prévost et la tradition du roman noir." In *L'Abbé Prévost: Actes du Colloque d'Aix-en-Provence*, edited by Jean Fabre, pp. 39–55. Paris: Editions Ophrys, 1965.

———. *Lumière et romantisme*. Paris: Klincksieck, 1963.

Fairchild, Hoxie Neale. *Religious Trends in English Poetry*. 4 vols. New York: Columbia University Press, 1939–68.

Fayolle, Roger. "Quand? où? et pourquoi la notion de préromantisme est-elle apparue?" In *Pré-romantisme: Hypothèque ou hypothèse?* edited by Paul Viallaneix, pp. 38–56. Paris: Klincksieck, 1975.

Feise, Ernst. "Goethe's Werther als nervöser Charakter." *German Review* 1 (1926): 183–228.

Feugère, Anatole. "Rousseau et son temps. La Littérature du sentiment au XVIIIe siècle." *Revue des Cours et des Conférences*, 36, no. 1 (1934–35), 114–31; 267–80 [poetry]; 333–45 [Marivaux's theater]; 558–68 ["De la comédie larmoyante au drame bourgeois"]; 737–50 [Prévost]; 36, no. 2 (1935), 162–76 [Vauvenargues]; 653–64 ["Diderot: l'apologie des passions fortes"]; 755–68 ["La Bible des âmes sensibles: La Nouvelle Héloise"]; 37, no. 1 (1935–36), 273–88 ["Le Sentiment religieux chez Rousseau"]; 658–72 [Bernardin de Saint-Pierre]; 37, no. 2 (1936), 83–96 ["Le Mal du siècle au XVIIIe siècle"].

Fiering, Norman. "Irresistible Compassion: An Aspect of Eighteenth-Century Sympathy and Humanitarianism." *Journal of the History of Ideas* 37 (1976): 195–218.

Figlio, K. "Theories of Perception and the Physiology of Mind in the Late Eighteenth Century." *History of Science* 13 (1975): 177–212.

Finsen, H. C. "Empfindsamkeit als Raum der Alternative." *Deutschunterricht* 29.4 (1977): 27–38.

Folkierski, Wladyslaw. *Entre le classicisme et le romantisme.* Paris: Champion, 1925.

Foster, James Ralph. *History of the Pre-Romantic Novel in England.* New York: MLA, 1949.

Fox, Christopher, ed. *Psychology and Literature in the Eighteenth Century.* New York: AMS Press, 1987.

François, Alexis. "Romantique: le mot et le sentiment au XVIIIe siècle." *Annales J-J Rousseau* 5 (1909): 199–236.

Friebe, Freimut. "Von Marianne Dashwood zu Anne Elliot: Empfindsame Motive bei Jane Austen." *Anglia* 91 (1973): 314–41.

Friedman, Arthur. "Aspects of Sentimentalism in Eighteenth-Century Literature." In *The Augustan Milieu: Essays Presented to Louis A. Landa*, edited by Henry K. Miller, Eric Rothstein, and G. S. Rousseau, pp. 247–61. Oxford: At the Clarendon Press, 1970.

Frye, Northrop. "Towards Defining an Age of Sensibility." In *Eighteenth Century English Literature: Essays in Modern Criticism*, edited by James L. Clifford, 3rd ed, pp. 311–18. New York: Oxford University Press, 1959.

Fulweiler, Howard W. " 'Here a Captive Heart Busted': From Victorian Sentimentality to Modern Sexuality." In *Sexuality and Victorian Literature*, edited by Don Richard Cox, pp. 234–50. Knoxville: University of Tennessee Press, 1984.

Funke, Maurice R. *From Saint to Psychotic: The Crisis of Human Identity in the Late 18th Century. A Comparative Study of "Clarissa," "La Nouvelle Heloise," and "Die Leiden des jungen Werthers."* New York: Lang, 1983.

Furst, Lilian R. *Counterparts: The Dynamics of Franco-German Literary Relationships 1770–1895.* London: Methuen, 1977.

———. "The Man of Sensibility and the Woman of Sense." *Jahrbuch für internationale Germanistik* 14.1 (1982): 13–26.

Gaiffe, Félix. *Le Drame au XVIIIe siècle.* Paris: Colin, 1910.

Gaillard, Francoise. "Le Préromantisme constitue-t-il une période? Ou quelques réflections sur la notion de préromantisme." In *Le Préromantisme: Hypothèque ou hypothèse?*, edited by Paul Viallaneix, pp. 57–72. Paris: Klincksieck, 1975.

Gallaway, W. F., Jr. "The Sentimentalism of Goldsmith." *PMLA* 48 (1933): 1167–81.

Garber, Frederick. *The Autonomy of Self from Richardson to Huysmans.* Princeton: Princeton University Press, 1982.

Gardner, Elizabeth. "The *Philosophes* and Women: Sensationalism and Sentiment." In *Women and Society in Eighteenth-Century France*, edited by Eva Jacobs et al, pp. 19–27. London: Athlone, 1979.

Garland, H. B. *Storm and Stress (Sturm and Drang).* London: George G. Harrap, 1952.

Gassenmeier, Michael. *Der Typus 'man of feeling.' Studien zum sentimentalen Roman des 18. Jahrhunderts in England.* Tübingen: Niemeyer, 1972.

Gautier, Roger. "Le Thème de l'amour dans le théâtre de Jean-Jacques Rousseau." *Revue d'Histoire du Théâtre* 1986; 38 (3): 281–92.

Gazagne, Paul, ed. *Marivaux par lui-même.* Paris: Seuil, 1954.

Gillot, H. *Diderot l'homme: ses idées philosophiques, esthéthiques et littéraires.* Paris: Courville, 1937.

Giraud, Victor. "La Sensibilité de Mme du Deffand." *Revue des Deux Mondes* 4 (1933): 689–703.

Gläser, Horst. *Das bürgerliche Rührstück*. Stuttgart: Metzler, 1969.

Glotz, Marguerite and Madeleine Maire. *Salons du XVIIIe Siècle*. Paris: n.p. 1945.

Goldberg, Rita. *Sex and Enlightenment: Women in Richardson and Diderot*. Cambridge, England.: Cambridge University Press, 1984.

Graham, John. "Lavater's *Physiognomy* in England." *Journal of the History of Ideas* 22 (1961): 561–72.

Green, F. C. *Literary Ideas in Eighteenth-Century France and England*. 1935. Reprint. New York: Frederick Ungar, 1966.

———. "Medieval and Modern Sensibility." *Modern Language Review* 32 (1937): 553–70.

Greene, Donald. "Latitudinarianism and Sensibility: The Genealogy of the 'Man of Feeling' Reconsidered." *Modern Philology* 75.2 (1977): 159–83.

Grenet, André and Claude Jodry. *La Littérature du sentiment au XVIIIe Siècle*. 2 vols. Paris: Masson, 1971.

Grieder, Josephine. *Translations of French Sentimental Prose Fiction in Late Eighteenth-Century England: The History of a Literary Vogue*. Durham: Duke University Press, 1975.

———. "English Translations of French Sentimental Prose Fiction 1760–1800: A Bibliography." *Bulletin of Bibliography* 29 (1972): 109–21.

Gruenter, Rainer. "Despotismus und Empfindsamkeit: Zu Schillers *Kabale und Liebe*." *Jahrbuch des freien deutschen Hochstifts* (1981): 207–27.

———, ed. *Das weinende Saeculum*. Colloquium der Arbeitsstelle 18. Jahrhundert Gesamthochschule Wuppertal. Heidelberg: Winter, 1983.

Gunther, Hans. "Psychologie des deutschen Pietismus." *Deutsche Vierteljahrsschrift* 4 (1926): 144–78.

Guthke, Karl S. "Zur Frühgeschichte des Rousseauismus in Deutschland." *Zeitschrift für deutsche Philologie* 77 (1958): 384–96.

Habermas, Jürgen. *Strukturwandel der Offentlichkeit: Untersuchung zu einer Kategorie der bürgerlichen Gesellschaft*. Darmstadt, Neuwied: Hermann Luchterhand, 1962.

Hagstrum, Jean H.: "Eros and Psyche: Some Versions of Romantic Love and Delicacy." *Critical Inquiry* 3 (1977): 521–42.

———. "Gray's Sensibility." In *Fearful Joy: Papers from the Thomas Gray Bicentenary Conference at Carleton University*, edited by James Downey and Ben Jones, pp. 6–19. Montreal: McGill-Queen's University Press, 1974.

———. "Johnson and the *Concordia Discors* of Human Relationships." In *The Unknown Samuel Johnson*, edited by John J. Burke, Jr. and Donald Kay, pp. 39–53. Madison: University of Wisconsin Press, 1983.

———. "Pictures to the Heart: The Psychological Picturesque in Ann Radcliffe's *The Mysteries of Udolpho*." In *Greene Centennial Studies*, edited by Paul J. Korshin and Robert R. Allen, pp. 434–41. Charlottesville: University Press of Virginia, 1984.

———. *The Romantic Body: Love and Sexuality in Keats, Wordsworth, and Blake*. Knoxville: University of Tennessee Press, 1986.

———. *Sex and Sensibility: Ideal and Erotic Love from Milton to Mozart*. Chicago: University of Chicago Press, 1980.

———. "'Such, Such Were the Joys': The Boyhood of the Man of Feeling." In *Changing Taste in Eighteenth-Century Art and Literature*, pp. 41–62. Los Angeles: William Andrews Clark Memorial Library, 1972.

———. "Towards a Profile of the Word *Conscious* in Eighteenth-Century Literature." In *Psychology and Literature in the Eighteenth Century*, edited by Christopher Fox, pp. 23–50. New York: AMS Press, 1987.

———. " 'The Wrath of the Lamb': A Study of William Blake's Conversions." In *From Sensibility to Romanticism: Essays Presented to Frederick A. Pottle*, edited by Frederick W. Hilles and Harold Bloom, pp. 311–30. New York: Oxford University Press, 1965.

Hammer, Carl J. *Goethe and Rousseau: Resonances of Mind*. Lexington: University of Kentucky Press, 1973.

Havens, George R. "Pre-romanticism in France." *Esprit Createur* 6 (1966): 63–76.

Hayes, Julie. "A Theater of Situations: Representation of the Self in the Bourgeois Drama of La Chaussée and Diderot." In *The Many Forms of Drama*, ed. Karelisa Hartigan, pp. 69–77. Lanham, Md.: University Presses of America, 1985.

Hazard, Paul. *The European Mind, 1680–1715*. 1935. Reprint. New York: New American Library, 1963.

———. "Les Origines philosophiques de l'homme de sentiment." *Romanic Review* 28 (1937): 318–41.

———. "Un Romantique de 1730: l'abbé Prévost." *Revue de Littérature Comparée* 16 (1936): 1617–34.

———. "Tendances romantiques dans la littérature de la Révolution." *Revue d'Histoire Littéraire de la France* 14 (1907): 555–58.

Hertling, Gunther H. "Die *Werther*-Kritik im Meinungsstreit der Spätaufklärer.: *German Quarterly* 36 (1963): 403–13.

Hervier, Marcel. "Le Préromantisme au XVIIIe siècle." *Année Propédeutique* 6 (1954): 392–410; 478–90.

Hettner, Hermann. *Literaturgeschichte der Goethezeit*. 3rd rev. Edited by Johannes Anderegg. Munich: Beck, 1970.

Hirsch, Arnold. "Die Leiden des jungen Werthers: Ein bürgerliches Schicksal im absolutistischen Staat." *Etudes germaniques* 13 (1958): 229–50.

Hobson, Marian. "Sensibilité et spectacle: le contexte médical du *Paradoxe sur le comédien* de Diderot." *Revue de Métaphysique et de Morale* 82 (1977): 145–64.

Hohendahl, Peter Uwe. "Empfindsamkeit und gesellschaftliches Bewusstsein. Zur Soziologie des empfindsamen Romans am Beispiel von 'La Vie de Marianne,' 'Clarissa,' 'Fräulein von Sternheim,' und 'Werther.' " *Jahrbuch der deutschen Schillergesellschaft* 16 (1972): 176–207.

———. *Der europäische Roman der Empfindsamkeit*. Wiesbaden: Akademische Verlagsgesellschaft Athenaion, 1977.

Hönnighausen, Lothar. "Strukturelle Auswirkungen der 'Sentiment': Vorstellung im Schauspiel des 18. Jahrhunderts." *Anglia* 89 (1971): 439–55.

Hoog, Armand. "Un Cas d'angoisse préromantique." *Revue des Sciences humaines* (1952): 181–97.

Howells, Coral Ann. *Love, Mystery, and Misery: Feeling in Gothic Fiction*. London: Athlone, 1978.

Humphreys, A. R. "The 'Friend of Mankind' (1700–1760)—An Aspect of Eighteenth-Century Sensibility." *Review of English Studies* 24 (1948): 203–18.

Jäger, Georg. *Empfindsamkeit und Roman*. Stuttgart: Kohlhammer, 1969.

———. "Die Wertherwirkung. Ein rezeptionsästhetischer Modellfall." In *Histo-*

rizität in Sprach- und Literaturwissenschaft, edited by Walter Müller-Seidel et al, pp. 389–409. Munich: Fink, 1974.

Jamieson, Ruth K. *Marivaux. A Study in Eighteenth-Century Sensibility.* New York: King's Crown Press, 1941.

Jauss, Hans Robert. "Rousseau's 'Nouvelle Héloise' und Goethe's 'Werther' im Horizontwandel zwischen französischer Aufklärung und deutschem Idealismus." In *Aesthetische Erfahrung und literarische Hermeneutik*, vol. 2, pp. 585–653. Frankfurt/Main: Suhrkamp, 1982.

Jourdain, Eleanor F. *Dramatic Theory and Practice in France 1690–1808.* 1921. New York: Benjamin Blom, 1968.

Kadler, Eric H. "Eighteenth-Century Precursors of Romantic Poetry in France." *Lock Haven Bulletin* 4 (1962): 1–8.

Kaiser, Gerhard. *Aufklärung, Empfindsamkeit, Sturm und Drang.* Vol. 3 of *Geschichte der deutschen Literatur.* Munich: Francke, 1976.

Kaplan, Fred. *Sacred Tears: Sentimentality in Victorian Literature.* Princeton: Princeton University Press, 1987.

Kauffman, Linda. *Discourses of Desire: Gender, Genre, and Epistolary Fictions.* Ithaca: Cornell University Press, 1986.

Kayser, Wolfgang. *Entstehung und Krise des modernen Romans.* Stuttgart: Metzler, 1955.

Kelly, Gary. " 'A Constant Vicissitude of Interesting Passions': Ann Radcliffe's Perplexed Narratives." *Ariel* 10.2 (1979): 45–64.

Kieffer, Bruce: *The Storm and Stress of Language: Linguistic Catastrophe in the Early Works of Goethe, Lenz, Klinger, and Schiller.* University Park: Penn State University Press, 1986.

Kiely, Robert. *The Romantic Novel in England.* Cambridge: Harvard University Press, 1972.

Kory, Odile. *Subjectivity and Sensitivity in the Novels of the Abbé Prévost.* Paris: Didier, 1972.

Langen, August. "Zum Problem der sprachlichen Säkularisation in der deutschen Dichtung des 18. und 19. Jahrhunderts." *Zeitschrift für deutsche Philologie* 83 Sonderheft (1964): 24–42.

Lanson, Gustave. *Nivelle de la Chaussée et la comédie larmoyante.* 2nd ed. Paris: Hachette, 1903.

———. "Les Origines de la Sensibilité au XVIIIe siècle." In *Origines de Premières Manifestations de l'esprit philosophique dans la littérature française de 1675 à 1748.* 1909. Reprint. New York: Burt Franklin, 1973.

Lappe, Claus. *Studien zum Wortschatz empfindsamer Prosa.* Disseration, University of Saarbrücken, 1970.

Larroumet, Gustave. "Origine et développement de la littérature romantique en France au 18e au 19e siècle." *Revue des Cours et des Conférences* 1 (1892–93): 9–14; 68–71; 101–4; 129–35; 206–14.

Larson, David. "The Expansive Sensibility of Michel-Guillaume Jean de Crèvecoeur." *Exploration* 2 (1974): 36–51.

Larthomas, Pierre. *Le theâtre en France au XVIIIe siècle.* Collection "Que sais-je?" Paris: PUF, 1980.

Laufer, Roger. *Style rococo, style des "Lumières."* Paris: Corti, 1963.

Leigh, R. A., ed. *Rousseau after Two Hundred Years*. Cambridge, England: Cambridge University Press, 1982.

Leppinies, Wolf. *Melancholie und Gesellschaft*. Frankfurt/Main: Suhrkamp, 1969.

Lévy, Maurice. "English Gothic and the French Imagination: A Calendar of Translation, 1767–1828." In *The Gothic Imagination: Essays in Dark Romanticism*, edited by G. R. Thompson, pp. 150–76. Pullman, Washington: Washington State Press, 1974.

Lioure, Michel. *Le Drame*. 3rd ed. Paris: A. Colin, 1968.

Loiseau, Hippolyte. "Goethe en France." *Germanisch-romanische Monatsschrift* 20 (1932): 150–66.

Löwenthal, Leo. "Goethe und die falsche Subjektivität." *Goethe Yearbook* 2 (1984): 1–12.

Mabille de Poncheville, A. "Delille et les préludes de la sensibilité romantique." *Revue Critiques des Idées* 23 (1913): 540–57.

MacAndrew, Elizabeth and Susan R. Gorsky. "Why Do They Faint and Die?—The Birth of the Delicate Heroine." *Journal of Popular Culture* 8 (1975): 735–45.

MacFarlane, Alan. *Marriage and Love in England 1300–1840*. Oxford: Basil Blackwood, 1986.

McGuirk, Carol. *Robert Burns and the Sentimental Era*. Athens: University of Georgia Press, 1985.

MacLean, K. "Imagination and Sympathy: Sterne and Adam Smith." *Journal of the History of Ideas* 10 (1949): 399–410.

MacLeod, Jack, "Rousseau and the Epistemology of 'Sentiment'." *Journal of European Studies* 1987 June; 17 (2 [66]): 107–28.

Marshall, David. *The Surprising Effects of Sympathy: Marivaux, Diderot, Rousseau, and Mary Shelley*. Chicago and London: University of Chicago Press, 1988.

Mattenklott, Gert. *Melancholie in der Dramatik des Sturm und Drang*. Rev. ed. Königstein/Ts: Athenäum, 1985.

Matucci, Mario. "Sentiment et sensibilité dans l'oeuvre romanesque de Marivaux." *Cahiers de l'Association Internationale des Etudes Françaises* 25 (1973): 127–39.

Mauzi, Robert. *L'Idée du bonheur dans la littérature et la pensée française au XVIIIe siècle*. Paris: Colin, 1960.

May, Gita. *De Jean-Jacques Rousseau à Madame Roland: Essai sur la sensibilité préromantique et révolutionnaire*. Geneva: Droz, 1964.

Mercier, Roger. "Sur le sensualisme de Rousseau: Sensation et sentiment dans la première partie des *Confessions*." *Revue des Sciences Humaines* 161 (1976): 19–33.

Messinger, Edward. "*Sensibilité,* Time, and Character in Diderot." *Eighteenth-Century Life* 1 (1974): 55–61.

Miller, Nancy K. *The Heroine's Text*. New York: Columbia University Press, 1980.

Miller, Norbert. *Der empfindsame Erzähler: Untersuchungen an Romananfängen des 18. Jahrhunderts*. Munich: C. Hanser, 1968.

Mog, Paul. *Ratio und Gefühlskultur: Studien zur Psychogenese und Literatur im 18. Jahrhundert*. Tübingen: Niemeyer, 1976.

Monglond, André. *Le Préromantisme français*. 2 vols. 1929. Reprint. Paris: Corti, 1965–66.

———. *Vies Préromantiques*. Paris: Editions des Presses Françaises, 1925.

Montandon, Alain. "Laurence Sterne et le développement de l'*Empfindsamkeit* en

Allemagne." In *Proceedings of the Eighth Congress of the ICLA*, edited by Bela Köpeczi and György Vajda, pp. 325–41. Stuttgart: Bieber, 1980.

Moore, C. A. "Shaftesbury and the Ethical Poets in England 1700–1760." *PMLA* 31 (1916): 264–325.

Moravia, S. "The Enlightenment and the Sciences of Man." *History of Science* 18 (1980): 247–68.

Morgan, Charlotte Elizabeth. *The Rise of the Novel of Manners: A Study of Prose Fiction Between 1600 and 1740.* 1911. Reprint. New York: Russell and Russell, 1963.

Mornet, Daniel. *Diderot, l'homme et l'oeuvre.* Paris: Boivin, 1941.

———. Introduction. *La Nouvelle Héloise.* By Jean-Jacques Rousseau. Paris: Hachette, 1925.

———. "Un Préromantique: les "Soirées de mélancolie" de Loaisel de Tréogate." *Revue d'Histoire Littéraire de la France* 16 (1909): 491–500.

———. "Le romantisme avant les romantiques." *Annales de l'Université de Paris* 3 (1928): 125–44.

———. *Le Romantisme en France au XVIIIe siècle.* 2nd ed. Paris: Hachette, 1925.

———. *Le Rousseauisme avant Rousseau.* Paris: Alcan, 1912.

———. *Le Sentiment de la nature en France de Jean-Jacques Rousseau à Bernardin de Saint-Pierre.* Paris: Hachette, 1907.

Mortier, Roland. "Des larmes de la sensibilité aux larmes du sentiment: Baculard d'Arnaud, Diderot, Ballanchi." In *Das Weinende Saeculum,* edited by Rainer Gruenter, pp. 31–37. Heidelberg: Winter, 1983.

———. "Un Magistrat 'Âme sensible': Le Président Dupaty (1746–1788)." In *Studies in Eighteenth-Century French Literature presented to Robert Niklaus,* edited by J. H. Fox, M. H. Waddicor, and D. A. Watts, pp. 151–62. University of Exeter Press, 1975.

———. " 'Sensibility,' 'Neoclassicism,' or 'Preromanticism'?" In *Eighteenth Century Studies Presented to Arthur M. Wilson*, edited by Peter Gay, pp. 155–63. Hanover, NH: University Press of New England, 1972.

———. "Unité ou scission du siècle des lumières?" *Studies on Voltaire and the Eighteenth Century* 26 (1963): 1207–21.

Mounier, Jacques. *La Fortune des écrits de J-J Rousseau dans les pays de langue allemande de 1782 à 1813.* Paris: Presses Universitaires de France, 1980.

Moureau, François. "Les Larmes comiques de Nivelle de la Chaussée." In *Das weinende Saeculum,* edited by Rainer Gruenter, pp. 39–48. Heidelberg: Winter, 1983.

Mullan, John. "Hypochondria and Hysteria: Sensibility and the Physicians." *The Eighteenth Century: Theory and Interpretation* 25.2 (1984): 141–74.

———. *Sentiment and Sociability: The Language of Feeling in the Eighteenth Century.* Oxford: Clarendon Press, 1988.

Müller, Peter. "Epochengestalt und nationales Kolorit des deutschen Sentimentalismus in frühen aesthetischen Schriften Goethes und im *Werther.*" In *Parallelen und Kontraste: Studien zu literarischen Wechselbeziehungen in Europa zwischen 1750 und 1850*, edited by Hans-Dietrich Dahnke, Alexander S. Dmitrijew, and Peter Müller, pp. 108–39. Berlin: Aufbau, 1983.

Mylne, Vivienne. "Sensibility and the Novel." In *French Literature and its Background 3: The Eighteenth Century*, edited by John Cruikshank, pp. 45–61. Oxford: At the University Press, 1968.

Nakagawa, Makoto. "La Vie de Mme Riccoboni et sa sensibilité." *Ochanomizu U Studies* (Tokoyo) 27.1 (1974): 65–83.

Noel, Georges. *Une "Primitive" oubliée de l'école des "Coeurs sensibles": Mme de Graffigny*. Paris: Plon, 1913.

Nokerman, Jean. "La Sensibilité française et le préromantisme." *Lettres romanes* 2 (1948): 199–234.

Oates, J. C. T. *Shandyism and Sentiment*. Cambridge Bibliographic Society, 1968.

Ormant, F. "La sensibilité au XVIIIe siècle." *Enseignement chrétien* 6 (1953): 47–58.

Page, Alex. "Faculty Psychology and Metaphor in Eighteenth-Century Criticism." *Modern Philology* 66 (1969): 237–47.

Park, W. "*Tristram Shandy* and the New 'Novel of Sensibility.'" *Studies in the Novel* 6 (1974): 268–79.

Parnell, Paul. "The Etiquette of the Sentimental Repentance Scene, 1688–96." *Papers in Language and Literature* 14 (1978): 205–17.

———. "The Sentimental Mask." *PMLA* 78 (1963): 529–35.

Pascal, Roy. *The German Sturm und Drang*. Manchester: Manchester University Press, 1953.

Perkins, Merle L. "Destiny, Sentiment, and Time in the *Confessions* of Jean-Jacques Rousseau." *Studies on Voltaire and the Eighteenth Century* 67 (1969): 133–64.

Perry, Ruth. *Women, Letters, and the Novel*. New York: AMS Press, 1980.

Picard, Roger. *Les Salons littéraires et la société française*. New York: 1943.

Pichois, Claude. "Préromantiques, rousseauistes et shakespeariens (1770–78)." *Revue de Littérature Comparée* 33 (1959): 348–55.

Pikulik, Lothar. *"Bürgerliches Trauerspiel" und Empfindsamkeit*. Köln, Graz: Böhlau, 1966.

Pilon, Edmond. "Le Salon de Mme Goeffrin et le sentimentalisme philosophique." In *Portraits français*, vol. 1, pp. 79–93. Paris: n.p., 1904.

Pitou, Alexis. "Les Origines du mélodrame français à la fin du XVIIIe siècle." *Revue d'Histoire Littéraire de la France* 28 (1911): 256–96.

Platzner, Robert L. "Mackenzie's Martyr: The Man of Feeling as Saintly Fool." *Novel* 10 (1976): 59–64.

Poovey, Mary. *The Proper Lady and the Woman Writer: Ideology as Style in the Works of Mary Wollstonecraft, Mary Shelley, and Jane Austen*. Chicago: University of Chicago Press, 1984.

Pupil, Francois. "Aux sources du romantisme: le XVIIIe siècle et les ténèbres." *L'Information d'Histoire de l'Art* (Mars–Avril 1974): 55–65.

Radner, John B. "The Art of Sympathy in Eighteenth-Century British Moral Thought." *Studies in Eighteenth-Century Culture* 9 (1979): 189–210.

Rawson, C. J. "Some Remarks on Eighteenth-Century 'Delicacy,' with a Note on Hugh Kelly's *False Delicacy* (1768)." *Journal of English and Germanic Philology* 61 (1962): 1–13.

Ribble, Frederick G. "The Constitution of the Mind and the Concept of Emotion in Fielding's *Amelia*." *Philological Quarterly* 56 (1977): 104–22.

Richetti, John J. *Popular Fiction before Richardson: Narrative Patterns, 1700–1739*. Oxford: At the Clarendon Press, 1969.

Ridgway, Ronald. *Voltaire and Sensibility*. Montreal: McGill-Queen's University Press, 1973.

Riggan, William. "*Werther, Adolphe,* and *Eugene Onegin*: The Decline of the Hero of Sensibility." *Research Studies* 41 (1973): 252–67.

Rogers, Katharine M. *Feminism in Eighteenth-Century England.* Urbana: University of Illinois Press, 1982.

———. "Sensitive Feminism vs. Conventional Sympathy: Richardson and Fielding on Women." *Novel* 9 (1976): 256–70.

Rogers, Winfield H. "The Reaction Against Melodramatic Sentimentality in the English Novel, 1796–1830." *PMLA* 49 (1934): 98–122.

Rosen, George. "Forms of Irrationality in the Eighteenth Century." In *Irrationalism in the Eighteenth Century*, vol. 2, *Studies in Eighteenth-Century Culture*, edited by Harold Pagliaro, pp. 255–88. Cleveland: Case Western Reserve University Press, 1972.

Rosenberg, Sondra. "Form and Sensibility in *Les Liaisons dangereuses* and *Vanity Fair.*" *Enlightenment Essays* 3.1 (1972): 18–36.

Rosi, Ivana. "Madame Riccoboni: Le inquietudini della sensibilità." *Saqqi* 24 (1985): 329–72.

Rothstein, Eric. *Eighteenth Century Poetry: 1660–1780.* The Routledge History of English Poetry, vol. 3. London: Routledge & Kegan Paul, 1981.

Rousseau, George S. "Literature and Medicine: The State of the Field." *Isis* 72 (1981): 406–24.

———. "Medicine and Literature: Notes on their Overlaps and Reciprocities." *Gesnerus* 43 (1986): 33–46.

———. "Nerves, Spirits and Fibres: Towards Defining the Organs of Sensibility—with a Postscript 1976." *The Blue Guitar* 2 (1976): 125–53.

———. "Science and Literature: The State of the Art." *Isis* 69 (1978): 583–91.

Roussel, Roy. *The Conversation of the Sexes: Seduction and Equality in Selected 17th and 18th Century Texts.* New York: Oxford University Press, 1985.

Runte, Roseann. "Dying Words: The Vocabulary of Death in Three Eighteenth-Century English and French Novels." *Canadian Review of Comparative Literature* 6 (1979): 360–68.

Sagnac, Philippe. "Les Grands Courants d'idées et de sentiments en France vers 1789." *Revue d'Histoire Politique* 2 (1938): 317–41.

Salm, Peter. "Werther and the Sensibility of Estrangement." *German Quarterly* 46 (1973): 47–55.

Sauder, Gerhard. "Bürgerliche Empfindsamkeit?" In *Bürger and Bürgerlichkeit im Zeitalter der Aufklärung*, edited by Rudolf Vierhaus, pp. 149–64. Hiedelberg: Schneider, 1981.

———. *Empfindsamkeit.* Stuttgart: Metzler, 1974.

———. "Subjectivität und Empfindsamkeit im Roman." In *Sturm und Drang*, edited by Walter Hinck, pp. 163–74. Kronberg: Athenäum, 1978.

———. "Sterne's 'Sentimental Journey' und die 'empfindsamen Reisen' in Deutschland." In *Reise und soziale Realität am Ende des 18. Jahrhunderts*, edited by Hans-Wolf Jäger, pp. 302–19. Heidelberg: Winter, 1983.

Scherpe, Klaus R. *Werther und Wertherwirkung: Zum Syndrom bürgerlicher Gesellschaftsordnung im 18. Jahrhundert.* Bad Homburg: Gehlen, 1970.

Schings, Hans-Jürgen. *Melancholie und Aufklärung.* Stuttgart: Metzler, 1977.

Schmidt, Erich. *Richardson, Rousseau, und Goethe. Ein Beitrag zur Geschichte des Romans im 18. Jahrhundert*. Jena, 1875.

Schneider, Jean-Paul. "Science et sensibilité au XVIIIe siècle: essai sur une esthétique du paysage selon H.-B. de Sausurre." *Travaux de Linguistique et de Littérature* 7.2 (1969): 107–31.

Schöffler, Herbert. *Deutscher Geist im 18. Jahrhundert*. Göttingen: Vandenhoeck und Ruprecht, 1967.

———. *Protestantismus und Literatur*. 2nd ed. Göttingen: Vandenhoeck und Ruprecht, 1958.

Schofield, Mary Anne and Cecilia Macheski, eds. *Fetter'd or Free? British Women Novelists, 1670–1815*. Athens: Ohio University Press, 1986.

Schott, Robin M. "Kant's Treatment of Sensibility." *New Essays on Kant*, edited by Bernard den Ouden and Marcia Moen. New York: Peter Lang, 1987.

Schrecker, Hélène. "L'Esprit sensible dans les oeuvres de Marmontel." In *Roman et Lumierès*, edited by Werner Krauss, pp. 182–87. Paris: Editions Sociales, 1970.

Schulz, Dieter. "The Coquette's Progress from Satire to Sentimental Novel." *Literatur in Wissenschaft* 6 (1973): 77–87.

Schumann, Detlev W. "Betrachtungen über den Sturm und Drang." In *Aufnahme—Weitergabe: Literarische Impulse um Lessing und Goethe*, Hamburgische Philologische Studien 56, edited by John A. McCarthy and Albert A. Kipa, pp. 53–89. Hamburg: Buske, 1982.

Selby-Bigge, L. A., ed. *British Moralists*. New York: Bobbs-Merrill, 1964.

Sellier, Walter. *Kotzebue in England*. Dissertation, University of Leipzig, 1907.

Sgard, Jean. "Etat présent des études sur A. F Prévost." *L'Information Littéraire* 27 (1975): 57–61.

———. "Prévost: de l'ombre aux lumières (1736–1746)." *Studies on Voltaire and the Eighteenth Century* 27 (1963): 1479–87.

——— and Michel Gilot. *Le Vocabulaire du sentiment dans l'oeuvre de Jean-Jacques Rousseau*. Geneva, Paris: Slatkine, 1980.

Sheriff, John. *The Good Natured Man: The Evolution of a Moral Ideal, 1660–1800*. University: University of Alabama Press, 1982.

Showalter, English, Jr. "*Sensibilité* at Cirey: Mme du Chatelet, Mme de Graffigny and the *Voltairomanie*." *Studies on Voltaire and the Eighteenth Century* 135 (1975): 181–92.

Sickels, Eleanor M. *The Gloomy Egotist: Moods and Themes of Melancholy from Gray to Keats*. Columbia University Studies in English and Comparative Literature 110. New York: Columbia University Press, 1932.

Smith, I. H. "The Concept *sensibilité* and the Enlightenment." *Journal of Australasian Universities Language and Literature Association* 27 (1968): 5–17.

Smith, Louise Z. "Sensibility and Epistolary Form in *Héloise* and *Werther*." *L'Esprit Créateur* 17 (1977): 361–76.

Smith, Nelson C. "Sense, Sensibility and Ann Radcliffe." *Studies in English Literature* 13 (1973): 577–90.

Sokolsky, Anita. "The Resistance to Sentimentality: Yeats, de Man, and the Aesthetic Education." *The Yale Journal of Criticism* 1.1 (1987): 67–86.

Souriau, Maurice. *Histoire du Romantisme en France*, vol. 1. Paris: Editions Spes, 1927.

Spacks, Patricia Meyer. *The Female Imagination*. New York: Alfred Knopf, 1975.

———. *Imagining a Self: Autobiography and the Novel in Eighteenth Century England*. Cambridge: Harvard University Press, 1976.

Spink, J. S. "A propos des drames de Beaumarchais." *Revue de Littérature comparée* 37 (1963): 216–26.

———. "From 'Hippolyte est sensible' to 'le fatal présent du siècle': the position of 'bienfaisance'." In *The Classical Tradition: Essays presented to R. C. Knight*, edited by H. T. Barnwell, A. H. Divernes, G. F. Evans, F. W. A. George, and Vivienne Mylne, pp. 191–202. London: Grant and Cutler, 1977.

———. " 'Sentiment,' 'sensible,' 'sensibilité': les mots, les idées d'après les 'moralistes' français et britanniques du début du dix-huitième siècle." *Zagadnienia Rodzajow Literackich* 20.1 (1977): 33–48.

Sprague, Allen B. "The Dates of Sentimental and Its Derivatives." *PMLA* 48 (1933): 303–7.

Stanlis, Peter. "Babbitt, Burke, and Rousseau: The Moral Nature of Man." In *Irving Babbitt in Our Time*, pp. 127–54. Edited by George Panichas and Claes Ryn. Washington DC: Catholic University of America Press, 1986.

———. "Burke and the Sensibility of Rousseau." *Thought* (1961): 246–76.

Stanzel, Franz Karl. "Innenwelt: Ein Darstellungsproblem des englischen Romans." *Germanisch-Romanische Monatsschrift* 12 (1962): 273–86.

Starr, George A. "Egalitarian and Elitist Implications of Sensibility." In *L'Egalité*, edited by Léon Ingber, pp. 125–35. Brussels: Bruylant, 1984.

———. " 'Only a Boy': Notes on Sentimental Novels." *Genre* 10 (1977): 501–27.

———. "Sentimental De-education." In *Augustan Studies: Essays in Honor of Irvin Ehrenpreis*, edited by Douglas Lane Patey and Timothy Keegan, pp. 253–62. Newark: University of Delaware Press, 1985.

Steeves, Harrison R. *Before Jane Austen: The Shaping of the English Novel in the Eighteenth Century*. Chicago: Holt, Rinehart, & Winston, 1965.

Stemme, Fritz. "Die Säkularisation des Pietismus zur Erfahrungsseelenkunde." *Zeitschrift für deutsche Philologie* 72 (1953): 144–58.

Stewart, John Hinde. "Sensibility with Irony: Mme de Montolieu at the End of an Era." *Kentucky Romance Quarterly* 25 (1978): 481–89.

Stone, Laurence. *The Family, Sex, and Marriage 1500–1800*. New York: Harper & Row, 1977.

Suhnel, Rudolf. *Tränen im empfindsamen Roman Englands: 'Handkerchiefly feeling' bei Richardson, Sterne, Mackenzie*. Heidelberg: Arbeitsstelle Achtzehntes Jahrhundert Gesamthochschule Wuppertal, 1983.

Swiderski, Marie-Laure. "La Thématique féministe dans le roman sentimental après 1750." In *Aufsätze zum 18. Jahrhundert*, edited by Hans-Joachim Lope, pp. 111–26. Frankfurt: Peter Lang, 1979.

Tave, Stuart M. *The Amiable Humorist*. Chicago: University of Chicago Press, 1960.

Taylor, Samuel S. B. "Rousseau's Romanticism." In *Reappraisals of Rousseau: Studies in Honour of R. A. Leigh*, pp. 2–23. Manchester: Manchester University Press, 1980.

Temmer, Mark. "Jean-Jacques Rousseau's *Confessions* and Gottfried Keller's *Der Grüne Heinrich*." *Revue de Littérature Comparée* 44 (1970): 155–83.

Texte, Joseph. *Jean-Jacques Rousseau et les origines du cosmopolitisme littéraire*. Paris, 1895.

Thompson, L. F. *Kotzebue: A Survey of his Progress in England.* Paris: Champion, 1928.

Todd, Janet. "Reason and Sensibility in Mary Wollstonecraft's *The Wrongs of Woman.*" *Frontiers* 5.3 (1980): 17–20.

———. *Sensibility: An Introduction.* New York: Methuen, 1986.

———. *Women's Friendship in Literature.* New York: Columbia University Press, 1980.

Tompkins, J. M. S. *The Popular Novel in England 1770–1800.* 1932. Reprint. Lincoln: University of Nebraska Press, 1961.

Tornius, Valerian. *Die Empfindsamen in Darmstadt: Studien über Männer und Frauen aus der Wertherzeit.* Leipzig: Seemann, 1910.

Touaillon, Christine. *Der deutsche Frauenroman des 18. Jahrhunderts.* Foreword by Enid Gajek. 1919. Reprint. Bern: Peter Lang, 1979.

Trahard, Pierre. *Les Maîtres de la sensibilité française au XVIIIe siècle 1715–1789.* 4 vols. Paris: Boivin, 1931–33.

———. "La Sensibilité française au XVIIIe siècle." *Revue des Cours et des Conférences* 31.2 (1930): 1–15; 109–23; 227–47.

———. *La Sensibilité révolutionnaire 1789–1794.* 1936. Reprint. Geneva: Slatkine, 1967.

Trousson, Raymond. "J-J Rousseau et son oeuvre dans la presse périodique allemande de 1750 à 1800." *Dix-Huitième Siècle* 1 (1969): 289–310; 2 (1970): 227–64.

Trunz, Erich. "Seelische Kultur: Eine Betrachtung über Freundschaft, Liebe und Familiengefühl im Schriftum der Goethezeit." *Deutsche Vierteljahrsschrift* 24 (1950): 214–42.

Tytler, Graeme. *Physiognomy in the European Novel.* Princeton: Princeton University Press, 1982.

Ulmer, Gregory. "'Clarissa' and 'La nouvelle Héloise.'" *Comparative Literature* 24 (1972): 289–308.

Unger, Rudolf, *Hamann und die Aufklärung.* 2 vols. 1925. Tübingen: Niemeyer, 1963.

Utter, R. P. and Gwendolyn B. Needham. *Pamela's Daughters.* New York: MacMillan, 1936.

Van Bellen, E. C. *Les Origines du mélodrame.* Utrecht: n.p., 1927.

Vance, Christie McDonald. *The Extravagant Shepherd: A Study of the Pastoral Vision in Rousseau's "Nouvelle Héloise." Studies on Voltaire and the Eighteenth Century* 105 (1973).

Van Tieghem, Paul. *Ossian en France.* 2 vols. 1914. Reprint. Geneva: Slatkine, 1967.

———. *La Poésie de la nuit et des tombeaux en Europe au XVIIIe siècle.* Paris: F. Rieder et Cie, 1921.

———. *Le Préromantisme.* Vol. 1. Paris: F. Rieder, 1924. Vol. 2. Paris: La Nouvelle Edition, 1929.

———. "Le Roman sentimental en Europe, de Richardson à Rousseau." *Revue de Littérature Comparée* 20 (1940): 129–51.

———. *Le Sentiment de la nature dans le préromantisme européan.* Paris: Nizet, 1960.

Van Tieghem, Philippe. "La Sensibilité et la passion dans le roman européen au XVIIIe siècle." *Revue de Littérature Comparée* 6 (1926): 424–35.

Vaughan, Larry. *The Historical Constellation of the Sturm und Drang.* New York: Peter Lang, 1985.

Vial, Fernand. *Une Philosophie et une morale du sentiment: Luc de Clapiers, marquis de Vauvenargues*. Geneva: Droz, 1938.

Viallaneix, Paul, ed. *Le Préromantisme: Hypothèque ou hypothèse*? Paris: Klincksieck, 1975.

Viatte, Auguste. *Les Sources Occultes du romantisme*. 2 vols. Paris: Champion, 1980.

Voisine, J. "L'Influence de J-J Rousseau sur la sensibilité littéraire à la fin du XVIIIe siècle: Goethe, *Werther*, Bernardin de Saint-Pierre, *Paul et Virginie*." *L'Information Littéraire* 12 (1960): 38–41.

Wallman, Johannes. *Philipp Jakob Spener und die Anfänge des Pietismus*. Tübingen: Mohr, 1970.

Warner, James H. "'Education of the Heart': Observations on the Eighteenth-Century English Sentimental Movement." *Papers of the Michigan Academy of Science, Arts and Letters* 29 (1943): 553–60.

———. "Eighteenth Century English Reactions to the Nouvelle Héloise." *PMLA* 52 (1937): 803–19.

———. "Emile in Eighteenth-Century England." *PMLA* 59 (1944): 773–91.

Watt, Ian. "Sense Triumphantly Introduced to Sensibility (1961)." In *Jane Austen's "Sense and Sensibility," "Pride and Prejudice," and "Mansfield Park": A Casebook*, edited by B. C. Southam, pp. 119–29. New York: MacMillan, 1976.

———. *The Rise of the Novel*. Berkeley: University of California Press, 1957.

Weber, Peter. *Das Menschenbild des bürgerlichen Trauerspiels: Entstehung und Funktion von Lessings 'Miss Sara Sampson.'* Berlin: Rütten und Loening, 1970.

Weinstein, Arnold. *Fictions of the Self: 1550–1800*. Princeton: Princeton University Press, 1980.

Welz, Dieter. *Der Weimarer Werther: Studien zur Sinnstruktur der zweiten Fassung des Werther-Romans*. Bonn: Bouvier, 1973.

Wieser, Max. *Der sentimentale Mensch. Gesehen aus der Welt holländischer und deutscher Mystiker im 18. Jahrhundert*. Gotha, Stuttgart: F. A. Perthes, 1924.

Willey, Basil. *The Eighteenth Century Background*. 1940. Reprint. London: Pelican Books, 1972.

Williams, David. "Voltaire on the Sentimental Novel." *Studies on Voltaire and the Eighteenth Century* 135 (1975): 115–34.

Williams, Raymond. *Keywords: A Vocabulary of Culture and Society*. New York: Oxford University Press, 1976.

Wilson, Arthur M. "Sensibility in France in the XVIIIth Century. A Study in Word History." *French Quarterly* 13 (1931): 35–46.

Winandy, Rita. "Prévost and Morality of Sentiment." *Esprit Créateur* 12 (1972): 94–102.

Wittmann, Anna. "New Trends in the Form and Function of the Denouement; German *Empfindsamkeit* and *Sturm und Drang*." In *Man and Nature/ L'Homme et la nature*, pp. 101–11. Edmonton, Alberta: Academic Printing, 1984.

Woodbridge, Benjamin. "Romantic Tendencies in the Novels of the Abbé Prévost." *PMLA* 26 (1911): 324–32.

Wright, Walter Francis. *Sensibility in English Prose Fiction 1760–1814: A Reinterpretation*, Illinois Studies in Language and Literature, vol. 22.3-4. Urbana: University of Illinois Press, 1937.

Wunberg, Gotthart. "Sentimentalität. Bemerkungen zum Distanzcharakter ihres Begriffes." *Bildung und Erziehung* 16 (1963): 205–10.

Wuthenow, Ralph-Rainer. "Rousseau im 'Sturm und Drang.'" In *Sturm und Drang: Ein literaturwissenschaftliches Studienbuch*, edited by Walter Hinck, pp. 14–54. Kronberg: Athenäum, 1978.

Wynne, Edith J. "Latitudinarian Philosophy in Fielding's *Amelia*." *Papers of the Missouri Philological Association* 4 (1979): 33–38.

A Chronological List of Works by Jean H. Hagstrum

Books

Samuel Johnson's Literary Criticism. 1952. Reprint. Minneapolis: University of Minnesota Press. Chicago: University of Chicago Press, 1967.

The Sister Arts: The Tradition of Literary Pictorialism and English Poetry from Dryden to Gray. 1958. Reprint. Chicago: University of Chicago Press, 1974.

William Blake Poet and Painter: An Introduction to the Illuminated Verse. 1964. Reprint. Chicago: University of Chicago Press, 1978.

Samuel Johnson. *Sermons*. Ed. Jean H. Hagstrum and James Gray. *The Yale Edition of the Works of Samuel Johnson*, vol. 14. New Haven: Yale University Press, 1978.

Sex and Sensibility: Ideal and Erotic Love from Milton to Mozart. Chicago: University of Chicago Press, 1980.

The Romantic Body: Love and Sexuality in Keats, Wordsworth, and Blake. Knoxville: University of Tennessee Press, 1986.

Eros and Vision: The Restoration to Romanticism. Evanston: Northwestern University Press, 1989.

Articles

"The Sermons of Samuel Johnson." *Modern Philology* 40 (1943): 255–66.

"*La Figlia che Piange* by T. S. Eliot." *English "A" Analyst*, No. 3 (1947): 1–7.

"On Dr. Johnson's Fear of Death." *ELH* 14 (1947): 308–19.

"Johnson's Conception of the Beautiful, the Pathetic, and the Sublime." *PMLA* 64 (1949): 134–57.

"The Nature of Dr. Johnson's Rationalism." *ELH* 17 (1950): 191–205. In *Studies in the Literature of the Augustan Age: Essays Collected in Honor of Arthur Ellicott Case*, edited by Richard C. Boys, reprint, pp. 88–103. Ann Arbor: George Wahr for the Augustan Reprint Society, 1952.

"Some Opportunities for Research in Eighteenth Century Literature." *Newberry Library Bulletin* 3 (1954): 177–88.

"Romantic Skylarks." *Newberry Library Bulletin* 5 (1959): 45–54.

"The Poetry of Stanley Kunitz: An Introductory Essay." *Tri-Quarterly* 1. 3 (1959): 20–26. In *Poets in Progress*, edited by Edward Hungerford, reprint, pp. 38–58. Evanston: Northwestern University Press, 1962.

"William Blake Rejects the Enlightenment." *Studies on Voltaire and the Eighteenth Century* 25 (1963): 811–28. In *Blake: A Collection of Critical Essays*, edited by Northrop Frye, reprint, pp. 142–55. Englewood Cliffs, NJ: Prentice-Hall, 1966.

"William Blake's 'The Clod & the Pebble.'" In *Restoration and Eighteenth Century Literature*, edited by Carroll Camden, pp. 381–88. Chicago: University of Chicago Press, 1963.

"Blake's Blake." In *Essays in History and Literature*, edited by Heinz Bluhm, pp. 169–78. Chicago: Newberry Library, 1965.

"'The Wrath of the Lamb': A Study of William Blake's Conversions." In *From Sensibility to Romanticism: Essays Presented to Frederick A. Pottle*, edited by Frederick W. Hilles and Harold Bloom, pp. 311–30. New York: Oxford University Press, 1965.

"The Rhetoric of Fear and the Rhetoric of Hope." *Tri-Quarterly* 11 (1968): 109–23.

"The Sisters Arts: From Neo-Classic to Romantic." In *Comparatists at Work: Studies in Comparative Literature*, edited by Stephen G. Nichols, Jr., and Richard B. Vowles, pp. 168–94. Waltham, Mass.: Blaisdell, 1968.

"The Fly." In *Blake Essays for S. Foster Damon*, edited by Alvin H. Rosenfeld, pp. 368–82. Providence: Brown University Press, 1969.

"Kathleen Raine's Blake." *Modern Philology* 68 (1970): 76–82.

"Blake and the Sister-Arts Tradition." In *Blake's Visionary Forms Dramatic*, edited by David V. Erdman and John E. Grant, pp. 82–91. Princeton: Princeton University Press, 1970.

"Verbal and Visual Caricature in the Age of Dryden, Swift, and Pope." In *England in the Restoration and Early Eighteenth Century: Essays on Culture and Society*, edited by H. T. Swedenberg, Jr., pp. 173–95. Berkeley and Los Angeles: University of California Press, 1972.

"Dryden's Grotesque: An Aspect of the Baroque in His Art and Criticism." In *Writers and Their Background: John Dryden*, edited by Earl Miner, pp. 90–119. London: G. Bell, 1972.

"'Such, Such Were the Joys': The Boyhood of the Man of Feeling." In *Changing Taste in Eighteenth-Century Art and Literature*, pp. 41–62. Los Angeles: William Andrews Clark Memorial Library, 1972.

"Babylon Revisited, or the Story of Luvah and Vala." In *Blake's Sublime Allegory*, edited by Stuart Curran and Joseph Anthony Wittreich, Jr., pp. 101–18. Madison: University of Wisconsin Press, 1973.

"Christ's Body." In *William Blake: Essays in Honour of Sir Geoffrey Keynes*, edited by Morton D. Paley and Michael Phillips, pp. 129–56. Oxford: At the Clarendon Press, 1973.

"Gray's Sensibility." In *Fearful Joy: Papers from the Thomas Gray Bicentenary Conference at Carleton University*, edited by James Downey and Ben Jones, pp. 6–19. Montreal: McGill-Queen's University Press, 1974.

"Eros and Psyche: Some Versions of Romantic Love and Delicacy." *Critical Inquiry* 3 (1977): 521–42.

"Blake and British Art." In *Images of Romanticism: Verbal and Visual Affinities*, edited by Karl Kroeber and William Walling, pp. 61–80. New Haven: Yale University Press, 1978.

"Romney and Blake: Gifts of Grace and Terror." In *Blake in His Time*, edited by Robert N. Essick and Donald Pearce, pp. 201–12. Bloomington: Indiana University Press, 1978.

"Byron's Songs of Innocence: The Poems to 'Thyrza.'" In *Evidence in Literary Scholarship: Essays in Memory of James Marshall Osborn*, edited by René Wellek and Alvaro Ribeiro, pp. 379–93. Oxford: At the Clarendon Press, 1979.

"Johnson and the *Concordia Discors* of Human Relationships." In *The Unknown Samuel Johnson*, edited by John J. Burke, Jr., and Donald Kay, pp. 39–53. Madison: University of Wisconsin Press, 1983.

"Pictures to the Heart: The Psychological Picturesque in Ann Radcliffe's *The Mysteries of Udolpho*." In *Greene Centennial Studies: Essays Presented to Donald Greene in the Centennial Year of the University of Southern California*, edited by Paul J. Korshin and Robert R. Allen, pp. 434–41. Charlottesville: University Press of Virginia, 1984.

"'What Seems to Be: Is': Blake's Idea of God." In *Johnson and His Age*, edited by James Engell, pp. 425–58. Cambridge: Harvard University Press, 1984.

"Richardson and Blake." *Blake: An Illustrated Quarterly* 18.4 (1985): 236–37.

"Is There an Ideal of Marital Friendship in Western Culture?" *National Humanities Center Newsletter* 7.2 (1985–86): 1–8.

"Towards a Profile of the Word *Conscious* in Eighteenth-Century Literature." In *Psychology and Literature in the Eighteenth Century*, edited by Christopher Fox, pp. 23–50. New York: AMS Press, 1987.

Reviews

The Grand Tour in Italy, by Paul Franklin Kirby. *Italica* 29 (1952): 272–73.

"The Theoretical Foundations of Johnson's Criticism," by W. R. Keast. *Philological Quarterly* 32 (1953): 276–78.

Originals Abroad, by Warren H. Smith, and *English Travellers Abroad 1604–1667*, by John Walter Stoye. *Italica* 31 (1954): 253–54.

Young Sam Johnson, by James L. Clifford. *Modern Language Notes* 71 (1956): 131–33.

The Achievement of Samuel Johnson, by Walter Jackson Bate. *Modern Philology* 54 (1956): 66–69.

The Providence of Wit in English Letter Writers, by William Henry Irving. *Modern Language Notes* 72 (1957): 130–33.

The Italian Influence in English Poetry from Chaucer to Southwell, by A. Lytton Sells. *Italica* 34 (1957): 115–16.

English Miscellany, ed. Mario Praz. *Victorian Studies* 1 (1957): 196–97.

Literary Criticism: A Short History, by William K. Wimsatt, Jr., and Cleanth Brooks. *Philological Quarterly* 37 (1958): 307–9.

Italy and the English Romantics, by C. P. Brand. *Italica* 36 (1959): 149–50.

Things Common and Preferred, by Karl A. Olsson. *Book News Letter of Augsburg Publishing House* 308 (July 1959): 1.

A Philosophical Enquiry into . . . the Sublime and Beautiful, by Edmund Burke, ed. J. T. Boulton. *Philological Quarterly* 38 (1959): 306–7.

Mountain Gloom and Mountain Glory by Marjorie Hope Nicholson. *Modern Language Notes* 76 (1961): 48–51.

A History of Literary Criticism in the Italian Renaissance, by Bernard Weinberg. *Italica* 39 (1962): 140–42.

From the Renaissance to Romanticism, by Frederick B. Artz. *Philological Quarterly* 42 (1963): 314–15.

Research in Written Composition, by Richard Braddock, Richard Lloyd-Jones, and Lowell Schoer. *College English* 26 (1964): 53–56. In *Issues and Problems in the*

Elementary Language Arts, edited by Walter T. Petty, reprint, pp. 396–401. Boston: Allyn and Bacon, 1968.

The Two Worlds of American Art, by Barry Ulanov. *Chicago Tribune* 19 September and 3 October 1965.

Johnson on Shakespeare, ed. Arthur S. Sherbo. *Studia Neophilologica* 41 (1969): 435–38.

The Princeton Index of Christian Art. *UCLA Librarian* 23 (1970): 58.

The Seamless Web, by Stanley Burnshaw. *Comparative Literature Studies* 8 (1971): 271–73.

The Rambler, by Samuel Johnson, ed. W. J. Bate and Albrecht B. Strauss. *Studia Neophilologica* 43 (1971): 318–20.

The Art of Ecstasy, by Robert T. Petersson. *Modern Language Review* 66 (1971): 649–50.

Mnemosyne: The Parallel Between Literature and the Visual Arts, by Mario Praz. *English Language Notes* 8 (1971): 308–10.

The Notebook of William Blake, ed. David V. Erdman with Donald K. Moore. *Philological Quarterly* 53 (1974): 643–45.

Blake and Visionary Art and *The Romantic Rebellion*, by Kenneth Clark, and *British Romantic Art*, by Raymond Lister. *Blake Newsletter* 8 (1975): 143–44.

The Figure in the Landscape, by John Dixon Hunt. *English Language Notes* 15 (1978): 307–9.

Blake as an Artist, by David Bindman. *Blake: An Illustrated Quarterly* 12 (1978): 64–67.

Alexander Pope and the Arts of Georgian England, by Morris R. Brownell. *Eighteenth-Century Studies* 12 (1979): 391–96.

George Eliot and the Visual Arts, by Hugh Witemeyer. *Nineteenth-Century Fiction* 34 (1979): 217–20.

William Blake's Designs for Edward Young's "Night Thoughts," ed. John E. Grant, Edward J. Rose, and Michael J. Tolley. *Eighteenth-Century Studies* 15 (1982): 339–44.

The Paintings and Drawings of William Blake, by Martin Butlin. *Modern Philology* 79 (1982): 445–51.

Index